Black Love NOTES

ALSO BY DENIS GRAY

HARD GROUND

A BIGGER PRIZE

TEARDROP

DELLA'S DEED

LUCKY

BENNY'S LAST BLAST!!

Black Love NOTES

Denis Gray

BLACK LOVE NOTES

iUniverse books may be ordered through booksellers or by contacting:

iUniverse LLC
1663 Liberty Drive
Bloomington, IN 47403
www.iuniverse.com
1-800-Authors (1-800-288-4677)

ISBN: 978-1-4917-4093-4 (sc)
ISBN: 978-1-4917-4095-8 (hc)
ISBN: 978-1-4917-4094-1 (e)

Library of Congress Control Number: 2014912489

Printed in the United States of America.

iUniverse rev. date: 07/16/2014

Cover Art by Charles Lilly

"Have you ever killed someone, Modecai? Have you? It hurts all over."

—Delores Bonet

Chapter 1

Modecai Ulysses Jefferson was a jazz musician. There was nothing wrong with him being a jazz musician, but what *was* wrong was that Modecai composed jazz music at four thirty in the morning and Miss Tallulah Brown, his landlord, who lived at 10 Mulberry Street in Way City, Alabama, had asked Modecai (politely) to leave. In other words, he was being tossed out of his apartment with the overwhelming support and appreciation of his fellow tenants, who'd had enough of Modecai Ulysses Jefferson and his four-thirty-in-the-morning music!

Benny's Pit looked like a typical southern greasy spoon restaurant that had died and gone to hell.

"Delores, let me plop an extra mound of potatoes on that plate of yours!"

Plop!

How did Benny know? Delores Bonet thought. *Is it that obvious to everyone? He's come in here five times now, and five times I've taken his order—but why shouldn't I, come to think of it? I'm the only waitress in Benny's Pit.*

Tell me, what do my eyes do? Jump through hoops when I see him? Or do somersaults? Don't tell me, because if they do, they'd better stop, and fast!

He always looks like he's in a struggle, though, doesn't he? He always looks like he's a brush or two away from a disaster. It's like the world's about to crumble in on him at any given minute if—oh well, I'd better get over to his table before the poor guy's food gets cold or, worse, he starves to death.

Listen, tonight I'm going to ask him his name. He knows mine, right? Dee. When he asked me, I told him Dee, Dee Bonet, not Delores Bonet, but Dee. Only Benny calls me Delores around here anyway. I guess he's trying to give this greasy spoon joint some class.

"Here you are. Guess you thought I'd never get back over to you with your order."

"Uh-uh, Dee, not at all; you're good at your job."

"Pork chops, mashed potatoes, corn on the cob, greens, and … what—what's your name?"

"Oh, uh, Modecai." Modecai's knife sliced through the tender pork chop on his plate.

"Modecai? Why, I never would've guessed that, not in a millions tries."

"It's what my dear mother and father stuck me with, all right: Modecai Ulysses Jefferson."

"Modecai's a nice name, uh, though, Modecai."

"I like it." Modecai was talking with a mouth crammed full of pork chops, mashed potatoes, and buttered corn on the cob. "Even though my older brother's name is Charles."

"Oh, so you got the short end of the stick, not Charles?"

"Yes, the short end. But who's complaining? It grows on you after a while—if you let it."

"Delores, order's coming up!" Benny yelled from behind the counter.

"Be right there, Benny."

"Tell me, Dee, why does he call you Delores when everyone else calls you Dee, including me?"

"Class, Modecai. Benny probably thinks 'Delores' has a ring of class to it. Sounds, you know, better than Dee."

Cautiously, Modecai's brown eyes looked up at Dee. "Suppose I call you Delores, would you mind?"

"No, uh, not at—"

"Delores!"

"Be right there, Benny."

Modecai wanted to wink at her but thought better of it. He'd wink at a Dee but not a Delores. Besides, he wouldn't want to give her the impression he was coming on to her, in any way flirting with her.

Modecai's table was cleared of its mess.

Off in the corner of Benny's Pit, someone had dropped a nickel in the jukebox. A blues harmonica sounded like it held someone's fate in it like a muddy cup. The harmonica was singing like a Mississippi swamp mosquito that'd outgrown someone's thumb. It'd sting them if they got too close to it, that blood-fattened mosquito, so it was best to let it stay right where it was, singing in the tall, slack, lazy green grass, right at the edge of the mud-thick riverbank.

Modecai had come into Benny's Pit with a folded newspaper (the *Way City News*) sticking out his back pocket. He'd spread it across the table (half of it, at least). The paper, along with his glass of lemonade, took up most of the table's space.

He had to find a place to stay, didn't he? An apartment. Yesterday he wrote music for the entire day. Today, he thought for the entire day. He had the mind of a philosopher today and that of a musician yesterday. Way City, Alabama, was by no means a big city. Way City wasn't New York City or Chicago or—it was a small city, a rural town, for the most part, and how many places in Way City were there for a colored person to stay? For a colored person to rent out a room? The odds were stacked against him, big time.

But my days with Miss Brown are numbered, and I've got to find … there's got to be something in this newspaper for me. Some room vacancies somewhere. I've only been in Way City for two months, so I don't know too many places around here. But I have to think the rents go for about the same rate. I don't think there's too much difference from one place to the other. What, Miss Brown has six tenants in her apartment building, three to a floor. From what I've seen in the two months I've been here, Miss Brown's apartment is the biggest one on this side of town. I hope I'm not being thrown out a luxury building, because if I am I don't want to see the next building that could be in my future. Man, not for the life of me!

"Uh, Modecai, what are you smiling about, may I ask?"

And since another nickel had been dropped into the jukebox, and since it was two blues guitars dueling like two wild cats' fur flying on a bandstand, Modecai's ears hadn't heard what Delores had said.

"Uh, Delores, could you—"

"The music—"

"It's loud!"

Delores turned down the jukebox.

Modecai was relishing Delores's smile, something he thought was sexy about her too. It was a small smile on a small, dark face. But it was a smile big enough to light up a small room the size of the one they were in now, in Benny's Pit, with tremendous sex appeal.

When she got back over to the low-standing table, she saw the newspaper spread across it.

"Modecai, are you looking for a room to rent?"

Modecai's eyes shot straight up from the newspaper. "Yes, I am."

"Where are you staying now?"

"Over at 10 Mulberry—"

"Miss Tallulah Brown's then? So why's she—"

"Tossing me out my apartment? I make too much noise."

"You! Now that I can't believe. Heh. Heh." Delores laughed nervously. "You're pulling my leg, aren't you?"

"It's my music," Modecai said, strumming the table with his fingers. "Uh, you see, Delores, I'm a jazz musician."

"Modecai, I can't imagine your music making noise, ever." Her ears had taken note of how Modecai's fingers were strumming the table.

"Lookit, Delores, not at *four thirty in the morning*!" Pause. "Uh, it's noise then to most civilized people in the world—not music."

"So, uh, so why … why do you play your, uh …"

"Jazz music?"

"So early in the morning?"

"I must."

"Must?"

"I'm a composer. I write music. I hear music every second of the day. Honest I do."

"Right now? This instant? While I'm standing here? While we're talking?"

"Every second, like I said."

Delores's eyes paid even more attention to the *Way City News* on top the table.

"Maybe I can help you out of your fix."

"You—how?"

"In the building where I live, there's a vacancy." Delores felt her notepad loosening from her hips, so she adjusted it before it bopped off to the floor. "Two rooms and a bath."

"It's … why it's better than what I've got over on Mulberry, that's for sure. Is the rent, is it reasonable …?"

"It's a few dollars more. But it's worth it."

"But, uh, how much is a few dollars more in your vocabulary?"

"About six to seven dollars more a month."

Modecai seemed to be pondering the situation—actually doing more addition than subtraction.

"Can you afford that much, Modecai?"

"Uh, yes, I can—think I can, uh, fit it into my monthly allowance," Modecai laughed. "Even though it's already as tight as a shoe box."

"Oh, I forgot to tell you where I live. It's 9 Taylor Street. Know where it is in town?"

"No. Uh, near where?"

"Near here. It's …"—Delores angled her finger south—"over in that direction."

"How far is your finger actually point—or better still, how far, would you say, is it from Mulberry Street?"

"Oh … about half a mile, at least …"

"Good." An upbeat smile slipped over Modecai's face. "Miss Brown and her tenants are sure not to hear my piano at four thirty in the morning. Not from there!" Pause. "Thanks, Delores. A lot."

"Don't mention it, Modecai."

"But one thing," Modecai said cautiously, "I come with a piano. I don't travel alone. By myself, sorry to say."

"It's how the noise comes into play?"

"I carry a piano on my back."

"Modecai, don't worry, it'll fit in your room okay. So you can take it off your back anytime you want."

"If the apartment's available."

"Don't worry, I'll call Mr. Cankston now. Purvis Cankston. He's the landlord. How's that?"

"Oh fine. Here, Delores," Modecai said, handing Delores a nickel for the phone call.

"Thanks. It'll just take a second."

Was he ever relieved. His hands were in his pockets and a tune was in his throat as he walked up Bailey Street like a king of hearts. Sometimes Modecai did feel out of place—how about corny. He was a daydreamer, someone who always heard things, sounds, distant harmonies and rhythms and stories not yet told. *I'm hearing the moon as it smiles, even if last night was when it visited me while I slept; and the wind whistles wildly like a witch on a broom sweeping across my sheets. I hear the morning's sun spur me awake and tell me to rise, get up so I can go about the world and do great, great things.*

Loose change down in a pocket sounds like cymbals clashing, or sometimes an orchestra playing out of tune, but it's music, always a song to my ears. And it's everywhere: in a cough, one, two, three coughs; in a sigh, short or long—a note, then notes—tracing something on the periphery in the ear, catching fire, filling my head and heart and the blank page, making my pencil move fast, quick, at top speed, my mind racing into darkness, only to see light again, a flame burst open and the song's mine, the tune, crackling, then controlled, then contained, yes, mine, suddenly and happily, thrilling me like a fresh scent of spring from head to toe.

Modecai had to take a huge breath just thinking about it on Logan Street in Way City, Alabama—that, Delores, and renting an apartment at 9 Taylor Street from Purvis Cankston, he hoped, with all his heart.

Chapter 2

Modecai found Jake the moving man. (Hallelujah!) It was never hard finding Jake in Way City, Alabama, so it seemed. And the moving price for the piano going down the three flights of stairs was the same price for it going up three flights of stairs: three dollars. And then, of course, there was moving the piano into 9 Taylor Street, which meant two flights up, but Jake still charged three dollars even if it was short one floor!

Modecai sat in the room's shadows as the day shifted through another brilliant color in the sky.

Knock.

"Delores?

"It's me, Modecai."

He was dressed. It represented the whole nine yards of being "dressed."

Delores was expected.

"Good evening, Delores."

"Modecai, a red tie?"

"Do you approve or disapprove?"

"You are looking in my eyes, aren't you?"

"Then, uh, you most certainly approve."

Delores entered the apartment.

"Modecai, is this what it means to be a jazz musician too?"

"My room—uh—I need a housekeeper, don't I? Someone to clean up my mess."

"Your music's—"

"Everywhere. All over the place."

"I thought by now, after a week …"

"Why, it's been a week already?"

"You'd be settled in."

"Uh-uh," Modecai said, shaking his head, earnestly, hopelessly. "Uh-uh, not me, Delores. I wouldn't know what to do if my room wasn't weighted down with music, music, music. Everywhere. If I had to look at a neat, uncluttered room, I think it would kill me, or at least offend my senses."

"Well, as they say, to each his own," Delores said, seemingly indulgingly. "But as for me, I—"

"You're as neat and precise as the dress you're wearing."

Modecai liked the look of Delores's body (what was there not to like about her body?). Delores had what would could be considered a V-shaped waist, solid legs, nice-sized breasts, a backside round and fully packed (as they say), and, well, that should cover it, the waterfront—shouldn't it?

All of this beautiful black body was in a black dress. All of Delores looked like a black plum, juicy and sweet to the core.

Modecai strummed his suspenders as if there were a song in them; his pant bottoms kind of bounced above his shoestrings in perfect tune.

Delores winked at Modecai as if ready for anything tonight, anything in the way of fun and adventure.

* * *

Lights, what damned lights!

A person could barely see a crystal chandelier in Charlie's C-Note Club. It was darker in this room than the bottom of a dresser drawer.

"Uh, can you see all right, Delores?"

"I can hear you, Modecai, b-but can't see you. Really see you."

Delores groped for Modecai's hand like she was down inside a coal miner's shaft.

"Come on, Delores, it's not that bad."

Delores's hand had located Modecai's hand and was holding onto it for what appeared for dear life.

"Uh, is this how musicians live, Modecai?" Delores asked with apparent wonder. "Without electricity? Like in the Dark Ages? With all the lights turned off?"

"Uh, can't afford electricity, Delores. We jazz musicians, as you call us, have to make out the best we can without it. Fumble in the dark. Yep, we jazz musicians."

"The music's good," Delores remarked. "I really do like it. How it sounds. I—"

"Uh, Delores, but you really have to listen to it. You really do."

Delores laughed to herself—she got the subtle hint.

Her hand stayed on top Modecai's.

As the music played, Modecai's hand warmed. At first it was barely perceptible to Delores, but soon, after a while, it was if it'd been transformed into a hot, steamy radiator almost too dangerous to touch.

These guys are good, Modecai had repeated more than once to himself.

Delores did like the music. It was good music. Delores was a rhythm and blues gal herself.

"Pardon me. Be right back."

The bathrooms (men's and women's) were off to the rear, but Modecai was heading up to the bandstand. The four musicians were on break. The houselights in Charlie's C-Note Club were turned on.

Shortly, Modecai was back at the table.

"Everything's copacetic."

"Oh, right," Delores said as if she'd entered into a magic, enshrouded, coded world of jive talk.

"Right, copacetic as you say, Modecai." Delores winked. "Copacetic."

The houselights dimmed, and then the solid wall of black was back in a snap.

The band was back and had played for a while, and then Modecai stood. Delores, she was expecting Modecai to head to the back where the bathrooms (men's and women's) were for sure, this time.

"Excuse me," Modecai said, bending over, whispering into Delores's right ear.

And for some inexplicable reason, Delores saw Modecai's red tie, but not his white shirt, in the dark.

"Psssst ..."

"The bathroom, Modecai?"

"Pssst ... no, Delores, the bandstand."

Modecai slid his long, thin frame like a sylph into the darkened space.

Delores didn't understand this, was dumbfounded, in fact. Why was Modecai going up to the bandstand? What for? To do what? And what if the musicians up there didn't take kindly to him up there with them, because colored folk in Way City, Alabama, had a predilection for fistfights and knife fights over much less than what Modecai was doing, approaching the bandstand—much, much less, Delores thought, worriedly.

But when Modecai got to Charlie's C-Note's bandstand, the piano player stood up, and Modecai sat down in his place on the piano stool.

To Delores, it seemed perfectly timed, as if Modecai and the piano player were wired by invisible puppet strings that someone timely jerked.

Delores listened to the music. It's what Modecai had told her to do, listen to the music.

Play, Modecai! Play your piano, man!

Boy oh boy, did Delores like the way Modecai played the piano, for her money's worth. His head was down. He was mesmerizing in so many complex ways difficult to explain. His body, his head, his everything seemed to be bubbling up sweat together, out of one huge pocket in his skin. In fact, she could feel his soul even when it sped at incredibly high speeds. In fact, she felt Modecai's genius jump up on its hind legs and leap out of him. Her eyes closed, her body rocking tightly in the chair, a lovely power washed over her. The music cooling her, soothing her, relieving her of whatever pain she knew, had been through—whatever journey she'd been on at this short stage of her life.

It's what Modecai's piano playing was doing to her. It's how right it felt. How much it was guiding her inner spirit.

Now Modecai was playing without the band, in some kind of solo, solemn way, it's what Delores thought. She was not a musician, so how was she supposed to know about any of this musician stuff? Rules, regulations. Rhythm and blues was her meat and potatoes, where there was background, a lead singer, but other singers or musicians in the background. But not a solo, a solo figure whose solo was making her black skin glow, whose light was shining out of somewhere, maybe out of an enlightened darkness or something.

Play, Modecai, play! Play! Play!

Modecai's head was down, hanging as loose as a candy apple at the end of a string. His head was bobbing up and down, up and down. His long fingers were digging into the piano keys. His sweat, from his forehead, was dripping down onto his red tie, his white shirt, and most of his plain blue suit at a furious pace, in a furious assault.

Play, Modecai! Play!

It's all Delores could think.

Maybe Modecai had heard her and maybe he hadn't, but at least, now, she was beginning to understand what a jazz musician was, and this was becoming more and more important to her by the minute or, maybe more accurately, by the second.

"Did you expect this to happen tonight, Modecai? So soon?"

Modecai's arms were wrapped around Delores's bare shoulder. Her arms were wrapped around his bare waist. Modecai and Delores were lying in Delores's bed naked—they'd made love after they'd left Charlie's C-Note Club.

"I know I didn't."

A mental picture of Delores in her skin-tight black dress, which Modecai figured could be found somewhere (but didn't know where) in the room, flashed immediately into his mind's eye.

"I don't do this kind of thing, Modecai. I'm not a loose woman. I do get my share of sexual remarks from men in Benny's, but I don't—"

"Delores," Modecai said gently, "you don't have to explain yourself. Because this, well, frankly, I'm no lady killer. I don't go around seducing every woman I first come into contact with either."

"But with your charm and good looks, Modecai …"

"I know, Delores, but that's not me. I'm not into that style of living. It's not copacetic."

Delores's head was on Modecai's shoulder; she kissed his neck.

"Copacetic? You've used that word twice tonight, Modecai. Where'd it come from? And what does it mean?"

"Oh, uh, that everything's okay, I guess. First rate. Up to snuff. Is on the square. And as far as its history, I heard a jazz cat from Philadelphia use it. Some jazz musician who was blowing through Hamlet, North Carolina. And it's stuck with me ever since, like glue."

"Modecai, f-forgive me, okay? For what I'm about to say."

Modecai's body remained calm.

"I'm shy at this, Modecai, so let me catch my breath and, I guess, my courage."

Delores's head rose off Modecai's shoulder until hers was equal with his. Inwardly, Modecai turned his face to Delores. Her full lips touched his. Their lips held to the kiss for a few seconds.

"Were you making love to me from the bandstand tonight? Is that how you wound up in my bed so easily? Why we made love?"

Modecai didn't know how to answer Delores's question, just where to begin.

"Tonight, every night I play what's inside me, Delores, I suppose. I play what's beating me up or giving me joy—or whatever makes me feel sexy—"

"And passionate? That too ...?"

"Yes, I agree. Passionate too."

"Were you making love to me tonight from the bandstand? Were you?"

And now, right now, Modecai could actually see that he was. That those five nights he'd eaten at Benny's Pit and he stopped calling Delores "Dee" but "Delores" and she'd helped him find a place to live and she knocked on his door every day before going to work, that tonight from Charlie's C-Note Club's bandstand, that yes, he was making love to her and only her—it's where it'd all led to. That Delores was right. That her question wasn't a dream puffed up off pillows, wishful or naïve.

"Yes, Delores. I must have been."

"Modecai, can you stay here with me for we can rest or, or, uh—do whatever?"

"Do whatever covers a broad area, Delores. At least for me."

"I love the way you play the piano."

"Then, as it stands now, you're my biggest fan in Way City."

"I love jazz."

Modecai thought about Delores's black skin-tight dress, which was somewhere in the room, and Delores's body in it.

"Modecai, don't tell me I, just now—did, did I feel something move?"

"I think so, Delores," Modecai laughed. "You're right."

The jazz music drifted into Delores's ears. She licked her lips. Am I dreaming? Did I leave the radio on? The sound sounded the same as—

Delores propped herself up on her elbow; her right hand patted the side of the bed where she knew Modecai's body's imprint was. Delores realized she was alone, without Modecai—that he'd left her, gone down the hall to his room adjacent to hers. Lightly, Delores lay back on her back. She listened as Modecai had taught her to do tonight at Charlie's C-Note Club—listen.

Maybe I should go down the—

But quickly Delores canceled out such a thought—to get up out her bed, put on a robe, and go down the hall and knock on Modecai's door. Wouldn't it ruin everything she and Modecai and the night's magic had created for them? Wouldn't it turn the night back into some real place and not a place where the fantasy felt real?

The melody came to mind. She was catching on fast, Delores thought. Listen, yes, listen—tonight she was taught by Modecai how to listen to the music. Really, really listen to the music.

"It's what Modecai played at the club. It's what he told me he soloed on tonight."

Why should she tap on his door, ask him to come back down the hall with her, for them to lie in her bed and for them to make love when Modecai was already in her bed, when his arms were already wrapped tightly around her, holding her, his fingers already making all kinds of crazy love to her black skin, delighting her.

Modecai stopped for a second. His mind was inspired by a new thought, a new energy, a new idea. The pencil came out his mouth. Teeth marks were grooved in it.

"That's the one! It's where the sound I've been hearing in my head, I've been after all night, goes. There, man, right there!"

Modecai's hand was a blur. It was like it was striking the air fantastically, and sparks flew from it. The colors were bright, in Technicolor, almost like you could actually hear and see them integrate one into the other. Modecai's mind was creating a pathway, and then making music on paper, where this note should go, and that note should go. Instinctually, he was orchestrating sound, notes, steering them—where each note should go, fit in in the scheme, pattern of the incomplete yet complete construct. The notes were manifest, had already been created in some mystical, subconscious, abstract way; and now they had a life of their own to fulfill, turn over, render responsibly to the creation.

Oh, it might sound pretentious and off-putting, but it wasn't, because you had to know more about it, the musical process, the musical universe, how sounds bounced around in Modecai's head like Ping-Pong balls, wild and free, untethered, not integrated but dispersed and foreign, never really making any sense to anyone, least of all to Modecai at the time of their invention and, at the same time, waywardness, abstraction.

But Modecai would keep listening to them as they tumbled around in his head, and then they became echoes, made shadowy, mysterious substances not until at some point they weren't; they had a force, a might to them, full, bright, complete, total continents of color, adornment, and his mind could see notes, actually see them, catch them, put them down on paper, let them breathe and live there. They were now earthbound, captured to a source. They were now an E-sharp or an F-flat or a C-natural, but black love notes, always black love notes, and it was on Wilson Street in Way City, Alabama, where he heard some of them, and Joyce Street, and now this morning from his room on Taylor Street.

And then came Delores, Delores's sound, when it came from out of space, the universe; it was low, earthy, breathy (a B-flat, maybe?)—like, yeah, like her voice. Yeah, dark like her skin color. He could riff the blues off her sound. When he touched her, when they made love, he felt the music he'd played in Charlie's C-Note Club inside her. It was as soon as he entered Delores's bedroom that the music was inside her. It was the first time he touched the skin on her bare legs (the black love notes, his fingers knew, had played before); but they lay there naked like a keyboard on Delores's legs, radiant in the moonlight—there was a moonlight, wasn't there? Yes, there was moonlight, Modecai thought, remembering it all, how it took place, unfolded between him and Delores in her bedroom.

"And we were lovers, weren't we, Delores? Black lovers. We became black lovers like black love notes on a musical page. It's what it felt like when I made love to you tonight."

Modecai's hand was shaking with the pencil still in it. He began laughing to himself. It was enough for one day. It was enough black love notes for anybody today.

"I'm hitting the sack. I really am thinking too much. It's enough confusion, I think, for one day. Even for me."

Modecai stood up from the piano stool and stretched his arms above his head.

"Delores, see you later on this morning. But not before eight. Not after tonight. Wow ..."

Yawn. Yawn.

Chapter 3

Knock.

"Come in, the door's always open," Modecai said in a welcoming voice.

Before his head could turn to the door, Modecai was greeting his a.m. visitor and heard something large and heavy roll across the thick hardwood floor.

"Brought the super express along with me. My super deluxe, Modecai. So good morning!"

"Good morning, Jimmy Mack!"

Modecai was off his piano stool, and he and Jimmy Mack Burgess glad-handed each other.

"Glad to see you, Jimmy Mack."

"Said I'd be by last night at the C-Note. What I told you."

"I know, Jimmy Mack."

"Don't expect you'd think this early, huh?"

"Ten o'clock's not early. Uh, at least not for me."

"Last night was a gas, man. So I had to haul my black ass over here! Man, I liked what you was putting down last night at the club. Like you was serving up some deep-fried chicken out my mamma Bea's oven!"

Jimmy Mack unzipped the bass case, and then like a magician hiding away thousands of pigeons before a spellbound audience, Jimmy Mack unsheathed his potent-looking instrument.

"See, the super express, Modecai, is at your service!"

"It's a beautiful piece of wood you play on. And you make it ring like a bell, Jimmy Mack. Beautifully."

"Aged wood, Modecai. Even know the forest it was cut down from." Jimmy Mack grabbed the top of his bass fiddle. "Okay now, enough with the sca-diddle-do; let's tag onto some sca-diddle-dee!"

"What, Jimmy Mack? Anything special you'd like to play?"

"Uh, be my guest, Modecai. But maybe we'd better not jump off on nothing too sudden, harsh," Jimmy Mack said, rolling his fingers some. "First, I gotta get the circulation in my fingers going, that arthritis thing, then haul us some ass, man!"

Jimmy Mack and Modecai'd met last night at Charlie's C-Note Club—of course. He was the jazz band's leader. He called his jazz unit "Mack's Men." They were, by no special order of appearance or favoritism, Billy Shivers (the cat who gave up his piano stool to Modecai); Ron Bishop, reeds; and Marshall Douglass, drums. These were Mack's Men. Modecai didn't know them before last night. Billy Shivers and Ron Bishop were local musicians. They came out of Way City, both homegrown.

It was two hours later. Modecai had made himself and Jimmy Mack ham sandwiches. By now, they'd been wood shedding (practicing) for a little over an hour and a half.

"Who says time flies, Modecai," Jimmy Mack said, chomping down on his ham sandwich with pickles with one pudgy hand and holding onto his beautiful piece of wood with the other.

"You make a damned good ham sandwich, Modecai! Damned good!" Jimmy Mack snatched the bottle of beer near him.

"Thanks, Jimmy Mack."

"Modecai, how you keep yourself in the pink, may I ask?" Jimmy Mack said, smacking his lips before laying waste to the rest of his ham sandwich with one incredible-sized bite.

"What, uh …"

"Pay your rent. Your monthly check to the almighty landlord. For the cat don't sneak up on you. Ain't gotta dog parked outside your door at night with a baseball bat."

"Oh, I …"

"Hell, who the hell am I to be asking you that, Modecai—when I know how hard it is on us jazz cats to scrape up a living. Lucky if we can pay to put a decent part in our hair in the morning!"

"You're a funny, real funny cat, Jimmy Mack!"

"You know us bass players—say we all crazy as hell. Lookit, we don't have no keys to view like the rest of you cats do. Reeds got valves. Trumpets got valves. Pianos, keys—right? Lucky you. But string players ain't got nothing, Modecai. String players finger their fingers around on a three-inch fingerboard like blind mice skittering in a box of fried rice, man.

"No wonder we crazy as all hell. You go around being funny'n hell too, if every time you played something, it depended one part on chance and the other on nerve."

"Sounds like a tough life for a bass player, Jimmy Mack."

"Oh no, oh no, not at all, Modecai—us bass cats get along quite fine. Quite fine. Thank you."

Jimmy Mack put the beer bottle down on the floor.

"You write you some hep stuff, Modecai. Lock it right in the pocket. Lock it tight as hell. You don't belong in no Way City, Alabama, Modecai. No horse and pig town like this.

"New York, New York City, Modecai. You belong in the Big Apple, man. The Big Apple Twist."

Modecai's body trembled slightly. "Y-you, are you sure you don't want another ham sandwich, Jimmy Mack … w-with pickles?"

"Hell, Modecai, eat too damned much now. My body's beginning to look like a damned bass fiddle. Spin like one too! But seriously, Modecai, uh, seriously …" Jimmy Mack had paused.

"Your black ass oughta be up in New York City. Oughta be up in one of them jazz clubs up there laying down your shit. Them tunes and you oughta be working your way over to Fifty-Second Street and Broadway, man. On over to Swing Street."

And for a second time, Modecai's body trembled, but more seriously this time.

"You've been, you've been up to New York City, Jimmy Mack?"

"Hell, yes, ain't I though."

"Fifty, Fifty-Second and, and Broadway? On Swing Street?"

"Sneak me a good peek at it. Old country boy like me—wasn't so old then." Pause.

"H-how was it, Jimmy Mack? How—"

"Got some pretty-looking women up there in the first place. Number one," Jimmy Mack said while folding his arms around his bass. "Come in all sizes, shades, and colors. Shit, ain't prejudice 'bout nothing—just the white man is."

"Did you sit—"

"Darn tooting right I-I sit-in. Shit! With my big mouth? Stick it in somebody's ear and they get the message loud and clear."

"How was it? How'd it go down, Jimmy Mack?"

"Uh, great, Modecai. Rumbled and roared, as I call it. Me and this fine piece of wood of mine. Me and her, we rumbled and roared up there, man. New York City!"

Modecai stood. He walked over to Jimmy Mack's "fine piece of wood" and touched it.

"Yeah, me and my bass been up there in the Big Apple, on Swing Street. Can say that much about me and her. Keep score."

He couldn't, Modecai thought. He and his upright piano couldn't say that much about themselves, "keep score."

Modecai walked back over to the piano.

"Fast life up there, though. Man … Fast life on them streets. Fast women. Fast cars. Just like they say. And them cats drink like hell, Modecai. Drink a drunk under the table.

"Too damned fast for a old country boy like me. My feet get pinched in them big-city shoes. Got to admit." Jimmy Mack smiled sweetly.

Then Jimmy Mack's fingers strummed something on his bass strings.

"Me and my girl, lady here, rumbled and roared up there. Yes, siree, Modecai. Yeah, man, me and her done rumbled and roared up in the Big Apple, man. New York City."

Modecai was alone. Jimmy Mack and Mack's Men had left the apartment. Yes, the rest of Jimmy Mack's band came by to visit Modecai, one dragging behind the other. Mack's Men had visited Modecai. Now all of them knew where he lived in Way City, Alabama.

Modecai went to the store down the street but was back. Those cats can eat! Modecai'd chuckled. Did they come to play this morning or for some freebies?

Man, it was great playing with them last night and today (sharing piano duties with Billy Shivers), *but now, I've got a whole lot of work to catch up with,* Modecai thought, looking at the music piled up everywhere around him and looking at it like it had eyes but no ears, but little green horns sticking out, and would devour him whole as soon as his eyes shut.

"There's this tune I want to revamp. Maybe if I put it in the key of … well—I want it to have a lighter texture. Got to work that one out."

Man, he said to himself again, *Mack's Men can eat! Eat some ham sandwiches!*

He had to watch his pennies, that's for sure. Those four cats went through a week's worth of groceries in one sitting like termites through a wood pile. Already, Modecai was thinking about changing his address or just going on a bread and water diet for the next five days.

"Uh … New York City, man …"

Modecai stopped short and let what he'd just said suspend itself right there. He walked over to the window. It was summer in Way City, so the window was open. He sat on the windowsill. Being summer, folk on Taylor Street sat opposite the sun. His two-story apartment building sat in the shade. He couldn't believe he had two rooms—man, was he living!

"New York City …"

Jimmy Mack's been there, he thought. He'd stepped into the Big Apple. Put his feet down in the Big Apple. His shoes have actually touched down on its soil.

"Man …" Modecai's voice wavered. "Man …" He looked over at the piano. "Don't worry, you go where I go. We aren't parting company anytime soon."

How long had he had the dream in his head? What, since he first heard the words "New York City." Has it really been that long ago? It seemed like it'd been since he was in knee pants. Probably—maybe it was.

Who said it first? Mr. Eustace Sylvester?

"Been up there, Miss Estelle. New York City, Brother John."

It's when he first heard the name, when Mr. Sylvester from down home was talking to his mother, Estelle, and his father, John, one Sunday morning outside Lazarus Baptist Church.

"Tall buildings, Miss Estelle. Made me feel like a pipsqueak (Mr. Sylvester was but so tall anyway). Call them skyscraper buildings, Brother John. What they make of them. 'Cause they scrape the sky, Miss Estelle. They sit so high off the ground. Are they high."

"It was the first I heard of New York City, through Mr. Sylvester."

And, of course, over the years he learned just what New York City represented to a jazz player. First it was New Orleans, and then Kansas City had to be included too, and Chicago—and then New York City.

New York City, a city that could make or break a jazz cat. It's what jazz cats said about New York City. It seemed all the great jazz talent was there. It was the breeding ground, the hotbed for jazz music, where it was all mixed and manufactured from—the talent.

They said cats rode in on Greyhound buses, arrived at Forty-Second Street every day of the week. Young jazz cats coming to play, to dig, to gig—to make a name, reputation for themselves, as if their very lives depended on it. New York City was the jazz scene where young jazz cats convened. New York City was the trophy everyone was out to steal. The trendsetters were in New York City, the cats who would fight you down at the bottom of the barrel to get to the top. It's where the jazz wars were won or lost, the jazz battles were fought, waged—the best and worst of a jazz musician's life was up there in that big northern city, metropolis.

Modecai looked down on Taylor Street. He was on the shady side of the street, out the sun, the day's sweltering heat. He got up off the windowsill. He walked over to the piano; his shoulders slumped when he sat on the piano stool. He worked so hard at his jazz music. What, for a day in the sun, for glory, notoriety, recognition? How many times had he asked himself this? How many times had the question pierced his gut?

He was tired of the question. Sick of it. Fed up with it. It just sat there like a big lead balloon in the middle of his mind going nowhere. He wanted it to go somewhere, fly, skim the sky, answer questions for him—why him, why music, why was he chosen to lift the big jug of water onto his back and lug it up the mountaintop, not knowing if he'd reach the mountain's top or determined or strong or dedicated enough, not knowing if there was a top to be reached.

If it meant him sitting around all day thinking about what kept him and his music going—as he was now doing—he'd go nuts. Because it was always a project not work, but a project. It was always striving for something, yes, that mountaintop, wasn't it? Pursuing something. But just what? Who gets to swallow the golden apple? Whose appetite's finally satisfied, man?

"New York City."

Skyscrapers. Broadway. Fifty-Second Street. Fast women. Fast cars. Big boozers. Shoes pinching a country boy's feet. Jazz cats going East for exotic reputation, for mythic duals in smoky nightclubs, fierce gunfights on the bandstands. Cats going East to blow their horns, axes, to place their unique, individual stamp on the jazz scene, one no one had ever seen before, cast themselves in bronze. Every day it happens. Every day there's a new busload of jazz cats streaming into New York City to be heard, seen—to shoot the dice, blow on them good and hard and hot, fling them like fireballs; for the winner can take all, win the pot of gold at the end of the rainbow, the sky full of rainbows to reach out and grab hold of.

Yeah, man, it's all a crap shoot, Modecai thought. All of it. Yeah, life's nothing but a big crap shoot. Now, at this young, tender age of his, he was beginning to realize this more and more the older and wiser he got. Life's a big crap shoot. Everybody has a pair of dice in the grooves of their hand. A pair of dice to toss to the wind. The back alleys were crawling with crap shooters, with people taking a chance on life. A toss, a fling at life in a game they're trying to win—trying like heck not to lose. Maybe they do understand the odds and maybe they don't. Maybe they do understand a lucky seven, snake eyes, and maybe they don't. But everyone starts out equal, with a pair of dice to toss onto the crap table.

Modecai knew he was tossing his dice. He knew he only had but so much time to do it before the game was called off, was ruled over. Music, it came to him easily. Black love notes came to him easily. But there was New York, wasn't there? There was always New York City lurking in the backdrop, its siren call. There was always New York City swinging in the seat of a golden swing offering up the moon for sale like a piece of Swiss cheese.

"Jimmy Mack, when he spoke of New York, his eyes sparkled, man. 'Sitting-in.' Taking part in a jam session. Who knows who he played with? Who knows? Who knows who's going to be the next new star, the next new Louis Armstrong, Billie Holiday. Nobody at the start does. When it's all beginning."

You could be jamming with anyone in those jam sessions up in New York City. You could be jamming with anyone famous or who just got off the Greyhound bus at New York City's Port Authority—there was no telling. Nobody had been tagged or given a special number marking them for success. There was no passport in their pocket or keys to the city to open up doors; and if you thought so, you might as well leave your bags unpacked on top your bed as soon as you got there and head back to where you came from—even Modecai knew that much about New York City's hard-as-nails reputation, the necessary struggle pending.

But Modecai still felt his skin tingle at the prospect.

* * *

When the room door down the hall closed, Modecai popped to his feet. His door opened. Delores was in the short hallway.

"This is becoming a daily thing. A routine, isn't it?"

"I guess so," Modecai said, grinning.

"I like it," Delores said.

"Me too," Modecai said.

"This could become a habit."

"I think it already is."

"By next week, Modecai, the bloom will be off the rose."

"Whose rose, Delores?"

"Uh, I heard you playing earlier. Umm, maybe I should say, I heard the band playing earlier. And they sounded good. You are teaching me to listen, Modecai. There were a lot of familiar things I heard."

"That's great."

"It means a lot to you, doesn't it? I mean I'm only a waitress at Benny's, but I know what it feels like to be appreciated. A nickel tip feels just like, I guess, what a dollar tip would feel like if I ever got one."

Pause.

"It's not like you make a lot of money playing jazz music. Often, but certainly not a great deal of the time, none at all, Delores."

"H-how do you survive then, Modecai?" Delores asked timidly. "H-how do you make it from day to day? Month to month?"

"I don't rob banks, if it's what you're suggesting."

It's when Delores realized she'd asked the wrong question, hit a raw nerve in Modecai.

"Modecai, I—"

"I got tossed out Miss Brown's apartment because of my music, not because of the rent … I couldn't pay my rent or … or was late on my rent. I take care, pride in taking care of my responsibilities. I don't shirk any of them."

Delores *had* stepped on a big, raw, sensitive toe. How was she going to dig herself out of this hole?

"Uh … I saw Miss Brown at, matter of fact, at church service j-just last Sunday, Modecai."

Modecai's face maintained its grave look.

"S-sorry," Delores said.

"For what, Delores?"

"I'm still trying to catch on, I guess. To a jazz musician's life. His ways."

Modecai slouched and then stood erect and then stood somewhere between the two opposite extremes. "It seems I'm always going against the tide. The fish swim upstream to breed, but it's like I'm always swimming downstream. Away from everything and everyone."

"Did I hear your heart break a little, Mordecai, or, or am I exaggerating?"

"No, no, it's not a complaint, just a fact, Delores. M-my life's fine. There's no reason to complain about my life."

"It's something I try not to do. I'm twenty-six—"

I'm two years younger than her, Modecai thought.

"And I've had some rough times. But my momma had it rougher than me. You see, I didn't know my father when I grew up. But he must've been a bastard like he made me. But when I go to church, I pray for him, but I'll never forgive him—or hope to ever see him. I left home and have been scratching out a living since I was sixteen, Modecai. I don't have a natural talent, you might call it, like you, just a talent for surviving, I like to say."

* * *

Modecai hadn't moved from out his room all day. It was dark outside. He'd eaten. The dishes were washed (he'd managed to do that much in the apartment today). After Delores went off to Benny's Pit, she left him with a lot to chew on—actually, a mouthful (like a cat with an old balled-up sock).

Bastard. *Bastard.* She'd chosen that word to describe her father, a person Delores didn't know. She'd never known. Up until now, it was the most profane word he'd heard her use. Man, she must hurt like hell inside. Her face actually burned when she said it, "bastard," like her father had ripped something precious out her heart and the hole has not been filled.

At least her father didn't cause her to hate men. At least it didn't seem to have that kind of effect on her. But it was still too early to tell. Sometimes they say things like that work just the opposite for a person: somebody like Delores starts looking for love in the wrong places. They begin looking for a man's, a lover's love to replace their father's.

Am I that man? After last night's lovemaking, has Delores made me that man? And what about her past: does Delores have a trail of ex-lovers, of men picked, selected to replace that "bastard" her heart's ice-cold for?

Am I the pick of the litter this time, because if I am, I don't know, man. Honestly, I don't know. See, I don't make commitments. Last night was last night, after all. It was like ... spinning on a dime, beating the drum until the sound falls out the air. This morning I woke up with Delores inside me, but by this afternoon I was full of Jimmy Mack, Billy

Shivers, Ron Bishop, and Marshall Douglass. By this afternoon there was no confusion, no suspense or mystery.

"When Delores gets in from Benny's, the two of us will have to sit down and talk about this. I have to apologize to her about the money thing anyway. Set the record straight. Uh, I was rude with her. I was taught better than that.

"But Delores has to know that my tomorrows all look the same. That I'm a slave to music. She has to understand how it feeds me and me it. See what I mean, Delores?" Pause.

"Man, Jimmy Mack came here to my apartment at ten o'clock, uh, just to jam on some of my tunes. He carried that big old bass fiddle in here with him. We jammed and jammed. We talked for a while, ate ham sandwiches (well, he had two to my one), had a beer apiece—but we played and played until the rest of the cats showed up. They ate me out of house and home, but we mostly played."

Delores, why, she heard what we were doing in the room today.

"You see, Delores mustn't get the wrong idea. The wrong impression. A jazz musician's life is his own. It's his own, Delores. When you're one with the music, when it's gotten that far—then it's all over for you. There's nowhere else to turn. No one can set you off course. Pull you out of that kind of beauty. There's nobody's hand you can reach for, you can grab onto to save you.

"You're down there sparkling, glowing, embedded in diamonds. You shine. You're polished. You're everything and more. No other thing comes to mind. No one comes to mind. You're lost in a sunset. Jimmy Mack and the band were shimmering. We were all shimmering. We felt better than gold. We felt richer than Rockefeller. We were on, tapping our toes, snapping our heads—swinging through tunes like crazy. Like crazy, man!

"Jimmy Mack took us to Broadway and Fifty-Second Street. We were sitting-in on Swing Street. We were up in the Big Apple. Fast women. Fast cars. A five-cent shoe shine and a ten-cent tip. Man, now that's living. That's what a jazz musician is—playing until the string snaps."

* * *

Benny and Delores were the last ones out Benny's Pit. They were in its back alleyway, making their way through the usual dark back there. Then, as usual, it was about time for Benny and Delores to part company at the next corner, Benny going right, Delores left.

"See you tomorrow. And be on time, huh, Delores? Not like you was tonight, huh?"

"You're not going to let me forget it, are you, Benny? Late one night in how many—"

"It don't matter. You a late bird, girl," Benny said in his thin, screechy voice.

"Gotta keep both my eyes on you, young lady. One day turns into two and, and so on and so forth …"

"So on and so forth my foot!" Delores laughed. "You know I've been the best waitress who's ever worked in the Pit."

"Listen, and you just ain't whistling to a pig stuck in mud neither!"

"So my job's still safe?"

"Sure is. Safe as a queen bee in a hive." Pause. "Now, uh, you get home safe now, girl."

"You too, Benny."

Delores watched Benny walk away (someone who was tall, long, and as light as a feather duster) and when she turned:

"Boo!"

Delores practically jumped out her skin (as the saying goes).

"It's me, Delores!"

"Who is—"

"Modecai!"

And now Delores recognized Modecai's voice and frame. "What, t-this is how you have fun? By scaring a poor girl out her wits while walking home from work at night!"

"Scared, why it looked like you were about to bat me silly. Knock me down for the count."

"Heh … heh … right."

"Who taught you to ball your fist like that? Joe Louis would probably duck you."

"You can run, but you can't hide."

"Delores, how'd you know Joe Louis's line?"

"Oh"—Delores smiled—"I know all about Joe Louis. 'The Brown Bomber.' I have a radio too, Modecai. I've cheered for him whenever he steps into the ring to fight. Like every other colored person who owns a radio in Way City, Alabama."

"That, you do," Modecai said shamefaced. "I've seen your radio in your room."

"And it works as good as anyone's."

"What a fighter," Modecai said.

"Deadly." Pause. "By the way, Modecai …"

"Yes …?"

"We are going back to our apartment building some time tonight, aren't we? Because we haven't moved in, let me see …"

"Okay, forward march. It's just that I guess we were enjoying our little conversation so much that …"

They began walking.

"Why are you here anyway?"

"Uh, yes, Delores, there is. In fact there … I just want you to know how sorry I am about this afternoon. I wasn't myself. Who wouldn't be curious, want to know how I pay the rent. Feed and clothe myself. Get on from day to day."

"It had to come up, Modecai, don't you think?"

"My mother, she's the one who sends me money every month. She wires me money from Hamlet, North Carolina. From the farm. It's how I live. It's what I live off of mostly." Modecai stopped walking. "I'm lucky, luckier than most."

"She's given you a kind of freedom to do—"

"To work at my music. Not have to do anything else."

"That's a faith, a testament of faith, isn't it, Modecai?" Delores sighed.

"My mother's always been there for me."

They began walking again.

"W-what about your father?"

"It was nine years ago that my father died of tuberculosis."

"You loved him?"

"A lot."

"He loved you?"

"A lot."

"I can tell."

Modecai picked the pace back up.

"Modecai, about this afternoon, you're forgiven. Completely," she laughed.

"Uh, there's something else, though …" Modecai's voice sounded serious. "I am a jazz musician."

Delores stopped walking. She and Modecai were out in front of the apartment building.

"You see, it's what I am."

They walked into the apartment building. They walked up the stairs and onto the building's second landing.

Delores walked past Modecai's apartment door.

"Delores, y-you heard me, didn't you? Did—what I said? Just said, didn't you?"

Delores was at her door. Her keys were out her pocketbook. She inserted the key into the lock.

Slam!

Modecai stood in the hallway speechless.

Tap. Tap.

"What are you afraid of, Modecai? What!"

"Can you at least open the door? We don't have to talk through the door like this, d-do we? Me in the hallway, you—"

The door snapped open.

"You have to know that. That's all. It's all I'm saying. You just have to know that."

Delores stood in the middle of the room, her back turned to Modecai.

Modecai's arms were outstretched, gesturing, trying to make his point. But Delores beat him to it, turning to him.

"I'm not after you, Modecai. I'm not trying to take you away from any damned thing!"

"Last night. But—"

"Are you that damned stupid! Dumb! Are you!"

"No, but …"

"You couldn't spend the night with me. You couldn't even spend the night with me in my bed. You couldn't even let it get, go that far last night." Pause. "I patted the bed where you were supposed to be this morning—and you weren't there. Gone. Gone. Modecai. Gone. What do you think? I'm a fool? That stupid!"

Modecai's fear didn't seem as vital as before. Not as urgent as to set him off from his apartment like a speeding bullet and to Benny's Pit to tell Delores what he thought he must tell her—where she stood in his life right now, today.

"Sorry, sorry, Delores."

"Don't hand me that 'sorry' routine. I've heard enough of it for a damned lifetime!"

"B-but, Delores, I am sorry."

"Just leave, go. We'll pretend last night never happened. You men. You treat everything as if it's a triumph, as if—I don't know, maybe I'm not that smart.

"Why did you think I had sex with you last night? Why, Modecai? Why do you think we made love last night? Was it supposed to happen? Did someone write it in—on, on a wall, in the sky … that it was supposed to happen? No, no," Delores said, now answering her own question. "No, it happened to us between the time we left here until the time we came back from our date.

"It happened when you touched my hand, smiled, walked up to the bandstand, t-talked to one of those musicians of yours at Charlie's C-Note—w-whatever. Under the stars, Modecai—whatever, whatever it was. Whatever it was, it just happened, happened, happened, Modecai."

It did happen in those ways, those particular, special ways, didn't it? Modecai thought. He had to put last night back together. It had to be reassembled, put back in order a second time in his head, and then thought through. He wasn't in a room alone, solitary, thinking by himself, but was with Delores, trying to find real answers to real complex, difficult questions.

"You've been in love before, haven't you?"

"Haven't you?"

"Haven't you?" Modecai asked again.

"Yes."

"I haven't."

Delores shut the door.

"It's all I'm saying. It's what I think I'm—it's me, not you. But me."

"There'll come a time, Modecai."

"Maybe, w-who's to say."

"Tonight tore you away from your music. Or I should say, last night, what happened between us."

"It did."

Delores walked over to the open window and sat on the windowsill. She looked out the window.

"I'm not trying to steal you away from … what's yours … Belongs to you …"

Now Modecai felt sure enough about himself to walk over to where Delores sat.

"I hear it, its beauty. I've never heard anything so beautiful as what you play."

"Some-sometimes it scares me."

"What?" Delores said, turning to Modecai.

"Distractions. Uh, thinking there could be something else other than my music. Uh, for me. It's like the smallest thing can threaten it. And yet it's so strong that it, I mean my music, can defeat anything. It's not fragile. Why, that's the paradox."

"Whoa, Modecai. Wait a minute. I consider myself a pretty smart cookie, pick up on things pretty quickly, but that word you used—you're going to have to help me with that one."

"Paradox? It just means a situation, one that can produce contradictory things, uh, results from it, than what you intended."

"You're smart, Modecai. Awfully smart."

"What," Modecai laughed, "just because I happen to know what the word 'paradox' means? Looked it up in a dictionary?"

"Did you go to college?"

"No. Just, as a kid, I read a lot. Something, I regret, I don't have much of a chance to do these days."

Delores began humming something, and to Modecai's surprise, it sounded darn good!

"Delores, don't tell me you sing?"

Quickly, Delores quit humming.

"Come join me."

"Delores, I can't sing. I'm a piano player, remember?"

"No. Here. Here on the windowsill. There's enough room for two."

And so there was.

"Let's look at the stars."

Modecai sat opposite Delores.

"Delores, think they're smiling down at us?"

"Could be. That itsy-bitsy one way over there is. Way ... way over in the corner of the sky there."

"W-where?" Modecai said, stretching his neck, twisting it at an extreme right angle.

"Modecai, you know I'm teasing you. And you're acting no better than a big kid."

"But I was looking for the itsy-bitsy star. And I wasn't acting like a 'big kid' either."

Delores's hand landed on top Modecai's knee; for Modecai, it was like last night renewed and retrieved.

"I know a lot about you after just one day. Is that good? Or is it too much too soon between us?"

"Sometimes, there are times, Delores, when I doubt myself. When I think I'm just spinning my wheels. That what I am, what I do is all ... just a waste of time. Too big for me to handle, that is."

"Why, don't think that. Don't ever think that. Listen to your mother."

"My mother?"

"She has faith in you. She proves it every month. Can't you see that? By wiring you money from the farm."

Modecai looked at Delores. He was stunned by what she'd said.

"I never looked at it in that light before. Not quite like that."

"Modecai," Delores laughed, "you couldn't even find an itsy-bitsy star in the sky just a few seconds back—and now here you're talking about seeing the light!"

Now was like last night. Both sensed it. There was no real reason now to deny it. Delores's hand squeezed Modecai's knee, but it felt like much more than that. Modecai took her hand off his knee and kissed it. Delores wore a short skirt and heels. The skirt was hiked, and her tight, muscular legs were in full view. Delores's lips, they brushed Modecai's.

Last night was playing melodies in their minds.

Modecai's hand touched Delores's nyloned thigh, and Delores's dark flesh trembled.

"Last night was beautiful, Modecai. So beautiful," Delores said, leading Modecai out the front room and into the bedroom. When they stopped just short of the bed, Delores slipped into Modecai's arms. Their tongues locked. Modecai's hand held Delores's buttocks as she began pressing her body more and more into his, her breath exciting his cheek's skin.

"Last night I saw a thousand stars."

"Tonight we'll see a thousand and one, Delores. One thousand and one in the sky."

Delores's moan tickled Modecai's ear as his fingers felt how moist she already was below her waist.

"Oooooo … baby …"

Delores hummed in, what Modecai imagined, was the key of A-natural, in his ear. Or was it A-sharp?

It was déjà vu. Delores awoke to music. Modecai's music. She didn't bother taking her hand to pat down to find Modecai in the bed, to see if he was still there. This time, she just rolled off to that side of the bed, occupying it as if she could make two bodies—clone Modecai's with hers.

What time is it? Who cares? Every night she'd slept alone. Every night since Johnnyboy had been gone; it no longer bothered her.

Two nights in a row she and Modecai had made love in her bed. She tried explaining that fact to Modecai, but he'd said no explanation was needed. They'd clicked, that's all. It was the most explaining both knew was needed.

Was he writing a song for her like he said he would? *Ha. I really hit a high C tonight! It's what Modecai told me. I don't know what a high C looks like on a piano—but it's what Modecai said I hit!*

I told him I wound up seeing a thousand and one stars in the sky as, as he'd promised me. So I was singing high Cs and seeing a thousand and one stars in the sky all at the same time, wasn't I?

Delores rolled onto her back. Her hands held onto her ample breasts. Her lungs burned when she breathed. Then, gently, her fingertips flicked both nipples.

How she wished Modecai would come back to her bed, just come back one more time down the hall, she thought. She'd hear him, his door open and close and his footsteps enter the hallway as well as she heard Modecai's music enter her ears from his room. Each step of Modecai's she'd hear. And she'd make room for him in the bed, next to her—it'd really be that simple, easy, wouldn't it? The whole thing, wouldn't it, for them?

Chapter 4

"Got it! I can't believe I got this record in Way City. Not this record in a record store in Way City, Alabama!"

"Me and my shop, son, try to stay up with the times." He was a straight-backed older gentleman. He was receiving monetary payment from Modecai.

"Got me a pipeline straight to New York City. Wichita, Kansas, too. Just kidding about Wichita. But got me a cousin who owns a record shop up there in Harlem. Doing quite fine for himself. Old Cecil. So he calls me from week to week. Keeping me updated as to what's going on. Posted on the current trends up there. What new buggies I should buy for my baby. Record shop here!"

Modecai was outside the record shop. He was carrying a slew of records, not just the one he'd plucked out the record bin. He strode the street in the bright sun like a king graced and adorned in a white shirt and chocolate-brown suspenders buttoned at the waist to the same colored pants. The shine on Modecai's shoes could blind an American Eagle looking down from Pikes Peak.

Suddenly, Modecai shifted from striding up the street to downright swinging up it like he had a few drops of fresh oil in each of his bodily joints. His arms and shoulders swung like Buddy Bolden swinging a high and mighty tune out his horn. Modecai felt the music permeate him. It came from out the record albums, the jazz albums he was carrying waist high in his hands with all the care of someone carrying a cache of china from China.

Modecai had a big collection of jazz albums. He had his heroes. Buddy Bolden was one (even though he'd never recorded live or in a recording studio while alive). But Modecai knew of Buddy Bolden and his hot horn (cornet), knew he was responsible for King Oliver as King Oliver was responsible for Louis Armstrong. Modecai maintained a keen history of events, when and how the "circle" was formed. He took great pride in owning this kind of knowledge of jazz music.

New York City (Harlem, in particular). It'd come up again, Modecai thought. It was beginning to sound like a broken jazz record playing in his head. The word "New York City" even came out of a simple commercial transaction, one with a record store owner in a place seemingly so remote as Way City, Alabama. New York City is the hub of everything—isn't it? New York City is the center of everything—isn't it? New York City has this lure, Modecai thought, as sly as a green-eyed snake slithering on top of sand.

So many musicians had gone up there and failed. New York City's full of dashed dreams. New York City's littered with jazz musicians, broken dreams shattered like glass.

But for now, nothing was motivating him to go up to New York City, to be a part of its jazz scene. He wasn't a poor, hungry, starving musician. He had his monthly stipend from his mother. Monthly, the money was wired from home, Hamlet, North Carolina, by Estelle Jefferson. He could pay his rent. He could buy his food. He could take care of his clothing and other personal expenses and still have a few dollars left over in the till at the end of the month for a few fun items for himself. He could buy jazz albums pretty much whenever he wanted.

Why must he think he had to push himself off to New York City? Take the first bus out the bus station? What was the rush? The urgency? He could write his music in a two-room apartment building in Way City as well as in a two-room apartment building in New York City. His black love notes had to sound the same in Way City as they would in New York City. The sun, every morning, set in him in Way City. He never felt in conflict with or at odds with anything or anyone. There were no sharp angles in Way City, nothing to rub him the wrong way, go against the grain. Things were, for the most part, smooth. And for now, he and Delores were hitting it off pretty good. He and Delores had a kind of understanding about things since last night's conversation.

New York City was like a sly, green-eyed snake, all right, full of lure and curiosity; but once its exotica shed its skin, was it just a big snake pit? Did you fight from the bottom of the heap to get to the top of it and still get swallowed up in the end? Was that all there was to it? What was at the bottom?

"Damn, man, you beat my black ass to it, Modecai!"

Modecai was spinning the platter he'd bought on his turntable. The phonograph boasted a new needle. Modecai always made sure his phonograph had a new needle whenever the old one wore down.

"My dough's been short on me, so I ain't been over to Platter Palace in a long while now," Jimmy Mack said. "Else I woulda bought me that record too."

"Earl 'Fatha' Hines at his best, Jimmy Mack."

"So how many times you ac-quaint yourself with the man's musical offerings by now? Since you bought it out of Platter Palace, from Josh Emory's store, Modecai?"

Modecai couldn't suppress his guilt. "Uh, need you ask, Jimmy Mack?"

Silence centered the room and then was broken when Modecai exclaimed, leaping to his feet, "Listen to this tune, Jimmy Mack, and the trumpeter playing it. His solo, the tune, and the trumpeter's solo is, it's incredible, Jimmy Mack. Just incredible, man!"

Jimmy Mack was all ears. And when the trumpeter's solo ended and the tune ended, Modecai saw Jimmy Mack's grin was as wide as the Gulf of Mexico.

"Jimmy Mack, uh, you, do you know who that was! Honestly! Who was playing the trumpet solo! And who wrote the tune!"

"Sure do, Modecai. Got the goods. Inside track on it. Bunny Greensleeves is raising cane up in New York City, ain't gonna be a deep, dark secret for long!"

"Greensleeves, Bunny Greensleeves? I-I've never heard of him."

"Oh, that don't mean nothing. 'Cause you will. Bet my last pair of boots and drawers on that. Been up in New York City with Fatha Hines's band for, uh, let me get my facts straight now … okay, for a few months now. All I know on the subject."

Modecai knew Jimmy Mack had a pipeline from Way City to New York City too, like if anything moved on New York's jazz map, it was sure to pop up on his radar screen as an unidentified object.

"What a solo. What chops."

"Bunny Greensleeves is full of wild invention, Modecai. Word on the New York scene is, the cat's been chewing up the furniture in New York City. Spitting cats out his mouth like they's sunflower seeds!"

Modecai was at the phonograph. Carefully, he lifted the phono's short arm.

"Man, that was sweet, Modecai. Boy can blow. Sure blow that horn of his, all right. Think he's gonna be one of them great ones. Make you tap your feet with your heart."

Modecai put the needle back to where Bunny Greensleeves's solo began.

"I-I've got to hear that solo one more time, Jimmy Mack. One, just one more time."

"What, for you can hear it ten times more before you turn into bed tonight, right? Turn that phono off for the night."

The silence enveloping the room was spooky.

"Wow!"

"Word on him is Bunny Greensleeves writes up a storm too. Got him charts galore. Say the cat's gonna be a composer of the highest merit, establishment, one of these days."

"And I can see why, Jimmy Mack."

"You know, uh, uh, you belong up in New York City with him, Modecai. With this Bunny Greensleeves cat."

Jimmy Mack's remark was like a punch to Modecai's gut.

"You heard what I just said, don't you, Modecai? Said you belong in New York City with Bunny Greensleeves playing your stuff, man. Making the rounds. Shooting the breeze. Making a name for yourself."

"I-I …"

"What you waiting on? Bunny Greensleeves up there. You belong up there with the cat. The young boy. You ain't table waiting down here, is you? Way City, is you? Bunny Greensleeves, the young cat's making a name for hisself.

"Hell, man—so what's stopping you, Modecai? What in hell—your shit's as good as his. There ain't no big-deal difference between the two of you that I see. Hell …"

"I-I …"

"Don't know how you wound up in Way City no how. Down here in this slop. Way City is for a old plow like me. For old cats like me. Or for cats who got them a family to feed every night and want to stay local. Way City's a place where they put old cats like me out on a cow pasture with the cow manure, or shoot us.

"Ha. How about that? Now it ain't that bad, but we play in a club like Charlie's C-Note Club. Charlie's trying to make it something, I know, happen, and I love him for it, but it ain't even close. Up for good conversation. Chew the fat with." Pause.

"But you oughta be passing through, Modecai, you hear me? Not staying. A young genius cat like you. Building up steam, not losing it. Like a locomotive speeding off to somewhere on greased tracks."

Jimmy Mack slammed his bass with his hand.

"Ha! 'Slam' Stewart hisself taught me how to do this here little number. In New York. With my bass. Ha! 'Slam' Stewart, hisself."

Modecai seemed to need that pause, that break, that interlude—that humorous, timely note.

Jimmy Mack picked up his bass fiddle and then leaned it against the wall and then walked over to Modecai. He put his big arm around Modecai's square-boxed shoulders.

"Modecai, Way City ain't on nobody's jazz map. You ain't gonna find it. Not even a fly. Way City, Alabama's for a old hoe like me and Billy and the rest of the cats in the band, like I already put to you, but it ain't no place for you. Not no young bad-ass kicking cat like you."

Jimmy Mack felt Modecai's body shake under the weight of his arm.

"We all gotta take baby steps in the beginning. Ain't nothing wrong with it. Not a damned thing. B-but sooner or later we gotta let the mare out the barn, man. Can't keep it wrapped in blankets for too long. It's gonna wanna run. It's what's natural to do, Modecai. Sees them fields, that open space, and it's gonna wanna run like hell.

"It was built for running, nothing else. To run free in the fields. Seen it in my life, natural born life—you too, Modecai. Taste the wind or, hell, make one!"

And Modecai's ears heard Bunny Greensleeves's trumpet soar through another octave. The record was still spinning on the turntable.

"Bunny Greensleeves's free, Modecai. He's up in New York playing, bumping up against life at its best and its worst. You get me, Modecai? Hear me, man?"

Modecai nodded.

"Motivation, Modecai. Motivation, dammit. What you need, motivation? Or are you like all of us jazz cats once was? Just plain scared to death?"

Jimmy Mack walked away from Modecai and back to his bass fiddle, his eyes glancing admiringly down at it.

"Well, all the same—Bunny Greensleeves is up there in New York City cutting a album with Earl 'Fatha' Hines's big band that we is listening to. Putting heat in our pants. Are all ears about."

And Bunny Greensleeves was blowing his trumpet through Jimmy Mack and Modecai's ears, all right. He did sound like some kind of lure, like he'd captured or seduced New York City's jazz scene and was turning it quite literally on its ear, upside down like an apple cart whose apples were spilling all over New York City's cobbled streets with unleashed relish.

Chapter 5

The ten-floor tenement sat in the middle of the block on 116th Street in Harlem.

"Bunny, you took that solo so high, thought you was talking to God. Damn!"

"Says who? Sticks? What dictionary? Let me tell you something from my mouth to your ears: I *was* talking to God. And the Big Cat in the sky was listening with both ears!"

Bunny Greensleeves and John "Sticks" Cooper had been working out some rhythmic things between them. They lived together. They shared the apartment with one other person though, a nonmusician cat (didn't know how they worked that one out, how he got on the bandstand with them, but the other nonmusician cat they lived with loved jazz).

"I could've juiced it up some more if I wanted. But you know I gotta save some for tonight. Don't want to give everything away for free—"

"When, ha, you can give it away for nothing. I know," Sticks laughed. "How it goes. Them tricks, man."

"Who said you can't get rich by digging a ditch, Sticks? It certainly wasn't no jazz cat playing jazz who said that off-the-wall shit!"

Sticks Cooper sat behind his drums looking like a long, wet, slippery shadow.

Bunny Odecai Greensleeves looked like a small, bouncy rubber ball you bounce against the wall and hope to catch on the first hop.

"We picked the wrong occupation, profession, man."

"Looks that way."

It's when John "Sticks" Cooper, this jazz vet, executed a sad drumroll on his drum with his drumsticks.

Bunny fingered the trumpet's valves and then blew into its mouthpiece not in any way to make ordinary sound but as if, weirdly, to echo it.

"But not me, Sticks. Uh-uh, man! I'm gonna make me some bread. Libby Greensleeves's little baby boy from Philadelphia, Mississippi—the one she diapered, fed, and raised—is gonna be rolling in dough. In a big haystack of sticky green dollar bills one day."

"You got it all figured out for yourself, huh, Bunny," Sticks said, his drumsticks executing another sad drumroll. "A young boy like you. Swing the world by its tail. Got the socks matched to the shoes already, huh?"

Bunny grabbed his golden-tinged trumpet. "Me and my baby, Sticks. We know the score." And then Bunny Greensleeves pointed his finger to his head. "And this, Sticks. What's locked up in here."

"The tunes, your compositions—"

"I ain't wrote yet. Yeah. But I know they're in my head under lock and key. In safekeeping. Just keeping cool as a cucumber sitting in the shade."

"Mr. Hines thinks—"

"Thinks I'm a young genius—and who can blame the man, man!"

"You ain't modest about nothing, are you, Bunny?"

Bunny Greensleeves, if you studied the young cat's eyes, really studied them from the inside out, front to back, you wouldn't come away thinking he was studying Sticks Cooper's question, only indulging it.

"There's only one way to think, Sticks. And if I don't think that way, then I might as well pack my ego in my trumpet case and catch the first Greyhound bus out of New York City and back to Philadelphia, Mississippi. Back to where the hell I came from."

Sticks performed another sad drumroll.

"We country boys don't scare easy though, do we, Bunny? Seen so many blue days down South, the way, New York City looks like a birthday cake with candles."

Then Bunny raised his trumpet and blew on it. "Can't seem to blow them candlesticks out, Sticks!"

"Sometimes, Bunny, it's good when your eyes seen them worse, so they can see what better looks like."

Bunny looked around the drab, gray apartment.

"But better's gonna be better than this shit for me one day, Sticks. You know what I like. You know my style."

"Women and clothes—and not necessarily in that order."

And Bunny Greensleeves looked dapper in his clothes: red pants, white shoes, and a chalk white silk shirt that was embroidered in all the right places.

"Hell, clothes attract the woman, Sticks—"

"And then Bunny Greensleeves takes over from there, huh, Bunny?"

"Yeah, man. Yeah. Square to the peg, Sticks. Shit's square to the peg!"

Sticks was napping.

"Hey there, Big Booty!"

Al "Big Booty" Bailey lumbered through the apartment door. (Al "Big Booty" Bailey had him one big booty, man!)

"Say, what's happening, Bunny?"

Big Booty was the apartment's third listed tenant on the lease and mailbox (the nonmusical one, of course). Bunny and Sticks did a three-way split with Big Booty on the rent. Big Booty worked as a boot black on Broadway. Midtown. Big Booty's reputation on Broadway was that his seat was the broadest seat anyone had ever seen or sat on on Broadway. Big Booty sat in it whenever a customer wasn't getting his shoes shined from his rag, polish, spit, and brush.

"Sticks snoozing, Bunny?" Big Booty asked, his mouth busy chomping on a fat, plump piece of drumstick he just got out of the refrigerator, reducing the drumstick bite by bite to a partial representation of its former self.

"Yeah, Big Booty. Sticks's baby browns counting little Bo Peep's sheep in his sleep by now."

Quickly, efficiently, Big Booty's mouth had chomped through the drumstick.

"Damn, Big Booty, bet you your big black ass would fight a mouse over the cat's last scrap of cheese if you and him got in a fight—even if you are afraid of mice."

"You ain't seen none of them frisky little critters running around the apartment lately, have you?"

"Nope, can't say I have. But it don't mean shit. Don't mean Sticks ain't."

Bunny walked out the kitchen. He sat down on a chair in front of a music stand holding his music. He shut his eyes. He was lucky to be here, in a mouse-infested tenement in Harlem, he thought. He was lucky to be here, a boy from Philadelphia, Mississippi—someplace that, to him, now, sounded like it was on the other side of the equator. He was lucky to get out of there—but luckier that he had a talent, a gift from God that got him out of there. His family was still in Philadelphia, Mississippi. Bunny Odecai Greensleeves never liked to think about that fact for too long, for any stretch of time.

"Bunny …?"

"Yeah, Big Booty?"

Big Booty came into the front room. He looked well fed for now.

"What time you and Sticks get in this morning?"

"I don't know about Sticks, but I got in much later than him."

"The Hotel Lorraine again?"

"Yeah. Made a deposit at the front desk. Man, the Hotel Lorraine's got all my change. Is spending the shit like crazy. My green is what's keeping its sheets clean."

"What the babe look like?"

"You mean 'young lady,' 'young lady,' don't you, Big Booty?"

"Okay. Okay, yeah, yeah—whatever."

"Stacked as a—"

"Stack of pancakes?"

"And long and tall as—"

"As, as a ten-inch straw. I know. I know, Bunny. Hey, man, tell me something I don't already know."

"So why'd you ask if you—"

"You jazz cats, man," Big Booty said with envy. "Sleep all day, play all night, and party all morning."

"Yeah, that's about the size of it, Big Booty. How we cats skin the bear."

"Yeah, what a damned life!"

"Compared to what, Big Booty?"

Big Booty cracked his knuckles. "Compared to mine. Compared to a bootblack on Broadway slapping shoe polish on shoes all day with a shoe rag, Bunny—that's what!"

"You mean, when you and your big ass ain't sitting around watching them fine-as-wine chicks swinging their hips up Broadway. What your big ass meant to say."

"Yeah, yeah." Big Booty blushed uncontrollably. "You caught my black ass, Bunny. All right."

Bunny lifted the golden trumpet to his lips, and the trumpet produced a round, golden sound.

Man, Big Booty thought to himself, *Man, can Bunny play that trumpet!*

"What the hell, Bunny?" Sticks said for the fiftieth time it seemed since it happened. "I thought a five-alarmer had gone off back in the apartment. I swear, man. Cross my heart and die twice."

Sticks was setting up his drum set at Berl's Pearls. It was another gig on the Harlem jazz map in this thriving world of nightclubs and jazz music.

"No, it was just me, Sticks, talking to the angels for Big Booty's sake."

"Man, Bunny," Sticks said disagreeably, "and I was sleeping good. Sound like an angel—if you don't mind. Mess with a man's sleep it's like messing with his money or his woman or his food or his—"

Earl Watson, the leader of the horn section, tapped Bunny on his shoulder. "Hey, listen, Bunny, Mr. Hines says you got the solo on 'Brown-Eyed Baby' tonight. All right."

"Right. Thanks," Bunny said.

"Brown-Eyed Baby" was a Bunny Greensleeves composition. An original.

"Did you hear the man's voice, Bunny?" Sticks shrugged his shoulders. "Like Mr. Hines was gonna let him blow your solo. The dudes got the *J* word written all over his forehead. Could see it as far away as Alaska."

"Cat acts like he's jealous, I'm gonna take over his gig soon, trumpet chair, Sticks. Hell, I don't want his gig, man—cat can have it. Got me bigger plans than leading a horn section in Fatha Hines's jazz band, man."

"You do?"

"Yeah. I've got to breathe, Sticks …"

"What you mean is, is a change, don't you? Be your own man, man," Sticks said, looking into Bunny's brown eyes. "Call the shots. All the shots all the time."

"It's who I am, Sticks. Just don't know no better, I guess. Brash, I know I come off as brash at times. Cross the line."

"At times?"

"Okay, I know I'm a pocketful. A handful to handle. A big pain in the ass. But, I know what I want, Sticks. Know what I'm after."

Sticks beat out some mean rhythms on his drum set. Then he took his drumsticks and began rubbing them up and down with his hands.

"Trumpets always out front, Bunny. Leading the pack. Drummers, we just sit in the background. The shadows."

"But we cats know who does all the work, Sticks. Who's knocking us dead. Clubbing us over the head."

"Guess so." Pause. "But you're a frontline player, Bunny. The star. Right, smack dab in the middle of everybody's eye. Audience can't miss you. You get to wear the pretty clothes."

"No … the audience can't, Sticks. Don't miss nothing." Bunny beamed. "Tie or tux. Belt or suspenders."

"Got that clean-looking horn looking like a golden chariot in the spotlight."

"Yeah, yeah, I know, Sticks."

* * *

The entire crowd in Berl's Pearls was standing, applauding Bunny. Even Earl "Fatha" Hines couldn't stop it, not until Bunny stood and took, for the eighth time, another low, slow, graceful, sweeping bow at the waist from the band's horn section.

Earl "Fatha" Hines pleaded for the crowd's attention. "Ladies, ladies and gentlemen, whoa … whoa, now. The band, we do have to take a break. Sorry, but we do. It's written in the boys' contracts and mine, in indelible ink, I might add!" Mr. Hines joked.

"And it also says that we have to come back. Something we just love to do: to play more music for you!"

Bunny sat back down. The band members began glad-handing Bunny, all of them but the section's horn leader, Earl Watson—he blew past Bunny.

Bunny was wiping himself with a handkerchief—how he was sweating, man. Profusely. A young man stood in front of him. His hand extended to Bunny's. Bunny's hand took the note.

"Hmm … She's—"

"Tall and long like a ten-inch straw."

"And stacked—"

"Like a stack of pancakes."

"So where can I find this fine, delectable, spectacular wonder of nature, Chummy? This sweet goddess of the night, man?"

Chummy Davis, the young man, who was Berl's Pearls emcee, smiled deviously.

"Table number seven, Bunny."

"Seven, as in heaven, Chummy?"

Chummy and Bunny had devised their own numbering system for the nightclub tables.

"It all comes up lucky seven for you, Bunny."

"As long as she's got—"

"Don't sweat it. The chick's legs are as long as a New York City telephone pole."

"Calling long distance, Chummy?"

Bunny's hand was stroking Sweet Sylvia's legs (it's what she told Bunny she called herself). Chummy was right, absolutely, Bunny thought: her legs were as long as a New York City telephone pole calling long distance. Sweet Sylvia had her a fine pair of black stems, man. Fine!

The moon shimmered off her black skin like diamonds glittering in a Tiffany showcase. She was curvaceous, had been full of fun and fire in the bed. But he'd put her to sleep, Bunny thought, from the sex they'd had.

He was wide awake. He was thinking about this fast life of his—how he fit into it as soon as he arrived in New York City, onto its shores from Philadelphia, Mississippi. Nonstop. It seemed as if he'd been going nonstop since he got to New York City eight months ago. Had planted his feet on New York soil. It was like he'd created his own pace, his own schedule, even quicker, more demanding than even New York City required. He was in this joint and that joint. He traveled the city like he had a New York City map drawn on his back.

"B-Bunny, honey …," Sweet Sylvia moaned, and then she rolled right back on her back—back on the soiled sheets.

"Man, you're stacked, Sweet Sylvia. Stacked like a stack of pancakes!"

Bunny was ready for his third helping of "pancakes" but stopped short of waking Sweet Sylvia. His hesitation seemed irksome for him.

"When am I gonna stop hopping around New York City like a bunny rabbit, man? When? What the hell drives me? I-I mean, what the hell really drives me, man!"

Bunny rolled over. He sat on the edge of the bed. His trumpet case was within reach; he got it.

Dirt poor. He'd always been dirt poor. Him and his folk, his brothers and sisters, of which there were eleven, including himself, were poor as Mississippi mud. But it was odd, because he knew he was poor by other people's standards but rich by his own. He always felt kingly, like he was dressed in ermine and lace. He always thought of it as a light, a bright, warm illuminating light shining out him.

But once he got to New York, the warm, bright light that burned inside him began to consume him. It began to rage inside him like a fire, out of control, and he couldn't dampen it. For him it was like his skin was burning up, burning up, burning up. He had to play everywhere. He had to be everywhere. He had to do everything. Bunny Greensleeves had to be on top!

Bunny laid the trumpet case down on his lap. Flea bag hotels, he thought. Cold tenements. Yeah, it would be winter in Harlem soon, and the cold would be cracking through his apartment building's red brick.

"Brrrr … man … Brrrr …"

Bunny Greensleeves ain't built for no New York winters, Bunny laughed. *Not unless they're in heated apartment buildings up on Fifth Avenue, man. Of course I've seen Fifth Avenue. Of course I've been over on the other side of Harlem, the white man's paradise, the white man's playground. Where the white man lives. Heated pads. Nice, warm pads, yeah, heated pads, man.*

A real cushy life.

Bunny opened his trumpet case. His hand reached into the case and pulled out his golden trumpet.

"B-Bunny …"

Bunny was surprised Sweet Sylvia still knew what man she was with tonight, had sex with, even remembered his damned name.

Sweet Sylvia put her hand up to her forehead, and then it fell away, limply.

"Yeah, that gin did you in, didn't it? That and Bunny Greensleeves tonight."

Bunny's fingertips stroked his trumpet.

Is it how fame is? Bunny wondered. A woman last night. A different woman tonight. Fast. Cheap. Nonstop. Always on the go, never catching my breath in my lungs? Chest? When do I sleep, man? When does Bunny Greensleeves have time to sleep? When does fame let you sleep?

Bunny couldn't answer himself. Or was it he didn't want to. A musician. Tonight. Tonight on the bandstand, he did things to people few people could do. For a moment, a minute, an hour or more, the way he played his trumpet, he was able to touch people, put them in touch with themselves. So wasn't he in touch with himself then? Couldn't he give himself that power? If he was able to extend it to others, couldn't he at least give it to himself?

Fame. Fortune. Power.

As long as he could blow mightily into that trumpet he held in his hand, he had it, man. He held the majesty. The magic. He held the gift. He held the power.

The band, Fatha Hines's band, would be going out on the road. Fourteen one-night stands, one-nighters, man. Fourteen cities, towns—wherever the bus, with its loosey-goosey springs, would take them.

Fourteen one-night stands. Bumpy roads. Fourteen nights of different folk who didn't know his name but would—after he stood in the horn section and blew his trumpet good and hard.

They'd do like tonight at Berl's Pearls, wherever he went, wherever he carried his horn. He'd touch them, man—would he ever touch them. He'd bring the crowd to its feet no matter where he went. No matter where he played. He had the power, man. He and his trumpet, what he had in his hand, was looking at—he had the power to do that, man.

Bunny lifted the trumpet to his lips. It was all mimicked out. But he heard the music he played tonight as clear as if it were being played in the mouth of a whale. "Brown-Eyed Baby" stole everyone's heart. Even put tears in his ears. Man, did he have the power. Did he ever.

There was more of that kind of music in him. He could compose that kind of music while sleepwalking in horse blinders, while tripping over a crack in the sidewalk, while juggling salt and pepper shakers on top a church steeple.

"Sometimes I think I do sleep with the angels, man."

He was already too big for Fatha Hines's band. Already, inside, it's how he felt. Already, he was too good for the band. The music he could compose would exceed what he was playing in the band. The music he could write would give jazz a new look, a new face—a fresh, new means of imagining itself and its genius.

It was just finding the time. Fame takes up your time, man. Living on Fifth Avenue, not in Harlem, takes up your time, man. Being rich takes up your time, man. Being Bunny Greensleeves takes up your time, man.

"Pardon me, sir—but can you break a hundred-dollar spot? What? You say, you only have a ... a—five singles and some change? My, my ... ain't that poor of you! Ain't it though!

Yeah, man, caviar's served after five. The silver spoon comes out after five. Rich white people on Fifth Avenue live after five. It's when the limousine driver arrives: after five.

A chauffeur's cap, a smile, and spit-shined boots, after five.

Chapter 6

They'd made love in the sweet part of the afternoon. It was the first time Delores and Modecai had made love in the sweet part of the afternoon before Delores went off to work. It was always at night when they made love, not the afternoon. But it happened naturally, without coercion.

Delores's face was on: the eye shadow on the eyelids, the red rouge on the cheeks, mascara, lipstick. Delores pressed her lips together for the red lipstick could do its job. Delores smiled, for her ears had been pricked like a dog's—Modecai was back at his piano playing music.

Delores checked her pocketbook's contents. She was really falling for him, she thought (or had she fallen for him?), for Modecai Ulysses Jefferson. Over the past few months, yes, she thought—she was head over heels in love with the guy.

Then a terrifying thought came to mind: Johnnyboy. Johnnyboy Daniels was the last man Delores thought she loved. Johnnyboy Daniels was in Foster City Prison serving a five-year stretch for second-degree manslaughter. She'd visited the prison a few times. It was a long, difficult bus ride to Foster City, Alabama. Johnnyboy had killed a man in Way City.

There were no witnesses to the murder. The man's throat was slashed with Johnnyboy's knife. Johnnyboy said it was in self-defense, but because of his past criminal record, he said, the judge ("that white, pig motherfucker") gave him prison time. Johnnyboy lived in Way City.

How Delores met him had now become—for her—why had she met him. He was primitive, wild, his violence ugly, frightening. Johnnyboy said she brought the best out of him. It's how he saw her, almost like an angel of good will and providence.

Five months ago was the last time she took a bus to Foster City Prison. Johnnyboy was happy to see her. He told her to go on living her life—that he wasn't coming back to Way City. He said he didn't want to return to that kind of life of violence he lived there. It was the last thing he told her. His hazel-green eyes looked kind and truthful. It was the last she saw or heard from Johnnyboy. Johnnyboy Daniels was illiterate; he could neither read nor write.

It was a huge relief for her. In Way City, she was known as Johnnyboy's girl (because she was). It was as if she'd been afflicted, cursed; it was "hands off." But over time things changed. Over time men in Way City began to realize Johnnyboy was in Foster City Prison, locked away—not in the way. She'd had one or two flings—sexual, not romantic.

But now Modecai. This was serious. This was no fling. They'd made love in the sweet part of the afternoon today before her going off to Benny's Pit.

Modecai's teeth gripped the sharp, pointed pencil.

The door down the hall opened and then closed. Modecai opened his door.

"You could've at least waited until I got to your door, M—"

"For you could deliver a coupla solid raps on it?"

"Taps, Modecai, taps. Not raps. They're always taps."

"Sound like raps to me when you tap."

"Your ears are bad, plain bad, that's all."

"Why, how, I mean how could you say that to a jazz musician?"

By now Delores was relaxing in Modecai's arms. Modecai was looking into Delores's eyes.

"You certainly look good."

"See what a little afternoon of—"

And then Delores caught herself and her tongue simultaneously, for her modesty seemingly prevailed.

Modecai kissed her lips and then laughed heartily.

"It was … heavenly," Delores said after a long silence.

"I thought the cat had caught your tongue for a second."

"But, still, we mustn't make it a habit, Modecai. It might interfere with your writing. All right, honey?"

"I'll pick you up at Benny's tonight, if it's all right with you."

Modecai lifted Delores's chin and kissed her a second time.

"You're spoiling me."

"I know."

"But this gal's not complaining. Uh-uh. Not in the least."

Delores turned and began walking down the hallway, and Modecai noticed there was an extra swing in her hips.

"Girl, shake that thing! Shake it!"

"Oh, Modecai!" Delores squealed. She waved back at him. "See you tonight, honey."

Modecai hustled back over to his piano. He sat back down on the piano stool. *Now where was I,* he thought. "Hmm ..."

Tap.

Modecai leaped off the piano stool. Was Delores back for another kiss from his sweet lips? Was—

"Oh, it's you, Jimmy Mack!"

"Who'd you think it was? Dee?"

"Shows, huh?"

"All over. Face couldn't hide a pimple on a mule's ass. Besides, bumped into Dee down in front of the building."

Jimmy Mack rolled his bass into the room. He began unzipping the bass case.

"Uh, Billy said he'd be by later. Wants to work out some new stuff with you, seems."

"Hungry?"

"Don't have my feedbag on today, Modecai. Besides, man, getting tired of eating you outta house and home. Keep forgetting you're scuffling, struggling just like the rest of us cats is. Trying to make ends meet."

Modecai hoped the joy that must be shimmering off his face (if he saw it in a mirror) wasn't offending Jimmy Mack; but since he, in Way City, had been inextricably linked to Jimmy Mack and his men, his food bill had shot up and up and up and up and—

"Ready to play?"

"Uh, yes, but maybe, Jimmy Mack, you can help me with this opening bar I'm having trouble with," Modecai said, handing Jimmy Mack a copy of the music.

"Ummm … yeah. This is some nasty shit already you done cooked up.

S-some nasty shit boiling in the pot."

"Thanks, Jimmy Mack. But there's something still missing."

"Okay, let me strum the bass line you got here, okay? Umm …"

"What, Jimmy Mack? What is it?"

"You know, Modecai, I could bow this. For you. Some. Add a little tension to it. Uh … to …"

Modecai turned back around to his piano.

"Okay, a one, a two, a one, two, three …"

And Jimmy Mack and Modecai met at the opening bar.

Modecai shut his eyes; Jimmy Mack's bowing was doing it for the tune, providing the right tone, feel—what, he'd felt, had been missing.

"Perfect, Jimmy Mack. Perfect!"

"Hell, wasn't in the construction of the piece, Modecai. Nah, uh-uh, not at all. You just had to hear it. That's all. This tune's bad, bad news, man!"

Jimmy Mack stopped bowing his bass fiddle.

"Got a bridge for it yet?"

"Working on it. That's next."

"Got a name for it?"

"'Delores.'"

All music stopped.

"She's breathing in your ear, ain't she, Modecai? Tickling it?"

"Yes, she is, Jimmy Mack."

"Which ear? Right or left? The tickle? Don't matter." Pause. "You know, she's nice, Modecai. She's a nice young lady. And she's a regular churchgoer too!"

Modecai laughed.

"But you can't take her with you to New York City, when you go. Uh-uh. Not Dee. Dee Bonet."

Modecai slammed the piano cover shut.

"I wish you'd stop it. Stop bringing up New York City e-every time you get a chance! You come here! To the apartment, Jimmy Mack!"

"Hell, like beating a dead horse, Modecai. Guess it's the old country boy down in me. Ain't your guardian angel, man—but I ain't the devil neither."

When Modecai's anger cooled down, he smiled.

"I ain't gonna appease you, Modecai. And ha, don't ask me how I learned that big-ass word, maybe it was up in New York—no, I ain't gonna make nice-nice with you, man. My black ass, my bones too old and tired and you too talented for any bull crap but the truth. The truth dyed blue. Out the wash."

"I-I …"

"And don't give me that, that you 'appreciate' it bull crap neither 'cause my ears ain't in the mood for none a that bullshit. None of it." Pause.

"Been bugging your ass about New City, I know. But as long as I come here, in your apartment building, and play music with you, it's how it's gonna be. You can expect as much. So get used to it. Ain't backing off—not for one day. Understood?"

Pause.

"Billy and the rest of the cats feel the same as I do about it, Modecai. So let me say that up front. It ain't just me. It's just I've been appointed the chairman of the board, might say, see. They know I got me a big mouth and'll ride your ass into … all the way into oblivion 'til you see it my way. Pitch a boogey 'til you do."

"Ha."

"But, uh, what's it gonna take, Modecai? What—you got all the talent in the world. You got true genius in you," Jimmy Mack said, looking at the sheet music in his hand. "Real genius. What I'm holding. Staring the hell at. And it's only gonna get sweeter, man, the older you get. Life. Experiences and all." Pause.

"But what's it gonna take for you to unsaddle yourself? For you to get on a bus heading for New York City, Modecai? What, man? Moving ten, twenty miles an hour, who cares—long as it's heading up the road. Outta here. This backwater, barnyard, hayseed town that ain't even worth the shit in your pants."

Modecai's eyes were practically tearful; he seemed so emotionally moved by what Jimmy Mack just said.

"I-I don't know, Jimmy Mack. I honestly don't know."

"But you can't take Dee with you. Already said that. Dee Bonet. You can't—ain't in the cards, in the deck."

And for a second time, this comment, opinion of Jimmy Mack's irked Modecai. And again, Jimmy Mack appeared unperturbed, could care less.

"That-that's personal, Jimmy Mack. T-that's between me and—"

"Dee can't go with you, Modecai. Plain and simple. That's all. New York City ain't her kind of town—she'll get in the way. You got to leave the girl behind here in Way City when you go, Modecai.

"Dee Bonet'll understand—Dee ain't gonna get in your way. Not one iota. For one damned second."

And now, all of a sudden, Modecai didn't like Jimmy Mack Burgess or his company. And not one word Jimmy Mack had to say about his music, his genius, his life, and, especially, about Dee … Dee Bonet … Delores.

* * *

It was quitting time at the Pit for Delores.

She was looking at Modecai from across the floor and could sense that struggle in him, something she hadn't seen in him in a long time.

"You and that guy over there is getting awful serious, ain't you, Delores?"

"I didn't want this to happen, Benny. I didn't go looking for it—but yes, I think this thing between Modecai and I is getting serious."

"Can't fight love," Benny said matter-of-factly. "Can't do nothing about it. Them feelings trapped inside you, young lady. Ain't healthy. Ruin your health if you try."

Delores kept looking at Modecai, this lonely figure who had no cure for his loneliness, not even if she handed him her heart or told him his pain tattered her insides too.

Delores waitressed the table where her last customer for the night sat. Then she walked over to where Modecai sat, was sitting in the corner for the past few minutes.

"Modecai, honey, what's wrong?"

Modecai's eyes looked up at the clock on the brown stained wall.

"I'll be off in five minutes."

"Yes, I know."

"But we can—"

"Uh-uh. It's all right. You finish up. What I want to discuss with you can wait."

Now this new bit of information caused Delores to worry. Discuss? Discuss what? What was there to discuss?

"Modecai," Delores said, trembling, "honey, you're making me nervous."

"Don't be," Modecai said, taking hold of her hand. "There's no need to, Delores, okay? All, all right?"

The lights inside Benny's Pit were all shut off.

The restaurant's back-door light was on. Modecai hung under the light like a moth.

As soon as Delores was out the restaurant door, she grabbed Modecai's hand.

"Hi, Modecai."

He kissed her.

"S-still in a panic?" There was some edge to him too. His voice.

"Yes, I haven't been able to calm down."

They'd not begun walking yet. Then they had to make room for Benny as he squeezed past them.

"See you, Delores, Modecai. You two kids have you a good night now."

Benny hustled up the dark back alleyway.

The restaurant's back door's light was off. The dark, suddenly, looked even more piercing ahead.

The dark didn't seem to bother them. They still had their hands locked together but were not going anywhere fast.

"Aren't afraid of the dark, are you, Delores?"

"Who? Me?" Delores said bravely. "Why, I'm afraid of my own shadow. Especially if it jumped out at me." Delores laughed some more but then seemed to relax. "No, the dark doesn't bother me, only the future, sometimes."

"Delores, d-do you know what you just said?"

"No, Modecai, no, tell me." Pause.

"Jimmy Mack was by the apartment today."

"Yes, I know … I ran into him on my way out the—"

"Right, right. He told me. On your way to work. Right—see, my brain is in flux, Delores. In a state of confusion." Pause. "You know, it's the same old thing, Delores. He won't turn it loose."

"New York City?"

"New York City. He's being a bulldog about it."

Modecai was looking at her dark skin in the dark alleyway.

"Jimmy Mack knows something, Modecai, it's fair to say."

"He called me a genius today, can you believe it?"

"I think so too." Pause. "I'm not smart about—"

"New York City is the jazz capital of the world. It's where the great jazz players go to become great. The hotbed for jazz. New York City."

"Are you going, Modecai? Is, is this what this talk is about? All—"

"I-I don't know. I don't know a-about going."

"You know," Delores said, "you should've seen yourself at the corner table tonight. In Benny's just now." Pause. "You're used to being alone, aren't you?"

"Yes—in a way I am."

"What do they call it? A, a—"

"An occupational hazard," Modecai laughed.

"It doesn't bother you, does it?"

"What? Being alone? No, no, it doesn't."

"You're used to it."

"Uh, yes. It's my world, Delores. Where I live. It's a quiet, deep world. It's where I go when I compose, in a world where no one can reach me but me."

"It's a beautiful world, honey?"

"It never promises beauty, Delores, just—only, I think, some kind of reward. Substantial, uh … Yes." Pause.

"Delores, you've entered my life like a storm. You're in my life, well into it now."

"Something you never wanted, right?"

"Yes—it's not something I planned on. A woman in my life. But New York. N-New York ..."

"And we, they, they don't mix. Don't add up. Don't—"

"Delores, no, I'm not saying that." Anxiously, Modecai's hand was rubbing Delores's back. "I'm just saying—I don't know if I want to go off to New York City. And if I do go, when do I?"

"You're that confused, honey, mixed up about it?"

"Yes. But what it is I want to know—is bothering me more than anything is—"

"Will I go to New York City with you when—"

"If, Delores, if ..."

"When, Modecai. It's not a question of 'if.'"

"All right—when," Modecai said. "I won't fight you on that point. When, then." Pause.

"Then will you, Delores, go off to New York City with me when the time comes?"

"Can we start then, uh, walking back to Taylor Street then, Modecai, back home, honey?"

Modecai looked up at the dark sky. "There's no light back here, is there?"

They held each other at the waist.

"I didn't think this would happen, not in a million years. But I've fallen in love with you. Head over heels in love with you, Modecai."

The alleyway was dark and littered by beat-up trash cans spilled over onto their sides. Modecai and Delores were walking on top loose, shifting dirt. Even once outside the alleyway's small radius, there was another seventy-five or eighty yards more of unlit ground.

Modecai and Delores walked in total silence. Both coveted thoughts. Both were trying to fix this thing properly between them. Both were trying to nail down this situation, this relationship they were now owning up to as best they could. If they had to find themselves, each felt, individually, collectively, now was the time. At some time, somewhere there would be change, and both knew they had to be sure about it—that there would be no backing out or second-guessing themselves.

It was near the break in the alleyway when the silence between them was broken. Delores just hoped her voice wouldn't betray her.

"M-Modecai, honey, I want us to—"

And with no warning, Modecai's body was snatched from Delores in the alleyway's darkness.

"Motherfucker, what you doing with my girl!"

"Johnnyboy!"

"Nigger, oughta slit your throat!"

Johnnyboy's long, sharp blade was at Modecai's throat.

Modecai's eyes rolled back into his eye sockets.

"Johnnyboy!"

"Oughta kill you!"

"No, Johnnyboy, I'll—"

"Get back, woman—or this motherfucker's dead! Your fucking boyfriend's a dead man! Back! Back! Get the fuck back!"

Johnnyboy's foot kicked a trash can off to the side and then pushed his back up against the adjoining building's cracked wooden frame after dragging Modecai with him.

"Johnnyboy! Please let him go! Let him go!"

"Nigger, nigger's gonna die, Dee. Tonight—with this! This!" Johnnyboy slanted the knife more into Modecai's throat.

"But it's not worth it, Johnnyboy. You just got out of prison. Foster City Prison. Didn't you? Haven't you, Johnnyboy!"

"Yeah. Just got out. My black ass out that motherfucker. What, what … yeah, Dee."

"When, Johnnyboy? When?"

"What's today? Dammit, goddammit … What's—I don't know, girl," Johnnyboy said, shaking his head painfully. "I don't fucking know!"

"Thursday, Johnnyboy. Thursday. It's, today's—"

"Thursday, it's Thursday already … T-Tuesday, Tuesday. It's fucking Thursday, Dee? I was let out Tuesday!"

"You weren't supposed to come back. You said—"

"But I'm back. Look at me, Dee. I'm fucking back. Had a change of heart. Back, my black ass. Back bad as a motherfucker. And I want what's fucking mine back!"

Modecai couldn't move.

"This nigger got him a fucking name! Do he!"

"M-Modecai, Johnnyboy, M-Modecai!"

"Country. Real country. Ha. Real fucking country boy!"

His grip loosened, but the knife's blade was still at Modecai's throat.

"Johnnyboy, when did you—"

"Just now. Seen Benny. Scared nigger. Nigger run like a scared jackrabbit when he seen me come looking for you. F-for my fucking woman." Pause.

"Come here. Come to daddy. Your fucking daddy, girl. Even in the dark, your black ass look fine! Even in the dark!"

Johnnyboy pushed Modecai aside, and Modecai fell forward, out of control, stumbling.

"Modecai, M—"

"You ain't going nowhere, girl," Johnnyboy said, grabbing Delores's wrist, "but to me!"

Modecai had regained his balance.

"Delores, Delores, are you all—"

"Run off, motherfucker. Lover boy. Better run your black ass outta here 'fore I run you through with this," Johnnyboy said, blustering with the knife. "Get your ugly, black ass outta here. This ain't none of your fucking business, nigger. Shit, hear me, motherfucker!"

"Go, Modecai. Go. Just go. Y-you don't need trouble. N-not this kind of trouble. Go!"

"D-Delores …"

"Go! Pleeeease, pleeeeease, Modecai …"

"Better listen to her," Johnnyboy said, thrusting the blade out in the dark. "Get the fuck outta here. Get going!"

"I'm, I'm going, n-not because I'm afraid of him, but—"

"Just go, Modecai. Pleeeeease … pleeeeease …"

Delores's eyes followed Modecai until he reached where the light pole could light his face, and saw how pale it was, the picture of fear in Modecai, where it had manifest, when Modecai had turned back around to her.

Go, Modecai, Delores said to herself. *Please, honey, please!*

Then Modecai turned back around. He was walking up the street.

"Good fucking thing, Dee, your boyfriend don't decide to come back here. Have a change of mind. Make trouble."

Johnnyboy let go of Delores's wrist. He swaggered.

"W-what do you want, Johnnyboy!"

"Don't I, don't I explain myself good enough to you before, girl?"

"Johnnyboy, y-you said you weren't coming back to Way City. That I could—"

"Get to starting your life back over. B-back to normal. Yeah."

"Yes. It, it's the last thing you said to me in Foster City Prison, Johnnyboy. The—"

"Yeah, I know, girl. Know what I told you when I was sitting in prison. Behind them fucking prison bars. Y-you ain't gotta remind me."

Johnnyboy folded the knife's blade back.

"Ha. Was gonna kill that nigger," he said, looking back up the street. He put the knife in his back pocket. "Had me a fucking mind to." Pause.

"Need you …" Johnnyboy's voice softened, even if the swell in his burly chest added muscle to his words. "Gotta confess, don't know how to start a life over new. Don't, Dee. Don't know how to do that, get that far without you, baby. Don't, Dee …"

Johnnyboy walked over to Delores; his hand reached out for hers, but Delores rebuffed him.

"Why you act like that? Fucking for, Dee?"

"You haven't changed, Johnnyboy!"

"'Cause I caught you with your lover boy? Chase him off? Was hearing y-your voice in the alleyway … Teared me up, Dee. See, hearing you talking to 'nother man scared the shit outta me. Never hear that before. Everybody in this fucking, motherfucking town know you my woman. Johnnyboy's girl.

"Fucking why Benny run off scared, 'cause he know. Why that old nigger Benny run off scared like he done. Knows Johnnyboy's back. Knows Johnnyboy's back for his woman … Knows if I find 'nother man, any man with my woman, I'll cut the motherfucker's throat. Benny knows I'll kill any man, any man I find with you, Dee. Any man I find with Johnnyboy Daniels's woman!"

* * *

Modecai was blind, half-blind with fear, with rage, with worry. He'd stumbled through Way City's streets, up his building's stairs, into his apartment. The dingy room's light was on. The musty smell in the room—but the window was open. Where did all of this come from? The explosion?

Modecai stumbled over to the piano, falling against it, all his body's weight. He could still feel the knife's blade on his skin, about to slit it open. But Delores, Delores was with that violent man. But she knew him; they knew each other.

Erratically Modecai was breathing. He'd never had someone put a knife to his throat. Knife fights were common in the South, but he'd never come close to dying before, had looked at death.

Delores. Delores. But now he must think of Delores. She had to be the sole object of his thinking, because what was this Johnnyboy person doing with Delores? Would she be coming home tonight? Or … or maybe she'd be coming home with him tonight.

Modecai raised his hand up to his neck. Slowly his fingers traced over where the knife's metal blade had been. He could feel the weight, the pinch of the blade, even now, as if the blade were sinking into his throat and blood was spurting out the slit the knife had split open and the knife had his blood on it. No, he'd never been that close to dying before—never.

Maybe I should go back there. Back to Benny's. No. No. I'd have to kill him. I've never killed a man. This Johnnyboy person would have to be killed. This Johnnyboy person would want to kill me s-so I'd have to kill him. There could be nothing less in the exchange. No compromise.

Where did he come from? Prison. Delores said prison. For what? What for? What did this Johnnyboy person do to go to prison?

Delores knew him—but from where? From Way City? Way City, Alabama? Or was it some past place? Some past episode? But he knew where to come for her: Benny's Pit. This Johnnyboy person knew where to find Delores.

Modecai's body came away from the piano. He didn't want to have anything to do with it. He looked at the music, it was everywhere—he didn't want to have anything to do with it. But it was all his, Modecai thought. But the music was all his, his musical creations, his world. The world he lived in, inhabited, retreated to daily.

But now it'd been invaded, it'd been impacted upon—compromised, corrupted. How much did he want Delores? Was he willing to fight this Johnnyboy person for her? Was he? Was he!

It was going to come down to him and this Johnnyboy person, for he knew he wasn't going anywhere, would let him and Delores return to each other as lovers—not anytime soon.

It's what tonight was all about, wasn't it? He'd put it to her. New York City. The jazz capital of the world. He asked Delores the question, but she never answered him. She had the time. They had the time. But they kept walking in the alleyway, back there. In the dark. In the silence that he knew now was stealing time from them—that, now, were bleak minutes.

They were thinking. New York City. Her going with him to New York City. He'd fallen in love with Delores. He'd told her so. Delores had fallen in love with him. She'd told him so. Out of nowhere, he came out of nowhere. Like a bolt, a thunderbolt. Out of nowhere.

My eyes must've shut off—died. They had to. What was happening to me? What was this evil thing that had come upon me, possessed me? A beast? And Delores was screaming "Johnnyboy, Johnnyboy," b-but I still didn't know why she was saying that. Using the name "Johnnyboy." Johnnyboy.

"I have to get off my feet. I must get …"

He stretched his body out on top the dusty hardwood floor. His left foot pushed at the stack of music, pushing it back, some of it, from the top, toppling over, falling off to the floor.

"Let me think. Think. Think."

But I'm doing too much of that already. Thinking. Thinking. Delores is out there with him, with this Johnnyboy person. But … he won't hurt Delores. God, God, don't let him hurt Delores.

Modecai could hear himself breathe. How did … It sounded weak, pale, sickly, pulverized by fear? His heart had beat beyond anyone's belief in the back alleyway.

"I'll wait for her. I'll fight for her, fight this Johnnyboy person if I have to. B-but I'm afraid. God I'm afraid. Afraid …"

Modecai shut his eyes and then opened them. Nothing, he felt, was going to let him rest, find a moment's peace.

* * *

Delores was still dazed.

The scare in her resonant, vibrating. Johnnyboy was back in her life. He was back from prison, Foster City Prison. Delores was at the corner of Taylor Street. This city, it felt so closed in now, so narrow, this little southern town.

From where she was, she could see the light in Modecai's apartment. What was he doing? He wasn't at his piano, was he? He wasn't making music while all of this madness, insanity was going on around him, was he? No, he couldn't—she meant more to him than that.

Tonight he'd told her he loved her. If she'd had her way, she would've told him first. But they weren't supposed to get serious; it wasn't supposed to come to this, not this—love.

Johnnyboy, though, had left her with an ultimatum. His knife might as well have cut out her heart.

Damn Johnnyboy Daniels! Damn Johnnyboy Daniels!

Delores stood in front of Modecai's door.

Tap. Tap.

"Delores!"

"M-Modecai …"

She fell into Modecai's arms. It felt like he was rescuing her from everything tonight. The mean, dirty, evil world. He was going to take her to his bedroom.

"N-no, Modecai. Please take me to—"

"Your room?"

"Yes. Please. Please."

Modecai helped her down the hall.

He wanted to turn in an opposite direction, toward Taylor Street, and pretend his bags were packed and her bags were packed and they were leaving for New York City together, that it was a different hour, a different day, and all there was to worry about was Benny was without a waitress. But instead, he was hearing Delores's hand dig down into her pocketbook, and he heard her keys jangle, and the key went into the lock, and Delores twisted the door handle, and his shoulder brushed open the door, and the bands of dark enveloped them; but they made their way through it like they made their way down the hall, with maybe his fantasies, but he knew they weren't Delores's.

Inside the apartment, she was too emotionally fenced off, something he was before she got there; but now it was her turn, now that she was away from that monster. But she was so deep inside herself he wanted his lungs to scream and bleed for her.

He laid her on her back on the bed. He looked up from her and out the window. Modecai thought of Taylor Street again, but he didn't want its music, its dance, its rhythm. No, he didn't need it. He was just glad Delores was okay, that she'd come back to the apartment. She'd made it back.

But where was Johnnyboy? Where the hell was he in all of this? What had Delores done with him? Such a horrible person as him. Where was John—

He felt her arms grab his waist, only to drop away.

"Oh, Modecai …" Modecai felt Delores's breath penetrate his shirt. "M-Modecai …"

His mind was edgy, jumpy; it couldn't land anywhere. He felt his tongue slip past his chest and down to his stomach—but he hadn't swallowed, Modecai knew he hadn't swallowed, not once—at all.

"I'm sorry, Modecai. We used to be lovers. He's been in Foster City Prison. His name is Johnnyboy Daniels. He killed a man with a knife—"

Modecai trembled.

"In self-defense he, he said. There were no witnesses, Modecai. He was sentenced to five years, b-but it's only been three. T-they let Johnnyboy out of prison in three years. I don't know why.

"Johnnyboy, he told me a while back to go on with my life. T-to make something out of it without him."

Modecai couldn't imagine this man, this Johnnyboy Daniels person saying that.

"He said when he got out of prison, he was going to go off to another town, to, to …"

"Start life, life over again, Delores?"

"Yes. Yes. T-to start life over again."

Delores tried to stand but couldn't.

"No, no Delores, no. Don't."

"Then hold me, Modecai. Hold me. I need you to hold me."

He held her. She buried her head into Modecai's shirt and began crying.

"Why, Modecai? Why! Why … why is Johnnyboy back!"

"For you, Delores. For, w-why he's back. For you!"

But Delores knew this. If anyone knew why Johnnyboy Daniels was back in Way City, Alabama, it was Delores. Johnnyboy had told her that and more before he left her back at Benny's Pit. There'd been an ultimatum he'd issued tonight for her and Modecai.

Delores drew her head out Modecai's shirt.

"But why now, Modecai?"

He wiped her tears. "I don't know why. I don't know why now."

Modecai kissed Delores's forehead.

"He said I brought the good side out of him. He used to say that to me often when we first met," Delores sobbed. "It's what …"

Modecai didn't want to know how they'd met, Johnnyboy Daniels and Delores Bonet. But he did know Delores hadn't tamed him.

"I don't know. H-he never hit me, Modecai. Struck me, not once. He never put his hands on me. Yes, I can say that much for J-Johnnyboy, Modecai. He never beat me."

She's saying it like it's some consolation, or some moral prize, Modecai thought.

Modecai came off the bed. He was on his feet.

"Modecai …"

"I saw the man: he's an animal, a beast."

"The knife …"

The cold steel, yes, for a second, third, fourth time tonight, Modecai could feel it against his neck.

"I don't own a knife, Delores."

"I told him about our, our relationship. A-about us, Modecai."

"He didn't come back with you. To the apartment."

"No."

"Why?"

"He left."

"But he'll be back."

"Yes."

"Left, left for where, where, Delores?"

"I-I don't know."

"Back home?"

"Modecai, this is Johnnyboy's home."

Johnnyboy, Johnnyboy—Modecai was beginning to hate the sound of Johnnyboy Daniels's name!

Delores crawled out the bed.

"Don't, I told you—"

But Delores was on her feet.

"I told Johnnyboy where I live," Delores said, grabbing Modecai's shirt, shaking him. "That you live down the hall from me!"

Modecai grabbed Delores by both wrists.

"Johnnyboy told me he wants you out of here before he comes back to Way City. In two days, Modecai. He said if not, if you're not gone—he'll kill you. Kill you this time!"

It took all the strength in Modecai to stand and not fall.

Delores's fists pounded Modecai's chest.

"D-do you hear me, Modecai? Hear me!"

And then Delores fainted, collapsed back into Modecai's arms. Modecai put her back down on the bed.

"Delores."

Delores didn't answer.

"Delores," he said again.

He could feel her pain. He could feel this knife sticking out her. He took her hands and arranged them, at least made them look comfortable atop her stomach.

"You rest, Delores. You've been through so much tonight. So just rest, Delores."

Two days. Two days.

"I'll, I'll be here. I'll be right here, Delores. I'm not going—"

Johnnyboy Daniels was giving him two days to get out. It's what his ultimatum was. Was it two days to move out the apartment? Or was it two days to move out of town? Way City, Alabama? Which? Delores hadn't said. Delores hadn't said which! Which!

"I don't own a knife. I'm not a fighter. I never fought anyone in my life. Not even Charles, my brother Charles."

Modecai looked into the dark and felt defeated. He was always protected. His parents protected him. Charles, his older brother, protected him. This was a part of his background. This was a part of his personal history.

Modecai looked down at Delores. Just how important was she to him?

Modecai'd been lying on Delores's bed for some time.

"M-Modecai …" Delores voice was groggy, lifeless—just waking.

Modecai was off his back.

"I'm here, Delores. I'm here. I haven't left."

"I know you are, Modecai. I knew you would be even though m-my mind must've shut down. I-I don't remember thinking anything when, when …"

"When you fell off—"

"Yes, fell off to—"

"You needed the rest, Delores."

"Yes, my mind. My body couldn't take it anymore."

Modecai kissed Delores. His hand ran through her hair. She took his hand and kissed it.

"Your beautiful hand, Modecai." She took his other hand and kissed it. "These beautiful hands."

Then Delores laid them across her breasts.

"Oh, Modecai, when they play, they play so beautifully. When they make love to me they, they …"

What was Delores doing to him? Johnnyboy gave them two days.

"Delores …"

"Nothing must happen to these hands, Modecai. These beautiful hands."

"Johnnyboy …?"

"Nothing must happen to you, Modecai. Nothing must happen to you."

Modecai wanted Delores to snap out of it—just snap out of it, dammit!

"You must go, Modecai. L-leave. You must do, do as Johnnyboy says."

"Like you do. You!"

"You mean you don't understand? Johnnyboy's killed a man. He's a murderer."

"But we can't let him do this to us, Delores. We can't let Johnnyboy Daniels—"

"There, but there's nothing we can do. Nothing any of us can do."

"I can fight him, Delores. This Johnnyboy Daniels character, Delores. Can't I? Can't I!"

"He's not a character. Johnnyboy's real. He'll kill you. Johnnyboy's lived a life of crime. It's the only life Johnnyboy knows."

Delores held onto Modecai, rocking him.

Modecai was hearing his voice again when he'd said he could fight Johnnyboy Daniels, but it didn't sound real—it sounded flat and punchless.

Modecai was in tears.

"Go, Modecai. Go …"

"But, but you, Delores, what about you? What will happen to you?"

"I'll be all right, honey. As long as you're safe, I'll be all right. I will, Modecai."

Chapter 7

It was daybreak.

Modecai was in bed.

If he'd gotten two hours of sleep, it was a lot. His eyes were the color red; he didn't have to look into a mirror. He still hadn't answered his question from last night: did Johnnyboy want him to get out the apartment or out of Way City, Alabama? All of a sudden someone he didn't know was controlling his life, how it would evolve from this day forward.

Modecai wanted to smash his head against the wall and see it bleed.

Delores. Now there was Delores again. Now she was back in his mind in full dress, vision. He had to use the bathroom. He had to get to the bathroom before he peed on himself.

Modecai got up. It's as if he hadn't eaten in so many days. His body was so weak. Delores is going to be pushed around again, isn't she? Isn't she! This person is going to push her around again without laying a finger on her, a hand on her—he's going to push her around again. Johnnyboy Daniels doesn't have to hit her, beat her; he doesn't have to knock her around with his fists—put his hand on her. He already owns her—she was already in prison.

He had to get to the bathroom. His bladder.

"What does a person l-like Johnnyboy Daniels want from a person like Delores Bonet? How does Delores make him better? It's what she said he said. How?

"What mystery does love hold? The kind in Johnnyboy's heart?"

He didn't know what'd made him ask that. What, his innocence, his youth …?

He burst through the door.

"Johnnyboy's back!"

It was ten o'clock. Modecai's head came off the piano cover.

"Jimmy Mack!"

"Modecai! Thank God you still alive!"

"How did you—"

"Everybody knows Johnnyboy's back in town. Come back last night. And now he ain't nowhere to be found!"

Modecai stood.

Jimmy Mack ran across the floor. He grabbed Modecai. He hugged him.

"Damn—was worried sick, sick as a dog."

"Then you know, you know what Delores and—"

"Their relationship?"

"Yes, yes—"

"She's his girl, old lady, Dee."

Modecai stepped away from Jimmy Mack. He opened the piano cover. He struck a note, a black key, a minor key on the piano. "Why didn't you … why the hell didn't you tell me? Y-you could've at least told me a-about Delores and Johnnyboy Daniels."

"Was supposed to be ancient history, Modecai. Past—you see everybody in Way City knows that. This fucking town. Word was out that Johnnyboy, he give Dee her walking papers, man. Life back. All back. It wasn't for me to spoil nothing for the girl. It ain't none of my concern or business."

"But he's back."

"Yeah, Modecai. The black bastard's back for Dee." Jimmy Mack's eyes bubbled. "Did he catch you with her? Man, it's what worried me so. The hell outta me. Why I run over to the apartment soon as I find out."

"Last night, Jimmy Mack, in Benny's alleyway, he put his knife to my neck."

"That knife, fucking knife of his. One he slit Silas Wilber-Lee Blue's throat with, I figure."

Modecai shuddered.

"You lucky to be alive, ain't dead. That Johnnyboy boy is mean as—"

"Delores told him she knew he, he didn't want to go back to prison."

"Man."

"He, he told Delores I-I have to—"

"Leave town. Way City, Alabama."

"No, out, out of here, this apartment, Jimmy Mack. It, it means out of—"

"No, it ain't what Johnnyboy said. What Johnnyboy meant. He don't make it easy on you and Delores. He seen you and his girl together—Johnnyboy wants you out of town. Way City. Johnnyboy don't play halfway at nothing. Not fucking Johnnyboy Daniels."

He had his answer. Why didn't Delores tell him, tell him what Johnnyboy Daniels had meant, said? But he knew all along, didn't he, what Johnnyboy Daniels meant? Didn't he!

"W-when he want you out of here, Modecai? When!"

"Huh, huh?"

"Uh, I said, when does the boy want you out of Way City, Modecai? Johnnyboy?"

"Johnnyboy! Damn Johnnyboy Daniels! Damn him!"

"Now listen, you get this and you get this straight: you don't wanna fight him. Mess with that boy. You ain't gonna win. He'll stick you. Stick you like a pig on a stick. Boy'll stick you with that knife of his, not unless you fucking shoot him. And you ain't built for that. Shoot a man. No man."

"No, no, Jimmy Mack. I can't. I—"

"Got to shoot him, not knife him, 'cause he'll win, Modecai. Fucking hands down."

It's as if Jimmy Mack had to say it again to make sure it was out his system and that Modecai understood and had been warned beyond a shadow of a doubt what his only option was—cut and run.

Modecai walked over to the window and then came back.

"Jimmy Mack, you, you didn't bring your bass," Modecai asked aimlessly. "Today with you. Why? Why didn't—"

"Modecai, this ain't no ordinary day. You got to face up to it. Make it clear. Gotta think all of this that's looking at you through an' through. This ain't no normal day."

"Think—how can I think, Jimmy Mack? Tell me? Tell—"

"'Cause you gotta think, Modecai. You owe it to yourself to think. Think about New York City now. It's where your head's gotta go. Gotta be. New York—"

"New York? New York!"

"Yeah, yeah, New York, city, Modecai!"

"Jimmy Mack, Jimmy Mack …" His stomach was churning much too fast.

"This is it, don't you see, Modecai? Gift wrapped. This ain't cellophane. This is what you've been waiting on, for, dammit, Modecai. I see your future sitting in my eyes clear as a Chinaman's fortune cookie!

"This is how it's got to go down, Modecai, for you to get outta here. Climb out the barrel, this pig hole. For you to get outta Way City, Alabama. For you to hitch yourself to a star and ride clear on it. Ride right on the tail of it." Pause.

"Johnnyboy Daniels have to come back to town, Way City, Modecai. To shake things up. You see, don't you, Modecai? You see, don't you, man!"

Jimmy Mack had left the apartment building but said he was coming back. How true this was, Modecai didn't know. Jimmy Mack had a nice, decent look on his face like he knew he had to let him be alone to really think all of this New York City stuff thoroughly through.

New York. New York City.

Modecai stood in front of his clothes closet. *I don't even have an overcoat,* he thought. *What about an overcoat? What … y-you've got to have an overcoat in New York City.*

His eyes were looking at what was scant in his clothes closet: clothes. New York, how do people dress in New York, up there—what do they wear? What, man, what?

He wasn't ready for this. Delores, he hadn't seen her all day: her life was rotting like his. It only takes one day to take the freshness out of spring, out of a day, out of clothes in a closet—out of an apple.

"Why did Jimmy Mack say New York City? Why not some other place, some other town? I-I'm scared, weren't you? An overcoat, I-I don't even own, have an overcoat to wear in New York City. L-look in my closet, Jimmy Mack, look!"

Modecai grabbed a shirt, a pair of pants—he didn't care. He was throwing the clothes to the floor. His hands went blindly after whatever they could in the closet. Modecai didn't give a damn.

"New York! New York!"

Jimmy Mack barreled through the door. He sensed something was wrong. "Modecai!"

The mess Jimmy Mack saw right away. Both messes: the clothes and Modecai.

"I'm going, Jimmy Mack! You, you and Delores and, and … Johnnyboy Daniels have won! You've all won. I'm going to New York City!"

"Modecai, Modecai." Jimmy Mack grabbed Modecai's hands. He literally locked Modecai in place. "You ain't gonna die. It's gonna be all right."

"It will, Jimmy Mack? It will, won't it, Jimmy Mack? Won't it?"

Jimmy Mack let go of him.

"I can think now."

"Ha. That Chinese fortune cookie's looking you dead in the eye, Modecai. Know your heart's broke, man. That love drifts in but not out your life that easy. Know you love Dee. That she get that much under your skin."

"I told her last night, for the first time, I love her."

"It's rotten luck, I know, but Dee, she wasn't gonna go with you no way. 'Cause you was gonna go to New York on your own one day. Just don't know it."

Now Modecai was picking the clothes up off the floor.

"Let me help you with them."

When Modecai and Jimmy Mack finished, Modecai walked over to the piano.

"Jimmy Mack, h-how does this get to New York?"

"Why, I don't know, Modecai. Ain't got a—helluva good question."

Modecai opened the upright piano's cover. "I'm not going to New York City without it. My piano."

"But you can't take it on a bus, Modecai. Ain't no bus seats big enough to handle a pi-ano, man!"

Modecai was laughing along with Jimmy Mack. It was the first he'd laughed since last night.

"Not unless I rent out the whole bus. Even though I probably, barely, have enough money for my own bus fare to New York City." Pause. "How much—what is the bus fare to New York City on the Greyhound bus anyway, Jimmy Mack?"

Jimmy Mack smiled so sweetly it looked like he might have a sweet tooth. "Don't worry, Modecai, you got you enough bread, dollars stuffed down in your pocket. You can pay the bus fare on the Greyhound bus from here to New York and back, round trip, if you have to."

Then together, they spied the upright piano.

"Gotta store it, Modecai. Plain and simple. And then come back to Way City for it."

"But where in Way City?"

"Don't know. Ain't no room in my place. And you can forget about Billy and the rest of them cats," Jimmy Mack laughed. "All about them."

Both pondered the matter more.

"Hmmm ..."

"How about Charlie's C-Note Club, Jimmy Mack? Charlie has a basement, doesn't—"

"Uh-uh. Bad idea. Atrocious. Charlie likes music, all right, but likes money better. Charlie'd probably sell the damned thing before you board the bus for outta here, man. Before the bus tires hit a patch of road. And then all of us cats have to wind up beating the boy's ass—and then be out a damned gig at the C-Note!"

Modecai pressed his finger down on a key on the piano.

"Don't worry, Modecai. We gonna find a place for it. We ain't gonna let a thing happen to it." Pause. "It's too, too pretty for that."

* * *

Maybe with Benny seeing Johnnyboy last night, Benny didn't expect to see Delores at work tonight, because her door hadn't been opened all day.

But his door opened, and Modecai looked down the hall at Delores's door. No one had gone in her apartment, and certainly not Johnnyboy. Johnnyboy said two days, and maybe he meant it, like it seemed he meant everything else.

Tap.

There was no answer.

Tap. Tap.

Yes, Modecai knew Johnnyboy wasn't in the apartment—he was sure of that much. If he was, Modecai reasoned with a slick grin, then he had to slip in through the back window.

Delores's door was unlocked. She left it unlocked whenever she was in the apartment.

Modecai pushed the door open. The room was cast in late evening shadows. Delores was not in the front room. Modecai steadied himself.

"Delores," he said while moving anxiously into the bedroom. "Delores …"

Her head rose up from the sheet. Then she tried hiding her face with the top sheet as if it wasn't hers or Modecai had never seen it before—at least not in its current condition.

"Delores …"

"Go away, please." Her voice was strident. "Haven't you forgotten me by now? Fallen out of love with me? Haven't you …?"

Modecai walked over and sat at the side of the bed. "I didn't hear your music. I haven't heard it all day," Delores said. "I've been listening, Modecai."

Modecai said nothing. Then he touched the sheet Delores's fingers held onto so stubbornly.

"Don't, don't, Modecai, don't … Okay, look at me!"

Modecai didn't flinch.

"I've cried all day too, Delores. All …"

"Jimmy Mack, I heard him go in and out the apartment."

"Jimmy Mack helped. He really did."

"You're going, aren't you, to New York City, Modecai, aren't you?"

"Yes."

"When, Modecai?"

"Tomorrow."

"Why? Why do we have to listen to Johnnyboy? Why? Tell me why, Modecai!"

Delores snatched the sheet back from Modecai and hid her face and began crying.

"Have you eaten today? At least eaten—"

"Have you?"

"I'm thinking crazily. I don't know what I'm thinking."

But Modecai had to think that she'd been in that room all day, alone; and when you're alone like that, like he was before Jimmy Mack came to the apartment, that reality doesn't stand a chance against the mind when it's alone in a room, thinking "crazily," as Delores said, making small lies stand large. When you begin to believe them even when you don't want to, there's no reason in God's name to.

"Benny—"

"He knows I won't be coming to work tonight."

Both were hopscotching, seemingly trying to summarize the day.

"Johnnyboy ...," Delores said faintly.

"You don't love him, do you, Delores?"

"No, I love you, Modecai. You and only you."

"Then come with me. Come with me, Delores. Come with me!"

"No, Johnnyboy'll find us, Modecai. He'd hunt us down like dogs."

"No, b-but not in New York City. Not there!"

"Where would we hide, Modecai? W-wherever it'd be, Johnnyboy would find us."

"But not in New York City, Delores. Not—"

"Where can you hide from someone like Johnnyboy Daniels, that he can't find you?"

* * *

Delores and Modecai had eaten. It was Modecai who'd cooked something. Delores was coming out the bathroom.

Modecai was at the edge of the bed. He got up when Delores reentered the room. Delores walked straight up to him.

"I want you to make love to me. The last time before you go, Modecai."

It's when Delores's body pressed against Modecai's, and she began unbuttoning the front of his shirt.

Just like that? Modecai thought, stunned. He didn't feel that safe—that nonthreatened by Johnnyboy Daniels.

"Delores, this isn't happening, is it? I know it isn't," Modecai said as if he were in a surreal world, not the world he thought he was in.

"I can't help myself, Modecai. I can't …"

The body Delores had seemed to be hiding from Modecai only hours ago, she was letting Modecai see, as she opened her robe and her full black breasts had come to life in front of him.

No, neither had expected this, not in their hearts, but it was happening, and neither was willing to stop it.

"This will be our last time together, Modecai. I don't want to think about tomorrow. To think about you leaving me and Johnnyboy coming for me."

Tightly Delores's hands held onto Modecai's waist. And then Modecai began falling backward onto the floor as Delores crawled into his arms.

"Modecai, make me forget everything, honey. Wash it out my mind. Please, please. Just for now. That this is happening to us, Modecai. That Johnnyboy's back."

Modecai's bare back was down on the floor. He shut his eyes. He didn't think about Johnnyboy Daniels, only Delores. They had to make love before they said good-bye, Modecai thought. They'd been lovers—this had to happen between them tonight.

Delores mounted Modecai and felt all of his penis that was inside her wet vagina and his mouth sucking her breasts and how love feels.

* * *

Maybe Modecai was thinking too heroically. He was holding Delores; he hadn't gone back to his room, thinking if Johnnyboy Daniels burst through the bedroom door, he would, if not, fight for Delores, at least die for her.

"Modecai?"

"I'm here, Delores."

"You didn't go off to your room. Down the hall."

They'd made it to the bed after making love, to rest.

"No, not tonight, Delores."

Delores wet her lips. She swung her body around to Modecai's.

"It-it's not tomorrow yet—is it, Modecai?" Delores asked, dreamlike.

"No, uh—it's not."

"Modecai, what about your piano!"

Modecai couldn't believe his ears, what they'd heard—Delores was thinking not only about him but the piano too.

"I don't know. Jimmy Mack and I have to find somewhere in Way City to store it. It's what Jimmy Mack's working on for—"

"Benny's, Modecai! Benny's Pit! Benny has a basement! He'll store it there for you!"

"You think so? B-Benny won't have to hold on to it for long. As soon as I'm settled in New York City, I'll be back to Way City for it."

Before Modecai could blink an eye, Delores was out the bed.

"Delores, where are—"

"I'm going to throw some clothes on and go outside and call Benny from the street, that's where!"

"I see that expression on you face—you don't even know what time it is. Benny's at—"

"It's, it's eleven ten," Delores said, looking at the clock across the room on top her bureau. "Benny should be home in about three minutes. I'll throw some clothes on, brush my hair. I'll be down the street at the phone calling Benny at home."

"Delores, it can wait," Modecai said as if trying to slow Delores down for some reason.

"Uh-uh, Modecai, not on your life. I'm taking care of this right here and now." Pause. "I love that piano as much as you."

Delores bent to pick up a shoe off the floor, and when she rose, Modecai stood over her.

"Thank you, Delores."

Modecai kissed her.

The shoe fell out Delores's hand.

* * *

As far as Modecai was concerned, the apartment was empty. The piano was gone.

But it didn't matter; he wasn't going to be there, in the apartment, no more than a minute more. But he looked around the apartment—it had served him well. He laughed devilishly. No, he didn't have to find Jake this time around. He and Jimmy Mack moved the piano out the apartment and into Benny's basement (he'd saved three bucks!).

Benny's basement was clean except for cobwebs. Benny and Delores said they'd take care of the piano. Especially Delores, she said she'd pull out a dust rag anytime she saw any hint of dust on it. He told Delores he didn't want her to take it to that extreme, that the piano just might get spoiled; and he didn't want that, a spoiled piano, not under any circumstances.

Yes, it's time to go, isn't it? Modecai was nibbling at time, trying his best not to bite too much of it off at one time but knew time doesn't work like that: it's not that cunning or calculating.

The apartment door opened. Modecai was in the hallway. He held onto two big leather suitcases (one with all clothes, the other with all music). He'd done this a couple of months ago, he knew; but right now, for him, it felt brand-new.

He and Delores had said good-bye this morning. They'd wanted to do it that way. They agreed to say good-bye from the bed. Delores didn't walk him to the door; she had stayed in bed. He saw it was six seventeen when he got into his room. It was the longest and latest he'd stayed in Delores's apartment with her. They didn't want any of that, Delores walking him to the door. They rejected the idea.

But now he did—he did wish she'd walked him to the apartment door, for what it meant, symbolized. But they'd cried enough in one day. They'd anguished enough in one day. They knew they truly loved each other.

Modecai looked down the hallway, down at Delores's door. Delores is behind there, isn't she? Isn't she, Modecai? Modecai thought.

"If, if I-I …"

And then he thought of Johnnyboy Daniels going through that door today.

"One last peek. If I could take, get one last peek of her."

Modecai knew the door was unlocked. He put the suitcases down. He began walking down the hallway at a quick clip. He wanted to see Delores this one last time.

The hell with Johnnyboy Daniels!

He was practically sprinting down the hall when the door flew open and she flew at him, and no words were spoken, only Modecai lifting Delores in his arms, holding her to him and feeling her lips kiss his skin.

When Modecai brought Delores down, he held her gently at the back of her head as she shook in her cotton robe.

"Delores …"

"I'll be all right, Modecai. I promise."

Modecai's hand left the back of her head.

"I know it's time for you to go."

And so Delores let go of Modecai.

Modecai turned. He began walking away, up the hall.

"Modecai!" Delores shouted. "Benny's, Modecai. Benny's!"

"Benny's?"

"You can write me. I know we didn't talk about it, any of this last night, but you can write me at Benny's, honey. Benny'll make sure I get your letters."

"Of course, of course!" Modecai said, his spirits lifting. "Of course I'll write you, Delores. And often. As often as I can."

Delores's spirits lifted too.

"Of course you will. And often, Modecai, often like you said. I know you will. It'll mean I'll always know where you are."

Modecai was back at his suitcases. He picked them up.

"Good-bye, Delores."

Modecai didn't look back at Delores, who was standing in the hall holding the robe's front panels.

"Good luck, Modecai, in, in New York City."

"Thanks, Delores."

"I love you."

Modecai wanted to turn around but looked at the stairwell before him and knew he had to walk down it under his own power. But his heart was devouring "I love you, Modecai."

Now Modecai was down the stairwell and out the building. He wasn't going to look back up at the building. He was only going to look straight ahead like the wind was in his face and the day could not shed its skin fast enough. He picked up speed when, out of the blue, he was snatched by the back of his suit jacket—someone yanking him, then dragging him and his suitcases, in broad daylight, back into the alleyway.

"You better leave, MOTHERFUCKER! You better get your nigger ass outta here!"

Modecai's body had been dragged off to the side of a building in the alleyway. Then Johnnyboy Daniels twisted him around and looked directly at him.

"Scared as a blue-eyed monkey, ain't you!"

Yes, Modecai's eyes stood paralyzed in his head. His hands released the suitcases; they hit the dirt. "What do you want!"

"Want! Shit, man, I got what I fucking want!" Johnnyboy gloated. "What I come back to Way City for!"

His incredibly powerful hands hadn't released Modecai, but it was better than Johnnyboy's knife at his throat, Modecai thought.

"Got what's mine back, nigger. Scared nigger. Got my girl back! I give you two days. I-I don't know how you and Dee say good-bye. Don't fucking care. But I give you and her two days."

Johnnyboy let go of Modecai, but it didn't mean anything to Modecai: it was still as if his large, bruising hands were still wrapped around his neck.

"See, I don't give a damn what you and Dee do the last two days, 'cause Dee is mine now. Belongs to me. My black ass. Johnnyboy Daniels," Johnnyboy said, thumping his chest. "From now till eternity. From now till the end of Earth!"

Modecai didn't reply, for suddenly he felt unafraid of Johnnyboy Daniels. It was him and Johnnyboy Daniels in the alleyway, yes; no witnesses, yes. But Johnnyboy Daniels was living for Delores to own something—he didn't want to go back to prison. Foster City Prison again.

"I'm going to New York City," Modecai said, brushing the wrinkles out his suit jacket. "I'm a jazz musician. I was going eventually."

"You and—you and Dee was going? You was taking Dee with you?"

Modecai lifted his suitcases.

"I asked Delores to go, but Delores never gave me an answer one way or the other, man."

Modecai began walking out the alleyway. Johnnyboy was trailing him from behind.

"L-listen, I'll treat her good, man. I'll, I'll take care of the girl. She's my girl. Motherfucking—I-I love Dee, man. I …"

Modecai was out the alleyway, back on Taylor Street, walking toward the bus station—"Love the girl, man."—with his two big suitcases, heading for New York City.

Modecai was at Way City's bus station. It wasn't much of a bus station. It was a brick building with cracked brick. There wasn't one good chair in the station to sit on and wait for the bus, just a short, splintered bench bolted to the middle of the floor. Some of the cracked, broken-at-the-legs chairs stacked in the corner gave the strong impression they'd been there waiting garbage removal sincc the first day the station's doors opened and the town's ceremony ended.

The colored porter sauntered into the bathroom with a bucket and wet mop.

Modecai's bus ticket stuck out his right hand. He said New York, he was going to New York. The cashier at the window told him his ticket would take him to the next station over, and then he'd have to buy a new ticket, another one, and so on and so forth until he got to New York City—"straight through," was how he'd put it, "straight through." Modecai'd laughed—nothing was easy, he'd thought, not even getting to New York City once he decided to go.

It was two eighteen.

He thought of Jimmy Mack. Jimmy Mack had knocked on his door at nine o'clock saying he had no luck in finding a home for the piano, but Modecai told him about Benny, and out the apartment the piano flew and into Benny's basement once Jimmy Mack got his uncle Samuel's pickup truck kicked up and ready to go. Modecai stood in the middle of the bus station's floor, knowing the bus was scheduled to pull out the station at two forty. There were but a few people inside the station.

The porter came out the bathroom, the mop was still wet, dripped with water; the porter began mopping the floor over in the corner, a ways away from Modecai.

Jimmy Mack, where was Jimmy Mack? After they'd moved the piano (it was after ten o'clock), Jimmy Mack said he'd be back to the apartment to say good-bye to him—this was the first time Jimmy Mack hadn't lived up to his word on something.

Modecai wasn't used to this, having idle time on his hands. And he seemed, by no means, to know what to do with it. Right now, he didn't feel like a jazz musician—in fact, he didn't feel like anything. He had no music in him, just a bowl-size of sadness. This wasn't music, he thought, but sadness. It could make music, but sadness wasn't music, just the manufacture of a bitter truth.

Modecai always thought that way about music. Music was joy and now he was joyless. He was going onto the greatest adventure of his life, and he was joyless. This sad figure with too many regrets, of too many what-ifs. What if this, and what if that, and—

Cut it out! That's not me, man. I'm not a melancholy person. I'm not a brooding person. Those people aren't me!

Modecai walked away from the middle of the floor and off to the wall and put his head in his hands. New York City is all he should be thinking of. The tall buildings. The bright lights. The fast cars. The fast women. The jazz clubs. New York City: jazz capital of the world. Hotbed of jazz. It's all he should be thinking of, not Delores. Not Delores Bonet and Johnnyboy Daniels.

"Listen … listen. I'll treat her good, man. I'll … I'll take care of the girl. I'll take care of her, man. I-I love Delores, man. I-I love the girl."

How could he take care of her? He couldn't even read or write; he was just out of prison. He had no job. He would be Delores's eternal burden. Someone Johnnyboy Daniels didn't have to bully with a knife.

Modecai had no wristwatch (he kept promising himself he'd buy one, one day), so he looked at the bus station's dust-clad clock. The bus he saw and presumed he would board at two forty was docked in the station. The bus driver had gone into the bathroom. It was two twenty-seven.

"Anybody that's gotta go," the tall, husky white bus driver said coming out the bathroom, "now's the time. Otherwise, the bus and me don't make no stops 'long the way. Not 'less for an emergency—and them come rare as a good spare tire and inner tube." He laughed.

Modecai headed for the bathroom with alacrity. Power of suggestion, he laughed to himself.

Modecai was out the bathroom when he saw Jimmy Mack and the guys storming into the bus stop.

"Modecai, Modecai, we here, man!"

Was Modecai ever glad to see Jimmy Mack's men.

"Them suitcases of yours, look like a jazz musician's all right."

"How come, Jimmy Mack?"

Jimmy Mack grinned like a tuna on a platter. "Plenty of mileage already on them, it's how come." And then he sniffed like a blue-blood cat to his men and to Modecai. "Got a reeeal skunky smell to them too, all over!"

Mack's men and Modecai laughed uproariously.

They'd formed a tight circle on the bus station's floor, making sure Modecai was stuck right there in the middle of it.

"We love you, Modecai. Think the world of you. And we hate to see you go, especially under the circumstances you're leaving."

Jimmy Mack and his men took in deep breaths like a band's horn section and then tipped their heads like sad hats.

"But before you board the bus, uh … Billy!"

And Billy Shivers stood at attention and then handed Jimmy Mack a bag that Modecai could smell like heaven had just touched Earth.

"We figure we ate you out of house and home while you was here in Way City, so the least we could do was to cook up some barbecue and pork chop sandwiches for the trip. In case you get hungry along the way. Your stomach starts humming like a bluebird.

"Benny fixed them and sauced them down with his hot sauce. Done all the work he could on them, Modecai."

"Thanks, Jimmy Mack, fellas, thanks," Modecai said to one and all.

Modecai was about to head for his suitcases.

"Ron and Marshall got them, Modecai." Pause.

"Modecai, why I don't come back to the apartment, was I have this to do." Jimmy Mack's hands went into his overalls, and he pulled out a sheet of paper that was folded, but which Jimmy Mack's fingers were fast unfolding.

"Names, Modecai. Contacts of cats I know in New York City." Jimmy Mack was going to joke and say the list would've included dames too but knew what Modecai was fresh from.

"I know cats all over New York City. High and low. From downtown New York to uptown Harlem, man."

The list in Jimmy Mack's hand was as long as a country road.

"Once you hit Forty-Second Street, Modecai, New York's all yours, man, courtesy of Jimmy Mack and his men!"

"Thanks, Jimmy Mack. I'm sure New York's all set to roll its red carpet out for me. And I'll be on a first-name basis with city hall and the mayor too, before long."

They all laughed along with Modecai.

The bus driver was on the bus. His body tilted to the right, taking the customer's bus tickets.

"Guess this is it, huh, Jimmy Mack?"

"Uh, yes, this is the beginning of a new life for you, Modecai. One day it-it's gonna feel like old legs. Like you walked a thousand miles before you walked your first. Let that sit in your head, well in it, and don't forget it, Modecai. Strike any of it out."

Ron and Marshal handed Modecai his two suitcases

Modecai waved good-bye to the four of them.

"Wish I was going with you, Modecai," Jimmy Mack said. "But had my turn at it."

Modecai boarded the bus. A few passengers had boarded the bus with him. Modecai sat at the open window. Jimmy Mack and his men gathered by the open window. They looked up at him.

"On that list, Modecai," Jimmy Mack said, pointing at Modecai; Modecai then held up the list in front of the clear window, "it'd do you good to look up Lawrence 'Sweet-Tone' Johnson first thing. Sweet-Tone's sweet as potato pie. Or if not him, then Milton 'Bones' Hammonds. He plays, uh, trombone. Ha. Got a heart of gold. The size of a chunk of liver too."

The driver closed the bus's doors.

"And, oh, Jimmy 'Shorty' Miller, say hello to Shorty for me. Shorty's on that list of names. Shorty's 'bout as short as a pi-ano stool. At the bottom, Modecai, bottom there."

Everyone seemed satisfied, their faces wide-open smiles.

Everyone waved.

Then Modecai sat back in his bus seat at the back of the bus, where "colored only" sat, and looked straight ahead.

The bus driver revved up the engine. Then the bus kicked up some serious ruckus out its rusted pipes.

Gas fumes flew up, shot right up into Modecai's nostrils. He couldn't smell Benny's pork chops and barbecue lathered in hot sauce if he tried.

Tears blanketed Modecai's eyes. And there was nothing that could quiet Modecai's heart.

* * *

This was the third Greyhound bus Modccai had been on to get to New York City. By now, to Modecai, they all looked and felt and smelled the same. Modecai'd had one pork chop sandwich and one barbecue sandwich. There were plenty more sandwiches—it was a big bag.

Modecai was in ordinary clothes. *Maybe I should've dressed, spruced myself up a bit better since I'm going to New York City, if I ever get there.* Modecai laughed. The sandwiches left his mouth hot, but otherwise, they were, as he'd put it, "smoking."

The Greyhound bus was traveling in the dark. He hadn't asked the bus driver how many more buses he must take to get to New York City, but maybe he should. What, three, four more, maybe? It was all right though, as long as he hadn't run out of pocket money.

Cash. Cash. Just how much cash would he have to have in his pocket once he got to New York City? How expensive is New York City compared to other cities? Southern cities to be more specific.

"Will momma's money hold up? Will it be enough for me in New York City?"

That's something he hadn't thought of. But with things happening so alarmingly fast, so damned rapidly to him, he hadn't had a chance to think about or reconcile anything, certainly not his financial situation. *Sweet-Tone Johnson probably is a sweet man, but I don't want to impose on anyone. The same holds for Bones Hammonds. But this is the way, isn't it, how a lot of young jazz cats hit New York City in stride: looking for other jazz cats to help them out. Looking for what is a refuge, in a way,* Modecai thought.

Modecai looked at his brown bag of sandwiches that'd left dark grease spots outside the bag. His mouth was red-hot (smoking!). He was going to pass on any more sandwiches until he got to the bus station—his mouth felt like it was at hell's gate. Benny and his darn hot sauce! Modecai winced.

* * *

This was the last Greyhound bus Modecai would board. The bus driver had proudly announced, "New York City, folks, it's right around the bend"! even if the cashier had advertised his ticket as one to New York City. So this was it, the final leg of the long, exhaustive journey.

The bus was full. It'd been hard for Modecai to locate a seat. On the other buses he'd gotten a seat by the window, but on this bus, he had no such luck. On this bus, heading for New York City, he was sitting in an aisle seat, and there'd been no mention of "coloreds only" since about two buses back. His suitcase was in an overhead rack. He had his brown bag of sandwiches in his hands. He was down to two: one pork chop and one barbecued rib (he'd kind planned it that way). The passenger next to him nudged Modecai's elbow for more elbow room with no resistance from him.

It was maybe twenty-five minutes into the trip when Modecai thought of Delores. His eyes had popped open. Delores was with Johnnyboy Daniels now, wasn't she? She went to Benny's tonight. Johnnyboy wouldn't let her miss a day's work, a day's paycheck from Benny's Pit.

They'd made love last night (or was it two nights ago?—maybe he'd lost track of time by now) and then into the morning. Johnnyboy was going to make love to her tonight. Johnnyboy was all man. He was the baddest man who ever lived. He was the baddest man who ever walked the face of the earth. He was going to make sure Delores remembered that—that she remembered that too. He was going to return in full force, at full scale, in full glory. He was going to try to prove himself above all proof, above all doubt. He was the baddest man on Earth. The greatest lover who ever lived.

Delores said they'd been lovers for over two-and-a-half years before Johnnyboy wound up at Foster City Prison, before Johnnyboy killed Silas Wilber-Lee Blue. She was supposed to be free of him (it's what he'd told her), but now her life was back to where it'd been all along with him: nowhere. He was simply back.

He would write her a letter as soon as he was settled in New York. He'd send the letter to Benny's. Benny's Pit now had two things he loved in it: Delores and his piano, Modecai thought. Only, he'd be back to Benny's Pit for the piano but not for Delores; that would never happen. Not in Way City, Alabama.

Modecai looked out the window from his aisle seat. All of a sudden the road's light had become steady. The roads were better built than before. The bus's tires seemed to grip the road better than before, the road much smoother. If you wanted to sleep on the bus, it seemed the best time for it was now.

But instead of sleeping, resting, whatever all the other people were doing aboard the bus, Modecai felt restless. And maybe the bus driver somehow sensed his restlessness too, for suddenly he announced with great vigor and in excellent voice.

"New York! New York City is ten miles down the pike, ladies and gentlemen! Just ten more miles to go!"

And there was a great cheer that rang out in the bus, enough, probably, to create an earthquake. And Modecai was a part of that cheer—his voice had risen in cheer like a champagne cork had just popped out a giant champagne bottle.

Modecai looked up, back, to his side and saw a wide sea of smiles. There was an excitement on the bus. They weren't all jazz musicians, Modecai thought, or were they! Modecai slapped his knee in response to his corny little joke. Hey, maybe they are. Just maybe so!

The bus buzzed.

Modecai felt himself in the company of friends, companions. He felt he was in the company of others who maybe were feeling some kind of tremendous adventure sinking into their skin too. Modecai sat up more in his bus seat. New York City, New York City, man! His shoe was going to give New York City a big boot in its pants too.

Ten miles to go—well, maybe more like eight by now. Man, how close!

Modecai, he'd not looked out the bus window, not since the bus driver said they'd entered the Holland Tunnel, crossing them from New Jersey to New York. He'd shut his eyes when entering the Holland Tunnel (a sight he'd never seen before—it was so amazing!). He'd told himself he didn't want to see New York City until his soles touched its soil. Modecai was going to be absolutely resolute about this; it's how he wanted to feel the aura of this great, open city: it was to be tactile first and visual second, for the historical record, he'd laughed.

The Greyhound bus was slowing down. A starry smile sat on Modecai's face as the sound of the bus decrescendoed to a whisper while his heart hummed "New York City, New York City" repeatedly.

"Forty-Second Street, folks!"

Modecai opened his eyes.

"I'm in New York City!"

"Yes, we are, buddy. Sure are!" the gentlemen said, walking down the aisle carrying his luggage.

Modecai and his row partner had to wait before they too could exit into the aisle to take their suitcases down from the overhead luggage rack.

Modecai stood. He got the suitcases. He smiled. He was just about to head up the bus aisle when the person who he'd sat next to said, "Good luck, Joe."

"T-thanks. You too."

"Say, by the way, what you got in that bag of yours that smells so good? Pork chop sandwiches?"

"Uh, close," Modecai replied. "Pork chop and barbecued rib sandwiches. With plenty of sauce."

"Now that was gonna be my second choice. Uh, the sauce too."

"Good luck, folks."

The bus driver was saying it to everyone, so he'd said it to Modecai too.

Modecai's shoes dropped down on New York City soil. Modecai couldn't believe it—he felt like doing a St. Vitus Day dance, but after that long trip of bouncy buses and loose springs and bad bumps, his body felt out of rhythm, out of sorts, so he just kept smiling as wide as a circus tent's top.

"Why, I'm here. I'm really here. Modecai Ulysses Jefferson is really here in New York City!"

Modecai held onto his suitcases and his bag of sandwiches and looked in total awe, amazement, rapture at what he saw. His eyes spotted a clock, and it said three o'clock. It was three o'clock in the morning in New York City, and it still felt like shops and stores were just opening up, setting up, and the sidewalks were being swept clean by city sweepers with fat handled brooms, and anyone who was asleep was really sleeping with one eye open and the other eye shut.

Modecai never felt more alive, more ebullient and at the same time overwhelmed. He never felt the music in him flow more than now. He never felt so many chords crash and melodies swell and harmonies collide.

Modecai collected his senses.

He felt as athletic as a cat on a midnight chase. He could scamper up Forty-Second Street. He could scamper up the tall, lean skyscrapers to their very tops. He could sit on a flagpole and look down and watch New Yorkers scurry below him like ants zigzagging wildly from street corner to street corner.

Even standing in the alleyway of this mighty canyon with his fat leather suitcases, he felt New York City welcoming him, giving him the once-over, and then saying, "Welcome, Modecai Ulysses Jefferson." No longer did Modecai feel like a country hick from the sticks. New York City had seen his kind before, thousands and thousands times over. He wasn't this new sight to behold for its sore eyes.

Honk!

Even the car horns in New York City sounded golden, like a Fatha Hines's horn section. Like a blast to Modecai's heart that made his feet want to tap out a tune as busy as Broadway.

Modecai continued to soak in this New York City ambiance from head to toe. He asked himself, "Is this how sparkling champagne feels on your skin?" New York was embracing him, letting him slip comfortably into its arms. It was giving him a chance, he felt—an opportunity.

Soon Modecai snapped out of his wonderment, but not all. First, he had to find Lawrence "Sweet-Tone" Johnson or Milton "Bones" Hammonds, one or the other—set a course of action. Have a plan of attack. Modecai looked around Forty-Second Street. But first, first maybe he'd walk around Forty-Second Street and Eighth Avenue (it's what the sign said) and then ask someone where Broadway was and then who knows where else. He didn't feel like a stranger, a pilgrim, even though others might think him one, gawk at him like one when he looked at things with a crooked neck and a restless eye, say, than they did—or most did.

But once his sightseeing was over, done with, he'd have to head off to either Sweet-Tone's or Bones's place. He hadn't decided which. Both names he liked, so it was going to be a hard choice. It was just a matter of choosing which he liked more. Maybe if he thought of it more as a contest, he thought, or … The fear of knocking on someone's door at whatever hour in the morning had all but deserted him for now—that dreadful feeling. Besides, there wasn't a respectable jazz man alive that he knew of who wouldn't appreciate a fellow jazz man knocking on his door at three or four o'clock in the morning when he was just getting in from a gig.

"Hmm … I think I will take that walk around town. Around this grand oasis called New York City, man. Who knows, I might just be lucky enough to bump into Bunny Greensleeves, or him lucky enough to bump into me. Whichever way it happens, it'd be great. Just great.

"Man, I really dig Bunny Greensleeves's music, a lot!"

But Modecai couldn't resist looking up at New York's sky one more time and swoon at the silvery moon.

Chapter 8

Bunny Greensleeves and Sticks Cooper had just crashed through the apartment door with their luggage.

"Catch any mice in the apartment while we was away, Big Booty!" Bunny Greensleeves asked.

Big Booty was scarfing down grit off his plate.

"They was running wild around here, Bunny!" Big Booty said between bites. "Man, I could've lassoed some of them cats, and—"

"Ride them piggyback, huh, Big Booty—they was so big!"

"Uh, yeah, yeah, Bunny, but—"

"You was too scared to. Them mice might throw your big ass!"

Big Booty got up from the kitchen table, wiped his hands on his T-shirt, and went to hug Bunny.

But Bunny jumped back like a frightened alley cat.

"Uh-uh, Big Booty. Hell no, man. No grease on my crease—pleeeease!"

"Welcome back, Bunny! Sticks! I missed you cats, man!"

"Likewise, Big Booty," Sticks said.

They shook hands. But Big Booty hugged on Sticks; Sticks had let him get near him.

Bunny hit the refrigerator.

"Man, if we ain't bushed, Big Booty."

"And hungry," Sticks added. "Big Booty, he leave any food in the fridge, Bunny?"

"About enough for a skinny crow or a one-eyed pigeon, Sticks. Slim pickings all the way around. Should've known we should've come fortified with a cow and some chickens under both arms, man," Bunny said, looking over at Big Booty. "How about you running to Slim's joint down the road and getting Sticks and me something to eat, Big Booty?"

"You mean Mr. Hines paid you cats?"

"Hey, don't be funny," Sticks said. "You know Fatha Hines is like a father to us cats!"

Sticks fished inside his pocket for some change.

"Uh-uh, treats on me, Sticks. Since I'm the star in this aggregation!"

"You sure are, Bunny. Man..."

Bunny was handing Big Booty the cash. Big Booty looked down at Bunny.

"What, you and your trumpet put on a show, Bunny? For y'all selves?"

"And them chicks down in them sticks was wailing like crazy to them trumpet licks, right, Sticks? Them barnyard babes."

"So what you want from Slim's, Bunny?"

"Ha," Sticks laughed, "you know our likes and dislikes, Big Booty."

"Uh-huh. Anything that's dead and we can cook, put in a pot, will do. Serve me and Sticks just fine!" Pause.

"And by the way, Big Booty"—Big Booty stood at the front door—"you can buy yourself something from whatever's left of the five spot I slipped you, man."

They all laughed.

It was just Sticks and Bunny in the apartment. They'd headed back into the generous-sized kitchen.

"Seriously, Sticks, my butt's sore, man." Bunny walked over to the kitchen window rubbing his butt. "I'm tired of riding them bouncy buses, man."

"Hey, Bunny, you just starting and you're complaining? What, I got to constantly remind you of that?"

"Sure. But, man, it seems like I've been riding in the back of a bus for a hundred years."

"Maybe a segregated bus," Sticks cracked, "but not Fatha Hines's."

"Yeah, say what you want, Sticks"—Bunny shrugged—"I'm tired, tired of them damned buses already, man."

It was like Bunny felt a big dent in him.

"You are serious, ain't you, Bunny?"

"Shit, serious as a Prez solo, Sticks. Yeah. I know I'm young, man, but the road is already making me feel old. I hate it, man!"

"Bunny, hey, you know the deal. You know it's the only way a jazz cat can survive, make a steady income, cash, by living on the road. Hell, take it from me, an old cat like me."

Sticks laughed. "Don't enjoy getting wrinkles pressed up in them threads of yours, huh, Bunny? Your crease crushed in them damned suits of yours."

"Hate it like hell. Ain't nothing worse than a wrinkle in a silk suit. Naaah, man, that shit ain't for Bunny Greensleeves. Not me."

Bunny walked back over to the table and sat down with Sticks. His pretty brown eyes looked more confused than confident.

"I don't know, Sticks. I just don't."

"What is it, is eating you, Bunny—that's so bad?"

"I think, I think it's time. Time, that's all."

"Not that again," Sticks said worriedly.

"Yeah, that again. I think me and Fatha Hines are gonna have to part company. I think I'm gonna drop out his band, man."

"But why? The hell why!"

"Been in the band too long already."

"Two months … what, two months is too much?"

"Two months and one week and three days, man."

"And that's too long. In a top-line band like Fatha Hines's is?"

"Got to do it, Sticks. Feels like I got a charley horse in my leg."

"But why, Bunny? Answer me—"

"It's who I am, Sticks. Hell, that's all. It's who Bunny Greensleeves is. I don't like to stay in one place too long. Feel cooped up. It's like death. A drag, man. A … yeah …"

"It puts food on the table, don't it? Pays the bills. Steady work, steady employment. It—"

"I'll find me a band. You know that for a fact. Hell, I can stand on a street corner tooting my horn to the wind and make five bucks in an hour. If the wind just blew one way, west."

"Sure, sure, but …"

"But I ain't, Sticks. I ain't no pauper. I don't beg from nobody. Don't go out with my pockets turned inside out to the wind," Bunny said, pushing himself away from the table. "That you'll never see Bunny Greensleeves do."

"Yeah, but Fatha Hines is a steady gig. How many musicians can say they got that in New York City? A steady gig? Source of employment?"

Bunny opened his horn case.

"But it's old hat for me now. It just ain't my style. Ain't the way I'm accustomed to doing things … It ain't hep to me no more."

Bunny had the horn in his hand.

"What is, Bunny?"

Bunny now hit what was a golden tone on his trumpet.

"Hell, I'm coming, Bunny, with the scarf!" Big Booty yelled, lugging the bag of food from Slim's into the apartment. "You ain't got to sound the trumpet, blow your horn to remind me when its dinnertime, man!"

* * *

"Brother, Buster's Chicken got the best damned chicken in town, man. Clean, crisp, and cheap. Of course I'm laying particular emphasis on the, uh, cheap part, Modecai—if you ain't noticed, picked up on it by now," Sweet-Tone Johnson's voice said in a low, sweet hushed tone.

Lawrence "Sweet-Tone" Johnson was showing Modecai Harlem's sights. He'd been doing just this for the past few days. Modecai had decided to knock on Sweet-Tone's door at four in the morning four days ago—Sweet-Tone just happened to be awake. Standing outside Sweet-Tone's apartment door, all Modecai said was "Jimmy Mack sent me," for Sweet-Tone to open the door and embrace him like a long-lost son coming out the cold.

"You're gonna remember all these joints I've been showing you the past coupla days, ain't you, Modecai?"

"Uh … sure, sure, I will, Sweet-Tone."

"'Cause, brother, this is just Harlem. There's still downtown. And that'll take another four to five days of touring too. Wheeling you around town."

"When you say 'wheeling,' Sweet-Tone, uh, you mean walking, don't you?"

"Uh, yeah, Modecai. Don't get the two confused. Can't accuse me of not being athletically fit, even though I do carry some extra butter in the basket. And cargo in the caboose. Sure as hell do."

Modecai laughed too, for Lawrence "Sweet-Tone" Johnson was a large man.

"Yeah, me and Jimmy Mack used to wear each other's clothes way back when. In the day. Yeah, folk used to look at us twice, brother. Think we was twins until they caught on, that is. Thought me and him, at first, was sharing the same haberdasher. Tailor cat in Harlem. The cat was cutting the same yard of cloth from the same fabric and selling it twice on the sly.

"Like we was two colored cats who don't know no better. Step straight off the banana boat. Brother, did we have them all fooled for a while. Bamboozled between us."

Sweet-Tone and Modecai crossed 125th Street and Lenox Avenue.

"Tell me honest now, Modecai"—Sweet-Tone stood in the middle of the walkway as teems of Harlemnites streamed by like sardines—"do you think Jimmy Mack and me could fit in the same suit of clothes today if you was, say, doing the tailoring? Piecing together a pair of pants? Stitching us a new suit? Want you to be honest with me now."

Modecai's eyes measured Sweet-Tone's physical dimensions from peak to feet against those of Jimmy Mack's perspicaciously.

"Yes—I'd say so, Sweet-Tone, to the uh … uh T."

Sweet-Tone bent over and slapped his hands to his knees, laughing raucously.

"So Jimmy Mack's been staying too long at the feeding table too, huh? Trough. Exercising them armpits of his. Ha. Keeping the feeding bag on for too long too. Don't know when the meal's over. When to quit. Say no to 'no' neither, when it comes to them mashed potatoes and pork chops and smothered cabbage and ham hocks, huh … brother!"

Modecai thought back to Jimmy Mack and his men raiding his refrigerator during many a day during his stay in Way City, Alabama, and his dough sinking as fast as an anchor in water.

"Uh, Jimmy Mack and his men, Sweet-Tone," Modecai said strongly. "Jimmy Mack and his band. There were four of them, at one time—not just one. Mack's Men!"

"Who was ganging up on you, huh, with their feeding bag? Send you to the poorhouse?"

Sweet-Tone was out the apartment building. He'd run off to play the numbers at a local spot named Mr. Lucky's. Sweet-Tone informed Modecai he played the numbers seven days a week at Mr. Lucky's hoping to hit the big one, make the big score one day; it was habit for him.

Modecai wasn't going to form that habit. He didn't have to know where Mr. Lucky's was in Harlem. Modecai figured Sweet-Tone could leave that joint off the New York City map. Modecai's money, for now, was tight as a snake's skin. Because of this month's unexpected expenses (the multiple bus fares), he could barely afford a powdered donut with a hole.

Modecai was sitting on his bed (well, a cot, a bona fide cot, but it was comfortable). He wondered how many jazz cats had slept on this very same cot, and he wondered about Delores, and he wondered a lot about his piano in Benny's basement too.

After four days, his heart ached like crazy. Even though there was no better place for him but New York City, his heart ached. By now, Sweet-Tone had taken him to a lot of jazz joints in Harlem, and it was exciting, very. At every jazz stop there was always a late-night jam session and someone new to listen to. Sweet-Tone played tenor sax. Sweet-Tone's tone on his sax was sweet, which was obvious by his nickname, Sweet-Tone. Sweet-Tone lacked musical imagination, verve; but still, the cat's tone was as sweet as a sun-ripened peach.

Modecai's heart ached for his piano. It was so much a part of him. It was as if a part of him was cut away, out alone on an island drifting off somewhere. It felt this way every day. The ache in him was getting worse, for he didn't know how long he was going to be separated from the piano, or when he'd be able to go back down to Way City, Alabama, to get it, bring it to New York City. He told Delores and Benny and Jimmy Mack he'd be coming back to Way City for it. He told the piano this too, but he didn't know when or how it would happen. He had no plans, no logistics, no timetable—why, no nothing.

Modecai rolled his socks back past his ankles and off his feet. He took his left foot and rubbed real hard at it with his hand. He was a country boy, all right, but Sweet-Tone walked him to death; it was quite some walking tour of Harlem they undertook this afternoon. He could soak his feet in a tub of ice water, he laughed.

He hadn't touched a piano since he'd gotten to New York. Sweet-Tone was probably beginning to wonder if he really was a jazz cat or a fake, Modecai joked. But he had scores of sheet music in his suitcase to prove he wasn't a fake. It's just that he didn't want to touch another piano until he retrieved his piano from Way City.

Later, on the way back to the apartment, he explained himself to Sweet-Tone. Sweet-Tone kind of understood. He kind of equated it to him not having his sax. Only, he pointed out to Modecai how a piano player, at least a jazz piano player, (maybe not those famous classical piano cats), can't carry their piano around from gig to gig, that they have to play on what the house has.

"I know," Modecai had replied, "but I promised my piano I wouldn't touch another piano until it got to New York City. And I never break a promise to my piano, Sweet-Tone. Not ever, man."

But even without the piano, Modecai was writing his black love notes. He'd been as busy as before. That process hadn't suffered any. He was hearing everything in Harlem. He was like a cricket, a rabbit. He was jumping at every Harlem sound his ears heard, every time Harlem's heart beat.

And he was jotting it down on paper as fast as he heard it. Or memorizing it when he was away from pen and paper, padlocking it there, putting it under house arrest, if you will. New York smelled right, felt right. He hadn't been deceived by its lure, by the Port Authority Bus Terminal or Forty-Second Street or Broadway. It hadn't teased. It didn't wear false eyelashes and a glittery, Tinseltown wig and offer promises it couldn't keep.

New York City was opening the world up to him. His world was a knothole before, but now it was a skyline, a vista teeming with opportunity. He was going to be a bigger part of it one day, New York. Harlem.

"It'll take time, I know. But I'm not one to rush. When the time comes though, I'll be ready. I will have paid my dues. All of them," Modecai laughed while trying to find a wee bit more comfort on the old green army cot.

"Ugh!" Modecai said, quite dishearteningly, regarding the cot.

* * *

Bunny stood on the Cotton Club's bandstand looking like the Prince of Cool, as if he'd just formed a new principality that he'd not yet named.

"How'd Mr. Hines take it, Bunny!" Sticks said, practically running to him.

"Mr. Hines'll get over it, Sticks."

"Come on, Bunny. How did the man take it!"

"Mr. Hines ain't happy. But what the hell, Sticks. Had to be done. That's all."

"I hope like hell you didn't come off sounding like an ingrate. I mean, man, sometimes you get a little too cocky for your own good. Sometimes you think you're too big for your own britches."

"Think, you think so, huh, Sticks?"

"Yeah, yeah—I do."

"Hell, man, you can think the hell what your black ass wants, 'cause I really don't give a damn, man. Really don't. I'm Bunny Greensleeves. I do what's best for me. Earl 'Fatha' Hines got his band, got his reputation. Now it's my time to get mine. My time."

"Man," Sticks said disgustedly, but then let it remain at that.

"Sticks, you got me this gig, this trumpet chair in the band, and I appreciate it. But I ain't no puppet on a string jerking up and down every time Mr. Hines points his finger at me."

"You know it's how it's done, playing in a band, Bunny. I don't have to school you. Tell you something you already know."

"Yeah, I know that, but it ain't for me, man, even if it is Earl 'Fatha' Hines, the great Earl 'Fatha' Hines is doing the pointing. It ain't for me. No way."

"So what is, Bunny?"

"Let's get the hell outta here, Sticks."

Sticks had zipped his cymbal case.

"Man, am I bored stiff!"

Sticks and Bunny were back in the apartment. Big Booty was sleeping. Sticks and Bunny were in the front room. They'd scarcely spoken a word on the way home from the Cotton Club gig. Bunny's pretty brown eyes looked at Sticks.

"I always thought I was the king of the hill since I was little, Sticks. My momma couldn't tell me nothing. My daddy couldn't tell me nothing. My brothers, sisters—they couldn't tell me nothing. Mississippi Charlie couldn't tell me nothing. I just got a wild streak in me, I guess."

"It's what's either gonna make you great, or it's gonna be your downfall, Bunny. Cut you down. One or the other. Could swing either way, you know. At any time."

"I know I'm young and hotheaded. I ain't gonna lie to you, man. I know that much about life. That a young cat like me should listen to someone like you who's got more experience in life. A ton of it under his belt. Been there, Sticks. Know that."

Sticks nodded.

"But I got to take my chances. That's me, man. That's Bunny Greensleeves. I ain't afraid of life, what's ahead—don't you see, Sticks? I got a streak in me that ain't afraid of nothing, I just ain't."

"I, hell, I wish I was like you, Bunny."

"Why should you think that? I don't mean to say it's right."

"I know, Bunny, but it keeps you from a lot of stress. It beats the hell out of worrying all the time, over every little thing."

Bunny dug his hands down inside his pockets. "And another thing, I got to get back to writing. I ain't been writing nothing lately. Playing gigs on the road every night and sleeping on the bus, traveling to a new town every day, man—my writing's coming up short, way short on me."

"I agree with you on that score. Ain't seen you pen nothing in a while."

"In a long while. Yeah, man, I got to get back to stroking."

"What they call it now, Bunny? You young cats? Ain't heard that one before."

"It's what Bunny Greensleeves is calling it."

"Stroking, huh?"

"Yeah, stroking, Sticks. Pencil to paper."

Big Booty and Sticks were asleep but not Bunny. Bunny was at the kitchen table with a pen in his hand and sheet music out on the kitchen table stroking. It was all of six ten in the morning. Big Booty would be up at six twenty-five and out the door by seven fifteen and on his way to meet his Broadway customers and their Broadway shoes.

Bunny yawned. He hadn't yawned all night and took particular note of it. He was dead set on remedying his present condition. He was going to write something, a tune, even if he had to force one out of himself. This was something he never had to do, but tonight, if he had to, he would.

He loved writing music; now he knew why: it offered serenity and peace. Yeah, it slowed him down, upset the day's tempo, for this part of himself he liked too, Bunny thought, when his imagination could catch fire and burn quietly from within.

It wasn't easy, him approaching Mr. Hines tonight. Mr. Hines was a great, great pianist. He had a great, great band. He was a great, great man. Mr. Hines wasn't happy about the news—was badly pained by it, if the truth be told.

"I know I was flip with Sticks about how Mr. Hines took to the fact I was leaving his band, but I've got to protect myself. Got to protect the rash things I do, man. I know I lost a great gig tonight, I ain't no fool. No dummy. B-but I don't like, cotton to feeling protected. I just don't cotton to that kind of—just don't cotton to it, man."

If the risks weren't there for him, then he thought he would die. He always had to be the one on the high wire. He was always the high wire act the carnival barker at the circus bragged about. The daredevil act. Taking chances, daring the odds, possibilities, doing them one better. Telling things to go to hell. Daring to do things differently.

It's how he saw his role in life. Some people didn't see where they had any role at all, but not him. He'd already defined himself. He'd already staked his claim—how to live life. How life must be lived. He had to make music. Do it at a fireball speed, really run at it. It made the whole process, from here to there, electric. He needed that, how he needed that electricity. He craved it. It set alarms off in him. He wasn't one to deny either his whims or his fancies.

He was always at the edge of everything, its margin, fringe, periphery. He was never in the center of it, the middle where it was comfortable, where the sweet cream rose—where it was cozy. No, not Bunny Greensleeves. No, Bunny Greensleeves couldn't sleep in a bed of roses if he tried. No, it wasn't his style. He'd rather stick his head in a hornet's nest and get stung by a pack of bees. He could survive life's stings as long as he was getting stung, could feel those bees' stingers actually stinging him.

Bunny sat in his peace, man, in his serenity, with a new day he would face. He had a tune in him. He had a thousand tunes in him. He had a melody. He had a thousand melodies in him. It was just getting back to the habit of writing music again. He had to catch a rhythm, that's all. It's all it would take for the music to leap out of him like a leopard off its leash, Bunny laughed, or shake him in his shoes like an earthquake.

Yeah, Bunny sat at the kitchen table knowing he put himself at risk tonight by quitting Mr. Hines's big band, a stylish, world-class band; but none of that stuff mattered to him for now. He thought of Big Booty beating those Broadway shoes with his shoe rag, and maybe that was the sound he was looking for tonight, seeking, his ears wanted to hear.

"Boppity-boop, boppity-boop, is that how that rag sounds slapping spit on the tip of each of them shoe shine cat's shoes, man, on Broadway? Boppity-boop, boppity-boop? Or, or is it more like, like boppity-bip, boppity-ba … boppity-bip, boppity-ba …?" Bunny laughed. "Yeah … boppity-bip, boppity-ba …"

Chapter 9

Two months later.

Modecai checked his cash, his financial situation carefully. And it checked out okay as Modecai peeled off a few choice bills from the top of his money roll.

Modecai was stepping out on the town tonight. Sweet-Tone was playing an out-of-town gig. Harlem, the night, was his. He was going to hang out alone … all by himself. Except tonight, Modecai wasn't going to hang out in Harlem but was setting sail and dropping anchor elsewhere. Far away from Harlem.

Modecai looked like a dapper Harlem sharpie with a requisite snazzy hat on (in keeping with the day). Last week was when he bought his cool-looking hat. It was a hat designed in the latest "uptown" hep cat style: broad brimmed, not stingy brimmed, not that that look wouldn't come back in vogue in Harlem, like the return of the '20s raccoon coat and ragtime.

Modecai was out his apartment building and shifting through the Harlem streets like he had three nickels for everyone else's dime. Modecai's nose did an upward tilt as it sniffed in Harlem's soft-textured night air like it was a fresh baked blueberry pie sitting out on the windowsill of some lucky cat's third-floor tenement.

"Aaah," Modecai said, "nothing like it, man. Nothing like it!"

Modecai loved these Harlemnites, the colored folk living in Harlem. For he was a Harlemnite himself after just two months aboard its shores.

Harlemnites chatted like parrots at a cracker and cheese party. Harlemnites walked like the kings and queens of spades. Over the past two months, it'd become the looks and sounds of Harlem that Modecai

Ulysses Jefferson had fallen head over heels in love with—never mind its exotic smells.

Now Modecai cocked his hat (and that was a heckuva sight to see). His fingers slipped up under his suit jacket. His fingers fingered his slack-fitting suspenders. Modecai was standing right smack dab in front of a Harlem subway station. He stared at it like it was a Harlem ghost, him shivering at the encounter.

Many times before, often, really, he'd heard this station's rumble rise from the underground above ground like a deep rumbling baritone sax. The sound it produced sounded like it could wipe out a twenty-piece jazz orchestra. Modecai had to see what this giant baritone saxophone looked like for himself (or was it Jonah's whale?), what horn section it played in.

He and Sweet-Tone had either walked or bused wherever they went in Harlem (Sweet-Tone was a "bus man" like him). Sweet-Tone was negligent in not taking him down to the, uh, orchestra pit (underground, a southern boy like him), and Modecai'd wondered why. But now was the time to see what kind of instrument produced this all-out, full-blown-scale, cacophonous sound—a sound no jazz musician's instrument he'd yet heard produce at a club date or record date.

You can do it, Modecai! I know you can, man!

There're no monsters down there. Lon Chaney ain't dressed up like the Wolf Man, man. They call it a subway. Harlemnites, colored folk up here ride it from home to work and back every day. I know they don't have anything like this back home in Hamlet, North Carolina, or, or any other place I know of, but ... but this is supposed to mark progress, Modecai, transportation for the future.

The station belched more than it rumbled this time.

"I wonder if that train was going uptown or downtown?"

Modecai was going downtown. He had a special treat in store for himself tonight. Modecai broke out into a cold sweat as the kings and queens of Harlem passed by, heading for the subway like it was a passing parade. The broad brim of Modecai's hat was thick with sweat, its powder-blue satin band and all.

Keep pretending it's a baritone sax, Modecai. Keep pretending the subway's a baritone sax, man. Keep pretending it's Harry Carney playing baritone sax in Duke Ellington's band.

Modecai was about to enter the subway station. And then Modecai did enter the station, because his body vanished from above ground like no one on Earth would ever see Modecai Ulysses Jefferson alive again, at least not up in Harlem, at least not at that subway station he'd been standing in front of.

Oh well …

* * *

Modecai was out the subway station. He was at the corner of Fiftieth Street and Eighth Avenue. And then, before he knew it, he was on the corner of Fiftieth Street and Broadway.

"Oh, man!" Modecai's pulse rate shot sky high. "Oh … oh, man. Harry Carney never sounded so good! I'm telling you, Duke. I'm telling you!"

He was trembling like a leaf. You could stir a sweet martini with the cat.

Modecai looked up at the tall buildings to his front. He was back down in this canyon of brick and steel, Manhattan. His skin tingled. From everywhere, night lights shone like clusters of small cities atop landing strips. There was a hustle in the streets. There was elegance, like a cachet of diamonds.

Modecai looked back at the subway station—he'd regained his composure.

"Heck, man, you don't scare me any. Not anymore!"

But still, Modecai took off his hat and wiped his forehead clean with his nervous hand.

Modecai was looking for Fifty-Second Street and Broadway and knew how to find it. His hand went down into his front pocket, and it touched on his money roll. *Aaah*, Modecai sighed to himself—he knew it was all there, like he'd just put it under his mattress.

Modecai began walking on Broadway, in Manhattan, like the kings and queens of Harlem walked their turf.

"Admittance for two, sir?"

Modecai wished he was wearing a black top hat for he could doff it at the pretty young lady at the door with the bright white teeth.

"Uh, one, please."

"The next set's in fifteen minutes. The band's taking a fifteen-minute break, sir."

A pause for the cause, Modecai said to himself. A pause for the cause.

"Thank you."

The club wasn't full. Modecai got a table as close to the bandstand as he could possibly get. If he'd gotten any closer, he might've been ticketed for trespassing.

"A drink, sir?"

"Yes, thank you."

"What'll you have?"

"A scotch and soda, please."

"Coming right up, sir."

Oh, the club has class. Class, Modecai thought. I'll probably have to leave a big tip. I'll probably walk out of here as broke as John D. Rockefeller—ha, how I wish!

He saw the piano on the bandstand; he wondered how it played. The bass was parked on the floor, but Modecai knew no harm would come to it. The drum kit was setup at the right spot, Modecai thought. You could draw a straight line from piano to bass to drums. There was a steel guitar on a guitar stand.

Modecai was in Howard "Big Hat" Morrison's jazz club: The Big Hat Club. Howard "Big Hat" Morrison was a colored jazz musician who played jazz guitar and owned a jazz club on "Swing Street" between Fifty-Second Street and Broadway in the jazz capital of the world.

The skinny on the cat, Big Hat, according to Sweet-Tone and the Harlem streets, was that Big Hat Morrison had hit the numbers so big that he owned half of Harlem and, now, clawing his way into Manhattan real estate like a crawfish digging its claws into sand.

He's not cheap about spending his money, Modecai thought after taking a longer look inside the elegantly appointed Big Hat Club.

"Oh, uh, thanks."

"You're welcome. And would there be anything else, sir?"

"Uh … for the time being, thank you, this will, uh, do. Do perfectly fine."

"If you need me just call me. I'm at your service, sir."

This club is tops, man. Tops!

Minutes later, the houselights dimmed. The Big Hat Club was full, at peak capacity—big hats and all (everybody was wearing a big hat in Howard "Big Hat" Morrison's Big Hat Club). Modecai couldn't keep his fingers still—he kept eyeing that gorgeous-looking piano sitting right smack in the middle of his eyes like a hypnotist luring him with a silver-plated watch and chain.

One, two, and then three musicians popped up on the bandstand. Drummer, bassist, pianist—in that order.

Modecai had to put his hand, the one that was itchy, inside his pocket. But now his right hand's fingers tapped the side of the whiskey glass.

The three musicians had been on the bandstand for a short time, and the club's crowd was getting antsy—very.

When Modecai saw him he knew it had to be Howard "Big Hat" Morrison. Man, was his big hat *big*!

Modecai's eyes landed on Big Hat. Big Hat bent over to retrieve his steel guitar off the guitar stand. He looked miffed, badly upset by something or someone. He strapped the guitar across his chest. He strummed a few chords. He looked at the piano player to give him the downbeat. And on the downbeat, Big Hat Morrison's Big Hat Club's bandstand came alive with music.

The guitar initiated the melody and then turned everything over to the piano player. Big Hat Morrison still appeared miffed on the Big Hat Club bandstand.

The piano player soloed. He was good, Modecai thought. He had a clear tone. He did a nine-bar solo and then turned everything back over to Big Hat Morrison. Big Hat Morrison nodded, seemingly jettisoning his anger and settling in on the tune he and the band were playing.

Modecai listened. It was a darn good thing Big Hat Morrison owned The Big Hat Club; otherwise he wouldn't be playing here tonight. He wasn't a good guitar player. He had to be a much better numbers player for sure—because there was no music coming out of him, just notes that made Modecai's heart beat cold.

Big Hat was in the midst of his solo, his hefty frame hunched over his guitar, making it seem small, insignificant in comparison, when, suddenly, there was a great hush, and then hysteria, followed by bedlam.

He bounced onto the bandstand like something impossible to catch on the first hop.

He was light skinned, looked like a blonde-wood piano.

It's Bunny Greensleeves! Modecai thought. It had to be!

Now Big Hat Morrison seemed miffed as hell this time. He looked like the last man on Earth with an argument under his big hat.

Bunny Greensleeves had a gold trumpet. Modecai loved it. He'd pictured Bunny Greensleeves (by his name) to be short and possessed with stupendous physical power. The trumpet at his lips, Bunny Greensleeves played a riff, a call-and-response thing with Big Hat Morrison.

Big Hat was rankled.

The crowd was going wild—fit to be tied.

Big Hat attempted to respond to Bunny on his guitar, but it came in off-key, out of pitch, his meager efforts falling far short of the mark.

Bunny Greensleeves offered something new; and Big Hat Morrison, when he did respond, came in late, the guitar off key, his clunky fingers being his own worst enemy.

So Bunny Greensleeves reeled off another incredible riff.

Big Hat sat draped over his guitar looking desperate, and then bewildered, and then hopelessly lost; and it was as if steam were actually jetting out his two big ears, ears even the cat's big hat couldn't hide.

Bunny Greensleeves waited and waited for Big Hat's reply … and when it finally came, it was like Big Hat didn't give a damn how bad it sounded.

So it's when Bunny Greensleeves took over the Big Hat bandstand. He stood in the bright spotlight. His white suit went with his white shoes and the white hat that was as white as a fresh splash of snow.

The trumpet's tone seemed to ride high in a cloud, flash, and then strike the Big Hat Club with a single blow, like a lightning bolt out the sky.

Modecai's hand practically knocked the drink over on the nightclub table. He was so excited by what he'd just heard from Bunny Greensleeves's golden trumpet.

Bunny's short legs were spread wide apart; his kneecaps were springy, bouncing brashly back and forth, back and forth. He was making the drummer sweat, work like crazy. He'd taken a slow tempo and then put this dramatic change in it—this force of nature that seemed out to sweep away any howling hurricane put in its path.

Bunny was swaying at the kneecaps now as if a fierce breeze were in his knees.

Modecai couldn't believe the sound this man's horn produced. If he didn't know jazz history, he would've sworn Bunny Greensleeves had just invented the trumpet and how it must be played just then and now, on the spot, improvised it all out for himself and then for everyone else.

"Go, Bunny, go! Blow, Bunny, blow! Blow your horn, man!"

Oh, and did Modecai agree with the roused crowd. Did the cat!

Bunny looked like a striped tiger in a white suit.

Modecai had come to the Big Hat Club to hear Bunny Greensleeves play his horn too. Sweet-Tone said he was down here. He'd finally gotten enough nerve to ask Sweet-Tone about Bunny Greensleeves, as much as he could ask about him without it coming off like he was a subject bowing, worshiping a god or a false idol.

And here he was at last. And there Bunny Greensleeves was at last. Modecai could practically reach out and touch the cat, pull him and his golden horn and powerfully packed muscle right out the Big Hat Club's spotlight and risk, what he knew would be, for him, a sorrowful fate or, much worse, certain death if he tried from the Big Hat Club's unruly, worshipful crowd.

Modecai'd heard enough of Bunny Greensleeves to come away knowing he was a genius jazz cat with a horn. And he'd heard enough of Howard "Big Hat" Morrison to come away knowing that "Big Hat" Morrison should donate himself and his steel guitar to the Salvation Army and use it for an end-of- the-year tax write-off for the IRS.

Modecai'd sat through two sets. By now, his money roll was thinning like a cheap rug, and he hadn't even tipped the waiter yet (YET!). He'd also been nursing the same drink at his table for the past hour like it was a baby down to its last diaper. The waiter, undoubtedly, had caught on.

"Another round, sir?"

"Uh … uh …"

Modecai began begging the waiter off, and right where he'd finished was where Big Hat Morrison announced, "That's it for the night, folks. Time for us cats to put our hats"—Big Hat tugged at the front of his broad brim—"up on the hat rack for the night. Thanks for digging and spending. Don't forget to come back, 'cause we ain't gonna forget to be here for you. So 'til then … we meet again …"

The pianist stood, the bassist laid his "hardwood" down on top the floor, and the drummer started disassembling his drum set. But then Big Hat shot a stare at Bunny Greensleeves that could starch a roach.

Modecai flinched; Bunny Greensleeves didn't.

Then Big Hat shot off the bandstand like an angry bullet.

Coolly Bunny Greensleeves turned, picked up his horn case, carried it over to the piano, and there it stayed.

Modecai, you can touch the cat, you can actually touch Bunny Greensleeves if you want to!

"Hi …"

Bunny turned around. Modecai was on the bandstand. Bunny's face shone. "Hey there!" Pause.

Modecai didn't know how to do this simple thing, thinking his unabashed admiration for Bunny Greensleeves was showing on his face like a fresh outbreak of freckles on a five-year-old.

Bunny turned back to his horn case.

"M-Modecai J-Jefferson."

Bunny turned back around.

"Bunny Greensleeves."

"I-I know."

Both laughed at the obvious.

"Guess I was one of—"

"Them cats—"

"Who was screaming, 'Go, Bunny, go! Blow, Bunny, blow! Blow your horn, man!'"

"Didn't see you but heard you," Bunny laughed. "Had my eyes shut. Was up in the stratosphere, man. Heard everything but seen nothing. Was on another planet. Out strolling the boulevard."

Bunny looked Modecai up, down, sideways, and backward.

"You a jazz musician?" Bunny looked around the bandstand to the drummer and the bass player. "You one of us cats, man?" Bunny asked, his thumb poking his chest.

"Uh—"

"Don't you ever pull that shit on me again, Bunny! You hear me, man! Don't you ever pull that kind of shit on me again. Ever!"

Big Hat Morrison stomped out onto the bandstand. Only a small portion of the Big Hat Club crowd remained, looked on.

"I run this fucking show down here! This is my club—my damned band, man. You ain't the man—I am. I hired your black ass. Your black ass works for me, motherfucker! For Howard 'Big Hat' Morrison, man—and don't you forget it!"

Bunny looked as cool as a snowbird; even his white suit looked cool.

"Coming out on the bandstand, pulling that kind of shit on me. Up, trying to upstage my ass, man. E-embarrassing me. Try-trying to make me look bad. Like a fucking fool. Don't you ever try pulling none of that kind of shit on me again! You hear me, Bunny! I let your black ass slide all night long. I got patrons to serve, who spend their bread in here. I let your black ass off the hook 'cause I was saving it for now. Ain't no music playing now, motherfucker! Ain't a thing!"

Bunny's eyes sat in their sockets as hard as diamonds.

"If you come back down here tomorrow night and pull the same shit on me again you pulled tonight, I'll spill your guts right out here on the fucking bandstand, man. I'll run my knife right through your black asshole like you're a New York City highway, motherfucker! A free fucking ride!"

Bunny didn't say anything but neither did anybody else in the club.

Then the tirade was over as suddenly as it'd begun. Big Hat Morrison seemed to have had his say, and so he stomped back off the bandstand.

Modecai, he was still tense, discombobulated; but Bunny, he noticed, the person whom all the rancor was directed toward, wasn't.

Bunny Greensleeves and his white suit were still as calm and cool as a snowbird on a branch.

"Hey, man, you forgot to answer my question," Bunny said, picking up the horn case, and apparently picking up where he and Modecai had left off before the Big Hat Morrison incident.

Modecai, still visibly affected by the aftermath of the passing storm, looked befuddled.

"Uh, uh …"

"Let me refresh your memory then …," Bunny said. "Like what I said before, are you a jazz musician? One of us cats?"

"Yes, I'm a jazz musician. I'm one of you cats!"

Bunny beamed. His hand was out.

Modecai grabbed hold of Bunny's hand. And then Bunny hugged Modecai and slapped his back.

It was one twenty-five.

Bunny hopped off the bandstand. Modecai hopped off the bandstand.

"What kind of tip you leave, Modecai?" Bunny quipped.

"Whatever it was, Bunny, it's gone now."

"So I see!"

Then they began winding their way out the Big Hat Club. Modecai seemed to be following Bunny.

They stepped out onto the street. There were some good-looking chicks standing beneath the Big Hat Club's lights; all of them were looking at Bunny.

"Got to beat them chicks, skirts, off me like flies, Modecai."

"I bet, Bunny."

"Got me a big ol' stick, Modecai, to do it with too," Bunny said friskily.

"Ha."

Bunny looked at Modecai. "Where you from, Modecai? Down the way? And are you visiting or staying?"

"I'm from down the way."

"Me too, man. Philadelphia, Mississippi."

"Hamlet, North Carolina. But I'm not visiting—"

"But staying. You came through the Port Authority, through Forty-Second Street on the Greyhound bus?"

"Yes—to all three."

"Yeah, same as me. It's about every jazz cat's story, Modecai. Who comes up here from down the way. Good old Greyhound bus, man. It's got style. Got a lot of mileage on it too. A lot of jazz cats coming in and going out."

They started walking up Fifty-Second Street, "Swing Street." After a few steps, Bunny turned—he winked at the girls lingering under the Big Hat Club's bright lights.

"Got to keep them dames, them skirts happy, Modecai." Pause. "So where you staying? Uptown or downtown?"

"Uptown. Harlem."

"Hey, me too."

"Thought so."

"Ain't been up there long though—right?"

"Right. How'd you know?"

"First you seen me play tonight, right?"

"Right."

"It's how!"

They were walking slowly, as if conversation was all that interested them, was their coinage.

"Uh, by the way, Modecai, what instrument you play? Man, hope it ain't the trumpet."

"Uh, no, no," Modecai answered, shaking his head. "Heck no!"

"Because if it was"—it seemed Bunny relished getting this shot in—"I know you'd quit playing it after tonight. Have a bad headache in the morning!" Bunny said, hoisting the trumpet case triumphantly above his head. "Sorry, Modecai, but my ego's as big as my sound, man."

"Uh, piano, Bunny. Piano."

Bunny stopped walking. He studied Modecai from hat to shoe top.

"Piano. Yeah, you look like a piano player."

So Modecai had to challenge that remark, what seemed such a clearly defined opinion of him.

"So … Bunny, just how does a piano player look?"

Bunny's pretty brown eyes twinkled, and then his nose twitched.

"Like you, Modecai. Exactly like you. No different. To the T. Total T."

"Gee, that's a lot of help."

"You good, Modecai?"

"I don't know. I haven't played for, for so long."

"How come?"

"My piano's down in Way City, Alabama, the city I just came from. Uh, left."

"Oh …," Bunny said with some surprise. "Hey, but every joint up here's got a piano. Everyone I know."

"I-I know. But—"

"You miss it, man."

"And I promised it … my piano, that is … I wouldn't touch another one until I brought her to New York. I-I know all of this must sound, uh, uh …"

"Coming?"

Bunny began walking again.

"Yes, yes, I'm coming."

"Uh-uh, man," Bunny said, grabbing Modecai's arm. "Hell, we've all been there. With that rotten luck. We've all been where you are when it comes to our instruments, Modecai." Pause.

"Got to breathe right. Have the freedom to breathe in the air right. Can't breathe right with no other horn," Bunny said, placing the horn case flat in his hand, "but this one. I ain't right—things ain't right without it."

Pause.

"But don't you worry, you'll get it back. It ain't gonna be for long."

They began walking up Fifty-Second Street again, leisurely, in no rush. They hadn't reached Broadway yet.

"I don't want you to get a big head, Bunny, but—"

"You mean you ain't noticed my head? Already big as a Zeppelin."

Modecai pressed on. "But I heard you on, on Earl 'Fatha' Hines's latest record, man. Y-you sounded great, Bunny. Just great!"

"Didn't I though?" Bunny winked. "Like an angel, man!" Pause. "I quit his band, Mr. Hines's band," Bunny said, stopping in his tracks.

Modecai was shocked.

"Why I'm playing at the Big Hat Club tonight. Had to get back on my own, Modecai. Freelance. Play it by ear, loose, the game fast and loose."

"There was no—"

"Friction? Naah. Working for Mr. Hines was like working, what it must be like working for—well, I can't think of anything now, which is even surprising to me—but Mr. Hines was a gentleman, a great man. I mean working for Mr. Hines was great. That recording …"

"Yes …?"

"Mr. Hines took me on on the fly, man. One of his trumpet cats ran off to Europe on him and left Mr. Hines high and dry, holding the bag. So I came in by reputation only. Mr. Hines never heard not a peep out my horn. Not only did he let me play on the record date but looked at the tune I brought in with me and put it on his album too."

"Yes, yes, it was great, Bunny, great."

"So I'm back out here kicking around, Modecai. Scratching it. Spinning the spindle as fast I please, man."

"Tonight didn't help, I know," Modecai said cautiously.

"You mean with Big Hat Morrison? With that cat? Him?"

"Yes."

"Screw that bigheaded, lame cat, Modecai. Screw him!"

Bunny bounced on the tips of his toes like a boxer ducking shadows.

"Big Hat may own Harlem lock, stock, and barrel—but that ain't got nothing to do with playing a guitar, man. That, his black ass can't play worth pigeon stew."

Bunny bounced into a new stance, even more elusive and intriguing. "You know the dope on the cat?"

"Yes."

"Numbers, man. Cat got lucky with numbers. Somebody sewed an extra pocket in his pants—"

"And filled it with bread," Modecai laughed.

"Ginger bread. Ginger bread cake. Ha. Y-you got the shit, Modecai. You got the shit, man!"

"But you, you did upstage him, Bunny."

Bunny liked Modecai for his obvious honesty. "Yeah, I know," Bunny replied softly, "the cat's gripe was legit."

Then Bunny looked up Fifty-Second Street.

"Hey, Modecai, at the rate we're walking, man, we ain't gonna reach Broadway until the sun comes up. Or goes down." Pause.

"The man, Big Hat, he ain't doing me right, Modecai."

Modecai put his hands in his coat pockets.

"The cat won't play any of my tunes. And he ain't lame. He's just, it's just that he's jealous as hell of me. All the way from here to Hoboken."

They kept walking.

"And I got me a satchel full of tunes too."

"I bet you do," Modecai said.

"I mean stuff I've been concentrating on. Tunes that'll knock your shoes out your socks."

"He was serious though, wasn't he, Bunny?" Modecai said. "Big Hat Morrison—"

"Fuck Big Hat Morrison, that cat and his big hat!"

"But he said he's going to spill—"

"Spill my guts!? Spill my fucking guts!"

Then Bunny's shoes went *screech!* in the concrete. And it's when Bunny's right hand dipped inside his white suit's back pocket as he put his trumpet case down on top the pavement. And then while rising in one seamless motion, Bunny jacked open the blade, and the knife's sharp metal shone in the Broadway lights as nasty as a two-day argument.

"I'll slit Big Hat Morrison's black ass from here to Philadelphia, Mississippi!"

And Modecai could feel Johnnyboy Daniels's cold steel blade sticking to his skin like cellophane—like it was going to cut into it, peel it as fine as the skin of a grape.

"I'm a violent cat, Modecai. A bad motherfucker, man!"

Johnnyboy's knife handle was ivory colored. Bunny Greensleeves's knife's handle was red, ruby red, Modecai said to himself.

"W-what's wrong, Modecai? Hey, man, I ain't gonna slice you at the knees. Was talking about Big Hat Morrison. I ain't got no argument with you."

Modecai's stomach was queasy. He hadn't forgotten that harrowing moment with Johnnyboy Daniels and his knife. He'd never forget

Johnnyboy and his knife. He still hadn't recovered from that night in the dark alleyway in Way City, Alabama; and maybe he never would.

Satisfied, Bunny stuck the knife back into his pocket. Modecai was relieved. Bunny picked his trumpet case up off the pavement. Modecai was glad.

They walked and talked some more until they reached the Eighth Avenue subway entrance. Once more Modecai's stomach was queasy and his face ashen white.

"D-don't tell me, Modecai."

"Yes, Bunny. This'll be my—"

"What, second …?"

"Yes, second time—"

"Riding the iron horse? How was it the first time around, man?"

Modecai was shaking.

"Oh." Bunny smiled, "That bad, huh?"

Pause.

"Hey, don't worry, the first time I rode the subway, hell, man, my knee joints rattled worse than them tracks. Sounded like a graveyard full of bones shivering in winter."

"But I kept thinking about Harry Carney."

"Harry? How come? What's that Duke Ellington cat got to do with riding the A train down from Harlem?"

"Aaah …I have my reasons, Bunny."

"Glad you're a piano player and not a trombone player, man."

"Why, uh, how come, Bunny?"

"Aaaah … I got my reasons, Modecai. Got my reasons."

Bunny dipped his hand down inside his snow-white suit's front pocket, and out came a token. Bunny flipped it.

Modecai did the same, exact thing as Bunny.

"Ready, Modecai, for the ride uptown, man?"

"Yeah, Bunny. Yeah."

Modecai Ulysses Jefferson and Bunny Odecai Greensleeves slipped into the Eighth Avenue subway station's entrance for they could hop on the A train heading for Harlem like they'd been doing just this for lifetimes and lifetimes together.

Bunny and Modecai were out the subway station. They were back in Harlem.

"Hey, Modecai, I got a great idea. Hey, man, there's got to be a jam session going on up at Smitty's Place on West 134th. You do know where Smitty's is in Harlem, don't you?"

"Yes," Modecai replied. "Sweet-Tone's taken me there."

Modecai, on the train, had told Bunny about Sweet-Tone. Bunny said he knew him, played with him on a few New York gigs.

"How about it then, Modecai?"

"Uh, yes, Bunny. But what time is—"

"It don't make no difference any. No never mind. You know them cats up there playing all night long. Hell, 'til the moon turns moldy gray. Or sets over Miami. Hell, them cats either be jamming like crazy or gambling like crazy. Either playing music or shooting craps. Or both!

"See you ain't wearing a timepiece on your wrist neither. Last one I owned got stolen out a hotel room I was in, man. Either one of them fly-by-night women of mine stole it, sweet Jezebels, or the cat at the hotel's front desk. Both of them was on my list of possible suspects," Bunny laughed.

"My short list, at least."

"You don't know the, uh, the woman's name, Bunny?" Modecai asked, seemingly, almost too innocently.

"Love them and leave them, Modecai. It's the Bunny Greensleeves motto, man. Don't leave no fingerprints for the police to find." Bunny began bouncing on his toes. "Pay at the front desk and leave out the back door. Skidididle-do, Modecai. It's what I do, skidididle-do, man."

Bunny frowned.

"But when I did go back for my watch—the same day, come to think of it—the same cat at the front desk did squint with a suspicious look in his eyes, even though I was checking his wrist for any newly acquired antiques, if you know what I mean, uh, getting at."

"And … Bunny …?"

"The front desk cat was clean," Bunny laughed. "Came up empty. Hey, man, I only got myself to blame, nobody else."

"Because the next time—"

"Yeah, the next time I'll just slip my drawers off my hips, not my watch off my wrist. Shit, the desk clerk can have my drawers, Modecai!"

Modecai, after one night with Bunny Greensleeves, loved the cat.

"Modecai, you and me, man, we're gonna have to buy us some new watches. Some downtown watches, man. Some downtown watches we can strut back uptown to Harlem and tell uptown time with. What do you say about that?"

"Okay. Okay by me, Bunny."

"Can't let no well-heeled cats like us beg nobody for time." Bunny winked. "Jazz cats like us got to keep their appearances and reputations up. No telling who's watching!"

Modecai had to agree. Yep, he had to agree, all right.

* * *

The after-hours joint, Smitty's Place at West 134th Street, was big enough to fit the necessary amount of people in it it had, and smoky enough to call on the New York Fire Department (engine companies #5, #6, #8—whatever).

But it was the music that Bunny and Modecai were in Smitty's after-hours joint for, and had. The music coming out of Smitty's Place was muscular, brawny, robust—all powerful. It could knock a super tanker out the water like a toy boat in a tub. Jazz cats were clustered together everywhere. It was like if you tried squeezing one more cat into Smitty's Place, the whole joint might split open like a fat man's trousers. There was fire in their eyes and in their bellies. A kind of madness quarantined.

And indeed the smoke in Smitty's Place could choke a horse (or kill it) and blind a bat (partially). But none of these cats seemed to mind. They were young and old. Black and white. Tall and short. Elegant, drab, graceful, clumsy. But they were emitting an energy in the big room that could light the world a million times over and make time never stop.

"Modecai," Bunny said, "we're going to have to get a little closer to the bandstand, man."

"Uh, it's okay, Bunny. I'm fine right here."

But then the music stopped, for everyone in the joint had spotted Bunny Greensleeves (now regarded as the baddest jazz cat in Harlem) in his white suit and hat, and with that black horn case of his in tow.

"Bunny!" One of the older jazz musicians motioned. "Hey, get your young ass up here and play something!"

"Hey, Mo, you know Bunny Greensleeves don't need no coaxing. Advertising."

Everybody in Smitty's Place laughed.

Then Modecai saw the jazz cats in front of him clear a precise path for Bunny. And Bunny strutted to the bandstand like he'd just bought a downtown wrist watch he was wearing uptown.

Comfortably, Modecai stood back in the crowd and smiled. He didn't wish what'd happened to Bunny for himself—but the respect from one jazz musician to the other, well, it would be hard not to like that.

When Bunny got up on the bandstand, he looked around the joint.

"Hey, Mo, you cats can get back to playing—the king's arrived!"

Modecai looked over his left shoulder and partly to his right where the crap table with the crap shooters were shooting dice.

"Roll, Jellyroll, roll! Roll for your sweet daddy, Jellyroll!"

Modecai laughed: were these men talking to their dice or Jelly Roll Morton? Because if it was Jelly Roll Morton—he was already on somebody else's roll call for now, and he wasn't about to answer them back for a long, long time!

But that was only a momentary distraction for Modecai, for his attention went back to the bandstand and the jazzmen up there. What talent, absolute genius he saw before him.

But now the buzz in the room had become almost unbearable. Everyone seemed to be anticipating Bunny. Was it because he had his golden trumpet cupped in his hand? Was it because he had his head (stuffed in that white hat of his) bowed as if in some mystical, East Indian prayer? Was it because he had a certain clear and defined hunch crunched into his shoulders? Was it because it looked like his short legs could straddle the Golden State Bridge and the George Washington Bridge at the same time? Or was it because his lips were buzzing lightly into his horn and, even so, was making a sound that could circle the planets twice around and make them sing as lightly as Ella singing Ellington?

And man, Bunny did step up to the edge of the bandstand. He did separate his short legs like he was straddling continents, and the sound his trumpet made—well, the crap shooters stopped blowing on their dice and stopped calling on Jelly Roll (or whoever) and started screaming.

"Blow, Bunny, blow! Go, Bunny, go! Blow your horn, man!"

Smitty's was rocking like a houseboat party with its anchor dropped out in the middle of the Atlantic Ocean for the night.

Bunny looked as pretty as God must look in a white tuxedo.

Modecai closed his eyes and snapped his fingers, and before he could open them, suddenly, Bunny stopped playing and was saying, "Modecai! Modecai! Hey, make a path for my man, my main man, Modecai Jefferson, man!"

And the men saw the jazz cat named Modecai Jefferson in the broad-brimmed hat, who was standing there monklike. And a path was cut for Modecai per Bunny's instructions. Men shuffling to opposite ends of the room in unison, a one-step dance on the dance floor. And Modecai did not hesitate at all, not one bit. His fingers really itched. And he was thinking about how it must feel to play with Bunny, with Bunny Greensleeves—with the man with the golden horn.

Modecai was on the bandstand and smiled. Bunny and Modecai shook hands.

"Hey, welcome back, Modecai. To the bandstand, man. Back home."

Bunny looked at the piano player. The piano player hopped up out the chair and made his own path off to somewhere.

Modecai sat down in the chair. He looked at the piano, just looked at it until Bunny snapped him out of wherever he'd been.

"You know where we left off, don't you, Modecai? The tail we're wagging. Where it's safe to jump in. Where it ain't too deep, man!"

Bunny, to Modecai's ears, made it sound as if they were about to jump into a cool pool.

"Uh, yes. Yes, Bunny."

And by mutual eyes and mutual magic and mutual consent, the musicians plucked, struck, and blew their instruments at the same time as if no one but them had such power.

Bunny was blowing his horn. Walking along the periphery of the bandstand, making the room silly with sound, making everyone in Smitty's Place make every human sound a foot, a voice, and fingers can possibly make. Folk feet tapping like the beaks of woodpeckers pecking wood; people's voices screaming like they were waking Harlem up out her sleep, telling her to get up out of bed and get off to work; folk fingers snapping like their first and last horse had just come in ("Jupiter's Daddy," "Poppa's Mistake," "Susie's Cake") paying one hundred dollars at the bettor's window, on the nose.

Bunny's trumpet was pointing to some illusionary object in the sky, but as he did at the Big Hat Club, he brought it down to point it directly at the next person who was to take the solo, run at the music, the equestrian course.

It was Modecai, man! Bunny had pointed his golden horn directly at Modecai. Modecai looked at Bunny's horn, brandishing a look of its own, as if to say "time to strut your stuff, man—put your cares up on the shelf and let all hell break loose!"

And so, after thunderous applause for Bunny, it became Modecai's turn to solo, do his spin, and all the jazz cats in the jazz joint looked at this jazz cat with dubious eyes while in some way hoping he was one of them, genuine—cut from the same musical cloth.

Modecai felt right at home. His body pulsed warm and light as his fingers skimmed over the piano keys lightning quick. Modecai'd grabbed everyone's ear and attention immediately. He didn't want anybody at Smitty's to have any lingering doubts about who he was (yeah, Modecai had an ego—yeah, he had an ego maybe as big as his piano!). Bunny stood there on the bandstand blown away. Digging his new friend in Harlem.

Modecai was getting involved in some serious music, reinventing harmonic patterns to the classic tune they played.

Bunny wanted to be with him on this. He began a call-and-response thing with Modecai, trading choruses. The bass player and drummer had to stop playing—they didn't have the chops (after all, it was a jam session) to play on what Modecai and Bunny were playing. It was turning into a duet, a two-man exploratory enterprise.

Smitty's Place was smoking.

Both Modecai and Bunny's eyes were shut as tight as a bank vault at midnight. They were going back and forth at each other, dueling swords. Not thinking but the fire in them burning freely, relentlessly, thirstily. They were driving the music into discovery, awareness, freshness, color, verve—of intellectual input, dimension, curiosity, and thought, new and alive.

Modecai had never felt his hands and head sweat with such joy.

Cats in Smitty's were stuck in a groove. Cats were swinging from star to star. The cigarette and cigar smoke in Smitty's Place was being blown out the air and into tiny corners of the universe. Smitty's Place was in a state of alarm!

Then it was like Bunny and Modecai were telling the other jazz musicians it was okay for them to come back to rejoin them as they coasted back into a different groove altogether, easing the other cats back into a safe harbor. It was so nuanced, performed with such consummate care, delicacy, Smitty's patrons applauded.

Lucifer, a crap shooter at the crap table shooting craps said to the other, "Them dudes blew the house down!"

"Every brick. They was bad as a"—the young cat blew on his dice; they rolled out his hand—"seven, seven come eleven, BABY! Seven come eleven!"

But the young cat's dice rolled out snake eyes as big as a baker's bread truck, BABY!

It was well after five o'clock. It's like Bunny didn't know what to do with himself. His body still had energy in it to spare. They were walking along 134th Street.

"You tired yet, Modecai?" Bunny asked in his high-pitched voice, like a shrill whistle was lodged in his larynx.

Bunny was hoping Modecai'd say no.

"No, Bunny. Not at all."

"Great, man. Great!"

In fact, talking about great, Bunny'd already told Modecai he was just that—*great*, a hundred times over.

"Man ..." Bunny was bouncing on his feet again.

Modecai pressed his hand down on Bunny's left shoulder, stopping Bunny in his tracks this time.

Modecai had this great, big grin plastered across his face. "Bunny, suppose I couldn't play? Suppose I couldn't play the piano worth a horse's lick, I mean—then what?"

"But I knew you could, Modecai. The minute I met you. Didn't doubt it for a minute, second. Knew you wasn't a trombone player, right?"

"Uh, right."

"Sometimes you know before you know 'cause you know, don't you, Modecai?"

"Yes, Bunny. Sometimes you know before you know 'cause you know."

They felt like a pair already as they hitched up and walked along the Harlem streets together.

"Ha …"

"Modecai …"

"Yes, Bunny?"

"You write, don't you? You write like hell?"

"It's all I do, Bunny, is write."

"Man, I was talking so much about myself before. Me and my tunes. Gabbing on and on, but forgot to ask you if you compose."

"I've got a satchel full of tunes too."

"Y-you do?" Bunny stammered. "I-I mean, I know you do, Modecai!" Pause.

"They're back home? Back in your apartment? Back at Sweet-Tone's place? Ain't they?"

"Uh, sure, sure, Bunny."

"They are!"

"Yeah, uh, yes."

"Then … what are we waiting on, Modecai? Get a step on or, better, in step, man. Shit, Big Booty and Sticks ain't seeing my colored ass this morning. Maybe this afternoon—but not this morning!"

* * *

The apartment door opened and closed. Bunny bounced across the floor.

"Where are they!"

"Uh …"

"The tunes, Modecai. The tunes. Why we're here. Your brain ain't screwed on backwards, is it!"

"No, uh, Bunny not, uh, no, man," Modecai laughed.

All the way over to Sweet-Tone's place, Modecai'd felt honored first that he was able to play with Bunny tonight and, second, that Bunny wanted to look at his tunes.

"Hope … hope I don't disappoint you, Bunny," Modecai said in a funny kind of twang.

"Get the hell outta here with that humble shit, Modecai, crap you dropping—when you know your tunes are as bad as a New Year's Day hangover, man!"

Modecai turned on the room's light.

"Sleeping on a cot too, I see." Bunny grinned. "Don't have to worry about lumps," Bunny clowned, "just sags and dips all night."

Modecai was about to say something, when Bunny said,

"Wow, Modecai! You must write 'til the cows come home!"

Modecai agreed.

"Stand back!" Bunny commanded Modecai. Bunny lifted one leg and then the other.

"It's how I sneak out the hotel's back door while them chicks are sleeping."

He began sneaking up on Modecai's store of music.

"Maaan," Bunny said as his lungs let go of all its air in a slow rhapsody of sound as if his mind had played through the music. "These, these are great, Modecai."

It made Modecai feel great. It made him feel all his toil, those hours and hours of pain and labor and ecstasy had finally been anointed by holy water.

Bunny turned, he was walking back into Sweet-Tone's front room with three pieces of sheet music. There was a music stand he placed them on.

Modecai had joined Bunny in the front room.

Bunny looked at his trumpet case.

Oh no, Bunny's not going to, not at—

The door popped open.

"Bunny!"

"Sweet-Tone!"

"Hey, Bunny, how you doing, brother!"

"Fine, Sweet-Tone!"

"How's the rent fitting you?"

"Tight. Too tight. Like a shark skin suit too tight at the elbows."

To Modecai, this seemed all rehearsed, like a cool routine between Bunny and Sweet-Tone.

Sweet-Tone swallowed Bunny up in his arms. Sweet-Tone was in from his out-of-state gig in Newark, New Jersey.

"Yeah, good, man, good. Just came in through the Lincoln Tunnel, brother!"

"Yeah," Bunny said, winking at Modecai, "still smell them gas fumes in your hair."

"Get out of here, Bunny. Brother, you ain't changed none since I last seen you!"

"Hell, who says I gotta, Sweet-Tone!"

"Hey, listen, Bunny, you know I can't beat you at talking—"

"Or playing!"

"So let's call it a draw for tonight at least, okay?"

Sweet-Tone had put his sax case down next to Bunny's.

"So I see you done met my man Modecai."

"You mean," Bunny said, "your man Modecai met me!"

"Yeah, oh yeah—it's what I meant to say, you know that, brother!"

Both looked over at Modecai.

"Me and Modecai hooked up at Big Hat's Big Hat Club down in Manhattan tonight."

"And wound up on 134th Street at Smitty's Place. I know, do I know."

"That's about the size of it, right, Modecai? Of the cute-looking dumpling, man."

"You look as pretty as ever, Bunny."

"Don't I though, Sweet-Tone!" Bunny said, batting his eyelashes back at him.

"Now don't you turn queer on me, Bunny. Got enough of them funny-looking cats up here in Harlem already. Swishing their tails like fish."

"Uh-uh, not on your life, Sweet-Tone. Not in my vanilla white suit. Even too pretty for that!"

The three still had their broad-brimmed hats on. Sweet-Tone tugged down on his.

"So what you think, Modecai, of the young cat live?"

"I should go into my room and break Fatha Hines's record, Sweet-Tone. For as they always say, 'Uh, ain't nothing like the real magilla, baby'!"

"Brother, didn't I tell you!" Pause.

"So what'd you do at Smitty's, Modecai? Sit on your hands like what you done when I took you there? Brother . . .," Sweet-Tone said, deflated.

"He played, Sweet-Tone. Modecai played, man!"

"You played, Modecai! You broke your—"

"Yes, Sweet-Tone, I broke my promise to my piano."

"Made him, the cat. It's like, like a big weight off his shoulders, right, Modecai?"

"Right, you're absolutely right, Bunny."

"So can the cat play! Romp! Can he, Bunny!"

Bunny eyed the sheet music sitting on the music stand. Bunny reached down for his trumpet case; Sweet-Tone did the same. Bunny took his trumpet out his case. Sweet-Tone took his sax out his.

"Shit, is there a man in the moon, Sweet-Tone, or is the cat pretending?"

"Hell, why last time I looked at it there was!"

"And can Modecai Jefferson—"

"Uh, forgot to tell you, Bunny: Modecai Ulysses Jefferson."

"Oh, sorry then, Modecai, 'cause I'm Odecai, Bunny Odecai Greensleeves, uh, but getting back, uh, and can Modecai Ulysses Jefferson write music, Sweet-Tone?"

"Brother, can he ever. Modecai writes him some licks, man. Some *heavy* licks, brother!"

Bunny began playing some of those heavy licks, and then stopped.

And there was a thump on Sweet-Tone's floor from the apartment below like the end of a broom handle had violently voiced its verbal complaint.

Oh, oh, Modecai thought, *we're in trouble with the law now.* And of course, it dredged up a dreaded memory of Way City and Miss Tallulah Brown and her tenants.

"Uh … I was tossed out of an apartment building by my landlord in Way City, Alabama, uh, not too long ago, Sweet-Tone, Bunny," Modecai recounted, "for making too much noise after—"

"Naah …," Sweet-Tone roared joyfully. "Not here, Modecai. Not in this apartment. In Harlem. The tenant downstairs, Mr. Blakey, the cat wants to hear him more music, not less."

"And ain't we here to o-blige Mr. Blakey, Sweet-Tone? The sweet-eared cat?"

"But it's, it's …"

"Six o'clock in the morning," Sweet-Tone said, spying his wristwatch.

"Six, six o'clock in the morning, Sweet-Tone, B-Bunny …"

"But not in Harlem, it ain't, Modecai."

"Brother, not in Harlem!"

Bunny's trumpet seconded Sweet-Tone.

Modecai thought of Miss Tallulah Brown again—and then he didn't. He laughed and then listened to Bunny and Sweet-Tone stir up a hornet's nest above Mr. Blakey's head and smiled as gorgeously and splendidly as if tickled by a feather.

Modecai was asleep, or was he? No, how could he sleep when he had the time of his life tonight. He heard Sweet-Tone snoring in his room like a bear in winter, though. The room's window shades were drawn to block out the sun. When Bunny left, Sweet-Tone checked his watch. It was nine ten, and by then, all of Harlem was awake. If only Miss Tallulah Brown could see him now, up in Harlem!

And what about Delores? What about Delores? He wasn't going to let her spoil his night, not the night he'd just had with Bunny Greensleeves. She hadn't written him back, had she? It seemed so long ago, so distant, Way City, Alabama—but when he thought about it, it didn't. He had written Delores two letters. The letters were sent to Benny's Pit, of course. Delores said it would be all right for him to write her there—why hadn't Delores written him back?

No, he wasn't going to let Delores spoil his night with Bunny, but she was. What was Johnnyboy doing to her? He played like all get-out tonight, didn't he? But Delores crept into his mind when the guys at Smitty's Place played a sentimental tune to quiet the crowd. And earlier, Bunny and his ruby-red-handled knife, it looked even more menacing than Johnnyboy's, like Bunny really knew how to use it (Bunny Greensleeves had powerful hands yet fingers as light as fluff). Bunny's energy is so powerful, so violent, untamed like it is on the bandstand, Modecai thought.

Delores, Delores, I can't get you out of my mind, Delores! I can't stop thinking about you! What's he doing to you, Delores! What's Johnnyboy Daniels doing to you!

And now Delores Bonet was roaring in his soul and not Bunny Greensleeves. Delores was there. She'd been unchained. He would write her again—a third time. She was getting the letters. What would Benny be doing with them otherwise? Everything was okay from that end. *Delores is getting my letters. S-she's read them.*

"When I sat at the piano tonight, oh how I miss you. Oh … how I miss you. I'm coming back for you, though. To Way City for you, though. You won't have to stay in Way City, Alabama, too much longer, in, in Benny's basement too much longer. I-promise. Promise you …"

Chapter 10

The apartment was three flights up. Modecai looked, but it wasn't for him—he could do better. Modecai was apartment hunting. He was doing it unscientifically for now. He was looking for For Rent signs hanging in apartment windows for now. There were plenty of those signs up in Harlem hanging in a window. He'd been in a lot of apartments the past two days (he'd worn a hole through his right shoe). Some of the apartments were too expensive (and Modecai kind of knew it beforehand), and some not at all livable—much like the one he'd just left from four blocks away. This apartment building business was frustrating, Modecai thought. But something he knew he had to do.

Sweet-Tone wasn't throwing him out, not by a long shot. No one should get the wrong impression about that, but Modecai knew when it was time to go, vamoose, scat—and it was time. He hadn't outlived his welcome, but right is right—and moving was the right thing to do.

He wanted to find the right place for himself simply because he was going to stay in New York City, Harlem, for a long, long time to come. Harlem was home. It was everything he'd dreamed it to be.

Modecai saw another For Rent sign hanging in an apartment building's window on this new street he'd traveled onto.

"Well … here goes, I guess," Modecai said mildly.

The apartment building looked decent from where he stood, not like it would crumble at the first sign of snow.

"Ooh, oooh, I know that look, Modecai. No luck, huh? Like trying to find a pickpocket in a crowd." Sweet-Tone was sitting on the front stoop of the five-story building.

It was a beaten-down look on Modecai's face, one prompting Modecai to shrug his shoulders. He took a seat directly below Sweet-Tone's on the building's front stoop.

"None whatsoever, Sweet-Tone."

"Ha, brother, these Harlem streets get hot when you're looking for an apartment, Modecai," Sweet-Tone said, handing Modecai a handkerchief out his back pocket.

"You're telling me," Modecai said, dabbing his forehead with the handkerchief.

"But when the Hawk shows up around here, brother, watch out, 'cause these streets get as cold as ice. Can ice-skate on them."

"T-the Hawk? What, who's the Hawk, Sweet-Tone?" Modecai asked.

"Oh, brother," Sweet-Tone's pearly whites chattered. "That's right, Modecai, you ain't been through no Harlem winters yet, have you? Know nothing about Mr. Hawk," Sweet-Tone patted Modecai's shoulders. "Don't, but don't worry, you'll get to know him, all right, soon enough. Get on a first-name basis with that chilly cat. Mr. Hawk's bad, bad news, Modecai—about as bad as they come, brother!"

"H-Harlem winters are, are that cold, Sweet-Tone!"

"Man, hold onto your hat, Modecai. Starch a roach, that cat dead away. Uh, right in his tracks. Before that bad cat can scoot behind the baseboard!"

Modecai shook his head in utter amazement.

Sweet-Tone shook his head as if his ears were hearing a Harlem funeral dirge for ol' Senor Roach passing through Harlem in a black hearse.

"Yeah, that bad, Modecai." Pause. "Going up? Okay, see you when I get upstairs."

Modecai was in the apartment. He'd struck out for the third straight day. He was at a card table Sweet-Tone let him use for writing. It was nice of him. Out on the streets, going from apartment building to apartment building in the hot noon day sun, he'd wanted to write down a thousand songs; and now that he had a pencil in his hand and a blank sheet of paper in front of him, he couldn't write one solitary note.

"Cold winters, I never thought of that, an overcoat, only down in Way City, I, why did I think of buying one in Way City? I … b-but I guess I'd better get one now, an overcoat now before the winter comes. Looks like I'm going to need one up here. Sweet-Tone even looked cold when he said it, 'winter.' He was turning a couple of shades of blue. Man, uh, I hope, I doubly hope I land an apartment by then." Modecai paused.

"I'm still trying to write a song for Miss Tallulah Brown. I still haven't been able to write one for her. Get to first base with it."

Modecai's pause was much longer this time around.

"And now I'm caught in this predicament: the apartment-hunting blues. Now, ha, that's a clever song title, isn't it? 'The Apartment Hunting Blues' by Modecai Ulysses Jefferson. I wonder how many jazz cats in New York City would appreciate that song title?"

Modecai looked at the green army cot in the room.

"Bet you, just bet you, a whole lot of them would."

Modecai said it like it would be an easy bet he'd win if he bet against himself.

* * *

A Saturday afternoon, five days later.

Bunny knew about Modecai's predicament. Bunny had beat his way over to Sweet-Tone's place. Bunny was yanking Modecai by the arm (the right one).

"Come on, Modecai!"

"Where, where to, Bunny!"

"Trust me, Modecai. You're gonna have to trust me on this one. Just put your faith in the Lord, man!" Bunny said like he'd just been ordained by a Bible and a preacher.

"O-okay, Bunny. If, if you say so, man," Modecai said as Bunny yanked Modecai out of Sweet-Tone's apartment.

They cut through Harlem streets (and a few back alleys too). They were in perpetual motion, on a mission, Modecai trying to match Bunny step for step, stride for stride, like two runners buzzing around an oval track. Bunny's brown-and-white shoes blurred into a light, cream-complexioned pudding.

"Bunny, is there any way we can just ..."

They were on 116th Street.

"Lighten our ..."

"Step! Hell no, Modecai," Bunny said without a bit of his breath breaking his stride. "This shit is too good to be true! Oh, yeah, Modecai. Yeah!"

Modecai's lungs were burning as hot as a furnace. "It-it'd better be, Bunny. Man, it-it'd better be!"

* * *

"All right, Big Booty. See you later, honey."

"Right, Earlene."

Earlene Bailey was leaving apartment 4D, turning abruptly to her right, trying not to bump Bunny with her big booty.

"Oh, hi, Bunny, honey," Earlene Bailey said while batting her round browns at Bunny.

"Oh, uh, hello, hello, Earlene," Bunny said shyly.

"Hello."

Modecai shot back a "hello" to Earlene Bailey.

"Hey, don't shut it, Big Booty! The door, man!"

So that's what Big Booty Bailey looks like, Modecai thought. Bunny had told him all about him. Big Booty's butt was big like Big Hat's hat was—

"Big Booty, Modecai. Modecai, Big Booty!"

"Pleasure, Modecai."

"Pleasure's, uh, pleasure's mine, Big Booty."

They were in Bunny and Sticks and Big Booty's apartment.

"How you like it, Modecai? The digs?"

Modecai's eyes kind of snooped around the apartment.

"It's fine, Bunny. Fine, but—"

"Let's get down to business then, shall we!"

"Uh, bear with him, Modecai. Bunny don't know to do nothing that's simple. Never."

"No, not at all, Big Booty. In the least, man!"

Bunny looked like he could kick the chair from under the pope; his eyes were so devilish.

"It's ours, Modecai. Yours and mine, man!"

"Ours!"

"Ours. Ours, if you want it. The apartment if you want to split the rent two ways."

"Wait a minute, Bunny, slow down. S-slow down some."

"Uh, Modecai, you want a drink of water, man?" Big Booty asked. "For yourself? Uh, before you answer the cat?"

"Yes, sure, p-please, Big Booty."

"Coming right up!"

"And while your black ass is in the refrigerator, make sure it's all you go in there for—water. Man, Modecai," Bunny whispered to Modecai as Big Booty rumbled out the room, "can that big countrified boy eat!"

Modecai remained dazed.

"Here, Modecai, take a chair."

Bunny pulled up a chair for Modecai.

Big Booty was back with the glass of water.

"Here, uh, Modecai."

Bunny pulled up a chair next to Modecai's.

"You okay, Modecai? Uh, water okay?"

"Yeah, yeah … Bunny, I-I suppose so."

"Okay, then, let me explain everything to you in sharps and flats then. Sticks is moving out the apartment. Called in from Chicago yesterday. Sticks's been on the road with Mr. Hines, but he got a juicy offer, uh, money deal from some cat in Chicago, so he's moving to Chicago. Be up here tomorrow to claim his stuff. And Big Booty here—"

"Explain it right, now, my situation right now, Bunny!"

"Yeah, man, yeah." Bunny smirked. "Uh … it goes something like so, Modecai. Big Booty's sister, Earlene, the one you just seen in the hall, just broke up with her sugar daddy, uh … uh …"

"Earl."

"That's right. Yeah, uh, Earlene and Earl. That's right. What a—so Earlene wanted to move in with Big Booty and me, but that wasn't cool. Not cool at all—"

"Not with Bunny around my sister, Earlene, it ain't, Modecai! Uh-uh, man …"

"Hey, Big Booty, I been meaning to ask you: how many toilet seats you and your family bust in a month, man? Where you lived? Maaan, your sister Earlene got herself a biiiig-assss booty!"

"Hey, Bunny, man, don't talk about my sister Earlene like—"

"So Earlene and Big Booty," Bunny continued, "gonna move in an apartment down the hall."

"Earlene's a beautician, and I'm a bootblack, Modecai. Both of us together, can make the rent on the first of the month. Handle it okay."

"Yeah, yeah, right, Big Booty, right, handle it—so you see the joint's ours, Modecai. Yours and mine, man."

"It is, Bunny?"

"Just, you just say, gotta say the word, Modecai."

Then Modecai hopped to his feet. "Yes, Bunny, yes. Yes!"

"That was the word!"

And Modecai latched onto Bunny, and they began this mean jitterbug thing while Big Booty clapped his hands as best as an unmusical, no-musician cat like him could in order to keep the music's beat in some kind of respectable time valuation.

Modecai and Bunny'd discussed the financial arrangement, the *fifty-fifty split*. It fit nicely into Modecai's budget. He could pull the monthly rent off without so much as a sneeze. Bunny said he could take care of his share without a problem also. Modecai and Bunny were soon to be roommates but felt more like soul mates.

Big Booty was off to Slim's corner store. Modecai and Bunny were humming out some tunes.

"It's gonna be just like this every day of the week from now on, Modecai, you and me working on tunes. Yeah, you and me, Modecai. Usually work, do all my composing at the kitchen table, if Big Booty's big ass ain't sitting there first!"

"Bunny, give Big Booty a break. You should—"

"Yeah, break the cat's legs!"

Pause.

"How's your writing coming along, by the way, Bunny?"

"Great, Modecai. If I could only convince Big Hat to …"

"Are things still, uh, better between you?"

"Yeah, it's copacetic. Well, like I told you last week, they're as good as they're gonna get. Man, Modecai, if only the cat would just let me play some of my stuff in his damned club. Shit, it's killing me." Pause.

"But it's bread, Modecai. Bread. I gotta keep thinking about the rent, especially since it's going up now. But my time's gonna come." Bunny's eyes looked like beautiful bright buttons. "I found you, didn't I—or you found me. However the hell the fate shit works itself out, man."

"Don't try figuring it out, Bunny, because you'll confuse yourself even more."

Modecai put his chin in the cup of his hands. "You know, Bunny, things happen s-so quickly, don't they? One minute I'm in Way City, Alabama, with Jimmy Mack and his men digging your sound, your style, on a Fatha Hines's record, and the next minute I'm up here, in New York City, Harlem, sitting at a kitchen table talking, and, and I'm talking to you."

"Yeah, man."

"Life is full of sweet surprises."

"Tricky, Modecai. The shit's tricky."

"Hey, Modecai, Modecai!"

Big Booty was back from Slim's corner store.

"Did Bunny tell you about the mice in the apartment? R-running around inside this joint!"

"What mice!"

"What? You didn't tell him, Bunny!"

"Don't worry, Modecai," Bunny began coolly. "Psssst—word out in the building, among the tenants is"—Bunny's hand partially covered his mouth—"them frisky cats is moving down the hall with Big Booty and his sister Earlene! Suitcases are already packed as of this morning! All packed and ready to go! Zippo!

"In fact, heard them scurrying, packing their stuff last night when I was in bed."

"Oh no, no, they're not!" Big Booty hollered at the top of his lungs, his big bag of groceries crashing to the floor. "No, they're not, *man*!"

"Big Booty, guess your big, black ass won't be eating no groceries tonight, now will *it*!"

* * *

Modecai had just showed up and had walked into his brand-new apartment on the fourth floor, 4D.

"Welcome."

"Thanks, Bunny."

Bunny took one of Modecai's suitcases.

"Bellhopped once. Include it in on my résumé," Bunny said. "Where to, Modecai?"

"Bunny, wherever you want me is fine by me."

Bunny pointed straight ahead to a connecting hallway. "The master bedroom then!"

"Are you sure?"

"It ain't the servant's quarters!"

And it wasn't. The room was tremendous. If Modecai were a fish, he'd think he'd just moved out a fish bowl and into an aquarium overnight.

Bunny put Modecai's suitcase down by the bed and then walked over to the window, whipping his hands through the air like a master of ceremonies.

"Even got a view out onto the world, Modecai."

Modecai walked to the window; he stood side by side with Bunny.

"Fits my style fine, Bunny."

"Man, makes you feel like you got a million bucks in your pockets, even if you ain't got but two pennies for a cup of coffee."

Modecai put his arms around Bunny's shoulders. Bunny jumped back.

"Hey, Modecai, watch the starch in the shirt, man!"

"So it's going to be like that, Bunny?"

"All day and all night, Modecai. I promise you that. Ain't letting go of the rope, not for a minute, a second of the day, man." Pause.

"Hungry?"

"Uh, yes … uh, yes—a little."

"Good. Then let me cook us up something. Got gourmet chef on my résumé too. What can't Bunny Greensleeves do!"

Modecai had to say it—he had to. "You mean Big Booty left food in the refrigerator before moving down the hall with his sister Earlene?"

"See, see," Bunny said, pointing his finger accusatorily at Modecai, "and you're the one who told me to lay off the cat! Shit's contagious, ain't it, Modecai? Like poison ivy, man!"

They'd gotten into the kitchen.

"Uh, Bunny, seriously, man—can you cook?"

"Hell, Modecai, please don't tease the crease in my grease," Bunny said, pointing his finger to the oil in his reddish brown hair. "'Cause you know there ain't nothing in this world Bunny Greensleeves can't do, man!"

* * *

The meal had been cooked, served, eaten, and digested. Modecai had to admit, Bunny was one heck of a cook! He wondered if he did all the cooking for Big Booty, even though big booties, apparently, were partial to the Bailey household, even before Bunny's arrival on the scene.

Bunny was looking at Modecai. He wondered what he was thinking. Where his mind was right now. This silence—it was the first time this kind of dreadful silence existed between them. For it felt, to Bunny, as if they hadn't said a word to each other for days, when he knew in actuality, it'd been maybe a matter of a minute or two, no more.

Quickly though, Bunny figured out the look on Modecai's face. Quickly though, Bunny made some sense out of it. Quickly he felt he was back in touch with Modecai like when they'd played the past two nights up at Smitty's Place.

"Modecai ..." Bunny was tugging Modecai's arm, urging him up from the kitchen table.

Modecai got up; there'd been no resistance from him.

Bunny walked Modecai into the front room.

"Miss it, don't you?"

"Like hell, Bunny."

"Uh, don't worry, man. We're gonna go down to Way City, Alabama, for it—you and me."

Modecai smiled.

"One of these days we're gonna make that trip. Get that piano of yours up here in Harlem. And it's gonna be soon. Hell, Modecai, I want to see what that gorgeous lady looks like for myself!"

Bunny shifted his feet.

"See that space, Modecai," Bunny asked, pointing his finger again. There was an open space in the front room. "It's gonna be sitting right there in that open spot where Sticks used to keep his drum set. Right there." Pause.

"Thanks, Bunny, for tuning into my feelings."

"And we ain't going down to Way City by mule and cart neither."

"Whoever said we were?"

"I don't know." Bunny pouted. "I just thought I'd let you know we ain't before you did think that," Bunny laughed.

"Thanks, Bunny," Modecai said sarcastically.

"Always gotta go first-class, Modecai. Luxury edition. Your upright ain't coming up to Harlem unless we do!"

"Oh, now I see what you're getting at."

"Yeah, man, we ain't going to Way City to get it by mule and cart. Only the best for that lady!"

"Yes, for her, Bunny!"

"Damn, you do miss that piano like hell, Modecai!"

"And it sounds, Bunny, a little like you do too."

* * *

Four days later.

Knock. Knock.

"Modecai, the hall phone's for you."

"Thanks, uh, Mr. Clarence."

"It's Bunny," Mr. Clarence laughed.

"R-right …"

"So you'd better hop to it. Make it snappy."

Modecai dashed out the door.

"Bunny keeps you jumping, don't he?" Mr. Clarence asked more with his bushy salt-and-pepper eyebrows than his pecan-brown eyes.

Modecai acknowledged Mr. Clarence in some kind of disoriented way.

Modecai picked up the phone. "Bunny?"

"Yeah, Modecai. Get down here, and quick. On the double!"

"W-where!"

"The Big Hat Club, that's where!"

"H-how—"

"Jinx got beat up. He's in St. Luke's. Big Hat needs a piano player."

"He does? Uh, uh, sure, Bunny, I'll be right there!"

"Take the A train, Modecai!"

"Sure thing, Bunny!"

Modecai was in the apartment, and then out.

"Maan … I hope I look all right …"

Modecai felt his nerves tremble through his clothes.

"My hat—the hat. I-I've got to get my, my hat. E-everybody in the Big Hat Club wears a-a hat. Everybody …"

* * *

Modecai was at Fifty-Second Street and Broadway. This time he really wanted to pinch himself—make sure all of this was real.

Modecai looked into the bright lights, the razzle-dazzle. He heard car horns honk. This was the real thing. Modecai was making his way down Fifty-Second Street when he spotted Bunny standing outside the Big Hat Club in his green suit looking like a grander version of a greenish parakeet. Modecai's footsteps livened—were tapping a lively tune, actually.

"Modecai, you made good time, man! Come on, we're about to go on. No time to rehearse nothing. None of the shit, man!"

Now Modecai felt so nervous that his saliva stuck to the roof of his mouth like bubble gum. And when he got in the Big Hat Club, there was this big crowd of people with big hats on their heads, and Modecai knew why the crowd was there, to see Bunny Greensleeves.

"Big Hat's negotiating some business in the back, Modecai—so I'll give you the old introduction bit after the first set, okay? The cat was about to call some other piano player in, but I called you, after I heard about Jinx's little mishap."

"Beat up? How did Jinx get beat up, Bunny?"

"Owed somebody some backs taxes (ha, bread). Don't pay to be late on your payments, Modecai. Jumped his ass up in Harlem." Bunny hopped up on the bandstand. "Wonder if it was one of Big Hat's own loan sharks who did it. Just wonder."

"Hey, man, the name's Cornelius Best," the bass player said.

"And I'm Scratch, Larry 'Scratch' Anderson," the drummer said.

"And you'd better sit your ass down, Modecai, and ac-quaint yourself with the keys, ivory … please!" Bunny said.

Instead, Modecai looked out at the audience and pretended he was up at Smitty's Place. He could play. The cats up there didn't bounce him out the joint on his ear (or was that his rear?) now, did they?

And then the club's emcee came out on the bandstand impressively mannered.

"Ladies and gentlemen …"

Modecai kind of brushed his fingers over the piano keys lightly.

"I-I guess I'm ready."

The houselights dimmed in the Big Hat Club.

Then Big Hat struck the pose to strike the downbeat.

"I'd better be."

And off the Big Hat Morrison Band charged like a racehorse with a hotfoot.

* * *

The houselights in the Big Hat Club were on, and the crowd was filing out.

"Oh, man, man, Modecai!"

At the moment, Big Hat was practically mugging Modecai's hand.

"Your partner claimed you was bad, b-but I can't say it enough: you are one bad-ass motherfucker, Modecai!"

Modecai felt Big Hat's big hand cracking the knuckles of his hand like roasted chestnuts.

"Kinda hope Jinx keeps his headache now, don't you, Big Hat?" Bunny said, packing his horn in his case.

"Yeah, Bunny, it's a shame, that Jinx thing, but Modecai here set the evening straight. Right, all right. Do you think you can—"

"Yeah, Modecai'll make the tour down here tomorrow evening. Yeah."

"Bunny, you can sit your black ass down and let the man talk for himself!"

Bunny's face didn't look like foul weather.

"Want to come back down tomorrow night, Modecai!"

"Yes. Uh, sure, uh, Big Hat."

"Then you're on. I got me a new piano player. Ain't that some good news!"

Bunny and Modecai were off the bandstand; they were mixed in with the tables.

The girl stood alone. The girl was white. Modecai didn't look at her but Bunny did. Bunny noticed Modecai hadn't looked at the white girl.

"Modecai, man, this here ain't the South," Bunny said. "Up here, man."

The tall, stacked white girl stared at Bunny. She was dressed nice, real nice.

"Excuse me, Modecai. I got something to do, man."

Modecai's eyes watched Bunny as he zigged and zagged between the club's tables. Modecai watched the exchange between Bunny and the tall, stacked white girl—her ear, then his.

Bunny came back over to Modecai. "You don't mind taking the A train, uh, solo tonight, do you, Modecai? I'm gonna make it up to Harlem also. But the white chick wants to stroll to the station before we board the train. Don't want to hold you back any," Bunny said, winking back at the white girl. "Know you got things to do back at the apartment, Modecai. Uh, things to attend to, man. For yourself."

* * *

This was the next day.

Bunny and Modecai were aboard the A train heading downtown to the Big Hat Club for rehearsal. Big Hat had the band rehearse in the club in the late afternoon (four thirty to six thirty) before each gig. Bunny and Modecai were making the trip together, enjoying the persistent clatter of the train tracks. Bunny was dressed to the nines. Modecai, conservatively appropriate—as always.

"Modecai, when are you gonna talk about her, man?"

It just came out the clear blue sky like an epiphany. There wasn't any hint or suggestion of this before—none whatsoever.

"H-how'd you know, Bunny?"

"Know you left more than just your piano back in Way City, Alabama. Knew it had to be a skirt, man."

"Delores."

"Nice name."

"I ..."

The train was scooting past another station.

"I'd fallen in love with her, Bunny."

"She didn't—hell, man, what, she wasn't—"

"No, she was in love with me. Delores *is* in love with me, still. B-but her man came back."

"Back?"

"Yes. You see, he was in prison."

"What for? The cat—"

"Manslaughter. Murder. He slashed a man's throat in a knife fight."

"Bad cat, huh?"

"Yes."

"So this bad cat came back to claim his property, what was his, his woman, and ran you out of town."

"Yes, you, you can say that."

"Unless you wasn't coming, planning to come up to New York City otherwise."

"No. I was planning to. I-I'd asked Delores if she wanted to come with me."

"And?"

"I never got a chance to find out one way or the other. Johnnyboy, Johnnyboy Daniels—it, it's his name, decided things for us."

It's when Bunny's eyes looked very dark and complicated, to the point of pure menace.

Bunny whispered it to Modecai. "Only, if it was me, Modecai, Johnnyboy'd be dead. My knife … the cats blood'd be smeared all over the fucking blade of it, Modecai."

And there it was. Modecai saw it for a second time since his relationship with Bunny—the violence in him that seemed to lurk just beneath his heartbeat.

"Stuck the shit in the cat's gut. Kill him for all time. Cat squeal out like a pig."

It sounded so final to Modecai, Johnnyboy's death.

"But I don't c-carry a knife, Bunny," Modecai said, twisting in his subway seat.

"I know that, Modecai. Been known that."

"Delores, she …"

"Delores knew that too."

"Yes, Bunny."

"She loved you. This woman, Delores, loved you, man."

"It's the only reason she went back to him, Bunny."

The train stopped; passengers boarded.

"Next stop's ours, Modecai."

"Uh-huh."

Bunny stood. He walked over to the subway doors.

Modecai was still sitting.

"She would've come to New York City with you, Modecai." Bunny's breath appeared against the subway door's glass. "But I still would've killed that Johnnyboy cat. Stuck the cat with my blade. In his fucking gut."

* * *

This was irregular: Bunny was not off with a woman or off at an after-hours jam session after his Big Hat gig.

Bunny had brushed his teeth. He was in powder-blue silk pajamas, ready for bed. He peeked into Modecai's room—Modecai had already turned in.

"Night, Modecai," Bunny said in a half-whisper.

Bunny was in bed in no time flat. If all of this was strange to him, Bunny didn't act it. He laid his head back on the pillow, propping up his legs. Modecai had a woman he loved, man—and that was great, Bunny thought. Had he ever fallen in love with a woman? No. "Ain't got the time—too damned busy."

He was glad he found that out about Modecai. He loved him like a brother. *Ha, I ain't even, man, me and Modecai ain't even compared ages yet, even though the cat looks older than me by ten years. Least that much. So I'll just say, I love the cat like an older brother—how's that?*

Bunny's legs came down.

Yeah, he was too busy to fall in love with a woman. And up until New York, Harlem, he was always shuttling from one town to the next. He wasn't going to drag a woman around town like a frying pan, man—he had that much respect for women. No, he'd bed them but not board them.

But then again, if Modecai had come to New York with Delores, would it have worked out for them? Modecai, lately, was strumming his fingers. Man, how he must miss that upright. Music, how much it takes of a man, the space it takes. Modecai loves Delores, sure, the cat does—but that piano, Modecai's piano, that upright, it's prettier than Delores.

A woman wakes you in the morning but not like music. Music's got a different sound in it, a different touch. A, a woman—

"I don't know if it would've worked, Modecai, you and Delores in Harlem. A woman gets jealous no matter how much she says she won't when you try your best to explain them things to her. Mornings and nights, they start adding up. Pile up like worn out mattresses, man.

"Music wears on love. It does. Wears on anything you touch. Only cats who living it every day understand the shit. It's ours, nobody else's. Can't, just can't be that, Modecai."

Bunny closed his eyes. He began imagining what Modecai's upright piano looked like—yeah, right, he was in love with it too, like Modecai'd said he was a few days back.

* * *

What am I doing, waiting for Delores to write me? I've got to write her again. I have to try again. "Delores's life isn't going well. That has to be the case. It has to."

Now Modecai was beginning to feel guilty. Now he was beginning to feel as if he should have taken a stand. Instead of Delores saving him, maybe he should have saved her. Maybe he should have sacrificed himself for Delores. He would've been dead. Johnnyboy would have been in prison. Delores would have been free. Modecai's body shuddered: it was a gruesome, horrific idea.

Modecai was out the bed. Quietly he walked across the floor. He didn't want to disturb Bunny. He had his pencil and paper. He turned the kitchen light on. When he sat, he sat heavy like he was going to sink down into the chair; the full weight of him would somehow make the chair's wooden legs wobble.

Bunny stirred. It was just too early for him to fall asleep. He looked over at his trumpet case. Bunny could see the case in the dark. In fact, you could bury it in one thousand black nights and he'd still see the case by some miracle of the mind and spirit.

Now Bunny was on his feet. He spotted the light burning in the kitchen.

"Guess who's up. Not unless Big Booty's back with them mice, man."

Bunny had music in him too. He didn't turn on the room light but got a piece of sheet music off the top of his bureau. A pencil was on top the bureau also.

When he got within range of the kitchen, he saw Modecai strumming his fingers on the table and his teeth gripped to his pencil. When he saw the piece of paper, it was blank.

He's writing Delores, Bunny thought. Modecai's not writing music. But he's strumming his fingers. Modecai's strumming his fingers.

"Bunny," Modecai said, not at all surprised by Bunny's sudden appearance, "don't tell me the kitchen light got in your eyes?"

"Modecai, I'm supposed to be the clown prince, jester in this act—hell, man, not you."

"Right. I forgot my place in the act. Of course, I'm the straight man."

Modecai saw Bunny's sheet music. Bunny sat down at the table. Right away it seemed as if the kitchen had undergone some divine intervention, for there the silence that reigned seemed golden.

And there they sat, Modecai and Bunny, in that golden silence, not until Bunny said, cracking the silence like a whip.

"Modecai …"

Modecai looked surprised that Bunny had broken this "unwritten agreement."

"Yes, Bunny?"

"Modecai, uh … uh"—it's maybe the first Modecai heard Bunny actually stammer—"h-how old are you, man? And don't lie, 'cause I know you're at least ten years older than me!"

* * *

Another two months had flown off the calendar. There was no stopping it. It was full of fun and merriment for Modecai and Bunny. The two jazz musicians seemed destined for each other. They were working steady at the Big Hat Club. They were pulling in a steady, heady wage. Uh-uh, Big Hat wasn't a cheapskate, didn't skimp on dollar bills—not by anyone's imagination.

Further evaluation of the month of September would reveal that Bunny was hustling overtime, man. Besides Big Hat's Club, Bunny was gigging (for money) whenever and wherever he could. Bunny was even teaching trumpet, squeezing that gig into his schedule when possible. Bunny, quite literally, was hustling like a big-time loan shark (*bag and cash man*) up in Harlem.

Modecai, quite frankly, was wondering what had gotten into Bunny. Was Bunny trying to build a small fortune or drive himself to an early grave? In fact, after Modecai had laughed about this frivolous assessment of the situation, it's when he gave serious thought to the latter—an early grave? He was going to talk to Bunny, and soon, man. Modecai didn't know who could blow taps at Bunny Greensleeves's funeral but Bunny Greensleeves.

* * *

It was one o'clock on the dot.

Bunny burst through the apartment door like Harlem was on fire.

"Oh, Modecai!" Bunny said, clapping his hands together and tapping his feet—acting the complete, total fool.

Modecai had a contemplative look on his face as he rose to his feet like a god about to produce great thunder and lightning and sparks in the sky.

"Finally, Bunny! I've got proof you've been overworking yourself! It-it's finally gotten to you. Laid you out for the count. The walls are beginning to close in on you. You're finally—"

"Modecai, don't even try to take my pulse, man! Don't you even go near my temperature!"

Bunny ran across the room like a madman. The window was open.

"Don't. Don't, Bunny. Don't jump!"

"Jump! Who the hell's gonna jump? Hell, the only way I'd jump out a window is if I lost my C-sharp on my horn, man, and that shit ain't gonna happen 'til I'm at least a hundred and two!"

Bunny bowed, rose, parted his arms—and it's when he let that infallible smile of his do the rest.

"Look, Modecai. Look!"

Modecai couldn't help but feel steam in his pants.

What was Bunny looking at out the window? What could produce a smile as beautiful as his? A woman? A beautiful colored woman?

And Modecai was at the window, and what shined up into his eyes was this Studebaker, this beautifully shined two-tone Studebaker whose glint could dazzle, persuade, and blind the eye.

"Isn't it gorgeous, Modecai? B-beautiful, man!"

"Yes, uh ...," Modecai muttered, "it's yours, Bunny? You bought it? It's why you've been working like a madman all these weeks? S-so you could buy yourself a brand new—"

"Uh, not buy, Modecai—rent. I ain't making no long-term payments on nothing but the rent. Rent. Cash and go!"

"Rent a car for what, Bunny?"

"We're going to Way City, Alabama. You and me and it, man, if you haven't heard from your bookmaker yet. We're going to get your piano out of Benny's Pit—out of that cat's musty old basement. It don't belong down in a basement, no morgue, Modecai, where nobody can see it or hear it!"

"No, it doesn't, Bunny!"

"It belongs in New York City. In Harlem. Sitting pretty. Sitting in the sunlight, the moonlight." Bunny walked over to the apartment's open space.

"Sitting right about here. Yeah, here!" Bunny said, spreading his arms and legs apart like he could measure himself out to the size of the piano.

Modecai wasn't looking at Bunny but at the shiny, blue, two-tone Studebaker down in the street. That thing, he thought, could get him and Bunny over to Russia and back.

The elation hadn't left Modecai (he'd looked at the Studebaker from the window down in the street a few hundred times by now), but the hundred and one questions were beginning to marshal themselves like wasps.

"Bunny, uh, I hate to say this, break this bad news to you, but we can't carry an upright piano, I'm afraid, in the backseat of a Studebaker—no matter how pretty it looks."

"I know that shit for a fact, Modecai. Hell, it's why I rented a van, man!"

"W-where, Bunny? Where!"

"What you expect me to do, ride around Harlem with a van hitched to the back bumper of a Studebaker? Bunny Greensleeves? Modecai, what, you must be out your mind, man!"

"Okay then, what about Big Hat? I mean what about the band, our gig, then?"

"That's square to the peg. Already took care of that little bit of business this morning with Big Hat. Woke up every horn player and piano player there is in New York 'til I got two cats to say yes.

"Got three-day reservations not to play at the Big Hat Club. A day down to Way City, a day back, and tonight, we're wheeling around Harlem in our two-tone Studebaker, Modecai. Knocking everybody dead."

"You're a trip, Bunny. A definite trip around Central Park, man."

"Skeedeedidididido, Modecai. Skeedeedidididooo."

* * *

Modecai had found out, through Bunny, that they were to leave for Way City at one in the morning. Modecai'd called Benny's Pit. He told Benny about what time they'd be in Way City. Benny said no problem, that he'd be there. Neither one had said anything pertaining to Delores. Modecai didn't ask and Benny didn't volunteer any information; it was quite awkward to say the least.

"Everything on the square, Modecai? Copacetic?"

Bunny had been playing his trumpet, running through some scales.

"Fine. Yes, things are fine."

"Delores didn't come up in the conversation, did she?"

"No, Bunny. It was strictly business between Benny and me."

"Well, sometime tomorrow all this shit'll be settled. Shake out the fleas and see what we got."

"Bunny. You, I …"

"That Johnnyboy, the cat's a dog, Modecai. He ain't doing right by Delores."

"I-I know, Bunny."

"The weight's heavy on you, I know, Modecai—so think about tomorrow, about the piano."

"I'd rather think about flesh and blood before I think about a damned piano, Bunny."

Bunny got up and walked into his room. He came back in a flash, though. He had his back to Modecai, and then turned.

"Look, Modecai! Look at this shit, man!"

"Bunny. Where'd you get that wild-looking thing from!"

"Man, it looks like a Picasso painting, don't it?"

"Do you think, who knows, Bunny …"

"The cat's liable to paint anything. One day this tie might be worth a whole lot of bread, Modecai. Yards. Parlez-vous francais?"

"Bunny, man, where, when did you learn how to speak French, a cat from Philadelphia, Mississippi, of all places?"

"Some of them old cats in Fatha Hines's band used to speak them some French, man. Brought it back with them. Taught me more than just *oui* and *si*."

"Uh, *si*, that's Spanish, Bunny."

"Uh, so what, Modecai? I'm trilingual. Sometimes I get them damned *si*s mixed up with them damned *ouis* and them—"

"Stop, man. Stop, before I topple over!"

Bunny was glad to see Modecai laughing. Tomorrow in Way City there would be a lot for him to deal with: the piano, Delores—the entire ball of yarn, he thought.

"Hey, Modecai, get dressed. We're dining out tonight."

"No, Bunny, you've done enough for me already."

Bunny pulled a fat wad of cash out his pocket.

"Modecai, you ever seen a jazz cat with this much serious bread before?"

"Well, uh, to be honest, uh, B-Big Hat Morrison, may-maybe?"

"Hell, Modecai, that big hat cat don't count—he ain't a jazz musician!"

"Well then, no, I haven't."

"Me neither, man. So we might as well blow it tonight. Make Harlem rich." Pause.

"And don't wear nothing lame, Modecai. To embarrass yourself with. We spinning through Harlem like a top and then stopping off at the Cotton Club. Already made reservations for eight o'clock on the dot for Bunny Odecai Greensleeves and Modecai Ulysses Jefferson, even if we got to get back here by nine for we can get our usual three hours of snooze before we take off for Way City. Gonna eat with them white folk, ain't playing for them tonight. You and me gonna pass for white tonight, Modecai—and they better serve our black asses at the Cotton Club, even if it ain't their policy to do so—even, if it's back in the kitchen!"

"And just think, Bunny, you almost said all of that in one breath."

"You mean it wasn't? I meant for it to be, man. Hell, I must be losing my breath control. A horn man can't lose his breath control, man. See, you piano players ain't gotta worry about breathing, no breathing, no breath control … See, you piano players just got to plunk them piano keys—"

Modecai was looking down at the blue, two-toned Studebaker for the 101st time and knew the Studebaker's engine must be getting cold and he'd better hurry up and get dressed before Bunny really got back his breath control and he'd miss out on his first visit to the Cotton Club. And …

Chapter 11

Modecai and Bunny'd arrived in Way City.

They'd traveled over smooth and bumpy roads on their way to Way City, Alabama. There were times, during the long trip down, when not only their physical but also their mental strength became a necessity; it was all according to which stretch of worn-down road was traveled. But whatever bumpy roads were negotiated, for Bunny and Modecai, they became a string, a series of small victories.

Both saw the plain sign at the city line.

"You just saw the sign, didn't you, Bunny?"

"Off to the right of the road, Modecai. Just big enough for it to squeal on itself."

Modecai couldn't tell you just how he felt. He'd listened to the car's emptiness, its hollow sound the whole trip down. But maybe three hundred, four hundred miles ago was when the sound grew increasingly its own, more distinct—singing a song of words, especially.

"Modecai ..."

"Yes, Bunny?"

"Hey, man, you got to guide me through this humpty-dumpty town, man. Don't forget, I've never been down this neck of the woods before. You've got to guide a big-city boy like me," Bunny said. "Don't forget, man, I'm used to big-city lights, big-city adventure, big-city ex—"

"I've got the picture, Bunny. You couldn't've explained it any better for me than you have."

It'd been this way the entire trip for Modecai and Bunny: quips, fun, playfulness, capriciousness. It's only when Modecai heard the van's hollow sound, and then its song, was there interruption, seriousness to the trip.

* * *

Severely the sign slanted, and it was the first time Bunny wished he had a paint brush parked in his hand and a bucket of paint parked in his lap; and the rest of Benny's Pit, he thought, he'd have to write a tune for: the bluest, saddest tune he knew or could imagine.

It was as if Modecai were looking at a white angel. His upright piano was within those four walls. His jazz. His music. It knew he was coming. It somehow knew he was there, parked right outside Benny's Pit with Bunny in the Studebaker's front seat.

Bunny braked the car. He glanced over at Modecai again and then twisted his body and looked back on the backseat at his horn case.

"You've got to be feeling like a million bucks, Modecai. Like you're panning for gold."

Modecai and Bunny clasped hands, and Bunny pulled Modecai to him. There was a soulful silence.

"Okay, man. Let's go. Enough of this shit—let's get on to why we're down in this town in the first place."

Modecai opened the car door and got out. When his shoes touched the ground, it was like he was walking on a cloud (as the cliché goes).

Modecai looked at the structure. "Benny, he's in the back, Bunny."

And when Modecai looked up the back alley he shivered, for he saw Johnnyboy's presence like he was a ghost with a bloody knife.

"What the hell's wrong, Modecai!"

"Nothing, B-Bunny, n-nothing."

"Nothing hell! Johnnyboy. The motherfucker, he—"

"Right there. He put his knife to my throat, right there, Bunny."

"The *motherfucker*!"

The memory of the event would never leave Modecai.

They were halfway up the alleyway when Bunny said. "Uh, wait a second, Modecai. You know what I forgot, what's on the backseat of the car …"

Bunny's legs churned to get back to the Studebaker as fast as the Studebaker's tires when he'd aired them out on the southern back roads.

Upon Bunny's return to the alleyway, though, he began strolling up it like this more-than-cool jazz cat who'd blown into Way City from New York City via taxi only for he could keep the taxi's meter running hot in front of Benny's Pit for a long stretch of time.

"Bunny, if only I could be as—"

"So damned cool! I know, Modecai. Cut in a groove." Bunny put his arm around Modecai's waist. "But you are, Modecai. The shit's rubbing off, man. I'm telling you, it's rubbing off on you, man."

They were at the back door of Benny's. Modecai gulped. Bunny heard it like a timpani drum.

"This is it, huh, Modecai?"

"Yes, Bunny."

"Paradise back in you."

Knock.

The door creaked open, and then—

"Modecai!"

"Hi, Benny!"

Benny grabbed Modecai's hand.

"Damn, it's damned good seeing you!"

Modecai turned to Bunny and introduced him to Benny. Then Benny pulled back the door. Modecai and Bunny stepped into the back room. Benny spotted Bunny's horn case.

"You a musician too?"

"Uh, yes."

Modecai walked over to the basement door.

"It's down there, Modecai. Just where you and Jimmy Mack leave it that morning."

"You're a good friend, Benny."

"Hey, Modecai, we're in this here thing together. All of us."

"Ain't nowhere to exit this place, until the Big Cat in the sky says so."

Benny laughed at Bunny's remark.

Then Benny took the lead. He turned on the basement's light.

Benny turned back to Modecai.

"Seems it cries itself to sleep at night, Modecai. From what I've been seeing from it when I come down here."

Bunny rubbed Modecai's back.

Modecai didn't want to cry but felt as if he could. On his way down to Way City, he'd thought about how he was going to meet this moment. Him and his piano. He should close his eyes, treat this as a complete surprise, he thought, think he was the luckiest jazz cat on the face of the earth.

For some reason, Bunny's hand held tightly to the horn case.

The piano's shine resembled a starburst of colors.

"D-Delores …"

"Girl dusts it with her cloth every night it's been sitting there, Modecai. On schedule."

"The piano's beautiful, Modecai. Just beautiful, man."

Modecai was the only one who was now speechless, shocked into submission. His eyes tracked across the piano's rich, solid black wood.

"Delores, she did this for the piano. Kept it in this condition."

"Every night of the week since you leave Way City, like I said, Modecai. The girl come down here to the basement."

Modecai touched the piano.

Bunny was opening the horn case.

Modecai had kept the piano stool with the piano. Modecai sat on the stool and then leaned his ear down into the piano keys. His body was at an awkward angle. He lifted his hand.

"Wonder, I wonder if she still sounds the same?"

And a finger became visible to the eye, and that's when Modecai did what he did.

"Oh … Bunny. Bunny!"

And Bunny's trumpet sang the same note out its bell. And Benny stood there stunned by the trumpet's beauty. And the room was transformed into music, one sound after the other. Modecai emptying everything out his system. All of it and more.

* * *

Bunny and Modecai both looked at the piano.

"Modecai, you take the front end, and I'll take the back, man."

"Bunny, it's the first time I've heard of a piano having a front and back end."

Bunny put his hands on his hips (he'd removed his suit jacket).

"The front is what I'll be carrying and the back you. Thought your lame brain had figured all them p's and q's and *x*, *y*, *z*'s out by now. Shit, Modecai."

"Oh, do forgive my blind ignorance, Bunny. I suppose I've been separated from my piano for far too long."

"Ready?"

"Ready."

Bunny bent his knees. Modecai bent his. Bunny grabbed the bottom of the piano.

"Oh, uh, three, on three we lift it." Pause. "Who's giving the downbeat, anyway, Modecai?"

"Who's the leader of the band?"

"Why—"

It's when Modecai and Bunny heard Benny's feet slipping down the stairs. He'd been upstairs for a short time before opening Benny's Pit for business.

"Moving it, huh?"

"No, we just do this for exercise every day. After we milk the cows and feed the chickens." Bunny bristled.

"Bunny!"

Then a sheepish grin fell over Bunny's face.

The piano still hadn't been lifted off the basement floor.

Benny had lightened his steps, had set himself off to the side of the basement almost as if he were not present; but suddenly, his hand touched Modecai, who now looked into a face and saw what he knew in his heart would be there, would surface to strike fear in him.

"We got-gotta talk, Modecai," Benny whispered. "You and me."

Modecai let go of the bottom of the piano.

"Delores?"

"Alone, Modecai."

Benny put his arm around Modecai. He was about to guide him over to a corner where thick cobwebs hung, where they could have a private talk.

"It's all right, Benny. We don't have to go over there—Bunny knows all about Delores. Everything about us."

"I-I don't know, Modecai. I just don't …"

"She's been receiving my letters—she has, hasn't she?"

Benny's black face blued. "Yes, uh-huh, Delores been getting them all right. From me, Modecai."

Modecai's body bent in.

"Three? Right, Modecai?"

"Yes, three, Benny."

"It's Johnnyboy, that fucking Johnnyboy! Delores tucks them letters of yours down inside her bra after reading them. Seen the girl. Three, four times a night reads them, Modecai. Slow—in, in a slow trance …

"I know she don't write you back. It's Johnnyboy. He's beating on her, Modecai. Taking to beating her!"

"What!"

"Beating her, man. Bad, down, down to the … He don't ever beat Delores before he go off to Foster City Prison, but he's beating her now."

"Where, Benny, where!"

"Everywhere. All over. Bad." Benny's voice was cracking. "Last week she come in here with a black eye. Was all swoll up. And this week her back. Delores's back was bruised. Black and blue.

"Now every week there's something new. Every fucking week Johnnyboy find a new part of her to beat on. Oh don't he! Don't he!"

Bunny had to steady Modecai. He looked on the verge of collapse.

"She ain't writing you back, Modecai, 'cause she can't. Delores ain't got nothing good to say. Ain't, she ain't gonna, won't lie to you. Rather go along and suffer in silence—I know the girl. Delores rather keep you in suspense, guessing then, then …"

"She said Johnnyboy never hit her, Benny, before. Put his hands on her. Delores said—"

"Must've come back from Foster Prison meaner—I don't know. Than when he—I don't know what the hell—"

"Me. It's me. He's beating Delores because of me!"

Bunny sat Modecai back down on the piano stool.

"You come into her life at the right time—don't you think no different. You make Delores as happy as I ever seen her. Turn her life around. For the good, the better." Pause. "You two have a chance, Modecai. A damned chance, not 'til Johnnyboy return. Come back from Foster City Prison. Oh … oh …

"Johnnyboy, Johnnyboy, that bastard, sonuvawhore's milk. He's the one who turn everything sour. Sorry as a pail of shit. Stinking … s-somebody oughta kill him. Shoot that bastard in the head. Kill Johnnyboy Daniels!"

Modecai was crying.

"I dream of it. One day somebody getting the nerve up around here to kill the boy. Shoot him dead like a dog. Get rid of Johnnyboy Daniels. Piece of dog shit once and for all. Do all of us living in Way City a fucking favor!"

* * *

The piano was upstairs in Benny's Pit, at its back door. Bunny had backed the car into the alleyway (he wondered why he'd not done so in the first place).

"On the count of three, Modecai!" Pause.

"Uh, one, uh, two (*grunt*), uh, one, two, *three*!"

In no time flat the piano was loaded onto the van and anchored down with rope for it wouldn't flop around like a giant fish. It was covered by a strip of heavy canvas.

Benny stood close by Modecai as he'd done down in the basement. His hands, he'd shoved down in his pant pockets. Then his left hand came out his pocket. He looked at his watch.

"Delores gonna be in here soon. For work." Pause. "She don't miss a day still—no matter how hard it gets." Pause.

"You keep writing her, Modecai. Just, you just keep writing to her—it's all Delores got left, now that the piano ain't here."

"Tell Delores, Benny. T-tell Delores that I—"

"Don't have to say nothing to the girl—Delores gonna know you come and gone. Off on your way to New York City again."

"See you, Benny."

"Yeah, Modecai. You too, Bunny."

"Yeah, Benny."

"Certainly can play that horn of yours sweet and pretty. From what I heard in the basement."

"Thanks. Thank you."

Bunny was in the driver's seat, Modecai the passenger seat. Simultaneously their heads turned to the backseat to where Bunny's horn case was. And there with it was a bagful of something that was actually sinful smelling.

"Rib and pork chop sandwiches!" Modecai shouted. "Benny must've put them back there when we weren't looking, Bunny."

Benny stood at the building's back door.

"Free of charge, men. Eat … eat and enjoy!"

* * *

Modecai was guiding Bunny through Way City streets again, not until he told him to stop the car across from a building Bunny already knew about. And there they sat in the blue two-tone Studebaker. And Modecai looked out the car's windshield, not hearing anything that meant anything.

"Delores, she lives in there, don't she, Modecai? That's the building—9 Taylor Street?"

Modecai was looking into his old room, not Delores's, whose room was in the back of the two-story building.

"What's he doing to her, Bunny? What's Johnnyboy Daniels doing to her! Delores said Johnnyboy Daniels—it's one thing he never did w-was beat her, Bunny."

Bunny looked to where Modecai was looking.

"I want to see her! Do you hear me! I want to see Delores!"

Bunny turned the car engine off.

"We'll w-wait here, Bunny. R-right here." Modecai sobbed. "We'll … we'll wait for her. De-Delores. Wait, wait …"

Pause.

"You don't want that, Modecai. No, man, for yourself. You don't wanna see her," Bunny said. "Man, not that—Johnnyboy's been beating on her, man."

"Bunny …"

"Benny told you, Modecai … Delores don't need you. Not you, just your letters."

Modecai fought harder.

"I'm no coward, Bunny. I'm not!"

Bunny started up the car's engine and began pulling the car away from the beat-up-looking building.

"Delores is up there."

The car was well past the building when Bunny answered.

"Know she is, Modecai. So, man," he said, clearing his throat.

* * *

They'd been on the road, back to New York City for some time now. They'd torn into some of those pork chop and rib sandwiches. Plenty still remained in the greasy brown bag. Benny had made enough for a cattle convention, even though no cattle conventions were ever convened in Way City, Alabama.

They were on a dark, bumpy road. The Studebaker's big, bug-eyed headlights were working vigorously against the dark.

"Man, it's a good thing I don't believe in ghosts, Modecai."

"Me either, Bunny."

"Man, did we come this way this—"

"But then it was light, Bunny. Sunlight."

"Boo!"

Modecai jumped.

"Yeah, Modecai, ghosts would have them a mean jam session out here, in this dark!"

Modecai's butt was feeling each bump in the road. He wondered about the piano back in the van.

"Thinking about that piano, ain't you?"

"Bunny, if you do that one more time, man, read my mind like that, I'm going to begin to think you're a ghost. Or a spirit or—"

"You was … wasn't you?"

"One hundred percent correct."

Modecai's fingers played something atop the car's dashboard.

"I'm going to have it tuned the minute we get back to New York City, Bunny. Do you know a good piano tuner in Harlem?"

Modecai, in the dark, could feel Bunny's eyes pressing on him.

"Now you know … man, Modecai, of course yours truly does. But not just any piano tuner, Modecai, but the best!"

"It's, uh, it's always got to be the best for you, doesn't it, Bunny?"

"Nine of us Greensleeves including myself."

The Studebaker's headlights still drove through the darkness, peeling it back.

"Nine in the band," Modecai laughed. "What number are you, Bunny?"

"Stuck in the middle of the pack. Wore me them hand-me-downs that I handed down. But even then, made something out of them. Told myself they were the best clothes anybody could wear because I was wearing them, had them on my back, so, quite naturally, they had to be the best. See what I'm getting at, Modecai?" Pause.

"Started off thinking that way. Momma and Daddy and the rest of them didn't teach me that: what I taught myself about the best, being the best, Modecai." Pause.

"Family," Bunny said, "what about yours? Your momma and daddy."

"Two. There're just two of us Jeffersons: Charles and me."

"Two! Not nine, man! A duet, not a nine-piece band!"

"Momma had two miscarriages and, and three still births. Daddy died seven years ago."

Bunny's eyes turned away from the road. "From what?"

"T-tuberculosis, Bunny."

"Oh."

"Momma took it hard. Momma …"

Modecai tried thinking of anything but his mother and how hard she took his father's death. Anything but her. The hard times on that farm in Hamlet, North Carolina, with his mother and Charles.

"Your Momma sends you the money once a month. Always on time like a good drummer keeping time, huh, Modecai?" Bunny said, seemingly trying to break up the tension.

"Yes, Bunny, Momma's a good drummer."

Bunny was going to say something else but caught himself—now wasn't the appropriate time, he thought. But sometime in the future it would be discussed—without a doubt.

"A few of us Greensleeves scattered like birdseed, Modecai. From the nest, man. Hightailed it off that farm and outta Philadelphia, Mississippi, like a jailbreak.

"Uh, but, got to admit, wasn't that bad."

"I'm sure it wasn't, Bunny."

"Was exaggerating. But for me, didn't cotton to farmwork. Marrying a farm girl a half mile down the road. Somebody smiling at me like she's milking a cow. Having a brood of kids, crying, feeding them, clothing them, then dying on a farm one day." Bunny smiled.

"But I keep in touch with everybody. The Greensleeves family. All my brothers and sisters. Momma and Daddy, man. Ones who left, know where all of them are too. Could point them out on a map. Think I'm lying, then try—"

"Charles, he left home. I don't know where my brother is, Bunny. To this day. He just vanished."

Modecai's eyes pointed straight ahead into the dark, but now as if looking for ghosts with a flashlight and living desperate, unforgotten dreams.

* * *

Modecai and Bunny were on the last leg of the trip. The rib and pork chop sandwiches were ancient history (freebies never do stand a chance around two grown men!)

"You see what I see before us, don't you, Bunny!"

"Been seeing it for the last five miles!"

"Bunny, Bunny, we made it! Made it home! Lady Liberty's standing in the sea!"

"Tall, man, standing tall. Hell, Modecai, soon as I get us into the Holland Tunnel and along the Harlem River Drive, we're home sweet home!"

"The New York City skyline is twinkling, isn't it, Bunny?"

"A two-day twinkle."

"It's a jewel at night. A sapphire, cluster—a cluster crown of jeweled lights, Bunny!"

Bunny mashed his foot down on the Studebaker's gas pedal.

The Studebaker and the van had just rolled onto Harlem's sacred ground.

Modecai felt like telling all of Harlem he had his upright piano back. He wished the Studebaker were a convertible. He wished he were sitting up on the Studebaker's backseat shouting it out to all the Harlemnites, to all the kings and queens of Harlem.

"Four of Benny's pork chop and rib sandwiches (that was between them), and we're home, Modecai. But damn, Benny's hot sauce was hot."

"Today feels like a tickertape parade, Bunny."

Honk! Honk! Honk!

"Somebody heard it, Bunny!"

"Shit, Modecai, everybody in Harlem heard it, know it's here!"

"Safe and sound, Bunny. Safe—"

"You mean—it knows it's back with you. The cat who owns it."

Bunny yawned. "Listen, don't wake me up for breakfast, don't care if you pile a stack of pancakes on my plate!"

The car was treading through Harlem nice and slow—easy now. Bunny and Modecai were in no rush. They'd been to Way City and were back. They were savoring their accomplishment, mission, their commitment to something they believed in, promised between them would happen. They felt like sweet wine at dinnertime, felt as mellow as a cello. One jazz cat's instrument is another jazz cat's instrument—that was their take on it, how it plays itself out in the key of C: warm and cozy in everybody's ears.

* * *

"There!"

Modecai had removed the canvas cover from the piano.

"Bunny, there's not a scratch on it!" he said, folding the canvas and putting it on the couch.

"Hell, Modecai, why don't you just kiss the damned thing and get it over with!"

The piano overpowered the empty spot, the one which, at one time, belonged to Sticks's drum kit.

Bunny rubbed his butt. "Them bumpy roads is murder. Ouch! Shit!" Bunny yawned. "Jeepers creepers, got to rest these peepers!"

"Bunny, you're a gem. I love you, man!"

"Hey, Modecai, you would've done the same for me if my horn was stuck in a pawnshop in say … Rolling Fork, Mississippi."

"W-where's that?"

"Hell, you don't want to know where Rolling Fork, Mississippi, is. Just skip it out your memory like bad vinyl playing some Muddy Water blues. Dash it out your brain for good, man."

"I-I owe you though, Bunny."

Bunny walked over to the light switch; he turned it off.

"If you say that one more time, I'm gonna tell Harlem's moon to stop shining down on it. That piano of yours."

"It does look beautiful, doesn't it, Bunny?"

"Like a birthday cake. Like a cat's birthday cake."

* * *

Modecai couldn't sleep a wink, and so, why should he try? He was sleeping on his side because his backside was sore too, just like Bunny's. Some of those bumps he and the Studebaker hit—Modecai rubbed his backside; need he say any more than what he'd just said?

Life is really funny, undependable, he thought. He went from happiness to sorrow and back to happiness in one day. Life *is* inconsistent—not something to be trusted. The piano was the happiness, Delores the sorrow, and the piano, again, the happiness. Life was flat, and then a bump, and then flat again—just like the roads he and Bunny'd traveled over from New York to Way City, Alabama.

He hadn't played one note on the piano since it arrived in Harlem. Could he pretend? Could he pretend Delores was down the hall from him? That he'd left her bed and she was waiting for the music, the black love notes to wake her. Could he pretend that in an apartment building in Harlem, away from everything in Way City, Alabama? Yes, he wanted to see her no matter how broken she was. Yes, he wanted to see her no matter how many times Johnnyboy had hit her, struck her, beat her, made her black and blue, made her even more embittered, depressed.

But what would it have proved? What would it have gained him, Delores—them?

She knew he'd been there. After all, the piano was gone, out Benny's basement—wasn't it? Was the piano an anchor for her? Was it some kind of island, a retreat she could go off to every night before she went back to Johnnyboy Daniels from Benny's Pit? Had he, Modecai Ulysses Jefferson, taken the last possible hope, thing Delores had left, from her?

If she'd walked out the building, saw him and Bunny parked on the opposite side of the building in the Studebaker, then what? It would have been crueler on her. She knew he was coming back to Way City for the piano, not her. Delores dusted and polished the piano nightly; she could see her reflection in it, the days withering, the tomorrows brewing like storm clouds.

In that apartment building, Johnnyboy was breaking her body apart. He was wreaking revenge on Delores his way, in a slow, deliberate, callous cycle of violence. Soon, how much of Delores would there be left?

Could he pretend she was down the hall from him—could he? That they'd done their nightly lovemaking and he and his piano and black love notes were waking Delores in tempo, in bright, colorful sound—to a new day kissing each cheek. Could he pretend that? Could he?

* * *

Bunny heard Modecai's feet on the floor. Bunny tensed and then relaxed. He hadn't slept a wink either. Modecai was reaching back. Bunny understood the problem. He understood the trials and tribulations, the intricate shaping of the day. Modecai's piano was home, but Delores Bonet was elsewhere.

He wasn't going to get in the way of Modecai. Not in Modecai's blue way. Any cat has to learn life's cues. Any cat has to learn when the music stops, dies, goes dead in his head.

* * *

Sun flooded the apartment's front room. Modecai sat down on the piano stool. The people of Harlem spun through his mind. Pretty colored women, handsome colored men. Modecai was imagining, pretending—seeing beautiful shadowy visions from his past.

When he sat down on the piano stool, he no longer felt the aches from the long car ride to Way City. His fingers struck a note on the piano for the first time in New York City, for the first time in Harlem.

"Delores, did you hear it?"

His fingers lay over the keys quietly and languidly and lovingly.

* * *

Bunny was on his feet; he couldn't resist the invitation to the dance. He walked into the apartment's front room.

Modecai heard Bunny but chose not to speak to him

Bunny opened his horn case.

"Bunny, I'm playing to Delores."

Bunny nodded. He played something over the top of Modecai's piano.

"You know what, Modecai?"

Modecai turned and saw Bunny's hand rub his backside.

"Travelling by car still beats the hell out of the Greyhound bus, don't it!"

Modecai did have to agree with Bunny on that score, even though more jazz cats were trooping through the Holland Tunnel and into the Port Authority at Forty-Second Street by Greyhound bus than by car even as Modecai and Bunny spoke.

Chapter 12

Even though it was two weeks later, Modecai and Bunny had determined that the upright piano was the apartment's one and only star.

Most conversation between them took place there. Bunny, who could play piano, monkeyed around with the piano some when he composed but, still, mostly at the kitchen table. But Modecai had forsaken the kitchen table; he did all his composing at the piano. Modecai was back in tune.

"Look, Modecai, got me a fifty-cent shine, for free!"

"Thought Big Booty charged a quarter for a shoe shine, Bunny."

"Had the cat apply an extra coat of polish."

Bunny had just come from down the hall.

"Caught Big Booty—"

"Before Big Booty did his Broadway hustle. His black polish dried up in his shoe box, man."

Then Modecai saw Bunny was wearing white shoes. Oh well, he thought. Oh well …

"Modecai, I heard what you were playing from down the hall. Man, your shit's getting sweeter and sweeter by the minute. It ain't got nothing to do with this, does it? The new love in your, our life," Bunny said facetiously, patting the piano like it was a pretty dame.

"Uh …"

"We gonna chase Count and Duke outta town, you hear me, man. We gonna chase them lame cats outta town with our hot tunes, Modecai!"

"Hold … n-now hold it, Bunny. Don't jump the—we're not trying to chase Count Basie and, and especially Duke Ellington out—"

"Like cocker roaches, Modecai. Like big, fat cocker roaches!"

"Come on, Bunny, we—"

"At the stroke of midnight, Modecai—then warning them cats they have got to go. Go, Joe! Arlene! Skideeadaddle-do, skideeadaddle-da. Scram, Sam. Mable. Heave-ho. Go. Leave. At the stroke of midnight, please. When the ticktock on the clock tocks twelve, we're gonna tell them lame cats to get the hell out of town. To get the hell out of Harlem, Modecai. Make tracks, man!"

"But there's enough room in Harlem for all of us cats, Bunny. There's e—"

"No, man. No. The hell there is. Them cats has got to go, man. Scram. Get outta town. Duke, Count—sorry, but you cats have got to go, *zippo*!"

Bunny was in a one-in-a-million pose. His body was angled in at least five different directions at once, while his thumb was raised directly over his right shoulder like he was tossing bad tequila out a whiskey glass.

"Your black ass can laugh if it wants, Modecai. But I already bought me a can of roach spray! Stop them cats dead in their tracks! D-don't move, 'cause I'll, 'cause I'll sprizz your ass, man!" Bunny laughed like he was looking down at a cockroach flipped on his back, perfectly starched.

Modecai twisted back around to the piano. Bunny stood behind him, studying the sheet music.

"Man, Modecai, you write a melody second to none, really."

"Are you kidding, Bunny? Give me a break, when I'm sitting in this room in the presence of a master melodist."

"I know, but your, your—what you call them again, Modecai?"

"Uh, black love notes, Bunny."

"Yeah, your, uh, black love notes, well, Modecai, shit, man, they're just that: black love notes." Pause. "Modecai ..."

It was said so lazily, Modecai thought, as if Bunny were going to take the time to explain more about himself.

"You know I think bigger than jazz tunes."

"You do?"

"Yeah." Pause. "Broadway. Broadway, man."

And Modecai saw the Broadway he knew, the Broadway he walked down every night to get to Big Hat's Big Hat Club in Bunny's eyes.

"You do, Bunny?"

"Show tunes, Modecai. No minstrelsy shit. Colored folk singing show tunes, man. Dressed up in Harlem finery." Bunny glanced down at the shine on his shoes. "Shoes shined. Polished!"

"Hey, like yours, Bunny!"

"Ain't nothing better than my shine. A fifty-cent shine on Broadway!" Bunny's fists punched the air.

"We can do it, Modecai. You and me. The way we write tunes. Man, show tunes—we were made to write show tunes, you and me."

"When, Bunny!"

"The time, it'll come. Just check it in with the rest of your dreams in the Dream Hotel. When the time is right, then that'll be the right time. You get me?"

Then Bunny scooted into the kitchen and came back with two glasses of water.

"Thanks," Modecai said, taking the glass of water from Bunny.

"Seen the smoke shooting out your smoke stack, man. Top of your hat."

Bunny took a sip of water.

"You know what, we've been writing a helluva lot lately."

"Every night since we got back from Way City."

"Leave from outta here, on the A train, hit the Big Hat Club, out the Big Hat Club, back on the A train, and *boom!*—we're back home." Bunny giggled. "Man, Modecai, I'm beginning to turn my black ass into a choirboy. And Bunny Odecai Greensleeves ain't nobody's choirboy!"

"Now, Bunny ..."

"Hell, it's true. I ain't had me a piece of, of juicy fruit in, man, can't even count back that far, it's been that long, man."

Modecai's hand covered his mouth to muffle his laughter.

"Tonight, Modecai, I'm gonna get back on track. Run the train over them tracks. I ain't coming back from Manhattan to Harlem without something dangerous swinging on my right arm. Ain't shaped like a soda bottle."

Modecai took the pencil out his hand and put it back between his teeth.

Bunny put his hands on Modecai's shoulders.

"W-what about you, Modecai? When, when you gonna get back on track, run the train?"

"I don't know, Bunny." His eyes were moistened by his tears. "I'm, I don't think I'm ready yet."

"Modecai, man—you're a man, man. You're a man. You're human."

"That I am," Modecai said, managing to smile. "I know."

"It … look, it ain't gonna mean nothing. No romance. Nobody cares for, for it to mean nothing, Modecai. You or the chick." Bunny took a deep breath. "Hell, them skirts just wanna know if you make love like you make music, Modecai—from the soul, man. What we play is sexy. Got sex written all in it—every note of it. Jazz."

Modecai looked over his shoulder and up at Bunny.

"You want to try tonight, Modecai? It ain't gotta be romance. I can set, set it up."

Modecai got up on his feet and walked over to the window. Bunny watched Modecai's head nod weakly

"O-okay, Bunny. Yes, okay. Do that. You can set me up with a girl. Young lady."

Bunny walked over to Modecai. He stood there by the window next to him.

"I know you ain't got over Delores yet."

"Right."

"But you can't be afraid of life. You can't run out of sight of it. Life, it don't, just doesn't operate that way. You know that, uh, by now."

"I am, are-aren't I, Bunny?"

"Man, you and that perfect English crap. Why don't you just say 'ain't' like the rest of us colored folk up here in Harlem do!"

"Uh, I am—ain't I?"

Bunny clamped his hand to Modecai's shoulder. "Just promise me you'll try tonight."

"I promise, Bunny. I'll try. Really try."

"Good." Pause.

"No matter how ugly the chick is! Cross-eyed and bucktoothed … and, and walk like a duck!"

"A duck! Maaan …"

The chase was on: Modecai chasing Bunny, lapping the piano as fast as they could.

* * *

But she wasn't ugly. And on top of that, she was white.

"Mindy, Modecai. Modecai, Mindy."

Modecai shook in his shoes.

Bunny mouthed the words "you promised."

Modecai shook Mindy's hand.

"Man, she dug your playing tonight, right, Mindy? Dug it to death."

"Yes. Did, did I!" Mindy said breathlessly.

She was classy looking, it's all Modecai could say. She was classy looking. Dressed "rich." "In the silk."

"Oh, and this is her girlfriend, Billie—like Billie Holiday, Modecai."

Except she was white, Modecai thought. A white Billie Holiday. White, and as pale looking as a sheet.

In no time, Bunny and Billie had vanished. It was just Modecai and Mindy in the Big Hat Club standing between two tables.

"Well, uh," Modecai said awkwardly, "looks, looks like it's just you and me, Mindy, d-doesn't it?"

She had strawberry-blonde hair and sky-blue eyes.

"Yes, it, it does, Modecai."

When Bunny set me up with my first white chick, Modecai thought, *he fulfilled any colored man's fantasy—any colored man but me, that is.*

"Ready, uh, ready to go?"

"Harlem, Bunny said you'd take me to Harlem, Modecai."

Modecai didn't take Mindy's arm, and he was sure she'd been to Harlem before—plenty of times.

As they walked up Fifty-Second Street heading for the subway station on Fiftieth Street, Mindy and Modecai, Modecai tried keeping the conversation at a minimum and distance between them at a maximum.

Whereas Mindy tried keeping distance between them at a minimum and conversation at a maximum.

"How do you get your fingers to … to move so fast over the piano, Modecai? *Zip, zip, zip*. I'd be afraid of chipping my fingernails if it was me, Modecai. Playing the piano. Your hands … are like a black blur."

When they got on the A train to Harlem, the train was crowded. The few colored faces in the car didn't stare at Mindy and Modecai. Modecai tried to sit somewhere away from Mindy, but by Mindy's actions, she insisted he shouldn't. Modecai felt like there were bricks in the bottom of his shoes.

"This is your first time dating a white woman, isn't it, Modecai?" Mindy asked.

Modecai looked at Mindy's strawberry-blonde hair and sky-blue eyes and remembered what it would mean for both of them if they were in Hamlet, North Carolina, and not in New York City on the A train, in Manhattan, bound for Harlem.

"I'm from North Carolina. From Hamlet, North Carolina. From a place where a colored man doesn't date a white woman. Dare do so."

"I've dated colored men before. This isn't my first time. Not at all."

All of them, I bet, am sure, were jazz musicians. Colored jazz musicians, Modecai thought cynically.

"I like colored men."

Modecai wasn't about to get into the physical, psychological, or sociological reasons for this white girl liking colored men like it was a medal of honor she'd just won.

Mindy's body inched closer to Modecai's on the subway seat.

"I'm not a dumb, blue-eyed blonde, Modecai."

For the first time, Modecai really looked at this white girl.

"Just like you're not a big, black brute of a man."

Mindy was humanizing them, he thought.

"I'm not a stereotype, Modecai. I'm just out on a date w-with a colored guy."

Modecai looked up at the subway car's ceiling, for so many years of thinking one way couldn't vanish in one night; but he tried to understand what Mindy had just said, laid out there for him.

They were out on Harlem's streets, and what they were about to do had seemed predestined by Bunny in the Big Hat Club, and by Mindy on Fifty-Second Street, on the train. They weren't an odd couple in Harlem. They weren't a mismatch of colors, odd socks. Harlemnites were used to colored men uptown swinging with their downtown/white women on their arms. Harlemnites were used to their racy bedroom eyes, this sex before the sex combusting them.

Modecai walked with Mindy. She didn't swing on his arm. Modecai wanted the Harlem streets to swallow him up—do him a favor. To put him out of his misery. He was going to have sex tonight with this white girl, and he didn't know how to do it, how it was done.

Bunny'd told him which hotel to go to. A cheap place. A place where no one listened to any of the sexual crudities between a man and a woman, not at the hotel's front desk where they took your money, handed you a key, and either sneered at you or smiled at you between tight teeth.

Modecai snuck another peek at Mindy—maybe, maybe if he pretended she was Delores, but she wasn't. She was Mindy, white, a white girl; he didn't even know her last name.

"Uh … you and your girl?"

The guy opened the hotel's register, that big, black tattered book of his.

"Uh-huh"—he paused—"got a room for you, Jackson! Just sign the dotted line. Right there—all you gotta do!"

This guy was cool, a hep cat—he had a name for him, Modecai thought: Jackson. Yeah, Jackson!

"Room 22, in the back. Far back."

Modecai saw the fee for the room in the "back." The lobby's sign explained this for him.

He looked at Mindy—she was enjoying all of this, he thought.

The desk clerk, whatever his name was, handed Modecai room 22's key. Modecai's hand fumbled it.

"Hold on steady now, Jackson! Can't let the plug slip out the hole that easy!"

The desk clerk and Mindy were enjoying this thing they were doing.

Mindy spun in front of Modecai.

"Here, Modecai, let me, oh, let me open it, Modecai … please." Her breath had rushed through Modecai's ears.

Suddenly she was a woman, a seductress who had learned the game well, Modecai thought.

He handed Mindy the key.

She hugged him. He held her.

Pretend. Pretend, Modecai thought. Pretend she's Delores.

"Ha." She laughed childishly, giddily.

She rushed to unlock room 22's door.

"Come in, Modecai. I won't bite you. I don't have fangs, jagged teeth. I'm not a female vampire. Dressed in black," she said, growling sexily. "Not me. Not Mindy. Me, Modecai."

Modecai saw her strawberry-blonde hair shimmer in the dark. It was of—it held no mystery, no intrigue for him, no allure. The hair was sun-bright.

She could sense his reluctance, reticence, his fright—couldn't she? She could feel Hamlet, North Carolina, in him—couldn't she? She could feel the South in him, years of it, generations of it—couldn't she? All his fears. But she was going to free him in this shabby hotel room on 128th Street in Harlem. She was there to free him. This white girl was going to make it her business to free him of all his troubles and woes, emancipate him—from the burnings, the killings, lynchings … and more, more, much more …

Bunny told him most of the colored cats who swung with the downtown/white chicks in Harlem were colored cats from the deepest parts of the South like him, Philadelphia, Mississippi—from the most racist, hateful, violent redneck sections of the South.

Mindy had shut room 22's door.

And they were swinging, man—those colored cats were swinging up in Harlem with their white girls on their arms, swinging up North, across the Mason-Dixon line.

"I'll undress you, Modecai. I know how to do it in the dark. I-I can do anything in the dark. Any-anything at all. You ask me to do. You'll see, see, Modecai."

Free me? Can you free me, Mindy? White girl? Break my chains? Free me, Jesus—JE-SUS!

"See. See, Modecai. See how good I am. See? See?"

Modecai stood naked, stripped down to nothing, of any clothing, ready for the whipping from the white master's whip, the lynching with the white mob's rope. The—

"Now me, Modecai. Me. It's my turn to … I'll, I'll undress myself in front of you. Right in front of you. You don't have to do anything. Nothing. N-nothing at all. At all. At all."

White skin. White skin. Every inch white skin. Not black. Not hiding away in the hotel room but white as a light, pale as the moon, a moon glow.

Her white hand held his black hand before slipping away.

He was following her as Modecai's manhood came alive, pulsed, hissed like a big, angry black snake.

"I'll be your first white woman, won't I, Modecai? Won't I? Won't I? Just think, I'll be the first white woman you've made love to. Love to, Modecai."

And I'll kill you. Mount you on my wall like a hunter's trophy. Something I slaughtered, tortured, killed—until you die away. Yes, until you die away. White girl. White girl!

"Oh … ooooh, Modecai. Modecai … Ooooooh … Aaaaaah!"

It was the first time Modecai's mouth had tasted a white woman's white skin or he'd heard a white woman scream at him but not out of fear of him but of her pleasure of him, his power.

"Oh … y-you're—aaaah … AAAAAAAH … in me, Modecai. In me. There in me. D-deep, you're deep inside me. Oh … oh, Mo-Modecai. Oh … oh … oh …"

Mindy's body was riding his, and her mouth was screaming down into the valley of his ear, screaming out his name; and Modecai was pretending, pretending it, that it was Delores whose black skin hid away in the night, who made him feel free—and not this white girl who too pretended she was free but was as pale as the moon and nothing more consequential or worthwhile to a colored man (him) than that.

* * *

It was the wee hours of the morning when Modecai entered the apartment.

"Bunny, you beat me home!"

"What you do, Modecai, walk the chick over to the subway station?"

Guiltily, Modecai admitted as much, shaking his head.

"Never walk them to the subway station after sex. Damn, Modecai, always slip out the hotel's back door before they wake. Always."

"The Bunny Greensleeves's technique."

"It works, don't it? Beat your black ass home, didn't I?"

Bunny hopped off the couch.

"Breakfast?"

"Yeah, I got everything all laid out. Figured you'd shoot in here hungry as hell. Am I right?" Bunny joked.

"Hungry, man—man, am I hungry, Bunny."

Bunny slipped into the kitchen. Modecai slipped right behind him like a spook.

The kitchen was already fit to a T—the eating utensils and things.

"Take a sit down. Pretend you're at the Waldorf."

Bunny got busy. "So how was that forbidden fruit you ate?" Bunny asked while cracking open an egg. "Taste?"

Modecai thought back over the night's terrain, its challenge. He'd tasted white skin, was in it—made love to it. His whole body shook with a quiet fever.

"So how was the shit, Modecai? The white chick—she was hep, wasn't she?"

"Yes, yes, she was hep. B-but—"

"But before you answer, Modecai"—Bunny's mood had shifted perceptibly—"I'm sick and tired of Big Hat's shit, man! His total shit!"

Modecai's body shifted in the chair.

"I showed him, you know, I showed him some of my tunes and … and some of yours too."

"Mine?"

"Yeah, I couldn't resist it, man. Had to show that lame cat what was going down!" Literally, Bunny tossed the hash browns into the frying pan. "This cat's as lame as a penguin on a crutch standing on a glacier. You hear me, Modecai? I'm fucking tired of his fucking shit!"

"He … he didn't like it, our … our tunes did—"

"The hell with Big Hat! That lame cat can't read music no way. He's jealous, that's all, Modecai—jealous as hell. He knows the club's packed to the gills every night because of me, man. I'm the main attraction. T-they're coming in the joker's joint to hear Bunny Greensleeves and, and you too," Bunny said deferentially.

"Thanks, Bunny. But it is you. They're there to see. The main attraction. Uh, not me. But thanks any—"

"That motherfucker!"

"Bunny …"

"But I'm fucking tired of it, Modecai, that big hat motherfucker's shit!"

Modecai tried to be the cool, the rational one—as always.

"There ain't nowhere where we can play our tunes. Nowhere. I ain't taking them up to Smitty's Place or no place like that. Nobody's jam sessioning on my tunes. Fumbling, stumbling over my charts, through my shit. Gotta be a tight unit. Tight like Mr. Hines's band. Gotta hear it like I wrote it. Gotta come out them horns right."

Bunny opened the refrigerator door, pulled out a bottle of orange juice, shook it good, and then stepped over to the table and poured some into Modecai's glass.

"Thanks, Bunny."

It seemed to be a tension breaker.

"You know, Bunny, let me talk to Big Hat about this. He and I hit it off pretty good."

"Yeah, I know."

"Maybe I can get him to see things differently."

"You mean our way, don't you, Modecai? Man, I let him see the tunes, that shoulda been enough for anybody. What I got to do, Modecai—teach that lame cat the alphabet from *a* to zoo too!"

"Ha."

"But I just got a feeling about him," Bunny said, once again seemingly centering things. "That's all …"

Then Bunny jumped, eliciting the same, exact reaction from Modecai.

"The sausage, Modecai! The sausage in the pan, man!"

Bunny looked into the frying pan.

"Lucky, they ain't burnt, just smell that way."

Bunny extricated the sausage from the pan, delicately.

"Uh, hey, Modecai, now back to you tonight." Bunny's eyes were twirling like flashy hubcaps. "How was the white chick? How was her forbidden fruit, man?"

"She wasn't colored, Bunny."

Bunny squared around to Modecai; and his short, powerful frame laughed like he had a giant rolling around inside his belly.

"Don't tell me you done," Bunny said in a slow Mississippi drawl, "brought your black ass all the way up here from the South to the North for you can be prejudice, boy!"

"Afraid so, Bunny," Modecai laughed mockingly. "That's about the size of it, Mr. Charlie. It's about how the shoe fits the foot," Modecai said in his best Hamlet, North Carolina, drawl.

* * *

Three days later.

The door was open.

"Hi, Earlene."

"Hi, Modecai," Earlene replied sweetly.

Earlene had a hair customer sitting in her chair. Earlene had a hot comb in her hand, but it didn't stop Earlene from waving back to Modecai warmly.

Modecai had some music tucked under his armpit, his and Bunny's. It was the third straight day Modecai'd carried his and Bunny's music under his left armpit. Two days ago he asked Big Hat if he could sit down and talk to him. Two days straight he got the same "shove off," cold shoulder. He was getting frustrated; Bunny was furious.

Last night Modecai had to calm Bunny down. Bunny had gone on one of his tirades. Bunny was more than anxious—it was more like he was desperate, like Howard "Big Hat" Morrison held a magic key to his future. It was like Big Hat had to play Bunny's tunes at the Big Hat Club or else.

He was going to insist he and Big Hat sit down and discuss this matter after today's rehearsal. This thing of tunes and Big Hat and Bunny had become serious. So serious, Modecai felt, it might explode into something really nasty, confrontational.

Dammit! Modecai said to himself. He knew he was late for rehearsal. He looked at a clock in a shop window: confirmed!

Modecai began running. New York's weather would be turning cold soon, Bunny had told him. His running was halted by a red light. Modecai had to obey New York's traffic laws: it knew nothing about music or how late he was for band rehearsal with Big Hat at the Big Hat Club.

He was going to be straightforward with Big Hat. And if he had to parry, he would. Modecai's left armpit held firmer to the music. *I'm not going to let Big Hat off the hook, man—uh-uh, not today, not on your life.*

The stoplight switched back to green (it wasn't soon enough for Modecai). Modecai was back into his running. He felt he had to get to the club, Big Hat, Bunny—there was no buffer for them.

Modecai ducked into the Big Hat Club. He heard the music. It sounded like the guys were grinding it out, the band, not playing it but grinding it out. Big Hat was in a chair, hunched over his steel guitar. He didn't look up.

"Subway, Modecai?"

"Yes, subway, Big Hat."

"And there was trouble on the tracks? All the way down?"

"Yes."

"Then you got to leave earlier than what you done to get here. That's all."

"Uh, right, Big Hat. Thanks."

"No problem, Modecai." Pause. "Listen, we was …"

Modecai put his and Bunny's music down on the piano bench.

"Playing through—"

"Some old, tired shit, Modecai. Stale, tired shit. Stale as hell, man!"

"So what … you got a problem with that, Bunny!" Big Hat said, turning his head around to Bunny, glaring at him. "What you got?"

Quickly Modecai sat down at the piano.

"It … it, uh, sounded good when I came in. It—"

"It sounded like shit, Modecai. Pure shit. Dried-out shit in farmer Jones's outhouse, man."

Bunny bounced to the front of the stage.

"How the hell can you make warmed-over shit taste like caviar?"

Ominously Big Hat rose from out his chair, this big plate of a man.

"This is the tune we should be playing," Bunny said, reaching down, grabbing the sheet music off the piano bench with his right hand and holding onto his horn with his left.

"So, you still trying to pedal them tunes of yours, huh, Bunny? Sell that piece of crap to somebody. Stink up their closet with them."

Bunny was glaring at Big Hat.

"You don't know nothing about music, Big Hat. You a lame cat, man. You got a tin ear for a ear," Bunny said, pointing to his. "Can't hear shit. Can't read shit. Don't know shit. Ain't—shit!"

"I know one thing for sure, Bunny: my band ain't playing none of that, what you got in your hand, man. 'Cause you a black motherfucker from somewhere where my yellow-ass piss can't reach!" Big Hat said, grabbing his crotch.

"What, your fucking peashooter? What, your weak pinch of piss, man?" Bunny said, laying the music back down on the piano and his horn on top the music. "You can't piss that piss on your own damned self, never mind me, motherfucker!"

Then Bunny thought about what he was doing. He couldn't win this way, not like this. It was all wrong, ass backward. He could do better. He walked over to Big Hat like he was carrying an olive branch to him.

"Hey, lookit, Big Hat, we can do ourselves better than this, man. Right?"

Modecai felt relieved.

"You and me got more dignity than this."

Big Hat's big, black eyes peeked from beneath the hat's broad brim, from out its shadows.

"Yeah, yeah—I guess so, Bunny," he said, shaking his head. "Guess you right."

"Hey, Big Hat, it's just music. It ain't a brick. It ain't gonna kill nobody—is it?"

Big Hat laughed; the band laughed.

"Here, man," Bunny said, handing Big Hat the sheet music and the rest of the players. "Fresh baked biscuits for you!"

One and all laughed again.

Big Hat put the sheet music on a music stand.

"Man …," he said, already seemingly exhausted by the music's obvious complexities.

"The melody goes like this here, Big Hat," Bunny said, raising his horn, about to let loose some licks.

"Hey, man, I know how the melody goes!"

Bunny backed off. "Yeah, of course, of course you do, Big Hat."

Bunny looked down at Modecai.

Big Hat caught him.

"Hey, what you doing, trying to make fun of me with your boy, Bunny? Boy here? With Modecai, man!"

"Hey, don't tighten your suspenders, Big Hat. Let them grip you, your pants ain't falling to the floor. About to—"

"Don't wear no suspenders!"

"Then, you should. They're great, man!"

Big Hat looked in a strange way at the music on the music stand, again.

"Okay. Uh, one, uh two, uh—"

"Hey, I'll count it out, Bunny. I give the downbeat around here. It's my damned band. Goddamned band!"

"Yeah, uh, sure, Big Hat. You do the drumroll, man. Perform the hat trick."

Bunny looked over at Modecai; Big Hat didn't catch him this time.

"Uh one, uh two, uh one, two … Man, you know I can't play this shit! You know that shit. What you trying to do? Embarrass me with this, this—you, you black motherfucker!"

Bunny's eyes bugged out his head.

"I'll, I'll …"

And the bandstand was too small to contain Bunny and Big Hat's acrimony as Bunny bounced off the bandstand and onto the club's floor, and his right hand dipped into his back pocket and drew out the ruby-red-handled knife, jerking open its long blade, slashing it through the air in front of him two times, his eyes traveling the length of Big Hat Morrison, and then stopping.

"I'll cut your big black ass from New York City to Mississippi and back if you mess with me, you bigheaded freak motherfucker!"

Big Hat froze; he didn't move. No one moved, but not for long.

"I oughta put a bullet in your fucking head, Bunny, but I ain't, motherfucker. That'd be too damned good for a Mississippi sharecropper's boy who's brung his black ass up to Harlem for what, Bunny? Fame and fortune? Yeah, yeah, that'd be too good for a low-life black-ass nigger like you." Big Hat's arms spread out in front of him.

"Bunny Greensleeves, Bunny Greensleeves in Broadway lights, huh, Bunny, huh?"

Bunny's blade remained where it was, smiling sweet as the devil.

"Ha. You're dead. Dead. Big Hat Morrison just killed your black, nigger ass, man! I just blew a hole in Bunny Greensleeves's motherfucking head. Ha!"

Modecai was confused, as well as the others witnessing this.

Big Hat picked up the music stand he'd knocked over. He straightened himself, coolly, calmly, his big hands making every effort to keep his clothes neat on his burly frame.

"Yeah, consider this, Bunny. This, motherfucker. Consider Howard 'Big Hat' Morrison just now, for all time, killed Bunny Greensleeves. Today. Right fucking now," Big Hat said, looking around at one and all on the bandstand.

And this vile look, like a vial of poison, had replaced the boast, the manly swagger.

"You'll never play your horn on Fifty-Second Street again, Bunny. Your black motherfucking ass. Not, not nowhere near here."

Big Hat picked up his steel guitar, strapping it on.

"Harlem. Yeah, Harlem. You can play your shit up in Harlem for them black jungle bunnies, for them black jigaboos, but not down here. Between Broadway and Fifty-Second Street. Not on Swing Street. Your black ass is gonna be banned down here like winter freezes over ice, man!"

And then Big Hat Morrison looked over to his right, over to Modecai who was still sitting at the piano. Big Hat nodded at Modecai, winking.

"You with this black motherfucker? He your boy? Your partner? Your nigger? You know this cat, man!"

Modecai stood, gathered his music and Bunny's horn and case.

"You a dumb motherfucker too, country boy. You a dumb, sharecropper's nigger from Hamlet, North Carolina. From down there too. Who ain't got no sense. Thought you was smarter than that, Modecai."

Modecai walked off the bandstand.

"Thought your black mamma jamma taught you better than that, motherfucker."

Modecai looked at Bunny and his knife.

"You can put it away, Bunny. Our business is finished here. Done with. Is over."

Modecai handed Bunny his horn and case.

"Yeah, know that, Modecai."

Modecai and Bunny began walking out the Big Hat Club.

"'Cause your black ass just been banned down here too along with Bunny's, Modecai. Ha. Blackballed. Just now. Ha. For life, Modecai. For a lifetime. An eternity. If I die and you two motherfuckers is still alive, I'm leaving it in my motherfucking will. Yeah, man, in my motherfucking will," Big Hat screamed. "With my fucking lawyers!

"Bunny Odecai Greensleeves and, and Modecai Ulysses Jefferson will never play on Fifty-Second Street and Broadway again!"

And then Bunny wheeled around while Modecai kept walking.

"Big Hat, you know what you can do for me? You can kiss my black, Philadelphia, Mississippi, sharecropper ass!"

Modecai and Bunny were back on the A train, going back up to Harlem. The train was loaded with people. Bunny and Modecai were standing, not sitting—it's how packed the train was.

Bunny had been in the greatest of moods since he'd left the Big Hat Club. He'd been as cheerful as a jailbird on the lam.

"How's it feel to be fired from a gig, Modecai?"

"Another first, Bunny. For me."

"Uh ... right ..."

Bunny then thought about Mindy, the white girl. Mindy and Modecai a few nights back.

"Ain't life grand? Ain't Bunny Greensleeves full of surprises, Modecai?"

"You had to do it, didn't you, Bunny?" Modecai said, looking down at Bunny, in a way commiserating with him.

"The cat was cramping my style, Modecai. Yes, had to do it."

"Bunny, you have to be on the razor's edge, don't you?"

Bunny sucked his teeth. "Uh-huh. Nowhere else. That's me for sure."

"It, uh, it was getting too comfortable for you."

"Too pat, Modecai. Man, felt like I was in prison, man. Marching off each day to the same tune to play in that lame cat's band in a prison suit. The, that cat was taking the spirit right outta my lungs. Outta the music."

"One good thing though, Bunny, it never showed in your playing."

"Uh-uh, Modecai, wouldn't let it. You know me."

"Once you're on the bandstand—"

"It's all business. Me and my horn and my music—and all that jazz, man!"

Pause.

"So you never answered my question, Modecai: how's it feel to be fired from a gig?"

"Lousy. How about lousy. My pockets aren't jingling, are they?"

"Seriously, Modecai."

Modecai had to laugh out loud, even if the train had a ton of people on it. "You're asking me, *me*, to be serious now, Bunny!" Modecai said disbelievingly. "Bunny Greensleeves is asking for Modecai Jefferson to be serious now?"

"Ain't I a gas, Modecai? A true gas, man!"

"Don't you mean you have a lot of damned nerve, Bunny!"

"Nerve then, man."

And while Modecai was recovering from his shock of all shocks, Bunny was wetting his lips and choosing his words carefully.

"Man, Modecai. I'd been waiting a long time, man."

Bunny seemed off in another world altogether. He seemed to be somewhere where his horn could blow free as a flock of birds.

"For what, Bunny?"

Bunny looked up at Modecai as if he were a mountain he'd just scaled with a pick and an axe and an armful of rope.

"To tell Howard Big Hat Morrison to kiss my *BLACK, PHILADELPHIA, MISSISSIPPI, ASS*—hell, that's what!"

And the A train exploded with applause.

"Why, there must be a whole lotta cats up here from Mississippi who ride the A train this time of day, huh, Modecai?"

* * *

Bunny and Modecai were on the corner of Fifth Avenue and 125th Street. The corner should have been a revolving door, the way Harlemnites would appear and then disappear in their travels.

"Like I said before, Modecai, we gonna have to hustle."

"Refocus ourselves, Bunny."

"Whatever, Modecai. What—the music, it's gonna be all about the music from here on out. Our tunes."

"I don't like that look on your face, Bunny. It-it's scaring me, it's—"

"A band, Modecai. A band, man!"

"Yes, yes, Bunny! A band!"

"We can pull it off. We two young, bad cats swinging the monkey by the tail!"

"OUCH!"

"Okay, a kangaroo then!"

"You are full of surprises, Bunny." Pause. "A band …," Modecai said dreamily.

"A battalion. A, a shit, Modecai—everybody's gonna want to play with us, who's anybody!"

Modecai felt the music, from the sheet music, play underneath his armpit.

"I'm gonna check with some people," Bunny said, bouncing on his toes (as usual) as if he knew all of Harlem. "I know me some people, Modecai. Up here. Bunny Greensleeves knows the whores and the pimps, the hustlers and the rustlers—and everyone in between up here in Harlem, man." Pause.

"Just don't burn the light tonight, Modecai—'cause Bunny Greensleeves's flight's gonna be late tonight."

"Hitting …"

"All the joints in Harlem. Scour them. Gonna listen to every jazz cat in Harlem who's got him an ax. Bought one. Nobody's getting off the hook tonight, man." Bunny touched Modecai's shoulder. "Don't worry any, Modecai, we're gonna get our tunes played."

Modecai felt good.

"See you in the a.m. Leave my slippers out in the hall, man. Neat as a pin." Pause.

"And, Modecai …"

"Yes, Bunny."

"Fuck Howard Big Hat Morrison! We'll play downtown again. Don't you worry any, man. We'll play on Fifty-Second Street, on Swing Street again. It ain't dead. Ain't nobody killed it. We'll play in them clubs again."

* * *

"Hi, Earlene."

"Hi, Modecai."

Earlene's door was open; she was working on a new head—Earlene and her hot hair comb, that is.

When Modecai got into the apartment, he put his and Bunny's music back where it belonged.

"Bunny, I didn't want to look. I knew Bunny had to get the best of Big Hat." Modecai paused. "How do I feel not with a steady gig? But I knew it was going to happen. I saw it brewing. Saw Bunny couldn't sit still."

Modecai sat at the piano.

Bunny has to hustle, he thought. He has to feel he's chasing after something all the time unless it's no good for him. *Well, at least I have momma's money coming in monthly. At least that's steady.*

A band, though. Why hadn't he thought of it? But if anyone would, it would be Bunny. Think big. Act big. It's how it all begins and ends, doesn't it? Think big, act big, be big. *I'm learning a lot from Bunny. May-maybe he's not learning a lot from me, but I sure am from him.* But Bunny, his knife, his temper—the violence contained in him.

"It's dangerous, Bunny. For you. You're always sitting on this powder keg that's about to explode. And there's nothing anyone can do about it, it's … it's just there. It's like his genius, Bunny's gift—it's just there. Waiting to explode once Bunny steps up on a bandstand. Once he raises his horn to his lips and spreads his legs apart and commands all to look and to listen and follow him off, off to …"

And suddenly Modecai snapped out of it. And since he had this spare time, benefit of Bunny, he was going to take advantage of it.

"I have somewhere to go, talking about going … going off to somewhere!" Modecai said, heading toward the hallway.

"Back to the Big Hat Club so early, Modecai?" Earlene asked, rolling a roller up onto the pretty young lady's hair who was sitting in the chair.

"No, uh, n-not tonight, Earlene."

"Oh, oh, don't tell me Bunny—"

"Uh, don't, I' don't have time to talk, to discuss it, Earlene. I've got to go!"

By now, Modecai was down the four flights of stairs.

"Oh well, looks like Bunny's lost another one of his jazz gigs. Big Booty said it wasn't gonna take long. Big Booty said it was just a matter of time … with Bunny," Earlene said to the young lady in the chair whose hair was being rolled tightly in rollers, neatly, precisely, who'd just nodded like she'd just become a jury of one presiding over Bunny Greensleeves's trial.

* * *

"I'm telling you, Modecai, them cats are everywhere! It's like drilling ground in a Texas oil field and nothing comes up but black gold!"

Modecai was in Bunny's room. The sun had risen but was gone for now. It was early afternoon. Bunny had called Modecai into the room after he'd come out the bathroom.

"Sorry I missed out on breakfast and lunch, but I was plain tuckered out after yesterday's happening, Modecai. I was totally zapped, man."

Bunny was in a robe (silk, not cloth).

"Modecai, what time is it anyway? You got?"

"Bunny ..."

"All right. Hell, you ain't got you a watch neither. You're as poor as me, man!" Bunny laughed. "When the hell are we gonna get us a timepiece to tell time with?"

"We are long overdue, aren't we, Bunny?"

"I'm just glad it ain't the rent we're behind on, man. Knocking us down."

Bunny slipped on his slippers. Modecai knew Bunny was planning on making a day of it now.

"Listen, Modecai, I spoke to some people, man. You know, business, Modecai, business."

"It looks encouraging, Bunny?"

"Better than that. This unemployment shit—we ain't gonna be at it long. I got people putting the word out for us. Circulating it through Harlem that Bunny Greensleeves and Modecai Jefferson are fronting them a band, man. A special band."

Bunny walked up to Modecai and grabbed him by the shoulders.

"Hope you don't mind, Modecai. But I had to give them cats a name. The name for the band, f-fancy it up. Excite them—"

"Okay, Bunny, what is it? You can let the cat out the bag," Modecai said with a sly, suspicious smile on his face. "Even though I see its tail."

"Uh ... uh, the ... the ..." Then Bunny said it lightning quick like he was playing his horn: "TheBunnyGreensleeves'sHarlemBoppers!'"

"Oh!"

"Like it, Modecai!"

"Love it. It is exciting!"

"Band's name don't mean nothing, though, Modecai. Anyway. It's still our band, man. Fifty-fifty on the shelf. My heart don't beat until yours answers. Is that close enough, Modecai?"

"Close enough, Bunny." Pause. "But I don't want to be the band's cynic, cast a cold, dour eye on things, Bunny—but we're some jazz band, Bunny Greensleeves's Harlem Boppers, without any jazz players to play in it yet."

"Cats are dropping over this afternoon for auditions. You mean to tell me I forgot to tell you at the door?"

The phonograph was on.

"Hey, what's that playing?"

"Ran out and bought a few records when I got home yesterday."

"Sounds like that Stravinsky cat. That Russian cat, Modecai."

"It's who it is, all right: Igor *Str-r-ravinsky*," Modecai said in a heavy, thick Russian accent. "You mean, you know about him, Bunny?"

They walked into the living room where the music was.

"Dig me some Igor. It's all music, ain't it? Melody, harmony, ideas, man. Invention. Him and Bartok, Bela Bartok, and Ives—them some hep classical cats, man!"

Modecai went over to the album jackets and picked them up.

"I bought Ellington and Stravinsky and, and let me see, some—"

"And we're unemployed? Standing in a breadline!"

"You did say temporarily, Bunny."

"And you, you trusted, believed me?"

"Oh yeah, Bunny, oh yeah."

"Even though you still got your mom's bread coming in," Bunny said softly.

"Yes, uh, yes, I do."

Bunny studied Modecai; he really studied him. There was something that was bugging him, really bugging him, was still at the back of his mind—but he knew it wasn't for now. He didn't know when it would be, but there was something mysterious about Modecai and his mother. Bunny wanted to ask Modecai, "When do you write your mother? Why don't you write her? You write Delores, I see you, but, hey, Modecai, why not your mother? Why not your own mother?"

"Hey, Modecai! Modecai!" Bunny was his overly hyper self again. "Man! Man!" Bunny was gasping for air.

"What is it, Bunny!"

"I heard a genius cat last night. I heard an angel with wings!"

"Where?"

"Up at Minton's. A cat who blew in from Toledo, Ohio—they say. Plays piano. Blind in one eye and, say, he don't see that much better in the other."

Bunny's description excited Modecai.

"Black as tar and prettier than stars. Move over, Mr. Hines, Mr. James P. Johnson, Mr. Fats Waller, Mr. Willie 'the Lion' Smith, Mr. Modecai Jefferson—'cause Mr. Art Tatum's in town!"

"He's that good, Bunny!"

"If you weren't my piano player, Modecai, I'd grab that bad-as-brown-gravy cat in a heartbeat." Bunny stood back and spread his legs. "Nobody, no piano player in the house wanted to touch them keys, ivory, man, when he finished playing. The cat got up, and them cats sat right back down. I'm telling you, Modecai."

"Did you play with him, Bunny?"

"No, Modecai. Uh-uh, I was too busy working the room. Setting up today's auditions. But I collared the cat before he left Minton's."

"And …"

"Welcomed him to New York City. And told him where he could get him a steady gig, a piano chair. Where they need a piano player, if he don't mind traveling downtown on the A train."

"Big Hat's club, Bunny?"

"Yeah, Big Hat's club, Modecai."

"Bunny, that was awful nice of you."

"Hey, Modecai, like I said, it's all about the music, man. All about what happens between them cracks and grooves in them piano keys. That black jewel's gonna raise hell in this town, man. So be prepared."

"Can't wait to hear him, Bunny."

"Man …"

"What, Bunny?"

"Man, we got to get us them timepieces, Modecai. I was just about to ask you the time again."

"Come on, Bunny, what, you can't be that lazy."

Modecai walked into the kitchen where a portable clock (which was moved from room to room, according to necessity) was.

"Oh, I've got plenty of time then. Told most of them cats to get here around four for the audition—but know how that goes."

"Uh-huh. We'll be lucky if we see them by six."

Bunny had his trumpet.

"Let's play something, what you say, Modecai?"

"One of your tunes or one of mine, Bunny?"

"You pick, Modecai. 'Cause it don't matter."

Then Bunny stopped; he looked like a blue-faced angel (speaking of angels).

"We're gonna be riding high soon, Modecai. The Bunny Greensleeves's Harlem Boppers are gonna be riding high in Harlem soon." Bunny had raised his trumpet high enough to touch the moon.

"You know, Modecai, I used to dream about moving downtown to Fifth Avenue. But lately, you know what, man? Park Avenue is far more fashionable, they say. These days. From what I hear. Know about it."

Riding high in Harlem. Modecai liked that, how Bunny made it sound. Bunny's horn hit a high note.

"Damn, Modecai! I guess you must've wrote that note just for me when you wrote it!"

* * *

Modecai and Bunny and Bunny's Boppers (yes, the name was later shortened by Bunny) were riding high in Harlem. Bunny had the right "in" contacts.

He knew the right people who could pull the right strings in Harlem. But Bunny Greensleeves (by then) had currency, persona, cachet; Harlemnites knew who Bunny Greensleeves was and were beginning to find out who Modecai Ulysses Jefferson was too.

Bunny was taking all this obvious success in like he was an Arabian prince born into a succession of kingdoms and royalty. Bunny believed he belonged where he was so much so that, already, he was preparing himself for the next step up to the next rung. Bunny's eyes would glitter like they saw gold. He was thinking about the big things as he'd told Modecai. Park Avenue was on his agenda, no longer Fifth Avenue but

Park Avenue, where the rents happened to be higher, steeper, more status worthy.

Modecai was taking his success in stride, in his usual unflappable way: with great humility. Modecai, not in his wildest dreams, had expected this kind of success so soon (even though he'd ridden on the coattails of Bunny's popularity.) Every night, Bunny's Boppers were playing to packed houses in Harlem. Every night they were creating a sensation, clobbering Harlem like a two-ton hammer.

And as far as the music went, Modecai and Bunny fit each other's musical styles to a T (indeed, of course, this was a given). These two young jazz cats were made for each other. They were like rum in coke, shapely legs in stockings, tea and crumpets, chalk and an eraser—Max Roach and Clifford Brown ("Brownie").

And as Bunny'd done only weeks before, Modecai was doing now, hustling like a pigeon in winter. And why? Who knew why? Modecai was giving piano lessons (as Bunny'd given trumpet lessons). And if there was a Sunday afternoon social in Harlem and it needed a pianist to play soft, pleasant background music, Modecai Ulysses Jefferson was sure to be there, hired (getting paid). Yes, Modecai was the man you'd call for the job, all right. The first piano player in line, all the time.

Yep, Modecai was down and out doing some heavyweight hustling. And why? Who knows why? Why, Modecai wouldn't tell J. Edgar Hoover if Hoover and his FBI agents wiretapped his phone to find out why. It's how secretive Modecai had been about all of this backroom wheeling and dealing—what seemed this infinite intrigue of his.

Modecai was up to something sneaky, underhanded, clandestine—but just don't ask him what, the cat.

Chapter 13

Bunny's hand patted the piano.

"If you ain't a piece of luck. A lucky piece, man."

Then Bunny stood back from the piano and looked at it as if he were looking at an African sunset.

"Modecai's writing like a fool. A crazy fool. Modecai's humming tunes like a bird and buzzing around here like a bee. Modecai's happy as hell."

Bunny dropped his hands down in his pant pockets and remembered the fat wad of stash that had sat, at one time, prosperously in his pocket before the eight brand-new suits, five brand-new pair of shoes, six pair of silk socks, five new dress shirts, eight new ties, Minnie's Mint (he and Modecai never did make it to the Cotton Club for dinner that night), and Way City came along.

"Hell, man, spent every last damned cent of the rent. Didn't leave a penny in my pocket for Lenny down at the cleaners to pick clean."

It was beginning to happen to Modecai, Bunny thought. Way City was beginning to ebb slowly from Modecai's insides. It was really Delores, wasn't it? Modecai would've been fine with Way City if it hadn't been for Delores Bonet. Bunny realized she was the one who still kept Modecai tied to Way City, Alabama, unless, for Modecai, it would be just another town, another stop on the jazz map. A town he had to wind through to get to New York City.

But there was one thing Bunny couldn't get off his mind, uproot: Modecai's relationship with his mother. He didn't write, so did … did he call? Call her? The money got there monthly, was reliable as hell. There had to be more to them than just that, the monthly money Modecai's mother sent him.

What was missing? Bunny thought. *What the hell am I missing out on? What the hell am I skipping over—missing like a magician's magic act happening right before my eyes, man, his hands moving but not moving?*

He had to pick the right time on the clock to get to the bottom of this mystery. Modecai wasn't handing it to him straight, right. But when was the right time? When could he dig up what had to be dug up out of Modecai's past? He didn't want to force the damned thing, hit a sour note. He didn't hit sour notes. He wanted to treat Modecai, this great friend of his, like his music: respectfully. Modecai and his mother, maybe there was some big problem between them that had gotten in their way, impeded them. And maybe he could help Modecai with whatever it was. Give it a chance to be discussed; it's what friends are for, after all.

Bunny's right foot patted the floor.

"Yeah, got to keep the beat I keep hearing. Yeah, last night, that chick Sally, she was kind of long and tall like that Dexter Gordon cat, man, that snazzy cat who blows that tenor sax up here. Yellow skinned like him too. Don't know why I like them tall—born that way. Long, tall Sally. Had that chick ..."

Bunny's right foot picked up the beat.

"Ooooo, man, I was traveling so fast in a twenty-five-mile-hour lane. Hell, I shoulda been ticketed by the cops. Making love to that long, tall, yellow-skinned chick was like jitterbugging to a jukebox. 'Cause me and her was jigging and, and shaking and ..."

Bunny paused, plunked a note on the piano, and then thought about Modecai and his mother again.

* * *

It was a Saturday afternoon.

Bunny had been kidnapped!

Yes, kidnapped!

But it was Modecai who was the kidnapper. Modecai had flashed a wad of dough in front of Bunny the size of a fat man's fist he'd earned from his many Harlem hustles (Bunny almost fainted at the sight), and then hustled Bunny out the apartment and into a cab (practically at gunpoint), and then into a taxicab speeding downtown.

It's where they were now, in the backseat of a speeding taxicab.

Modecai had whispered to the taxicab driver where to drive them off to in Manhattan, and the taxicab driver smiled like he'd just sniffed the scent of money up his nose.

Bunny, when he saw what transpired between Modecai and the taxicab driver, didn't cotton to anyone pulling a fast one on him—not even Modecai Ulysses Jefferson. Bunny always shot the eight ball in the corner pocket. Bunny always was the biggest splash in the pool. He always gave the horse the hotfoot. The stage was always Bunny Greensleeves's; the spotlight had nowhere else to fall but on him.

"Modecai," Bunny sniffed, "we've got to talk, man. We got to make a deal."

Modecai pinched his hat's stingy brim. "Uh, Bunny, I'm dealing the cards out the deck today, man."

"Listen, listen, Modecai, man, I know you're carrying the bread, the loot, the sweet ginger cake, but—"

Modecai's hand covered Bunny's mouth. "There're no ifs or buts about it, Bunny. I'm the head nigger in charge in Harlem today. The mayor of Harlem!"

Bunny's eyes looked like flying saucers, and then he shut them as if he were praying to the Pope for Modecai's soul and the devil's forgiveness.

As soon as Modecai's hand uncovered Bunny's mouth, Bunny said, "Modecai, if you're taking me out to lunch, if this is what this shit's about, then I ain't hungry!"

"Uh, cabbie, do you have a gag?"

"Need one, huh?"

"Maybe two."

No, Modecai wasn't going to let Bunny spoil the excursion; all of this was too special and too much fun. Modecai felt the roll of dough in his pocket; he could count it blindfolded. Every dollar, right down to the last blessed penny, was accounted for.

Was Bunny going to be in for a surprise. Bunny had made Way City possible for him, and the piano possible for him—and so many other things he couldn't begin naming. His association with Bunny had been the single most important musical and personal event in his life. They were young jazz cats learning things together. But there were times when Bunny knew more about, say, *x* as the hidden factor than he did. And there were times when he knew more about *y* than Bunny did. And there were times when neither knew anything about *z*—so they really had to improvise on the music, melody.

"We're here!" the cabbie happily announced.

Bunny was afraid to look but knew the cab was in midtown Manhattan and that—

"Hey, ain't we on Fifth Avenue, Modecai?"

"Uh-huh, we sure are, Bunny."

"Hey, what—the taxicab ran out of gas!"

When Bunny saw the taxicab driver's eyes cross, was when he knew he was in a big heap of trouble.

"Fifth Avenue, Modecai! Are you crazy? This ain't Fifth Avenue up in Harlem. Down here the streets are—"

"Paved with gold."

"And we're walking on them."

"Two colored cats from Harlem."

"Yes, two colored cats from Harlem," Modecai said, patting his pocket.

"Open the door then, man—and let me out!" Bunny said like he was about to conquer Manhattan with the charm of a leprechaun.

The cabbie hopped out the cab and opened the door.

"Bunny Odecai Jefferson and Modecai Ulysses Jefferson have docked ship!"

"Thank you," Modecai said to the cabbie and then followed Bunny. "You can keep the meter running, okay?"

"Why, yes, sure, sure thing, sir. Sure thing!"

"Do … do …" Bunny was stunned by the magnificent sight. Modecai had joined him. His arm held Bunny in place. "D-do y-you know where we—"

"Cartier's, Bunny. Cartier's. We're standing in front of Cartier's on Fifth Avenue, Bunny."

"And … and …"

"Here," Modecai said, opening the front door of Cartier's, "you enter first, Bunny."

It was the first Modecai had seen Bunny a nervous wreck, in shambles. He thought he just might have an accident in his pants but knew Bunny was made of much sterner stuff than that.

* * *

"Now I can tell if your ass is late or on time for rehearsals, Modecai!" Bunny said, holding firmly to his sparkling brand-new, gold-plated pocket watch.

And so Bunny had chosen a pocket watch over a wristwatch after much deliberation and Bunny having poor, young Reginald (Cartier's polite, courteous sales clerk) jump through circus hoops at a maddening pace.

"Man, Modecai, both of us cats got watches to tell time with!"

They were walking down 125th Street, extricated from the taxicab, passing the Apollo Theatre.

Looking at his "Harlem deluxe" or "uptown special" wristwatch (what Harlemnites called them), Modecai was more than pleased he had enough money left over from his wad (watch, taxi fare, tip), that he could afford a watch that was cheap compared to Bunny's but at least ticked and tocked on time.

Boorishly Bunny grinned. "Bet you a month's rent that your wristwatch loses time before my pocket watch does, man."

"You know what, Bunny," Modecai said after looking down at his wristwatch, "I bet it does too!"

After walking a bit more, their apartment loomed in the distance.

"Listen, Modecai, we've got to get back to thinking big, man."

Modecai stepped along with Bunny.

"Big band," Bunny said, hearing horns blasting in the Harlem air. "A big-band sound, Modecai."

The cars' horns impressed Modecai the same as when he first arrived in New York City. It was the second time Bunny had planted the bug in Modecai's ear.

"Man, writing for a trendy fifteen-, eighteen-piece orchestra would be a gas, Modecai. A real gas, man."

"I've dreamed of it, Bunny."

"It's the only way to go for cats like us. Stretch us out. A shot in the arm."

"A larger canvas to paint on for sure."

Bunny stopped in his tracks.

Screech! (That being Modecai.)

"Free us up even more. Ain't that nice. Hey, Modecai, skin it!"

Modecai gave Bunny some serious skin.

"Only thing is the bread department. We're gonna see a definite dip, reduction and deduction in our bread, man. At the end of the gig. All them cats to pay."

"But we can alternate, shift back and forth. We can alternate units, Bunny."

"But, hell, Modecai, I want the band to be tight. Nothing sloppy."

"We won't throw anything at them, Bunny."

"Not with the tunes we gonna write, Modecai. We're gonna write tunes that'll scare the shit out an elephant, man."

"Bunny, sometimes you scare me—you've got so much ambition. S-so much drive."

"How many times I gotta tell you, Modecai, my black ass can't sit still. If God put a windup toy in the universe, it's me. Had to be. Not a doubt in my mind."

"But disappointments, Bunny—do you think of disappointments, maybe? Biting off more than you can—"

"Negative, Modecai. Ain't got an hour in the day to waste on that shit, you know that. If you ain't leaning towards the brightest star in the sky, then what's the damned use? Ain't nothing worse than letting somebody else look back on your life for you."

Man, Modecai thought, now that was profound, very.

Bunny looked around 133rd Street, the street they lived on, his eyes taking everything in. "I breathe in the air, Modecai; it don't breathe me. I hear them sounds in the air, shit, Modecai—they don't even know I'm listening to them, who the hell Bunny Greensleeves is.

"Beginning to see my point?" Bunny winked.

"It's a good philosophy to have."

"You got it too. You just don't focus in on it like I do. But it's there. Quiet as a sunset. But it's drumming inside you too."

Bunny and Modecai were walking again

"Auditions, Bunny?"

"Yeah."

"When?"

"Soon."

"Where?"

"You guess where."

"Bunny, you're irrepressible!"

"What? You cursing at me again?"

"Don't worry, Bunny, I could think of a better word than that."

"A big band, man," Bunny sighed. "Already put a warning out to Duke and Count before, didn't I?"

"You sure did."

"Boo! Them slick-headed cats better watch their backs—better heard that, man. It's the last warning I'm giving them lame cats, coming from Bunny Greensleeves and Modecai Jefferson, not unless there're ghosts in Harlem!"

Quizzically Bunny looked at Modecai.

"You believe in ghosts in Harlem, Modecai? Up here?"

"Yes, uh—I mean, uh, I mean—"

And then Bunny took his gold-plated pocket watch out his pocket, spun it in the sun a few times on its chain like he had the moon on a chain, snapped open its gold-plated cover, and proclaimed in his high, sugary tenor, "It's Bunny Greensleeves and Modecai Jefferson time! Ha! S-since all of y'all Harlem jazz cats asked!"

And there were Harlem ghosts up in Harlem, Modecai thought, plenty of them, a whole busload of them. There just had to be!

* * *

Weeks later, Modecai and Bunny were still trying to put together the big band. Both were working exceptionally hard at it by holding auditions (what seemed around the clock) and listening to musicians whenever and whenever possible.

The band charts they'd been writing were extremely difficult—monsters that stared you dead in the eyes and dared you to flinch. Bunny had really opened Modecai up to a new musical vocabulary, to a new tapestry of language and colors. While Modecai's compositions required more of his time to compose (because of length and complexity), he'd become even more productive. Modecai's whole musical thinking had changed. His mind had become this tremendous laboratory, this active, grandiose ground for experimentation with sound, stretching it and arranging it in ways he'd not tried.

Modecai felt he was maturing rapidly as a man and a musician. But he still hadn't heard or seen this Art Tatum cat yet (but this would soon change).

And as for Bunny, he was working as hard as Modecai. After all, this big band business was his baby, his enterprise. Bunny was chasing the train too. Bunny was hungry to make it work for he could move on to new and bigger challenges for himself, it seemed.

Chapter 14

This morning, Modecai had gotten an early jump on Slim's corner store (Bunny and Modecai were still finding time to eat food despite composing so much—besides, the milk was low).

This afternoon, he was struggling to get the music down on the sheet music right. He was actually sweating out music. It was not a gentle stream. It wasn't this beautiful flow, lovely, seamless, and, seemingly, endless. Plus, he was under extreme pressure later from Earlene: she and Bunny, and even Big Booty, had been pushing Modecai to get out on a date.

This morning, coming in from shopping and passing Earlene's door, she'd opened it and said right out of the blue, "Modecai, when are you going to let a woman cook for you, honey? You know I do gorgeous colored women's hair all day in the apartment."

And so the name "Corrine" surfaced. And so Modecai was suddenly seduced by the name and this afternoon—

Knock. Knock.

Now who's that!

Modecai went to the door.

"Earl—"

"Hi, Modecai," Earlene, this big, pleasing-to-look-at woman, said. "Just dropping by to remind you about later, honey."

Modecai returned to the piano to look at that one note.

Earlene followed him.

"Don't worry, Earlene, I haven't forgotten about—"

"Corrine. Yes, like I said, this morning, Modecai—you two was made for each other!"

"I, look, I just appreciate you thinking of me," Modecai said, looking up at her. "That I'm on your mind."

"Boy, is Corrine a knockout, Modecai. Model pretty. Old Maybelline and me know how to grease that girl's hair up right, all right!"

"But I don't like a girl with greasy—"

"Just a little, a pinch," Earlene said, pinching her fingers together. "A dab—not the whole jar now. Ain't about to waste a whole jar of grease on no colored woman's hair!"

"Right, Earlene!"

Earlene walked over to Modecai and kissed his forehead.

"Corrine's appointment's for two o'clock, so I'll be knocking on your door around four."

"Uh … right, right, Earlene."

Modecai was back looking at the note he'd been struggling with for the past half an hour. It was as if Earlene was no longer in the room with him.

"And I know where you'll be, Modecai Jefferson—in front of that old piano of yours!"

Modecai was going to let Earlene get away with that insulting remark (old, old!), at least for now.

He struck the piano this time like they were having an argument. Modecai had been working on some other tunes but now had returned to the earlier one, that one note that would ultimately unlock the composition.

Plunk! Plunk!

"I can't get past this damned note, this one here (*Plunk!*)," Modecai grumped. "It's there, I know it—but I still can't get it!" Modecai said, frustrated. He felt like hammering the note into submission if necessary.

Knock.

"Oh, Modecai … Corrine's here," Earlene said sweetly, standing outside the door.

"Corrine. Yes, Corrine!" Modecai ran to the door and opened it.

"Modecai," Earlene whispered, "Corrine's sitting in the chair, well, oh my—wait until you see the job I did on that girl's hair. S-she's a living doll, darling. A living doll!" Earlene's cheeks bloomed.

"I'll be right down, Earlene, o-okay? Down the hall."

Earlene left; Modecai sweated. *Am I really ready for this?* Corrine—it was a name Modecai liked.

Modecai dashed into the bathroom. Did he look all right? he thought. This was like a blind date, wasn't it?

"No, no, Modecai, not really. Nobody's saying you have to date this girl. No … Earlene's not saying that at all. But it feels like it." Pause. "It seems Earlene's got her mind more set on this, her heart, really, than I do. It's like she's being a matchmaker, this cupid with a bow and arrow—and I'm his target!"

Modecai left the apartment door open just in case he had to make a hasty retreat back down the hall. Modecai wished the building were a little warmer—he could feel what Sweet-Tone had called a Harlem winter fast approaching. Already, it was stinging his toes.

Will she like me? Am I—will she find me attractive?

Modecai looked down at his shoes—if only he'd gotten a five-cent spit shine from Big Booty before he left for Broadway this morning.

* * *

"Modecai …," Earlene said.

Corrine was sitting in Earlene's chair. Her hair did look great: light brown, soft, and silky looking.

Earlene came over and hugged him.

Corrine stood. Modecai liked that.

Earlene still held onto him with one arm but turned sideways and said, "Corrine, this is Modecai. He's the handsome, young gentleman I told you who lives down the hall with Bunny Greensleeves."

She was light skinned, thin but shapely. Nothing like Delores, Modecai thought, not until—

"Hello, Modecai."

She spoke.

"I'm Corrine Calloway."

And her voice matched Delores's.

Modecai shivered but quickly recovered and answered.

"I'm Modecai Jefferson."

Then the three made small talk.

It was five, six minutes later. Modecai and Corrine had drifted up the hallway.

"Jazz—I love jazz."

"I'm, I haven't seen you in the clubs."

"I've been there."

"Where?"

"Where you've played."

She had black eyes, the kind any colored woman would die for: deep and passionate and sincere.

"How'd I miss you?"

"I don't know—guess it's the way you play the piano … with your eyes closed."

Corrine and Modecai were at the open door.

"It's where I live."

Corrine giggled. "So, uh, Earlene told me …"

"Uh, yes, uh, before," Modecai said, red-faced. "Would you like to come in?"

"May I?"

"Of course. Come in."

Modecai looked at Corrine; he'd say they were close in age. He probably topped her by a few years, but there was a level of maturity about her that appeared evident.

"Here, be seated."

There was that sofa of his and Bunny's that didn't look like much, like World War II had been fought atop it, and then left behind as some symbolic proof of the bloody, heroic battle.

"I hope I'm not intruding."

"No, not in the least."

"You sure?"

"No, it's fine."

Modecai could honestly say he liked Corrine's hairstyle—the one Earlene had styled and groomed.

Corrine took a deep breath. "So this is how jazz musicians live!"

Modecai couldn't help but laugh. Corrine had said it so brilliantly, so vividly.

"Yes, I guess this is how jazz musicians live."

"I can hear it."

"You can, Corrine?"

"Yes, I can, Modecai." Pause. "Did Earlene tell you what I do?"

"No."

"I'm a painter."

"A visual artist?"

"Yes."

Then Modecai looked at the way Corrine was dressed; she looked colorful, like a Renoir palette (Modecai'd been to art museums since setting foot in Harlem).

"You should see *my* studio!"

"Worse than mine?"

Shamefully, Corrine shook her head. "Much!"

They had something in common, Modecai thought.

"Do you smoke?"

"Uh, no, no, I don't."

"Do you mind if I do?"

There were a few ashtrays spread throughout the apartment (band members used them; Modecai and Bunny didn't smoke). Modecai stood and then got an ashtray for Corrine.

Corrine pulled the pack of Lucky Strikes out her pocketbook and then the book of matches. Slowly, the cigarette engaged her lips (Modecai liked them, her lips, that is). But it's when his hand took the matches from her and struck the match, was when the light from the match lit her light-skinned face, making it glow.

"Thanks, Modecai," Corrine said, puffing on the Lucky Strike. "I need these things," she laughed. "But don't ask me why."

"An artist …," Modecai mused as if he were thinking aloud.

Corrine took another puff. "A struggling one."

"Welcome to the club."

"Yes, I know," Corrine said, rubbing her bare arms. "Winter's on its way, and I'm still in short sleeves." Pause. "But I do secretarial work f-for I can get my hair done, at least once a month, by Earlene. I'm on call, an office temp."

Modecai more than enjoyed Corrine's wit, her ready-made sense of humor, not seeming to take herself too seriously.

"And the rent …," Modecai added.

"And food …"

"And clothes."

Corrine took another puff on her Lucky Strike, the gray smoke curled in the air. "We're struggling artists, all right."

"Are you looking for fame?" Modecai asked.

"Fame? Hmm …"

"Immortality?"

"Both wouldn't be bad now, would they?"

"Oh, not at all, Corrine."

"But fame first before immortality, Modecai."

"Oh … oh, yes, I want to enjoy my fortune, not someone else."

Corrine lay her half-smoked cigarette at the side of the ashtray.

"Seriously though, when I'm in my studio, it's the farthest thing from my mind: fame, immortality. It's work, hard work," Corrine said passionately. "Just me and my paints.

"It's the thing, one thing I run home to when I'm through with my office work. The thing I know is always there waiting for me once I'm there. I-I really don't know how to describe it any—"

"I think you just did, Corrine, and, I might add, perfectly."

Corrine took another puff on her cigarette. She got up off the sofa and walked over to the piano.

"Stuck?" she asked, looking at the one black, naked note on the page.

"Stuck!"

"I know the feeling. Things aren't going well, flowing for you?"

"Not at all. I've hit a brick wall."

"Tell me about it." Corrine winced.

"The music's there, sure. The tune. The melody line I'm after, it's there, but …"

"But it's being, what, stubborn? It's being its own boss right now? I guess it wants to hold out until the bitter end," Corrine laughed, seemingly knowingly. "Its sovereignty."

"But I'll keep my cool. My head. Persevere."

"Since you know you'll win in the end. We always do, don't we?"

He was beginning to like her laugh. It sparkled; maybe there were diamonds in it.

Corrine had walked over to the ashtray and doused her Lucky Strike. Modecai interpreted it to mean something symbolic, something—

"Modecai, I have to go." She laughed carelessly. "Guess what? I left my overcoat in Earlene's apartment."

Modecai didn't want her to leave, the heck with his music, his one naked note on the page.

"What kind of painting do you do, Corrine?"

"Varied. My ideas come from all over the place, different directions. Things. Say, why don't you come by and see my etchings sometime?" Corrine said flippantly.

"Wait a minute. Isn't it me who's supposed to say that? The man? Use that pickup line?"

"I don't know, Modecai, women are smoking cigarettes these days, out in public, even though we still let men light them, and—"

"That's enough. I get the point. I do, I really do."

Modecai took her arm and then began walking with her to the door.

"A-about those etchings, though …"

"Any-anytime, Modecai."

"But, uh, how do I get in touch with you?"

"Pencil, first."

Modecai went into his pocket.

"Got it!"

"Paper, second."

Modecai hustled over to the piano and tore off a piece of paper.

"Got it!"

Corrine lay the piece of torn paper flat to her pocketbook and began writing out her name and telephone number.

"Where I live has a common phone like here. But I'm always in in the evenings. Home after six, doing what—"

"I already know what."

Corrine half turned to shake Modecai's hand.

"It was really nice meeting you, Modecai. I mean, really nice."

Her eyes were worth any colored woman to kill for, Modecai thought.

"I have Earlene to thank for this," Modecai said.

"So do I."

"You'll hear from me—and, and soon."

"I-I hope so."

"I've got to see, uh, those etchings on the wall, after all, Corrine."

Modecai could've walked Corrine down the hallway, back to Earlene's apartment, but chose not to. It was much better watching Corrine while she walked down to Earlene's than vice versa.

And once Corrine had vanished into Earlene's apartment, Modecai dashed to the piano.

"I've got it!"

And the flow of music was instant. It could no longer resist Modecai's impulses, this freefalling of ideas and certain possibilities. And even though Modecai's mind and pencil were hectic, sprawling with ambition, the most lovely and sensitive notes emerged from it, tender, charming, caressing. Modecai heard Corrine Calloway's voice when she spoke, something sounding so much like Delores's—yet it wasn't.

Fifteen minutes later.

"Modecai …"

Bunny was back.

"Hey, what's that you're playing, man? Heard it down the hall."

"Sounds great, d-doesn't it, Bunny?"

"Yeah, man. Yeah. Great."

Bunny couldn't wait to get hold of his horn. But before he did, his nose sniffed the air.

"Cigarette smoke? Hey, who's been up here smoking, Modecai?"

Modecai swiveled around on the piano stool and threw his hands up in the air as if to say, "Why ask me of all people?"

But Bunny began conducting his own private investigation.

"Ha, caught you, Modecai, with your drawers down, man. Down around your ankles!"

Bunny was holding onto a cigarette butt. The butt had lipstick on it.

"Fine pair of lips, Modecai. Hey, a fine pair of lips, man!"

"Fine!"

"Thought I smelled a dame's cigarette smoke up here! The joint!"

Modecai had no knowledge that there was a difference between a man and a woman's cigarette smoke—only Bunny would.

"And her name is?"

"Her name's Corrine. Corrine Calloway."

Bunny's motor slowed down. "Nice, Modecai. Nice, man. Who did the honors?"

"Earlene."

"My girl!"

"Mine too—now."

"The girl's that sweet, huh, Modecai?"

"Yes, Bunny."

Bunny bounced. "Here I been trying like hell—uh, since that white chick, uh, d-disaster—to get you up and running, Modecai, and Earlene, she does the shit in one quick shot, take, man."

Bunny saw a look in Modecai's eyes. "Happy for you, Modecai. Happy as hell."

"Thanks, Bunny."

Again, Bunny bounced. "Now I've got some good news for you. We might be able to snag that Benny Carter cat!"

"What, really, Bunny!"

"Just came from talking to him. He's busy as hell but he wants to join the band. He's heard of our band charts—laid the cat out to rest!"

"What? Yours or mine, Bunny?" Modecai teased Bunny.

"Both, man! Both!" Pause. "He's a bad cat. Writes too. Some bad shit. Got some nice melodic shit going on between them two tiny ears of his."

"I love the way he plays."

"And can read as fast as Einstein can say, 'E equals mc square (E = mc2).'"

Modecai shook his head. "Your knowledge ceases to amaze me, Bunny."

"Now getting back to this new tune of yours, Modecai. Did it come …"

"Easily? Uh-huh. Real easily," Modecai fibbed.

"Yeah …" Bunny grinned. "Once that Corrine chick left the premises." Pause. "Wonder if the young lady's related to—"

"She didn't say, Bunny."

"Cab Calloway and her got the same last names, don't they?"

* * *

The crowd was big. The hour just right. Modecai was in the Big Hat Club. He was in a broad-brimmed hat (now totally out of fashion for the fall), dark sunglasses wrapping his face, and an overcoat with its tall collar pushed up to the side of his face (he didn't have it checked with the hatcheck girl).

He was not to be recognized in the Big Hat Club, not by anyone—not under any circumstances. But if for whatever reason he was recognized, no one would snitch on him anyway: Big Hat certainly was not one of the most well-liked employers in New York City.

This was about as high drama, foreign intrigue as it gets. Modecai looked like a spy who was trying to hide in the cold, not trying to come out. He'd told Corrine the story, the background of the plot, how and why Bunny and he were banned from Fifty-Second Street and Broadway by Howard "Big Hat" Morrison. Corrine liked Big Hat about as much as Big Hat's employees.

"You should see yourself, Modecai," Corrine said, laughter cracking through her face.

"Would I laugh?"

"Ha."

"Man, I know I should've worn my other pair of dark sunglasses."

Modecai looked around the club in his dark, wraparound sunglasses.

"Corrine, don't laugh too loud. Big Hat Morrison might see me!"

"Ssssh," Corrine said, putting her finger to her lips. "Mum's the word."

They'd ordered drinks.

Modecai lifted his coat collar more to the side of his face and then took a drink from the whiskey glass.

"D-don't, Modecai. Don't!" Corrine said, holding her sides. "I-I can't take anymore!"

Corrine had a Lucky Strike in her hand; Modecai lit it for her.

There was this murmur in the Big Hat Club. It sounded saintly. It sped through the Big Hat Club like greased lightning.

It was him, this black man who filled the stage even as his feet were feeling their way in their own patterned way forward toward the piano on the bandstand.

"Is that him, Modecai? Art Tatum?"

"Yes, Corrine," Modecai said like a man thirsty for water, "that's Art Tatum."

Modecai became more absorbed and transfixed by this man who sat down at the piano. His eyes had spotted an artist. It was the feeling of one artist looking at another one, knowing there was something making him see, even though Bunny had said his eyes were troubled, not at all reliable.

But it was how the bass player and drummer's eyes looked at him, Modecai thought. For there was this huge, enormous scare in them, this automatic thrill, this tremble; they were wired to him like electricity.

And Modecai and Corrine melted into the big crowd Art Tatum had made no outward gesture to, to assure the sacred quiet greeting him.

And when it happened, and as it happened, Modecai couldn't believe any of it, what he heard from the Steinway piano. Art Tatum was two people. Art Tatum had four arms, four hands, twenty fingers. Art Tatum came from outer space, another planet. Art Tatum was the baddest jazz pianist in the whole *damned universe*!

Folk were filing out the Big Hat Club.

Modecai's and Corrine's shoes were slapping pavement. Now there was that thrill in them, that terrible tremble—as if they were wired to Art Tatum in some weird, science-fiction fantasy.

"Dazzling, Modecai. My heart was racing like wild!"

"When he played—"

"'Body and Soul' …"

"Yes, 'Body and Soul.' I felt every note like, just like it was passing through me."

"Yes heaven and earth opened up. Each note he played, he put a true, bona fide experience inside it."

"It's, somehow, it's what we all try to do, don't we, Modecai? As artists?"

With heels on, Corrine's forehead was even with Modecai's.

"Me with my paints, the colors I use, how I light my subjects. You with your fingers."

Modecai loved this, how this conversation was going: art, and its intrinsic beauty.

"I could walk all night. It's like I'm walking on air. Umm …"

"Corrine, don't you think you ought to"—Modecai blew on his hands (*Man, I'm going to have to buy some gloves first thing—Sweet-tone didn't tell me that*, he thought)—"reconsider that."

"Not used to Mr. Winter, Modecai? The cold?"

"No. Uh, not yet. But I was told it's called Mr. Hawk."

"Oh, yes, it is—and this is just for starters. Just wait until Mr. Winter really starts stirring. What's in store for you."

Modecai thought about it—he could wait!

Modecai and Corrine made their way over to the Eighth Avenue subway station. This was Modecai and Corrine's first date. Modecai'd suggested the Big Hat Club. He'd called her two nights ago, and he and Bunny and the band weren't gigging tonight. Indeed, Modecai had to see and hear Art Tatum for himself. Did he ever.

"Have you got a token to get back to Harlem, Modecai?"

Modecai looked across at Corrine strangely. "Of … why, of course I do. What would make you ask me that?"

"Oh … I was hoping, really hoping we could walk back up to Harlem tonight, that's all."

Modecai knew Corrine Calloway hadn't suddenly gone loony tunes on him, their first date. It was just Art Tatum, after being in his presence—Art Tatum just did that to her, he supposed.

Swiftly Modecai took Corrine's hand, and together they made a mad dash down into the Eighth Avenue subway station, laughing all the way.

Corrine's apartment was on the top floor.

"I wish I lived on the roof," Corrine said. "Then I could smile at the moon all night."

Why are artists such romantics? Modecai thought.

Corrine, before turning on the apartment lights, warned Modecai by saying, "Modecai, are you prepared to see my mess?"

Then—

"Man, Corrine. you are about a neat as me!"

"But with much less room!"

It was a one-room studio apartment with a tiny bathroom and a kitchenette.

"You are gifted," Modecai said with emphasis as his eyes gazed upon a plethora of Corrine's paintings. Modecai stood closer to one of the paintings. "You really are."

Corrine took a drag on her Lucky Strike.

"It's what I keep reminding myself on those days when …"

"Everything seems to be falling apart, going wrong. Nowhere," Modecai bemoaned. "Like all the wheels falling off a milk wagon."

"Uh-huh," Corrine said, taking another drag on her cigarette.

Corrine wore a dark blue hat. She removed it. Then Modecai helped her with her pigeon-gray tweed coat.

"Where?" Modecai asked, looking around the one-roomer.

"The closet's over there." Pause. "And why don't you hang yours up while you're—"

"It, uh, it is late, Corrine. I don't think I should—"

"I'll make coffee, how's that? Uh, you like coffee, don't you?"

Modecai hung Corrine's coat along with his in the cramped closet.

"Light. You do know how to use light."

"Uh, beg your pardon."

"Light, I said light," Modecai said in a stronger voice, "you do know how to use light."

Corrine was preparing coffee.

"I'm getting there."

"I'd say you already are."

"No, I still have a ways to go yet. I'm still learning how to mix my paints, get the shades, the right shades I'd like from them."

Modecai moved over to another painting.

"Yes, you are good, Corrine. I mean," Modecai said unabashedly, "you are really good."

Modecai was sitting on a solid sofa. He stood.

"Be careful, Modecai, with this—it's hot," Corrine said, handing the cup of coffee with a napkin to Modecai.

"Thanks."

There was this thing resembling a coffee table in front of Modecai, so he took full advantage of it by placing his coffee cup on top of his napkin, which was on top of this thing resembling a coffee table.

Corrine came back with her cup of coffee. She sat next to Modecai on the sofa. At this point, there was a momentary lull in conversation. They were relaxed, drinking their coffee, seemingly, finally letting Art Tatum free them.

Corrine's cigarette was perched on her bottom lip. "Aaah," Corrine said. "I know that you don't smoke, but have you ever tried, Modecai?"

Modecai blew on the match.

"Nope."

"Good for you," Corrine said, touching Modecai's leg, and then her hand as quickly leaving it.

"The first time I smoked a cigarette, tried, at least, I choked on it."

"Everyone does that. The first time is always the worst experience a novice smoker will have."

"Well, it was the first time for me, Corrine. I didn't give smoking a second chance."

"I've been smoking since I was sixteen. Don't ask me why."

Modecai heard a sadness in Corrine's voice and looked around at the paintings on the floor, everywhere on the floor like his and Bunny's music.

"It gets lonely, doesn't it? Artists, creative people."

Corrine put out the cigarette.

Modecai didn't answer.

Corrine got up. "I'll be right back."

Modecai saw Corrine was going to the bathroom off to the side of the room. She shut the door.

Modecai sat on the sofa and looked at the paintings some more. There were all kinds of worlds to enter into in Corrine's paintings. She'd traveled everywhere in her imagination. It's what lonely people do, and he'd been where Corrine was. He'd traveled those worlds in his mind, in front of his piano. Even Art Tatum, tonight, traveled into those worlds, those mysteries and silences and wordless conversations between the mind and the spirit and the cosmos beyond.

Corrine came out the bathroom. Modecai'd finished his coffee. Modecai stood.

"Modecai, can you stay the night? O-over? The sofa folds out into a bed. It's about the only fancy thing I have in the apartment to really speak of."

She was lonely, but if he said yes, he wouldn't be saying it out of pity for her—he'd be saying it because he did want to stay the night with her.

"Yes, Corrine, I'd like that."

"Have you ever slept on a sofa bed, before?" Corrine asked while a gorgeous smile floated across her face.

"Uh, on cots, a pillow, and a floor, uh, hay, too, but no, not on a sofa bed."

"Then this'll be your first experience. So step aside, I'm coming through!"

"Can I do anything to help?"

"Yes. You can move that stack of paintings t-to over there. They'll fit—I think."

Everything was done. Everything was cozy. Modecai would sleep in his underwear, of course. He was already under the sheet and the blanket and his head resting on a pillow.

There was a wooden divider in the room that afforded Corrine privacy. She and her bed and whatever else was behind the room divider. Both Corrine and Modecai were awake, the lights still burning.

"In the morning, are you going to let me use your, uh, toothbrush, Corrine?"

"Why, of course, Modecai," Corrine shouted back over the room divider. "We can negotiate that."

"Like selling one of your paintings?"

A long silence ensued … then.

"Modecai, sometimes it's so difficult to let them go—of some of my paintings. I must admit."

"I know. It's like my songs. The song belongs to me first and foremost before it belongs—"

"It can never belong to anyone else as far as I'm concerned. The public. I don't feel it ever can. It'll always belong to me—be mine."

"Have you, uh, sold many paintings?"

"Quite a few," Corrine said, tugging on her robe. "I'm developing a small clientele. A small reputation here in Harlem."

"Be sure to add me to the list, okay—whenever I'm able to afford your prices."

Corrine got off the bed; Modecai heard her.

"I'd give it to you for free, Modecai. Whatever you want, I'd give to you free."

Modecai's heart jumped.

What was happening to him? he asked himself. Was he falling back in love with someone else this time? Was he that fickle? Could Corrine make him forget Delores and Johnnyboy Daniels, about him loving her—about Johnnyboy Daniels beating her.

"What are your dreams, Corrine, as an artist. Your ambitions?"

"Paris, Modecai. Paris. I want to go to Paris to paint."

"Where all the famous artists are."

"It's what the Parisians must say about Harlem's jazz musicians."

It was later in the night. The apartment's lights had been turned off. It was quiet, the night turning silence over as light as snow.

"Modecai …"

Her breath was warm.

"Modecai …"

Modecai saw this shining angel through his groggy eyes.

Corrine's lips touched his, parting, opening.

Modecai knew he wasn't trapped inside a dream, that this was real, the flesh he felt, that Corrine was lying next to him on the sofa bed.

"Corrine …" She was crawling atop him. "Ssssh … sssssh …"

Her lips were kissing him along his face and then down his neck until her teeth bit him teasingly, sending wild chills through him, Modecai feeling those chills down to his toes.

"Corrine …" Modecai rolled her over (there was just enough room on the sofa bed for that). Corrine looked up at Modecai. Modecai could see those deep, dark eyes in that pretty, light-skinned face.

"Corrine …"

Modecai let go of Corrine and then laid his head back down on the pillow.

Corrine shut her eyes and then opened them, seemingly reacting to what was this melancholy mood of Modecai's.

"Don't, I hope you don't think I brought you here to, up to the apartment—that I asked you to stay the night for you could make love to me, Modecai. F-for we could have sex."

"No, I know that, Corrine. You didn't—"

"D-did I, what I just did, has it changed your opinion of me, is that it? Is it? Because if it has, I don't do this kind of thing. I …"

"I know you don't. It just happened."

"Naturally, Modecai. It happened so very naturally between us, that how can I make apologies for it?" Pause.

"Another woman? Is that what's bothering you? Has you upset?"

Modecai ran his fingers through Corrine's hair that Earlene had groomed beautifully two days ago but now was mussed.

"Delores," Modecai said. "I'm in love with her. She doesn't live here, in New York. Up North, but down South. Way City, Alabama."

"Why'd you leave her?"

"It's a long story … But I had to."

"You are a special man, Modecai."

"Thank you." Pause.

"Can we, I don't want to go back to my bed."

"You don't have to. No need for you to."

"I just want to be with you tonight—no matter what."

Modecai was running his fingers through Corrine's hair. Corrine's head lay on Modecai's chest.

"I had to tell you, Corrine."

"What, Modecai?" Corrine said, raising her head off Modecai's chest.

"That I'm in love with Delores."

Corrine put her head back down on Modecai's chest.

"Modecai, I can wait."

* * *

Was Art Tatum still in him or what, man! Wait until he told Bunny what he did last night and who he saw. Wait until Bunny found out he was in the Big Hat Club. That he'd slipped past the club's tight web of security undetected. Modecai had his hand in his coat pocket, his hand squeezing the dark, wraparound sunglasses that'd been wrapped to his face last night.

Modecai was on 119th Street. He only had three more blocks to go to get to 116th Street (Corrine lived just six blocks from him). Modecai was exhibiting his best smile—he'd used Corrine's toothbrush this morning, free of charge. Last night, before both fell asleep, he told Corrine the Way City, Alabama, story. He didn't parse words, leave anything out, including, by last report by Benny, what Johnnyboy was doing to Delores. He said he was still writing Delores without her reply. Corrine was a good listener. He appreciated that. Maybe she knew what it meant to him that she listen.

This morning they'd agreed to continue to date. He wasn't going to close the book, shut down shop on someone as special as Corrine Calloway. And Corrine said she meant what she said in bed last night, about waiting.

This morning, October 28, to be exact, was cold. Modecai watched Harlem folk walk the streets far better than him. Veteran Harlemnites, Modecai thought. Seasoned. *Give me ten, fifteen years up here, and I'll be walking the streets of Harlem like them too, and not scampering the way I am.*

Earlene's door was open when Modecai entered the hallway.

"Now look what the cat just dragged in," Earlene said as she moved toward the door. Big, fat rollers were stacked in her hair.

"How'd it go, Modecai, between you and Corrine last night?"

"Uh, great, Earlene. Just great."

Earlene knew about the date, the first one; but from here on out, Modecai made it clear that he and Corrine would not be a topic up for discussion provided there were future dates between them.

Earlene clapped her hands like she'd just whacked a tambourine.

"Oh, I'm so glad, Modecai!" Pause. "And don't you worry, Modecai, this is the last of it. Last time I'll—"

"Stay up all night to see what the cat dragged in?"

Earlene yawned. "You got that right! Yep, been up all night." (Another broad yawn.) "Ain't good for business. A beautician needs her rest. At least eight hours sleep every night … sometimes ten …," Earlene said, turning as if she were heading straight for bed. "And that's the God's honest truth, Modecai. Especially up here in Harlem. After tackling with these colored women's hair all day!"

Modecai walked down the hall, and from where he was, he saw the apartment door was open. He looked at his watch: six forty-two! Modecai was shuffling along. And when he got to the door, he saw a beet-red Bunny staring back at him.

"The motherfucker, Modecai!"

Modecai's eyes were asking who, who, Bunny, who!

"Big Hat Morrison, Modecai. That big hat motherfucker!"

Don't tell me he saw me last night at the Big Hat Club, Modecai panicked. *Don't tell me Big Hat saw me with Corrine!*

Bunny was pacing the floor. Each step taken seeming to be chasing the last.

"That big hat motherfucker!"

"Bunny. Bunny. Please, man. Please … tell me what's wrong! H-happened!"

"We're banned! That motherfucker banned us. Sure as hell banned us from the motherfucker. Couldn't get a gig downtown, down there if I, I..."

Bunny pulled the knife out his back pocket. Bunny was slashing the air with it. And what Modecai saw was not just the air's blood, but Bunny's too, cursing it.

"But you knew Big Hat, what he said, Bunny. You knew the … the promise he made to us. You knew. His edict."

Bunny stopped with the knife.

"Thought it all was a threat. Not real. None of it. Wasn't gonna last, Modecai. Forgive and forget, Modecai. Forgive and for—fucking forget."

"Don't you remember what he looked like that day, when he said it, Bunny? Big Hat—h-how he said it?"

Bunny walked over to the piano and picked up his horn. Bunny sucked his teeth. "You know, Modecai, the white man, well, I know I gotta fight him for the rest of my life. Put up with his shit." Bunny looked down at his trumpet. "But the colored man, well, shit, Modecai—I figured him, the colored cat would cut another colored cat some slack, man."

Bunny slipped the knife back into his back pocket.

Modecai's legs felt whipped. He didn't expect that. He didn't expect Bunny to say something as close to the heart or as deeply felt as that. Modecai walked over to the couch and sat.

Bunny was at the window.

"Harlem, man. I love Harlem, Modecai. The sun doesn't rise or set any better than up in Harlem. But I can still see Park Avenue from here, this window—it's still clear as day. As a rainbow. Ain't no fog rolled in."

"It was the big band, wasn't it, Bunny? It's what started all of this t-to unravel."

"Yeah. I was trying to do our band debut gig down on Fifty-Second Street. Knew what white cats to talk to. They all hummed into the phone or cleared their throats like they got the flu bug—it just hit them, Modecai. Bad. Their tonsils, man."

"Big Hat."

"Yeah, Big Hat put the word out on us. Us cats. And he got all them white cats to clapping their hands like seals, man." Bunny turned to Modecai. "Trained seals. How'd he do that shit, Modecai? How'd a colored cat, black cat like Big Hat Morrison do the kind of shit, man?" Pause.

"I know how the black motherfucker did it, Modecai." Bunny's eyes glinted. "Cut them white motherfuckers into more of the same action up here they've already got but bigger—fucking how!"

"Well, what … what are we going to do now, Bunny?"

"Do! Do now, Modecai! Hell, we still got the Apollo Theater, the Cotton Club, man! They still got their lights turned on, burning bright. Bunny's Big Band Boppers appearing at the Apollo on November 3, man—that's what the hell we're doing!"

"You mean we're … we're booked, Bunny!"

"Solid, Modecai. Solid as a Fort Knox. Booked for two weeks. Two straight, solid weeks. Three shows a night. Plus matinees on Saturday and Sunday!"

"What are you trying to do to us, Bunny? Kill us!"

"We've got to make some bread, Modecai. A loaf, not no slice. At least a loaf!"

"We're ready for it, Bunny," Modecai said.

"Hell yeah. We got us some bad-ass cats. And with our charts ..."

"We could play the Apollo Theatre for two, four years and not run out of material. Music. Charts."

Modecai was at the upright.

"Bunny ..."

"Yeah ...?"

Modecai winked. "Guess where else I was last night?"

"Know you was promenading with Corrine. Skating—figured you got yourself a little juicy f—"

"No, I said, where, not who I was with."

"Oh, yeah, you did, didn't you?" Bunny bounced up on his feet as if he should be put under arrest.

"I saw the man, Bunny. The *man*, man!"

"Who? Tatum! You mean to tell me you went off to that big hat motherfucker's club and, and laid out your bread?"

"In disguise."

"So what? That's supposed to change the calendar, make a damned difference!"

Modecai walked over to his overcoat he'd put on the couch and reached into his side pocket. "In these, Bunny. These!"

"Ha. That big hat motherfucker—"

"Never saw me. Big Hat never saw me in the place." Pause. "And guess what else?"

"What, Modecai? You got more canaries under your cap?"

Modecai slipped his overcoat over his shoulders and put his sunglasses on.

Bunny laughed at the ridiculous sight.

"Big Hat didn't play last night. Not a note on his guitar, man."

"What! The cat didn't twang, twang on his steel guitar!"

Modecai played a fleet-footed cluster of notes on the piano.

"Maybe he's finally gotten the hint, do you think, Bunny?" Modecai suggested, charitably.

"Tatum probably told him, that's what happened. Threatened to kick Big Hat's ass, even if he's blind or almost blind. Go back to Toledo, Ohio, where he comes from, if the cat so much as got his ass close to him with that guitar of his. T-that"—Bunny looked around the apartment, seemingly searching for new words to describe Big Hat Morrison but came up short—"big hat motherfucker!"

And Bunny had the last authoritative word on Big Hat Morrison and Art Tatum and what was, more than likely, their current working relationship at Big Hat Morrison's Big Hat Club on Fifty-Second Street and Broadway.

* * *

And so the auspicious debut of one Bunny Greensleeves's Big Band Boppers at the Apollo Theatre, in Harlem, USA, on November 3, was a smash hit by all accounts. On opening night, the sky opened and every jazz musician in the world fell out of it (so it seemed). The band set Harlem on its backside. The music critics tried comparing the Big Band Boppers to other bands but, by consensus, could only announce, "Straight out of this world!"

The critics further concluded that the eminent composers, Bunny Odecai Greensleeves and Modecai Ulysses Jefferson, were "straight out of this world" and were rapidly encroaching on new ones. Both were labeled "one-of-a-kind finds," "one-of-a-kind composers." Fresh, unique, original, inventive—compositions which set new, high musical standards, musical charts that were opening music up to new trends and possibilities.

And the Apollo Theatre audience, on opening night, was on its feet more than in its seat. The band was tight. The band took care of business. But Bunny and his golden horn, as usual, brought the house down, stole the show—Bunny was the *boss*. He stood up there on the Apollo Theatre stage in a hep cat pink suit (a horn-bird that had laid a golden egg) like a pink flamingo flapping its wings. Bunny was the toast of Harlem, the people's choice. He was laying them uptown cats out to rest, putting them down for the count. The Apollo had never known moments like Bunny gave it: a jazz oracle speaking to all of Harlem through his music.

Modecai and Bunny were grateful for their success. The band's two-week Apollo engagement was wrapping up. The band members wanted to make their last night (not unlike opening night) special. But tonight, Bunny had something to tell the band. Bunny was bursting at the seams with excitement; but first he would tell Modecai since, of course, they were coequals in this musical cooperative of theirs, by most estimates.

Chapter 15

Bunny and Modecai were in the Apollo dressing room. Bunny, well, Bunny had to get one thing off his chest.

"Man, Modecai, this dressing room was built for mice, not men. Hell, a mouse got more room in a mouse hole than in here, man!"

"And why the last night at the Apollo to complain about the quarters, Bunny? Why not before tonight?"

"Uh, I don't know, maybe, ha, I've been blowing too many high Cs. Maybe, I don't know. So don't ask me."

Bunny was back in his pink suit, the one he wore opening night and tonight, closing night.

Then Bunny got jittery, because the special news he had to tell Modecai was shaking him like his body might fly away. So Bunny stamped his foot one time on the floor to make sure it was on solid ground.

"How's Paris suit you in a tux and tails, top hat, and cane, Modecai?" Bunny was still fingering his trumpet coolly, adeptly, when he said it. (Bunny's pink suit blushed, though.)

"P-Paris!"

"Got me a ticket in my hip pocket, man. Hot as a rocket!"

"When, Bunny, when!"

"Set it up today, Modecai. Made a call—"

"From down the hall?"

"Hell, yeah!"

"T-to Paris, Bunny!"

"Now don't start laying bricks! You know I ain't got those kind of nickels and dimes, that kind of loot laying in my pockets for me to call Paris."

"Paris! Wow, Bunny! Wow!"

Modecai grabbed Bunny and squeezed him and Bunny's trumpet to him.

"You're a dream maker, Bunny," Modecai said, now standing back to look at what had become his best friend in life. "You are. A person who makes dreams for everybody. Your horn plays dreams. I love you, Bunny. Love you, man!"

Modecai kissed Bunny flush on the lips.

"So now I know if you got bad breath or not, after that, man!" Bunny cracked.

"So, so?"

"The jury's out. Out deliberating the case."

"Yeah, yeah, Bunny, say whatever you want. Whatever … But … so when are you going to tell the guys the great news?"

Bunny bounced. "You mean 'we,' don't you, Modecai?"

"Oh, I see—it's back to 'we' again, is it?"

"Oui, oui, monsieur, we."

"That's right," Modecai said skeptically, "you know French."

"Exactament, monsieur."

"The cat's in Mr. Hines's band …"

"Oui!"

Modecai had to pinch himself again to make sure he wasn't dreaming all of this up.

"Paris! Paris! P—"

"Say it one more time, Modecai, and you ain't going nowhere. Keep you right here in Harlem. Chained to a bedpost!"

The band had received the good news. It was thrilled, as thrilled as Modecai had been when he found out about the Paris trip. And now the band had finished its last gig at the Apollo Theatre, at least for now.

The two of them were bundled up. The Harlem Hawk was talking.

"Corrine, let's take a cab home tonight."

Corrine's light skin was red.

"You won't get an argument from me. Not in this cold."

They were holding hands (or for more descriptive accuracy, gloves).

Modecai whistled, even though he felt his saliva freeze on his tongue. The taxi stopped.

"Modecai, practicing for Paris, huh?" Corrine said, stepping into the taxi.

Modecai'd told Corrine the good news right off. As soon as he saw her. Corrine was flabbergasted.

They sat in the taxi's backseat.

"Heat!" Modecai exhorted. "Heat!"

"And I thought I was going to have to heat you up," Corrine said with a hint of intent.

Modecai's entire being felt the potency of those words: He and Corrine, after so many weeks of dating, still had not made love. They still had not had sex. Modecai's body tightened.

Corrine frowned in the darkened space of the cab, realizing she had made a misstep, erred, even though she'd meant no harm by her remark—it'd just come out that way.

"Modecai," she said endearingly, "you played great tonight."

Modecai loosened up. "Bunny …"

"Didn't steal the show, not tonight, Modecai. Tonight was yours. You were fabulous."

Modecai reached for Corrine's hand again and held it.

"I'm jealous, though …" Corrine's eyes sparkled.

"J-jealous? What for?"

"You get to go to Paris before me. Remember, it's my dream too. Paris, France."

Modecai raised her hand to his lips—"No, I haven't forgotten it, mademoiselle"—and kissed it like any ordinary Frenchman would do on the Riviera.

"Oh … so chic, continental," Corrine sighed.

"Oui, oui," Modecai said in his best French, at least the little Bunny had taught him.

Both were in Corrine's apartment. Corrine was brushing her hair out, the very same hair that'd been crushed and mussed by her pillbox hat and needed attention.

"So this is the new painting you've been talking about."

"Yes," Corrine said from the bathroom.

"I love it."

Corrine turned off the bathroom light. "I haven't worked everything, all the details out yet—but I feel things emerging, beginning to come together, take on some personality in the painting."

"S-so do I, Corrine."

"I'll fix coffee for us."

"Thanks."

This had become kind of routine for them, Corrine fixing them coffee.

"It's funny," Corrine said over her shoulder, "how similar our disciplines are. Being with you, I've learned how, just how integrated it all is—the arts."

Modecai was still looking at the "emerging" painting with a creative eye and interest.

"Uh-huh. No wonder writers can talk to artists, and artists to musicians, and—"

"It's a bohemia, Modecai. A melting pot. A place for people and ideas. Paris has little bohemia's, enclaves—places where artists go to talk and share in new, exciting ideas."

Corrine was bringing Modecai his cup of coffee.

"I know. Besides, uh, the painters, artists are—"

"Everywhere you turn in Paris."

"Thanks."

Modecai was with his cup of coffee. Then Corrine was back with hers as they continued to chat more lively.

"Just think, Modecai, you're going to see all of that."

"I know. Uh, I still have to scratch my head over it."

"What? To see if it has fleas?"

"Ha."

"You know what, Modecai, I think Bunny would toss fleas on you, anything to give you a rise," Corrine joked. "Maybe Bunny's just kidding about Paris. Maybe he's just putting you—"

"Uh-uh, Corrine, no way. Not on your life. Bunny said he's already got ten suits packed for the Paris trip."

"How many days will, are you two be over there, by the way?"

"Uh, five. Five—not counting air time."

"Two suits for each day then, uh, huh?" Corrine laughed.

"That's Bunny for you, Corrine: teaching Paris, the fashion capital of the world, style. How to dress."

Corrine's body leaned back against the sofa.

"Modecai, I'm going to miss you."

Modecai wanted to say it would be for just a week, only had better sense not to.

Her body leaned forward. Modecai beat her to her pocketbook. Before she knew it, a Lucky Strike was on her lips and Modecai was lighting it.

"Thanks, honey," Corrine said, blowing out the match.

"You know, Corrine, my life has really changed, picked up momentum of late."

"Bunny's aggressive, isn't he?"

"Bunny doesn't waste time, no, Corrine, if it's what you're implying. I guess sometimes it's good and sometimes bad."

Corrine's eyes looked sharply through the lazy smoke at Modecai.

"You know sometimes a person can get things too fast, and then what, what's the next rung up?" Modecai said uneasily. "But with Bunny, he has to move at a certain pace, at a specific tempo. And, and it's ironic …"

Corrine's eyebrows lifted.

"It's ironic … in that it's the one freedom Bunny doesn't have, Corrine. The one freedom Bunny will never know. Really know."

"There're times, I must admit, Modecai, when I wish I had that kind of drive, burning ambition. Let out all the stops. Had the unstoppable drive Bunny has. When I could go and just … just make things happen. Sale myself."

"Bunny's a true master at it."

"I know."

"But there's a price to be paid, and I know it. There's that part of it."

Corrine hadn't finished puffing on her cigarette.

"It-it's something, uh, I worry about with Bunny. As if I can see it but he can't. As if it's there, Corrine—waiting its turn for some reason. I don't know. I just don't …"

"Modecai," Corrine said, receiving Modecai in her arms as he came to her, trembling, "I didn't know you worried for Bunny."

"I do, Corrine. I love Bunny."

When the minicrisis abated, Corrine picked up her cigarette, but slowly Modecai eased the cigarette from her hand.

"I know we haven't made love, Corrine. Had sex."

Corrine sighed.

Modecai doused the Lucky Strike. Corrine took his hand and kissed it, and then her lips nibbled his fingers.

"But it's going to change tonight. All of it. I'm going to make it change."

"I know, Modecai," Corrine said, now touching Modecai's leg. "I've felt it all night. In your playing, everything."

And Modecai felt a certain movement in his pants and his heart.

He picked Corrine up in his arms and carried her off to where the room divider was folded back and the moon dropped down on the bed and touched the room in a marvelous way.

Modecai began undressing Corrine.

* * *

Corrine puffed on her cigarette.

"Mmm …" Modecai rolled over to Corrine, yawned—and then stretched like a lazy lion lying in tall grass.

"Aren't you the picture of contentment," Corrine giggled. Corrine was in an artist's smock.

"Going to paint me?" Modecai kidded.

"Don't tempt me," Corrine replied.

Modecai rested his head on Corrine's bare leg. Corrine caressed the nape of his neck. This wasn't the first they'd spoken. They'd spoken after their first lovemaking, and their second.

"It's morning, isn't it?" Modecai said, clearing his eyes. "And you have to go to work."

"Well, at least call in this morning to see if my agency has a new assignment for me."

Modecai yawned again.

"Stop that …"

"Why?"

"It's catching," Corrine said, yawning. "Besides, I hope I'm not, you don't think me that boring."

Modecai's body shot straight up. His back was ramrod straight. "Not at all, Corrine."

Modecai took the cigarette from her lips and planted a kiss there.

"Y-you're a marvelous lover, Modecai …"

"But …" For Modecai had felt the linger, the pause in Corrine. "You know, I mean there is a 'but,' isn't there, Corrine? Let's not play cat and mouse with each other, okay?"

"No … I don't want us to do that. Not with you."

"Then …," Modecai said, his eyes coaxing her.

"You weren't with me last night, Modecai. Totally, all the way …"

"I know," Modecai said unhesitatingly. Modecai put his head against the wall in this small-statured bed with no headboard. "I wasn't, I know I wasn't."

"Delores, was it Delores, honey?"

"It-it's …," Modecai stammered, "beginning to sound like that, that dreaded name, isn't it, for you, Corrine?"

Corrine drew on her cigarette. "What made you say that?"

"Because it is. It's a simple fact, something plain as day to see."

Pause.

"My first time with a woman, a woman I really like and … and respect and admire—and I can't even—"

"You satisfied me, Modecai, beyond belief. D-didn't you hear me? My … what came out my mouth last night was-wasn't fake." Corrine smiled. "I can assure you: it was real."

What she'd said didn't seem to satisfy Modecai or erase his doubts.

Corrine put out the Lucky Strike and turned to Modecai.

"Dammit, Modecai, Delores gave up her life for you!"

The power and conviction of Corrine's words stunned Modecai.

"Y-yes, she did …"

"She loved you. She did something not many people would do, honey. Not for anyone."

"You do, you do understand then?"

"What's there not to understand? You don't have to draw me diagrams, Modecai. I'm a big girl. Okay?"

Pause.

"By the way, what time is it anyway?"

Corrine grabbed Modecai's wrist. "Six ten. Why I still have time to fix us—"

"You don't have to fix—"

"I'm hungry, Modecai. I don't know about you, but after the kind of sex we had last night, I'm hungry."

Corrine hopped out the bed in her artist's smock.

Moments later, Modecai was putting his underwear back on. Then he reached for his socks and twisted around to Corrine who was in the kitchen and whose back was to him.

"For the five days Bunny and the band are in Paris, I'm going to miss you, Corrine."

Corrine didn't turn around; she continued preparing breakfast—but it was like Modecai had already sent her a pretty postcard all the way from Paris, France, by post.

* * *

The day had come (Hallelujah and thank the Lord!).

Bunny was bouncing.

"We're gonna have a ball, Modecai!"

"I know, it's what you keep telling me, Bunny."

"Oh, man, you're as excited as me, Modecai. You know it, man. You just let me play the fool 'cause you know I'm so damned good at it!"

Modecai and Bunny were packed and were raring to go, set off for Paris.

"Modecai, got Earlene to collect the mail for us. Would've asked Big Booty, but that cat'd probably read through it first. Snoop through it like he was the FBI." Bunny performed a partial pivot. "Man, Modecai, can't wait to get to Paris to get me some of that French p—"

"Uh, paintings, Bunny. Paintings, man. Paintings, purchase paintings. Uh … some Picassos and uh—"

"Okay, Modecai, call it as you see it, man. Clean it up. But uh … uh … D-De …"

"De Gaulle ?"

"Yeah, that French cat," Bunny said with much disdain, "better lock up them French chicks. Or call out the Foreign Legion." Then Bunny poked his chest out. "'Cause you can tell that De … uh, De Gaulle cat, Modecai, that Bunny Greensleeves is coming to Paris for five days and four nights, but he might just stay on longer. It's according to how fine French wine tastes in wintertime!"

Then Bunny twirled his gold-plated pocket watch on his chain a few times like it'd fallen asleep and needed to be awoken.

"Time to step, Modecai."

"Yes, yes, it is, Bunny."

Modecai looked at his upright.

"Too bad we can't take her with us, on the trip. Don't worry though, asked Earlene to dust it for us."

"Thanks, Bunny." Pause.

"Okay, Modecai, let's get to stepping for real this time, man."

"Uh, right, Bunny."

And then Modecai and Bunny took one last look at the upright.

* * *

They were inside LaGuardia Airport's hub.

"Corrine, take it," Modecai said, folding some bills in her hand.

"Modecai, I was going to—"

"Pay your cab fare back to Harlem, don't be silly."

"Modecai," Corrine said flustered, "I mean I'm the one who invited myself to—"

"I wanted you to come. Last night, my eyes practically begged you to come to the airport with me."

"I know," Corrine replied coyly. "It's why I didn't call the agency today." Pause. "Nervous?"

"Uh-huh. There's a lot riding on this. Paris reviews can sink a ship if they're bad. And launch one if they're good. Bunny said French critics have a lot of pull in Europe. We …," Modecai laughed, "don't want to be banned from the continent too."

And then Modecai stopped laughing and so did Corrine: both thought of Howard "Big Hat" Morrison and his club on Fifty-Second Street and Broadway.

"Corrine—" Bunny had bounced back over to them—"let me bid you au revoir, mon cheri." Bunny then proceeded to peck Corrine on her left cheek and then her right cheek. "The French way."

"Oh, Bunny, you're a riot!"

"Spin me like a platter, and I just might make music in your lovely ears!"

Corrine laughed more.

"Gonna leave you two lovebirds to your own devices. You ain't gonna hear from me, Modecai—"

"Until you pull out your—"

"My timepiece, you bought me at Cartier's, nonetheless."

"What'd I ever do that for?" Modecai lamented.

"And I'll totally disregard that, what you just said, for now, Modecai—and tell you when it's time to get to stepping!"

Modecai turned to Corrine for explanation.

"It's a new word Bunny's been, uh, using lately, Corrine. 'Stepping.'"

"Oh."

"He's like a two-year-old with a new toy."

"Oh."

Heartily, Bunny laughed—and then bounced.

Modecai was holding Corrine's hand.

"You look handsome, Modecai. Did I tell you that?"

"Yes, you did."

"Oh, I forgot."

"I-I don't have to go, you know."

"Modecai, honey, it's only a week. For a week, hey, I can do a week standing on my head!"

Corrine looked over at Bunny and the rest of the band standing at the short, metal gate (what was the entrance to the plane).

"I meant to ask before, Modecai, but what's Bunny doing, advertising to the world?"

"Oh, come on, Corrine, what's wrong with a little, subtle advertising, uh for the band?"

"Subtle?"

Modecai took another glance at Bunny's traveling trunk.

"Okay, so Bunny went a bit"—Modecai was red-faced himself—"a little bit overboard."

"A little bit, Modecai? Y-you call that a little—"

"Okay, okay, Corrine, so Bunny got carried away," Modecai laughed. "It probably has something to do with him hitting too many—"

"Don't bother to explain, Modecai. You just have to accept it, if it's Bunny Greensleeves."

And their eyes snuck back over to Bunny's trunk. And what each saw in bold white lettering you could see from the planet Uraneous (if there is such a planet) was: BUNNY GREENSLEEVES'S HARLEM BIG BAND BOPPERS.

(Bunny had added Harlem to the band's moniker, only to give it a little more class and world reputation.)

"Man, Bunny's a gas!" Corrine laughed.

"Hey, better watch out, Corrine, you're beginning to sound like one of us. The band."

"A-a jazz cat?"

"Yes, ma'am."

"Honey …"

"Yes."

"I wonder what Paris looks like in winter."

"Like a winter in wonderland. And … and not as cold as Harlem, I hope."

"I want to go to Paris in the spring."

"You know what, Corrine, I never dreamed I'd ever go to Paris. Not once."

"Why's it sometimes these things happen these ways, Modecai? Those who dream the hardest are … sometimes their dreams—"

"You'll get to Paris. And it will be in the spring. It's not just a dream."

Corrine pulled out a Lucky Strike; Modecai lit it.

"The last time I'll be doing this for a while," Modecai said what seemed nostalgically.

"I will get to Paris, Modecai."

"That a girl, Corrine. That's my girl!"

"I will!"

It was as if the universe's clock clicked. Modecai saw the gold pocket watch flash from across the terminal's floor.

"Never should've bought Bunny that damn watch, Corrine! Never!"

"Time to step, Modecai. Get to stepping. Shake a leg, Modecai—Paris awaits, my man!"

The band smiled like silver eagles.

Modecai held Corrine in his arms.

"Say hello to Paris for me, Modecai."

Modecai was moving toward Bunny but waving back to Corrine.

"Tell her I'm coming," Corrine said. "Paris."

"I will, Corrine!"

"But in the spring, honey. In the spring. Tell her, in the spring."

Chapter 16

Modecai and Bunny had returned from their Paris jaunt.

"Food poisoning, Modecai. Took you all the way to Paris for you could get food poisoning. Can't believe that lame shit, man!"

Bunny was thumbing through the mail he'd collected from Earlene.

"Mine, mine, mine, yours!" Bunny said. "Mine, mine, mine, yours!" Bunny said, like he'd nailed the final nail in the coffin, since he was out of mail.

Both began catching up with things.

Modecai was sitting on the piano stool. He'd already greeted the piano with an "allo," something he'd brought back with him from Paris.

"F-food poisoning ..." Bunny was done with the mail, but not with Modecai. "Went, crossed the Atlantic Ocean, Modecai, for you could get food poisoning, man. Come down with it."

Modecai was bedridden for one day of the five-day stay in Paris; one of the other band members took over Modecai's piano duties.

Bunny was looking at the piano. "She missed you, Modecai. For those five days."

"Think so, Bunny?"

Modecai dropped his fingers down on the keys, playing a chord.

"Damn, Modecai, if we didn't conquer Paris! Them French cats didn't know what the hell hit them. Ran over them French cats like a French tank!"

"The band was in top form."

"Top form. Man, you'd think we were the king of Denmark."

And Bunny Greensleeves's Harlem Big Band Boppers (the name used for intercontinental purposes only) did take Paris by storm. The French didn't know what'd hit them: a Joe Louis jab or a Jack Dempsey haymaker. They just knew Bunny Greensleeves and "le hot jazz" had hit the continent and glad the Eiffel Tower was still left standing up under its own weight. unique

The French critics went gaga over the band. They said it was the finest American export since Josephine Baker and her shimmy-shimmy and banana costume at the Théâtre des Champs-Élysées (and that went way, way back when). Bunny and his horn got most of the French ink, though. Parisians and French critics fell head over heels in love with Bunny's peerless style. And Bunny paid a French translator to read all that French ink to him and tell him how inimitable he'd been (as if he didn't already know without English translations from a French interpreter).

Bunny removed his jacket, putting it on top the couch, saying, "Modecai, man, it feels great being back in Harlem, uptown, though. Shit, got tired of saying 'oui, oui.' Hell, Modecai, some of them French cats calling me every name under God's sun, and ha, I ain't got a clue in heaven to what they said yet. Just saying 'oui, oui, oui, mon, homme.'"

Modecai smiled.

"Heard Basie and his band's going over. Soon, real soon."

"Count is?"

"Yeah. Must be scared as hell." Pause. "Ellington'll be following him next, fast on his tail. Watch and see. Hightailing it over to the continent."

"Bunny …"

"Told you we'd chase them lame cats out of Harlem like cocker roaches, Modecai, didn't I!" Bunny laughed like a prophet. "Gonna be the last time you ever hear of Count or Duke in Harlem again, man. They better stay in Paris now that we're back in Harlem, Modecai. Keep it warm. Better get used to that Paris cuisine, if you know what I mean. Buy a French beret for every season!"

"You speak for yourself, Bunny. Not for me."

"Big things gonna be going down, Modecai. Big things gonna be shaking down now that we're back in Harlem, man. Mark my words. News travels fast, fast as Cheetah chasing Jane and Tarzan naked through the jungle."

"Bunny, Bunny h-how—"

"Ain't playing. Ain't lied to you yet, have I, Modecai?"

"Bunny, man, you don't know how to lie."

"Not unless I'm cheating at pool!"

Modecai'd put one of the envelopes on top the piano.

"Rent money, Modecai?"

Modecai nodded.

"From your mother?"

Modecai looked much more intently at Bunny. "Uh … uh-huh."

"Bunny! Bunny! Hall phone!"

Mr. Clarence hollered through the door.

"Where else is it gonna be! How the hell Mr. Clarence know I was home, man! Stepped back on to Harlem soil!"

But as Bunny walked across the floor he began answering his own question: "'Cause everyone knows when Bunny Greensleeves skaditty-do's from Harlem and ha, skidee-a-daddle's back, Jack!"

Now Modecai was in the apartment alone. He plunked a piano key. Who'd he miss most in Paris? Corrine? His piano? Delores? Who'd he miss most—it was a question he'd been positing to himself the past two days. Delores meant as much to him as before, but Corrine was beginning to ease her way inside him.

It was beginning to occur with some frequency, apparent ease. Like a river at rest. Like a shadow slipping over light. Corrine was beginning to connect to him, in him. Paris was a city for lovers, and he'd wished, at times, Corrine was in Paris with him.

Modecai plunked another key on the piano and then fashioned a chord and then shook his head, stopping there, not going any further.

"Modecai! Modecai!"

And it's when Bunny went zombielike, silent; and right off Modecai realized this was another cat and mouse game Bunny'd concocted as Bunny playfully twitched his whiskers.

"Bunny, it's that—"

"Outstanding."

It seemed Bunny could outstrut King Tut the way he was strutting the room's floor, first up and then sideways, and then crooked and then—

"Outstanding, outstanding, Modecai. Yeah, it's the right word for it. Outstanding."

Modecai figured two could play at this game, so he doodled with the piano keys.

Bunny looked at Modecai as if he were peeking underneath the brim of his hat to see if his eyes were still alive, hadn't gone as dead as a car battery yet.

"Curious, huh, Modecai? Curious, huh?"

No reply.

"Say it, Modecai. Say it, man. Ain't no fun un-unless you say it, Modecai."

Bunny sulked like a baby sucking its thumb and not its bottle.

"Yes, Bunny, uh, I'm curious. Am I."

"Ruby called."

"Who, 'Ruby My Dear'?"

"Aaaah, man, Modecai. What, you're the court jester now! No, Ruby, Ruby Records. Ruby Records. Them record cats!"

"That's—"

"Who I was just got off the phone with. They want to record us—the band!"

Modecai wiped at his brow (even though he wasn't sweating on the outside but bubbling with sweat on the inside).

"A recording, Bunny? When!"

"Two weeks hence!"

"I can't believe this!"

"Believe it!" Pause.

"Got to have at least thirty, forty tunes for them to pick from. Ain't gonna play with our shit like I know they do. Recording with Mr. Hines taught me that. I told them we're doing originals too—even though we might have to compromise with them some."

"I think it's all right, Bunny. We can do some standards. It's okay. All right."

"Eighty percent ours though, Modecai. Eighty percent."

"Agreed, partner."

"We ain't gonna make much bread off the record gig. Have to take a flat cut. A one-time deal. Shit, we play, they pay—then we walk."

"It's all right, Bunny. It's the next step."

"Yeah, man. Next step up. Records gonna sell in Harlem like chicken wings, and in France like French pastry."

"Oui!"

"You mean me," Bunny said.

"No, I mean oui," Modecai said.

"Oh, yeah, that's right, Modecai: you're a Harlem nigger who's been to France and back!"

* * *

Modecai stepped out of the cold and into the heated building on 122nd Street. He thought Harlem was cold; well, Paris was its equal, big-time. The Parisians were like the Harlemnites in that regard: they just took it all in stride, flicking it off their collar like dandruff.

Modecai blew on his hands. He was in the building for a purpose. It was early morning, and he was standing in an apartment building's lobby listening to the radiator hiss and holler and jump like it had the heebie-jeebies. Modecai put his hand inside his overcoat's deep pocket. He felt what was inside the pocket to make sure it was still there.

Modecai would wait down in the lobby; it wouldn't be long.

And it wasn't, as Modecai kept his back to the main door, and Corrine recognized his back, his hat, his coat.

"Modecai!"

"Corrine!"

And Corrine wrapped her arms around his neck, and they jumped around in the lobby like the radiator, hissing, hollering—doing the heebie-jeebies.

Now Corrine was straightening her dark-blue velvet hat with the feather back in place.

Before anything was said, Modecai put his hand inside his coat pocket.

"Here, Corrine, it's from Paris."

It was as if Corrine were smelling the bottle of perfume through its pretty, slender, gift-wrapped box.

"Romance is in the air," Modecai chuckled.

Corrine kissed Modecai. "You didn't have to bring it from Paris, France, Modecai. It's always been here."

Then Modecai glanced at his watch.

"Work?"

"Work."

"I'll walk you to the station.

"You'd better!"

"Ready?" Modecai said, armoring himself for the cold.

They made their way out the apartment building's lobby, Corrine holding onto Modecai's arm as if the mighty Harlem Hawk might whisk her away like candy paper.

"How was Paris's weather, by the way, Modecai?"

"Like this."

"It was?"

"Go in the spring, Corrine. Make sure you go in the spring, not winter."

"No artists on the streets, in the squares?"

"No, just pigeons."

Modecai waited for Corrine to stop laughing.

"Why didn't you call last night? You knew I'd be back."

"I—"

"You were waiting for me to call?" Modecai asked, cutting off any attempt for Corrine to reply.

"Yes, in … in a way."

"You got my postcard, didn't you?"

Modecai had mailed Corrine a postcard his first day in Paris.

"Yes, I received it, Modecai. Got it. Thanks."

"Just wanted you to know we, Bunny and the band and I, got, uh, there safely."

"Yes, I know. I was going to call, but I'm glad you decided to surprise me like this," she said as if somehow relieved.

They kept walking toward the subway station, riding on a wind that had picked up.

Was she competing with Delores? Modecai thought. Had Corrine, in her mind and soul, set the Parisian trip up as a test, a competition between her and Delores for his heart?

"You … then you did miss me?"

That was it—the clincher.

"Let me tell you something, Corrine, young lady: Paris opened up a new world to me. It dazzled me. Romance was in the air despite the awful cold. I thought of us a lot. You and me in the City of Love, Corrine. You and me walking arm in arm like now. It happened by the third day over there in Paris. I couldn't stop it if I tried."

Corrine and Modecai were in the subway station. They'd made plans for the night. The band wasn't gigging tonight, Bunny and Modecai had given it a night off. They were kind of out of tune since they had to fly through a time zone (jet lag).

"Seven o'clock, Corrine?"

"Seven o'clock, Modecai."

"And you'll wear …"

"My French perfume."

"Not the whole bottle, I hope?"

"Don't tempt me, honey," Corrine said, skipping blithely down the 125th Street subway station's stairs like it was springtime in Harlem.

* * *

To say over the last two weeks the band was busy would be like saying Billie Holiday wore a white carnation in her hair: it was a given. The band was blowing smoke out its ears. The Paris trip had really built up its confidence to a high point.

And talking about confidence—it was building up for both Modecai and Corrine. Their relationship had reached a new level of confidence and maturity. Delores Bonet still weighted Modecai's thoughts, but mentally, he was beginning to control her much, much more. He'd always love Delores (it was a given, like Billie's white carnation in her hair), but what he hoped lay ahead for him and Corrine was now beginning to feel less risky and more sure. Their lovemaking had improved by leaps and bounds; it meant a lot for both him and Corrine.

* * *

They were at Berl's Pearls on Eighty-Sixth Street and Lexington Avenue.

"Modecai, tomorrow morning, man, jump to attention soon as you get out of bed—we're heading downtown."

"See you in the morning, Bunny, Modecai."

"Okay, Joe. Glad you saved some butter for later. We're going to ball in the morning, man!" Bunny said.

Joe Crawford was the last musician to leave Berl's Pearls.

"Okay, Modecai, time to get to stepping, man!"

"Don't think I'll sleep a wink tonight, Bunny. No matter how hard I try. I'll probably go back to the apartment and talk to Corrine all night."

"You and that girl been tight ever since—"

"The Paris trip."

"Don't want to open no can of worms, but Delores?"

"Delores—she has a place. But the Paris trip made all the difference in the world for me. It made me face up to a lot of things …"

"Life, Modecai. Life's gotta go on. This space ain't none of ours but for so long no way. Hell, seen it in Paris, why them cats so crazy, wild over there. Dance and drink all night. All about having a good time all the time. French cats smelled death.

"It's in their eyes every damned day. War, it's still living inside them cats. Seen life flash at them, then die, man. Make anybody sick, Modecai. Downright, well, you know."

Yes, Modecai saw it. He saw how Parisians grabbed hold of life, how they gobbled it up. How Parisians squeezed blood out of its veins, understood it, just how splendid and special and magnificent and remarkable it is to live.

Bunny picked up his horn case.

"Tomorrow morning, Modecai, the band's gonna be immortalized, man!"

Modecai arched his eyebrows. "Why, I'm impressed, Bunny. I really am."

"Hell, been listening too much to you. You're beginning to ruin my vocabulary!"

* * *

"Of course, Corrine. I'll make sure I call you before Bunny and I leave for the studio. Of … of course—love, love you too."

Modecai hung up the phone. He sat back on the sofa.

(If there's anything wrong with this scenario, it is Bunny and Modecai bought a telephone—the hall phone was something of the past, a relic even though not everyone in Harlem had the new number. But in time they hoped to put Mr. Clarence out of work … permanently!)

Bunny entered the room in his silk robe and plopped down next to Modecai.

"Jittery as hell. Don't ask me why, Modecai. Shit, I couldn't answer you if I tried."

"Recording in a studio is different than, than performing before a live audience, isn't it, Bunny? Before people?"

"Hell, Modecai, like night and day." Pause. "Just don't like them producers, recording engineer cats fucking with me. Like I said before, they can be a pain in the ass. Think they wrote the music—the shit's theirs, ain't yours. You no longer have claim of it."

"Control, Bunny," Modecai said pejoratively. "Somebody's always got be in control, don't they?"

"Well, they can kiss my black ass 'cause I ain't taking no shit from nobody. I-I don't know about—"

"You don't have to worry about me, you know that, Bunny."

"Man, Modecai, I want this to be fun. A joy. But we ain't gonna get jerked around by Ruby Records or nobody else for that matter. We ain't no monkeys on a string. No lackeys, man. Thank God this shit is happening for us, but I ain't even gonna kiss God's ass, if he's got one, if I don't have to!"

"Bunny …"

"Okay, okay, maybe God's ass—but nobody else's!" Pause.

"But you know what this means, don't you, Modecai? We'll be cutting records like crazy, man. From now on."

"The proverbial foot in the door."

"Hell, whatever you just said, I second, goes double for me. But like I've been telling you, there ain't no bread in this shit, pancakes, just reputation."

"And posterity."

"Pos … what? Hell, help me, Modecai, before I jump off the Triborough Bridge!"

"We'll live on, Bunny. Live on after we die."

"On them records? That black piece of vinyl, unless it cracks."

"Uh-huh."

"I'll stick to immortalized and not that posterity shit, though. Sounds better. Like we ain't dead."

"Who, Bunny Odecai Greensleeves and Modecai Ulysses Jefferson? Dead? Why, we'll never die, Bunny. Never!"

"Nobody's blowing taps for me on my horn, Modecai. That's for sure!"

"I won't let them, Bunny!"

They were indeed nervous. All the signs were there. Both had put a lot into this jazz music, into this business of making jazz. Each new step they took was beginning to take them from being something ordinary to being something extraordinary. They could feel their ride to the top shortening, and the challenges to stay there increasing. Bunny wouldn't have it any other way, but Modecai wasn't so sure.

Bunny stood.

"Gonna give it one more try, Modecai. Gotta get at least an hour or two of sleep."

Modecai was glad about one thing though: Bunny was in his pajamas and not his pants and couldn't twirl that gold-plated pocket watch of his around like he was a licensed hypnotist.

Modecai stood.

"You're right, Bunny. It's worth giving it one more try."

Bunny patted Modecai on the back.

"And don't worry none, Modecai—we're gonna play Delores's tune, man, the one you wrote for her. Them white motherfuckers ain't gonna nix that tune, man. Okay?"

"O-okay."

Bunny went off to his room.

How did Bunny know it was Delores's song he would fight like hell for to make sure it was recorded at this morning's session? But he did know. If only Delores knew too.

Chapter 17

It had rained hard in Way City, Alabama, today, muddying the dirt. Benny had to touch her there. She'd winced.

Why did Benny have to touch her there? Benny knew not to touch her there. The dress, the outfit she wore, hid the marks, the bruises. She was black and blue: her back, her spine—he really hit her. He really teed off on her and hit her.

"Somebody oughta kill the sonuvabitch!" Benny had said. "This can't keep going on," he had said. "You can't let Johnnyboy keep beating you like he's doing, Delores!"

And then Benny touched her again, and it hurt. She winced like she'd felt Johnnyboy's hard, cement hand again.

But she'd had a conversation with someone this morning after Johnnyboy had left the apartment. She knew someone who knew someone. It'd all been arranged. The whole thing was being taken care of. It was seven fifty-two. The person said he'd be in the back alley of Benny's Pit by seven fifty-five when he called her. He said seven fifty-five and it would be taken care of.

Delores waitressed a table. Her face was still swollen from the other beating, not last night's but the one two days ago. It was the entire left side of her face then. It looked like a grapefruit, the size of a half a grapefruit then. Not one of Delores's regular customers passed comment since they knew Johnnyboy Daniels was her man. They knew Johnnyboy Daniels had been back from Foster City Prison for some time, for a number of months.

Delores took the orders. "Benny, Lucas, and Rufus on the Thursday Night Special," she said in a voice just above a whisper.

Her ribs hurt; sometimes she didn't want to breathe.

Johnnyboy wouldn't let her forget Modecai, she thought. He'd never beat her, not until Modecai came along. Did Johnnyboy know about Modecai's letters? *No, he would kill me if he knew. They're here in the restaurant, safe. I would never have gone to New York City with Modecai if … even if—*

He said he'd be of medium height. He said he'd be wearing a straw hat with a black band. He said he wouldn't give a name, so not to ask for one. He said the transaction was to be "quick, short, cash money." He said he didn't live in Way City but knew where Benny's Pit was. He said not to worry; he'd meet her at the back of Benny's Pit.

It was seven fifty-five. Delores sneaked out the side door of Benny's Pit, out into the alleyway. The man was out there.

"Miss?"

Delores had described herself over the phone.

"Yes."

"You got it? All of it?"

"Yes."

She had to walk to him, and even walking that short distance pained her.

The business in the alleyway was transacted. The money wasn't counted by the man; he just jammed it down inside his checkered jacket.

"Better be all there …"

"It-it's all—"

"If it ain't, gonna be back. There'll be trouble. Plenty."

He was as black as midnight.

* * *

Johnnyboy, she hated Johnnyboy, and now she must go home to him.

Delores and Benny were in the back alley and under the light.

"This the time of the night I don't wanna think of—in here, you safe from Johnnyboy Daniels."

Delores held onto the pocketbook's straps.

"Don't know how you gonna be when you come back here from night to night, Delores."

How many times had Benny said this very same thing? As many times as Johnnyboy had beat her?

"Don't worry, Benny, Modecai will write soon."

"Damn, the black sonuvabitch took it all from you. Took any hope of you living decent, a good life."

Delores refused to feel sorry for herself; she was beyond that point.

"What's he do? Wait on you?"

"Benny, I have to get home to Johnnyboy."

"Johnnyboy's gonna beat you tonight, ain't he? He's gonna beat on you!"

Delores looked like she was about to fall down into the muddied dirt.

"No, don't try to hold me, Benny," Delores screamed, slumping against the building's wall. "Don't!"

"He beats you black and blue. What he does!"

* * *

Delores was walking alone; she and Benny had parted company. He was waiting for her, but maybe, in her mind, she was waiting for him this time—for Johnnyboy to hurt her. To beat her. He would find some excuse, but even that, even that—he'd gone beyond even that.

But now she felt protected, no longer standing in fear of Johnnyboy.

If she could see the apartment from where she was, she'd know the apartment lights were on and Johnnyboy was standing beneath them. Delores shuddered. Was this what Johnnyboy had put in her? Delores thought.

"He's waiting for me—oh yes … he is."

She wanted to flee but couldn't. She thought about Modecai—Johnnyboy had chased him off to New York City. Modecai and his piano and his black love notes were there—it was comforting to know. And that Bunny Greensleeves was something else. She'd love to meet him. And the postcard she got from Paris: had Modecai really sent it to her from Paris, France? Paris, France, of all places!

Johnnyboy was waiting for her, or was she waiting for him this time?

* * *

Delores entered the apartment building at 9 Taylor Street in Way City, Alabama.

On the first floor, there was a racket going on down the hall. It'd been this way for some time. New people had moved into the building. They drank, partied, made a racket at all hours of the night every night.

Johnnyboy was waiting for her. He was going to beat her as sure as hell. He was going to beat her as sure as her body was black and blue. He didn't need an excuse, only Modecai. Modecai had made love to her, to his woman. He knew she loved him. He had forced her to confess it to him a thousand times by now, as many times as he'd beat her with his powerful hands

She was on the second floor. Her spine, she wanted to touch it, heal it with her hand, make it holy, give it the sacred power to heal. He'd even hear the key in her hand. Johnnyboy was waiting for her as sure as hell.

She stepped into the front room. She had a light coat on.

"You back, Dee!"

He was in the bedroom.

Since Modecai, all he wanted to do was beat her black and blue and fuck her.

"Come in here! You know what I got waiting for you!"

He would be in his drawers. His brute of a body would be as hot as coal.

She put her coat and pocketbook down on the chair.

"You coming, Dee? Or you want me to fuck your black ass on the floor in there!"

Delores picked up the pocketbook and walked into the bedroom.

Johnnyboy was in dirty drawers.

He was looking at a piece of drumstick he was eating as if it'd rotted his teeth.

He looked at Delores's pocketbook.

"What kind of tips you make tonight, huh? Enough to get your black pussy to New York?"

"Chicken's fucking cold as shit!"

Johnnyboy threw the drumstick at her. It struck Delores.

Johnnyboy leaped off the bed.

"Ain't never seeing that nigger again. Gonna have to kill me first!"

Slow hipped, he walked over to Delores. "But you ain't gonna do that, is you, Dee?" His hand went down inside his drawers. "Not as long as I got big Johnny hanging—"

"Stop it, Johnnyboy!"

"Oughta." Johnnyboy raised his fist over Delores but then ran and jumped on the bed feet first, stomping across it like he could break every spring and crack every plank of wood.

"Fucked that boy in my bed. Johnnyboy Daniels's bed!"

How many times must he say that!

"Good! Fucked my girl good! Dee, Dee … my girl …"

This is what she was used to—this daily diary. Him taunting her.

"Throw it on the bed, Dee. Fucking throw the money, fucking tips on the fucking bed!"

"Here!"

Delores tossed the coins at his feet.

"Take all of it!"

He grabbed up the coins.

"Yeah, pay me motherfucker. Pay me!"

Delores knew who Johnnyboy was talking to: this ghost—

"Pay me, nigger!"

Modecai.

"Pay me for my girl's *goood*-ass pussy! Pay me, nigger!"

Delores turned to go out the room.

"Where you going!"

Johnnyboy pulled down his drawers. His penis was swinging at her. "You and big Johnny here got you a date!"

"N-not—"

"W-what—"

"I want to take a bath first, Johnnyboy. A bath. T-tonight. I want to take a bath first."

"A bath? Like to fuck you greasy, girl. Greasy. Black and greasy. Yeah. Yeah, black, greasy-ass girl. Like one of Benny's greasy pork chops—that old nigger!"

"I …"

"I don't beat you enough last night—that it? I ain't beat you enough last night!"

Johnnyboy leaped off the bed again and began cakewalking.

"Your nigger ever beat you, Dee? Your nigger up in New York, he ever beat on you? Did he? Did he? Huh! Huh!"

"Johnnyboy—"

"I'm gonna beat you, you hear me, Dee! Gonna beat the living shit out you before I fuck you!"

Johnnyboy turned the room lights off.

"Come to daddy, girl. To your daddy!"

Delores could feel his hot breath, what she usually felt first as Modecai must have when Johnnyboy had put his knife to his neck. But it's his fists she heard, not his knife.

"Now I can see you again. Ain't so black. Can see—gonna break everything on you. Why … b-but why you holding that bag like that? Pocketbook? You don't give all of it, do you, Dee? Do you! You don't give me all the money, do you, you pussy-wetting whore! You, you … holding back …"

And it took one blow, and it was as if Johnnyboy had separated Delores's head from her shoulders.

He kicked her.

"Black bitch!"

He moved panther quick.

"Your New York nigger—do he beat on you? Do he? Do he beat on you, on you like me, Dee!"

"No, he loved me! Modecai loved me!"

"Loved you, loved, he gonna make you bleed like a motherfucking river!"

Delores struggled to her feet.

"And, and I loved him. L-loved him, Johnnyboy!"

Johnnyboy raised his hand and knocked Delores back down to the floor. Then her body began rolling across the floor as Johnnyboy continued kicking her with his foot.

"What you got in that fucking pocketbook? Think I forgot? What you—money to visit your New York nigger with! Money to visit your New York nigger with!"

Johnnyboy went for his knife. Now the knife was in the palm of his large hand. "Cut you and that New York nigger at the same time! Kill both of you niggers!"

And it's when the knife swooped down and the gun, coming out the pocketbook, pressed hard against Johnnyboy's right temple, and Delores's index finger squeezed the trigger, repeating it five times.

Three of the five bullets fired out the gun's chamber blew Johnnyboy's brains out his head.

* * *

"Modecai! Modecai! It's the phone!"

"W-what?" Modecai didn't know where he was. He'd wound back up on the couch and then fell asleep.

"Mr. … Mr. C-Clarence?"

"Yeah, yeah, Mr. Clarence—who else!"

Modecai was struggling up to his feet. "I-I guess so, Mr.—"

"Said it's urgent, Modecai, though. Some guy from Way City."

"W-Way City!"

"That's what the man said: Way City."

Modecai was awake and on the run.

Modecai ran past Mr. Clarence.

"Thought when you and Bunny got your own phone, thought you informed folk. Oughta move it down the hall anyways. Damn if I don't get no sleep around here!"

"Yes? Yes!"

"Modecai, Modecai, it's Benny!"

"Yes, yes, I-I know, Benny—"

"She shot him. Delores shot him. Plain done shot him dead. Shot the sonuvabitch's brains out!"

"Who, who—"

"Johnnyboy. Fucking Johnnyboy, Modecai. Johnnyboy Daniel's is dead! S-shot the sonuvabitch in the head!"

"D-Delores …"

"In jail, Modecai. City jail. Po-lice, they take Delores to the city jail."

"Jail … Johnnyboy Daniels? D-Delores?" None of it was sinking in; none of it was making sense.

"You gotta tell me something. Tell me I'm dreaming. Something. T-tell me this ain't real … even though that Johnnyboy get what was coming to him—he fucking deserve!"

Mr. Clarence was closing his door.

Modecai staggered up the hall, his body seemingly sawed into pieces.

"Delores in jail. Delores, *no*!"

Modecai was back in the apartment, his shadow was against Bunny's door. He opened the door.

"Bunny …"

"What is it, Modecai? What the hell's going on, man?"

"Bunny, Johnnyboy, Delores …"

"No!"

"He's dead, Bunny. Johnnyboy, not—"

"He's dead! Not, not—I thought Delores was—"

"No. Delores shot him in the head. She's in jail. The Way City jail!"

"Then we've gotta go, Modecai. Get to Delores, man. To Way City. Down there to—Delores needs you, Modecai. Delores needs you!"

* * *

Modecai was in the bathroom. He ran out into Bunny's room.

"Ruby Records! The recording session. What are we going to do about the recording session this morning, Bunny!"

"Call the cats and cancel it. Straight out cancel it. It ain't as im—"

"We can't do that, Bunny. Me, me—maybe, but not you. You've worked too hard. I won't let you, I—"

"You won't let me do what, Modecai? What the hell won't you let me do! Hell, Modecai, this is life, man. This is real life, man, played in real time."

"I know that, but this is my problem, not yours. This problem walked into my life, not yours."

Bunny walked out his room and past Modecai. He had a small black book in his hand. He was in the living room. He turned on the light. He picked up the phone. Patiently, Bunny stood there with the phone to his ear.

"Joe! Yeah, yeah, it's Bunny, man!"

"Yeah, I know what the hell time it is—I'm up too!"

"Okay … okay. What you want me to do? Why you wigging your skull for, man!"

"Now get this shit, and get it straight, Joe." Bunny paused for he could look back into the book. "Call Abe Meyerwitz in the morning and tell him the recording session is called off. Canceled!"

"That's right, that's right, you heard correct. It's called off—canceled as of now. The band ain't playing. Something came up, just came up, man. Modecai and me ain't gonna be in town."

"Yeah, shit, hell, man, it's all you got to know. And listen, Joe, call the guys, man, and tell each one of them cats the same. Same as I told you: we ain't recording with Ruby Records today. Give them our apologies. Send our regrets. Yeah, our apologies. Apologies."

"No, I don't. I don't know when we'll be back. But me and Modecai'll Western Union you cats."

"Yeah, soon as we know. Don't know how long a trip it's gonna be. Like this can take. Just know we going, Joe. Me and Modecai, man."

Bunny hung up the phone.

"If you need help packing, Modecai, I'm available. Know how you hate packing. It ain't your thing. Okay?"

Chapter 18

The car was rented. The trip was like before when Modecai and Bunny went to Way City to retrieve the piano, but this time, there was no trailer attached to the back bumper of the car to haul a piano. And this time, it wasn't a Studebaker but a Packard.

Fear was in Modecai the whole trip down to Way City, Alabama. His face was fixed in fear. He and Bunny hadn't talked much but thought a lot. Modecai knew Bunny's thoughts were pretty much the same as his. What were those thoughts? A thousand of them, a million of them, as if each existed in the life of the other.

"Passed by the sign, Modecai."

"Yes, saw it, Bunny."

"Remember how to get to Benny's a, a little …"

"The jail—it's on Emerald Street, near Anne Street." Then Modecai looked over at Bunny, disgusted with his ineptitude. "I'm sorry, Bunny, just go straight, man. Straight ahead."

The Packard could move but so fast in Way City, Alabama. The dirt roads were a series of twists and turns and then straight, flat, rugged ground.

"Anne, Anne Street is coming up next."

Bunny couldn't take it anymore—it was like him squeezing a note out his horn and then letting it scream, fill the void with madness.

"I got to know how you feel, Modecai," Bunny said. "Tell me how the hell you feel before I go crazy!"

"It's how I feel, Bunny. Crazy."

"Then tell me, Modecai, for Delores ain't gonna have to see it from you. For you don't make Delores's pain any worse from what it already is."

Modecai pounded his fist on the dashboard. "I've got to be strong, don't I, Bunny? Don't I!"

"Yeah, Modecai! Strong!"

"And ..."

"You can't get into blaming yourself. Moving back the clock, man. Trying to change things. Replace them things you can't replace. Nobody can do that shit. When the midnight hour comes, it's got a date with all of us cats."

And now the rented car rode on Emerald Street, and Bunny saw where they were going without being told. It's why Modecai felt the car's sudden deceleration take grip.

"Delores is in there, Bunny," Modecai said as if he'd just visualized Delores being handcuffed by the Way City Police in the apartment building at 9 Taylor Street and driven there by squad car.

Bunny parked the car.

"Bunny, d-do you think we can pray now, man?"

"Uh, sure, Modecai. Sure ..."

Shortly afterward, the car's doors opened and closed.

"The Way City jail," Modecai said, standing in front of it.

"A man always knows when he's in a rich town, Modecai. But a small town like this, always seems to have an Emerald Street with a jailhouse for colored folk at the end of it."

And into the dumpy, inhospitable-looking place they went, Modecai and Bunny. Bunny leading Modecai. Bunny trying to keep his steps crisp and clear and certain for Modecai would copy him.

"We're here to visit Miss Delores Bonet," Bunny said to the first person he saw.

"Who's 'we,' boy?" the white man asked, his voice gruff, his beard wiry.

"Mr. Jefferson and me."

"Tell by your accent you know how these here southern jails work, boy—even though I see you all prettied up in them fancy big-city slicker duds of yours."

Modecai stepped forward. "I'd like to see her, Miss Delores Bonet."

"That's right—but one visitor at a time. How it goes. Don't gotta give you no lessons in the law, seem like, boy."

Bunny was hot. Modecai grabbed his arm and whispered in his ear, "R-remember why we're here, Bunny. For Delores."

Bunny cooled down.

The jailer laughed.

"Boy get hot under the collar awful quick, don't he? Hot as a black mammy's pistol. Shot him three times, she done. Shot that nigra, uh … uh Johnnyboy three times in the head. He was a bad one 'round here. Bad apple, that Johnnyboy nigra. Bad as poison. Black s-son of a bitch!"

The jailer looked off to his right.

"Billy Bob, sign this here, boy, in the book. Why, he come from all the way up North to down here to Way City to see that Delores Bunet girl. The nigra woman who shoot that Johnnyboy Daniels boy dead in a lover's spat 'tween 'em. The one here," he said, pointing his finger directly at Modecai, "not the one in them big-city slicker duds, boy."

Bunny had just been reintroduced to why he hated a southern white cracker more than he hated a northern white cracker even though he knew each hated him equally.

"Tell him to come on over here then, Bubba. Know I can't move fast as 'em two colored boys."

Modecai walked over to where the yellow pad's pages favored the wall's faded paint.

"Name, address—where you from and all."

Modecai began doing just that.

"ID. Pocket ID, boy."

Modecai pulled out his wallet. He showed the man his ID.

"Look satisfactory, Billy Bob?"

"Uh-huh. Got his credentials in order. Up to date. Boy who he claim hisself is, Bubba."

And for a brief moment, it was as if time had stood still, for Modecai knew what the next step was—he would actually see Delores.

"Okay … then, boy …"

The jailer, Billy Bob, reached for the keys that had a jangle to them, a sound that undid Modecai.

"Come on, boy. Come along. Ain't got all day. You say you want, uh, here to see the nigra woman, don't you?"

"Yes … yes …"

"Hot dammit, Bubba!"

"What now!"

"F-forget to search the boy. Frisk him down for any of them weapons could be carrying him. Concealing him!"

"How you forget—"

"Spread them, boy—for I can see the sun ashining …"

Billy Bob began frisking Modecai, making sure there was nothing Modecai was carrying that Delores could use, maybe aid her in escaping from the pint-sized jailhouse.

The frisking was over. It's then when Modecai looked back at Bunny.

"Modecai, say hello f-for me, man. Tell Delores Bunny Greensleeves sends his best regards."

"You follow me, boy. Nothing more. Hot dammit! How I forget that? Frisk the … search the boy for them weapons concealments!"

How much was there to follow in a small place like this, Modecai thought. His eyes would meet up with Delores's the instant he got to where this short, pudgy jailer was taking him.

Modecai's heart beat insanely when the narrow key went into the rusted lock and the splintered door swung open and back. Modecai wanted to turn away from his midnight hour.

"It don't smell too good back here, boy. Admit. Foul, really foul. Can't do nothing 'bout that. You know how it is—the shit hole's back here also. Ain't for the faint of heart. Jail ain't built that way."

Modecai smelled things that soured his stomach more.

Delores was turning because her body felt Modecai's, and it felt like there was no more pain in it, no more of Johnnyboy's terrible beatings; her suffering had ended.

Delores's eyes expressed her embarrassment, and it did hurt her heart to look at Modecai.

"Miss Bunet, this here gentlemen fella, ma'am, here to see you. Checked him for weapons, uh, concealments—boy come up clean. Gonna step on over, right over here now. Ain't gonna listen in on your conversation, so any—so talk as personal as you like. Ain't got no ear for gossip, ma'am. Got me some scruples my folks raise me with."

Modecai was afraid to look at Delores, but when he did, he and Delores stared at each other in a way that startled them into realizing their reality, that one of them stood outside the cell's bars, and the other inside.

"Modecai, I can't stand this!"

"I've come, Delores!"

Modecai's hands were rattling the bars like a monkey's cage.

"Go away! It's done, don't you see, over with. I had to—"

"Kill Johnnyboy Daniels!"

Delores turned back around to him. Her eyes slanted down to the cement floor. Her jailhouse gown was a dirty brown. Her spine, her back, her ribs (a doctor down the road had patched) did nothing to impair her movement.

"Have you ever killed someone, Modecai? Have you? It hurts all over."

"Benny called me. Did you know that?"

"No."

"But you knew he would."

"Yes."

"Benny, he—"

She was crying. Delores grabbed Modecai's hands. She began kissing them greedily. Modecai wasn't going to stop her.

"I planned it, Modecai. Y-you see, I planned it from yesterday morning on. I, last night, I bought a gun from a man, a stranger." Pause. "If I shot him, I said"—Delores shut her eyes and then reopened them—"I'd spit on Johnnyboy's grave!"

"He beat you, Delores."

"Yes, beat me. Johnnyboy's hand was so hard, so"—Delores trembled—"he …

he kicked me. The things he said, he'd said before."

"All about you and me."

"Yes."

"Dammit, Delores!"

"I love you, Modecai."

"I love you too, De—"

"And now"—Delores broke away from Modecai—"this."

Modecai wasn't used to this arrhythmic pattern, notes being played out of order, sequence. But it was Delores's mind, not notes on a chart, not orchestration.

Modecai smelled the air.

"How can you stand it, Delores? The smell?"

Modecai knew it was the wrong question to ask, so depressing—like it had the power to drag Delores down more.

"Bunny's here, Delores. Bunny came down with me."

"Bunny!"

It was the first time Delores smiled, seeming to forget everything.

"Where'd you find him?" Delores asked, reaching for Modecai's hand.

"I don't know, but—"

"I have all your letters, honey. Benny he, he let me—they were the only things to keep me going. All of your and Bunny's jazz travels. G-going to Paris."

"I tried finding the prettiest postcard in Paris for you."

"I kissed it when I got it, honey." Delores laughed unevenly. "It's like I was there with you. Living in Paris. I never dreamed of a Paris, Modecai. Never—but you were there."

"Yes. Bunny, the band, and I."

"He's dead. I killed him. I killed Johnnyboy, didn't I—didn't I, Modecai? Didn't I!"

Her mind was scrambling again.

"I didn't know it would hurt like this, feel this bad. Killing someone."

This time Modecai kissed her hand.

"Benny, I called him. N-nobody in the building heard the shots. Gunshots. There're new tenants in the building. They make a lot of noise, a racket at night. E-every night.

Nobody heard the gunshots. I called Benny and told him to call the police." Then Delores looked harried. "Benny told me to run. Pack my bags and run—get out of Way City. No one would know the better. Only, b-but I told him no, honey. I told him to call the police—that'd I'd be there waiting for them in the apartment."

Modecai couldn't see Delores on the run either, a fugitive from the law, from southern justice. Neither could he envision that kind of life for her.

He only wished he could change her, transform her back to Delores—get rid of that dirty brown jailhouse gown she was wearing and her badly swollen and bruised face he kept hiding behind his fears and worry, pardoning over and over what, physically, Johnnyboy had done to Delores's beautiful face.

"The piano … Modecai. The piano—how's the piano?"

"Fine, Delores. Fine. I want to—"

"You thanked me enough. Your letters, in your letters. But it was yours, your piano, Modecai." It's the second time Delores had smiled. "It was ours. Your black love notes are made there, from there.

"I-I felt like a jazz musician every time I—w-when I touched it. Polished it, honey."

"You did?"

"Yes, Modecai. I felt what it must feel like to be a jazz musician. To own something as beautiful, lovely as that."

And then it seemed as if time were shrinking on them, for Modecai heard the jangling of Billy Bob's keys.

Delores wanted to kiss Modecai's lips, but then she wouldn't share such intimacy and privacy between her and Modecai with her white jailer.

And now Delores had to know something.

"Modecai"—the pause was long—"have you met someone? Are you seeing someone new?"

Modecai's heart shook in his shirt. What should he do? Say?

"Do you have a woman in New York City, Modecai?" Pause. "You're an adult, Modecai. A man, honey. A grown man."

Corrine, he hadn't even thought of her on the way down to Way City but was thinking of her now. Delores had killed someone. She'd lost herself. He wasn't going to let her think she'd lost him too. No, he mustn't do that. No, he mustn't let Delores's sudden fall be that great or severe or hopeless.

"No, Delores. I have—my music, it's still my music. It's all I can concentrate on right now. I haven't made time for anything or anyone else. There's only time for my music."

And now both heard the fidgeting, the jangling of Billy Bob's keys on the metal ring better than ever.

"Modecai, the smell—the smells back here do bother me."

She's alone. Dammit, she doesn't deserve this!

"I killed him, Modecai. I'm not a killer, a murderer—but I killed Johnnyboy, Modecai. And I'm going to live with it for the rest of my life."

Hearing the sound of Billy Bob's feet on the cement floor, Modecai knew he was heading toward them.

"All right, Miss Bunet. All right then … You and the gentlemen have y'all a good visit?"

Delores nodded.

Delores's hand left Modecai's.

"She's going 'fore the judge tomorrow."

Modecai backed away from the bars.

"Miss Bunet ain't contesting nothing, nothing at all. It's on the record. Uh, the fact that she done it, shot the boy, is you, Miss Bunet?

"Two, three days most, and everything'll work itself out. Court date. Bench trial. Verdict. Sentencing. Plain and simple. Like most cases of this type here do."

"Delores, Bunny and I packed."

Delores's face brightened. She wanted to kiss Modecai, hug him. She wanted to just hold him to her.

"Come on, boy, time to go. Visiting's up. I'll follow you this here time out."

"Oh, I almost forgot, Bunny told me to tell you, hel—"

"Now you 'bout to get yourself in trouble. Trouble, now—said, it's time to go, visiting's up!"

Delores was crying.

Bunny sprang off the wall when seeing Modecai.

"How is she, Modecai! How's Delores, man!"

There had to be shock on his face; he knew Bunny had to see the residue of it still there, Modecai thought. Modecai looked at the two white jailers, the one standing and the one sitting at the desk.

"Yeah, Modecai. Uh, I got all the info on the situation. Court date. Where …"

They were moving toward the jailhouse door.

"Thank you, gentlemen, for your hospitality," Bunny said sarcastically.

"Y'all boys come back now," Billy Bob said, grinning. "Always keep accommodations in the back for at least two more of y'all law-abiding citizens."

"And y'all boys watch your speed 'round here now," Bubba, who was sitting at the desk, said. "Down them back roads. Clock your black asses 'bout every fifty yards down the road, you know!"

"Fucking rednecks!" Bunny muttered under his breath.

Modecai and Bunny were outside the jailhouse.

"Modecai, Modecai, I'm sorry about before," Bunny said. "Man, of all people, me from Mississippi, should've known better. Shit, ain't supposed to show no white man no pain, man. Don't show that white motherfucker nothing!"

"Delores is hurting, Bunny. Really hurting. Just killing someone," Modecai said, looking out into a blank space.

"Even if it was a black motherfucker like Johnnyboy Daniels?"

"Yes. Even if it was someone like him."

They got into the car.

"It doesn't matter, Bunny."

"Delores ain't no killer, Modecai."

"It's exactly what Delores told me, Bunny. It's exact—"

"Because she ain't. Some people can kill. You ain't one of them. Delores ain't one of them … But me and Johnnyboy Daniels, him and me, Modecai, are, man. We can kill."

Modecai knew that.

"Kill a cat quick as he breathes. Takes a fucking breath."

Bunny started the car's engine.

"Where to now, Modecai, in this lame, one-horse town?"

"There's a hotel on Brisker Street."

"Think it's full?"

"Bunny, man, I'm, I'm trying to keep a straight face."

"Just as long as the joint got a phone and hot running water. A shower, man. Got to call Joe. Tell him we gonna be down in this one-horse town a few more days."

"Yes, yes, we must update Joe."

"And see what Meyerwitz says, Modecai. See if them Ruby Record cats up in New York set us up with a new recording date."

"D-do you think Ruby Records will ... will give us a chance, a second chance, Bunny?" Modecai asked innocently.

"Them cats ain't no fools, Modecai. No clowns. They smart as hell. Money, Modecai. Bread. They know how to smell that shit baking. Know the record's gonna sell like hot corn in Harlem on a stick. We ain't gonna make no bread, but the record business ain't about us, no way."

The car was back on the road.

"Okay, Modecai, where the hell'd you say this fancy Way City hotel was in Way City, man!"

Modecai was still trying to keep a straight face.

* * *

Both Bunny and Modecai had bathed. "Getting the funk off the skunk!" was how Bunny had artfully phrased it. Modecai was in the modest hotel room. Bunny was down at the front desk calling New York. *I'm going to have to do that next*, Modecai said to himself.

Corrine. He'd have to call Corrine. But he'd left word with Earlene to get in touch with her, to tell her he and Bunny had to go to Way City, Alabama—but he didn't tell Earlene about the tragedy in Way City. He didn't want to tell Earlene that. Besides, Earlene didn't know about Delores.

How would Corrine react to Delores killing Johnnyboy Daniels? Probably like any woman would: sympathetically. Colored men beat their women in Harlem, beat them everywhere. Colored men were always beating their women. No one said anything—it was just done. And when a colored woman turned on her man, reversed the tables, it was usually violent. It was usually the woman killing the man or vice versa. Delores killed her man; she'd won.

But the cost. Delores had everything, the murder planned out down to the last detail, everything but the cost. The emotional, psychological cost of what she did—killing a man. Tomorrow, in the courthouse, sitting before a white judge, would Delores show compassion or be as hard as stone? Thinking how Johnnyboy beat her, of beating her every day to a pulp. Or would she sit in front of the judge as a martyr for women or as someone who hated Johnnyboy so far down to the core, tract of her being that she bought a gun from a total stranger and shot Johnnyboy three times in the head with it, showing no remorse.

Or would she cry in court, in front of the judge, as she cried in front of him in the jailhouse. This torn person. This torn soul. Someone full of compassion and grief. Someone who had no other person to turn to but herself at a time she most needed someone else.

Bunny burst through the door.

"Lame motherfuckers!"

Now what! Modecai said to himself. What now!

"Don't tell me—"

"They don't want us. Ruby Records don't want us. Don't want to have nothing to do with us!"

"Okay … okay, Bunny, Bunny, calm down. O-okay, calm down."

Modecai grabbed hold of this bouncing bullet's arms, but Bunny broke away clean.

"Gonna regret this shit, Modecai. All the fucking way to heaven. First Big Hat Morrison, that black motherfucker, and, and now these, these lame white motherfuckers!"

"We're not banned, are we, Bunny! We're—"

"Pulled the same shit, lame shit as, as Big Hat Morrison on us. Except, it's just with them. Banned us from recording with them, f-for missing our recording date today. Banned our asses for life, for good … Life, Modecai. For fucking life, man!"

"Oh no, Bunny."

"Don't feel bad, b-bad, Modecai."

"They at least … they probably felt that at … at least you could've been there since it was my personal problem. For the date. You told them that, didn't you, Bunny, didn't—"

"Tell them what? I didn't tell them shit. They don't have to know shit. What happened. Lame motherfuckers. Lame as a crippled duck!"

"It's my fault, Bunny. It's—"

"Ain't nobody's damned fault. Told you back in New York, man. We play this crap game honest, legit. Life's the one who blows on the dice wrong. S-sideways. Shit. Can't run away from life, Modecai. We wasn't gonna do that shit—run away from life.

"Delores needed us. Had to know we were here for her. The shit was no more than what it was, Modecai."

Modecai sat on the bed. He dropped his head into his hands and then began shaking it from side to side. "N-now what, Bunny? What can happen to us next?"

Bunny's hand was on top of Modecai's shoulder.

"Somebody'll pick us up. Some record company's gonna want to record Bunny Greensleeves's Big Band Boppers. Maybe Columbia, Atlantic—one of them labels. We're hot, Modecai. A hot commodity."

Modecai's fingers felt the gruff hair on his face.

"Didn't shave, Bunny. For … didn't shave for Delores."

Bunny wouldn't intercept Modecai's mental state, how he was working his way through his problems.

"I'm, I'm glad Delores said s-she loved me."

Bunny sat down on the bed. He removed his stingy-brim hat and wiped the ring of sweat off his forehead. "Course Delores does, Modecai."

"What's going to happen to her, Bunny, now?" Modecai asked, looking at Bunny.

"Hell, man, these crackers down here! Hell!"

"But she bought the gun to kill Johnnyboy, Bunny. It's what she bought the gun to do."

"Blow that motherfucker away! Blow his fucking brains out his fucking head!"

"It, it was premeditated. Delores, I mean Delores wished it to, for it to happen this way."

"Johnnyboy Daniels would've followed her to hell and back, Modecai. You understand that, don't you? If she would've run from him. Made tracks. But if Delores ran off to you, came to New York, to Harlem, with him chasing her"—Bunny ran his hand back into his back pocket—"I would've cut him. Razored him clean. Cut the black motherfucker straight to the fucking bone!"

"Put the knife away, Bunny! I don't want to see it! It doesn't solve anything! Look where Delores is!"

Bunny closed the knife's blade, seemingly convinced of what he'd said. Bunny bounced up on his feet. "Better him dead than me. Johnnyboy Daniels in his grave, than me!"

Modecai laid his head back on the bed, and then his body sprang forward.

"I-I'd better call Corrine. She's probably home by now."

The fire was still burning brightly in Bunny's eyes as he said nothing back.

"Yes, she ... she's probably home by now," Modecai repeated rockily. "You know, Bunny, it seems like I'm beginning to make Corrine's life complicated."

"Modecai," Bunny said patiently, "you got to stop trying to treat people like you think they oughta lie in a soft bed, man. Corrine had her problems, troubles before you came along. She's got things to deal with. Corrine paints the world she sees, man. We play it. All of us know it." Bunny made a turn.

"Be in my room."

* * *

A big load had been lifted off Modecai's shoulders: he'd called Corrine. Corrine understood everything—what would make him think any differently. She was terribly worried for Delores. Corrine loved his devotion toward her, how he rushed right down to Way City to be by her side. He tried passing it off as nothing, but Corrine wouldn't let him. It almost sounded like hero worship from her, that level of praise. It was the first time today he'd found time to feel good about something.

But tomorrow. Modecai coasted over to the bed. What will tomorrow bring for Delores? The South, southern crackers, southern justice—what did it mean? Today Delores looked like she could serve one hundred years of jail time for killing Johnnyboy Daniels and it wouldn't be enough.

Modecai laid his head back on the bed. It felt funny, him and Bunny separated like this. Him in one room and Bunny across the hall. Bunny asked the desk clerk if he could play his horn when they checked in. The desk clerk said yes, but if the hotel guests complained, he'd have to stop. Modecai was surprised he hadn't heard Bunny play yet, but they'd lost their record contract with Ruby Records today, hadn't they? The past twenty-four hours had been a dark twenty-four hours.

Bunny had to be depressed, Modecai thought, despite his bravado, despite the never-quitting engine running inside him. There were certain things that collide, that hurt Bunny, he was sensitive to—but it was that indefinable something in him that kept him going. He wouldn't shut down the engine, give in to anyone. It was amazing, but now maybe he needed some rest. Maybe behind the hotel's closed door, Bunny had finally slowed down—just let it, everything, all of it drain out his system.

"If only I turn back the clock. Wind it back. Change things. If only—rearrange things. Why … why does there have to be a midnight hour? Things shifting, colliding, coming together, meeting headlong in space?"

If only I could give back to Delores what she had. If only I could go back to Miss Brown's on 12 Mulberry Street. If only I could go back to Benny's. I needed a place. A new apartment. I liked her right away. She said she liked me right away. Why not stay in the apartment building she lived in—why not? It was reasonable, the rent—not too expensive, within budget. It was easy to fall in love with Delores. She loved his black love notes, who he was, what he was—this jazz musician. This hep cat who played jazz. Whose music made her feel good when she woke to it.

"I wrote a song for you, Delores. I would've fought like hell for it, tooth and nail—it would've been recorded, on the album, Delores. Your song. I was going to send the record to you at Benny's. I don't know where you would've played it, but knowing you, Delores, you would've found somewhere to play it … somewhere."

Modecai heard the tune he'd written for Delores in his head. *Maybe if I listen to it, maybe tomorrow won't come. Maybe it will, can postpone tomorrow. Maybe, Delores—then you and I can be free. Free again, like before.*

Chapter 19

The Way City courthouse was old. It gave the stoic appearance to be a sentinel for southern justice within its jurisdiction. It was a dirt-white building, only it looked far cleaner than any other structure in a town as poor as Way City, Alabama.

"Hiya doing, Modecai, Bunny?" Benny said outside the courthouse. "This ain't like coming down for the piano. Is you up to it, Modecai?"

Modecai was nonresponsive.

"Had it coming, but I never thought to think Delores was gonna do it, shoot the sonuvabitch herself!"

"Did you see the man s-she bought the gun from, Benny?"

"Yeah, I seen him. Seen her sneak out to him. Peeked out the window. Don't bother long. Don't make nothing of it. Just think it awful strange, at the time."

"Ready, Modecai?" Bunny asked, taking hold of Modecai's arm.

* * *

Except for Benny, Bunny, and Modecai, the courtroom was empty.

Modecai, Bunny, and Benny had settled into their seats.

Delores entered the courtroom in handcuffs and then was uncuffed by the attending guard before she sat next to her lawyer. Her defense lawyer was short, was in a seedy-looking suit, and carried an overstuffed briefcase he put on top the desk in front of him like he was letting it hide his plump, pink-white face.

While she sat next to her defense lawyer, Delores looked over her shoulder. She looked at Bunny and Modecai, but her eyes remained impassive.

Delores turned her head back around to the front when the judge entered the courtroom. The court clerk called everyone in the court to rise to their feet and then announced the judge to be the Honorable Judge Prescott A. Webster. He was taller than most men and with round, slender shoulders. His black robe hung long and loose on him, almost sweeping the floor. He wore thin-framed glasses and had spoiled skin.

The courtroom was brought to order.

The prosecuting lawyer was a tall, stiff-jointed man who held onto his reading glasses with his right hand while speaking. He was speaking now.

How did Modecai sleep last night, get through it? *I couldn't sleep—I was afraid of the dark last night, afraid of sleep, of waking.*

What's Delores thinking? What must she be thinking? They took all the glamour from her. No makeup. Her hair barely brushed. They're presenting her as a murderer, a primitive black woman, unsophisticated—prone to violence. Never anyone, never anybody, never anything. Someone who was heading down that path, someone who'd shoot her black lover one day as sure as the devil was born and spread seeds of sin across the world.

"Bunny, I'm scared," Modecai said as Modecai watched Delores's defense lawyer now put his stuffed briefcase down on the wooden floor and stand to address Judge Webster.

"The Honorable Judge Prescott A. Webster, sir," he said in his tiny, pinched voice, "my client here, Miss Delores Bonet, will not have me plead her case in your courtroom, sir. She foregoes, uh, waives her Constitutional rights for a fair, deliberate, and impartial trial by her peers—and enters a plea of guilty for all and any charges, all counts filed against her by the state of Alabama for the unlawful death of the now-deceased plaintiff, Mr. Johnnyboy Edward Daniels."

Modecai gasped.

Judge Webster's red face brightened with quickened interest. "Based on the information before me, Mr. Pickens, your client's looking at, facing premeditated murder here, sir."

"Yes, Your Honor, I know full well the circumstance, sir."

"First-degree manslaughter."

"Yes, Your Honor—first-degree manslaughter."

"Now you're sure your client wishes to waive all her Constitutional rights in this case and plead guilty to all charges, counts brought by the state of Alabama and its jurisprudence in ruling on this case, Mr. Pickens?"

"Sure do, Your Honor."

"Would you kindly stand then, Miss Bonet."

"Has Mr. Pickens, here, your lawyer, advised you rightly of your legal, Constitutional right to stand trial before an impartial judge of this court in order to determine either your guilt or innocence in this case of yours, *Delores Bonet versus Johnnyboy Edward Daniels*, before this court, ma'am?" Judge Webster asked slowly, pushing his tall body forward.

"Yes, he, Mr. Pickens, has, Your Honor," Delores replied.

"And you're forgoing, waiving this Constitutional right for a fair trial, Miss Bonet, based on this fact? In favor of pleading to all counts of manslaughter? First-degree murder in the killing of Mr. Johnnyboy Edward Daniels?"

"Yes, I am, Your Honor."

"Well," Judge Webster said, leaning back uncomfortably in his chair, "well … I have no other judicial duty but to enter your plea of guilty, Miss Bonet. For the record. Premeditation, ma'am. First-degree manslaughter."

Judge Webster looked at Delores as if to say I'll give you one more chance to change your mind, but Delores didn't.

"Then you stand as charged by the state of Alabama, Miss Bonet, as guilty as charged for the murder of said plaintiff, Mr. Johnnyboy Edward Daniels on the, the night of …"

Judge Webster continued, until he said, "And so this court is adjourned until ten o'clock tomorrow morning, when I will render sentencing before this court."

Judge Webster rapped the gavel. He rose as well as everyone else in the courtroom.

Delores was taken away. The officer of the court recuffing her wrists.

"Modecai!"

Modecai's eyes had a vacant, faraway look in them.

"Bunny, Bunny, why? She never gave herself a chance, Bunny. Delores never gave herself a chance," Modecai said bitterly.

* * *

Bunny and Modecai had eaten. Modecai's stomach rejected the little food he ate. His stomach couldn't hold any of it down. He felt weak. Ten o'clock tomorrow morning was when Judge Webster's sentence would be meted out.

"It's still warm down here in, in November. N-not like back in Harlem, Bunny. Not …"

"When are you gonna let yourself talk about it, Modecai? Gotta talk about it—it ain't going away, man. Not for one day. Just ain't."

"Why didn't Delores try, Bunny?"

"I don't know why, Modecai. I …"

"She wants to pay the price, whatever it is."

"She doesn't want to get away with nothing, Modecai. Honest to the heart. What—"

"Why didn't I know it, figure it out before it happened? I shouldn't've been shocked." Pause. "If it were you, Bunny …"

"I'd try to get away with killing him! Not lose one night of sleep, a wink, a drop in the bucket. And if I had to kill that black motherfucker twice 'cause I didn't do it right the first time, I would!"

Modecai wanted to laugh at something so absurd but couldn't.

"Ain't trying to put down Delores or nothing like that … But a motherfucker like Johnnyboy Daniels only knows one way to die, and it's the way Delores killed him, with three bullets plugged in his fucking head!"

Slowly, silently, Modecai sifted through his thoughts.

"Redemption, Bunny. Redemption, man."

"W-what's that to mean? Got to do with it?"

"Delores's redemption. Delores making peace with herself and God too. Standing before God for killing Johnnyboy Daniels. Seeking God's forgiveness for taking another human being's life, for her sin—is … is for her not to try, Bunny. For her to turn herself over to man's law and be punished by it."

"Deep shit, Modecai."

"Yeah, it's some deep shit, is-isn't it, Bunny?" Modecai laughed sarcastically.

"Getting to know this damned place. Way City, Alabama. In that damned car. Ain't gotta look for street signs."

"Tomorrow will be our last day in Way City, Bunny."

"Yeah."

"Damn, Bunny, I thought things would have turned out better."

"Hell, she bought the gun. Ain't no doubt in anybody's mind what Delores was planning to do with it."

"Johnnyboy had to be stopped."

"Either cut or shoot the motherfucker. Delores shot him. I would've cut him. Either way, the motherfucker's dead. Six feet under. Pushing up fucking daisies by now."

And Modecai looked out the hotel window and wanted to see clear over to the jailhouse to where Delores was, but it was too far away even in a small city like Way City, Alabama. What a hopeless thought, he thought. What a chump he was to think such a thought, he thought.

* * *

It was Modecai and Bunny's third day in Way City, Alabama. The Honorable Judge Prescott A. Webster had rendered Delores Bonet's sentence as thirty years to life in Foster City Prison.

Billy Bob was standing at his post.

Modecai and Delores were in tears.

"You wouldn't try, Delores. You wouldn't even try …"

Both bodies were bent over. Delores was crying into the back of Modecai's fists that gripped the cell's bars.

"Why try, Modecai? My fate was sealed."

"You could've fought for your life," Modecai said bitterly. "It has to mean more to you than quitting, giving up on yourself."

"I did what I had to do, and no more. I had no right to ask anyone for more."

"But you had every right. You let Johnnyboy take your rights from you twice in your life: while he was alive and now when he's dead."

"I don't care what happens to me!" Her eyes looked dark and cold. "I'm only glad it's over, t-that all of this embarrassment, this humiliation is over with."

Delores pulled her head away from Modecai's clenched fists.

"Southern whites have heard my story before. There's nothing new, Modecai. A nigger beating his nigger woman until she turns on him and kills him."

Pause.

"What's new about it? Three bullets in Johnnyboy's head, not five? A gun and not a knife? Shooting him, not stabbing him? What's new to the story that whites haven't heard before? Tell me!"

"Thirty years, Delores!"

Delores rubbed her bare arm up and down with her hand. "I-I'll be an older woman, Modecai. By then. I'll …"

Delores broke down, her body sinking down onto the jail floor.

"Come here, Delores. C-come here."

"I can't, Modecai," Delores said from the floor. "I stood when the verdict was rendered, when the sentence was announced, but not now, Modecai, not now—don't ask me to stand now."

Delores's body trembled as if the concrete floor were dry ice.

Modecai bent down.

"Have you prayed?"

Delores's hands swiped at her tears, and her pretty black face looked broken, spent, and then perplexed.

"No, Modecai, I … no. I'm afraid to."

"God's forgiven you, Delores. He has."

"How can you say that? H-how do you know? W-what makes you say that? You can't say that, Modecai." Delores struggled to her feet. "You can't speak for God. Stand in his shadow. He's had his say. God's had his say."

Delores was on her feet.

"I haven't lost my faith, Modecai. When they come for me … t-to move me to Foster City Prison, I'll still have my faith."

"But when are you going to forgive yourself?"

"There'll come a time when I'll heal, when God will say it's time for me to. I'll wait for that day," Delores said confidently. "But today I'll …"

"You don't have to explain. You don't …"

"This'll be the last I'll see you, Modecai."

Modecai wouldn't lie to Delores. "F-for a while, but not f-forever."

"No, not forever."

"You'll call me. I gave Benny my new number—he had my old one."

"I can't call out of state from prison, honey. But I'll write. I know your address in Harlem by heart."

Modecai smiled.

It seemed they were at the point of saying the obvious.

"By the way, honey"—Delores's voice was cheery—"have you written a song for … for Miss Tallulah Brown yet?"

Modecai laughed. "No, I haven't, but I'm still trying at it, for sure."

"You know, Bunny Greensleeves is everything you said he was and—"

"More."

Pause.

"Black love notes. It all began with black love notes between you and me, didn't it, Modecai?"

Modecai took Delores's hand. "Yes, it's how it all began."

"You'd make love to me, and then, and then go off and play your black love notes for me. Letting me awaken to them."

"I couldn't sleep the night."

"I know, Modecai," Delores said.

"Those tunes move inside me."

"You're so lucky to be alive with them. To know them."

"Yes, Delores. I am."

"I'll be okay if you're okay. If you keep loving your black love notes, honey—then, then I'll be okay." Pause.

"You do understand, don't you, Modecai?"

"Yes … I do, D—"

"It's our music, Modecai. Yours and mine."

Modecai understood. Yes, he did.

And now Modecai must ask Delores something he'd promised himself he'd ask her, but now it seemed to matter to him more than ever.

"Delores, would you have gone to New York City with me if Johnnyboy, if he hadn't returned to Way City? Come back?"

"I ask myself that very same question every day, Modecai, and I still have no answer. You see, honey, I'm still fighting myself to know, to understand just what my future might have been."

Delores dropped her head.

* * *

"Hope like hell I never see Way City again!"

Modecai and Bunny had just crossed Way City's city line.

"Shoot it and bag it and throw it—oughta play taps for this sad, lame, square-as-Jane joint, man."

Modecai looked up at the sky and thought it looked swollen. Rain was about to come, he could feel it.

"Go ahead, Modecai, cry, man."

"Delores, Bunny, I'm deserting her again!"

"You ain't, Modecai. Life, it's gotta pick up speed again. It's gotta go on."

"I don't want it to stop, Bunny."

"But you can't change it neither. You've been thinking like that too much lately. Shit'll drive you crazy, insane, man."

"So what am I going to do, Bunny!"

"You're doing it now, Modecai. You've still got you business to take care of in Harlem."

"Joe and, and the band, uh, they're going to be, be upset with us, about—"

"The hell with them! Nobody lost nothing in the shuffle but some time. We're gonna make it up to them, though."

"Bunny … how?"

"You'll see. You know I'm full of surprises."

"Come on, Bunny, come on and—"

"Okay, okay, Modecai. Okay, man! Dig this—and dig it big: we, you and me, gonna write us a Broadway show! Like we talked about before. But now's the time, now, man, now!"

"You and me, Bunny? W-we are!"

"Hell, Modecai, hope you ain't hard of hearing, 'cause I know I ain't. Not in one ear or the other two!"

"Broadway," Modecai mused. "Broadway …"

"Yeah, Broadway, Modecai. The Great White Way, whatever they call it. It's our time. Now's the time for it, man."

"Jazz-jazzy tunes …"

"And leggy dames …"

"Yes, yes, I can see it, Bunny. See it!"

"Our names in lights, Modecai. Spotlights. Modecai uh … Jef, uh … uh, no, no, scratch that. Make that uh … uh Bunny Odecai Greensleeves and, and Modecai Ulysses Jefferson! Gotta keep it honest, Modecai. Square to the peg. Since it was my idea, after all!" Bunny giggled.

"Right, right, Bunny, right!"

The car was motoring along.

"Broadway ain't gonna know what the hell hit it. Broadway better pay its electricity, light bill, 'cause Bunny Greensleeves and Modecai Jefferson's lights ain't going out—burn on Broadway all night long, man!"

"Delores will be fifty-six w-when her sentence is up, Bunny. She serves her time. Is finally released from Foster City Prison. Did you know that? W-when they let her out, Bunny, Delores will be fifty-six."

"Yeah, Modecai, you said she was twenty-six, my age, man. Yeah, gonna be fifty-six when they let her out of Foster City Prison. You told me before back in the Brisker Hotel … remember, Modecai, when you said it, man?"

* * *

When Modecai and Bunny got back into the apartment building, it was late Sunday. But still, Earlene had a head in her chair. Her apartment door was wide open. Earlene was like a whirlwind in motion when she spotted Bunny and Modecai.

"Bunny, Modecai, you're back! God bless. Ex-excuse me," Earlene said to the head in the chair, "uh, for, uh, for just a second, a minute, I mean, Francine."

Earlene dropped the hot comb she'd been holding and ran to Bunny and hugged him and Modecai (it was like Bunny'd been swallowed whole by a whale, Modecai too).

When Earlene undid Modecai and Bunny, Earlene went back into her apartment.

"Got mail for you two," she said while handing all the mail over to Bunny.

Bunny and Modecai thanked Earlene. Earlene went back to her customer whose hair glistened about as lovely as an oil slick. Then both made their way to apartment 4D.

Bunny put his suitcase down, and Modecai his.

"Who's gonna do the honors, Modecai?"

"Mmm … let me see, uh, when we came off our Paris trip …"

"You did the honors, man. Put the key in the lock first and hopped in there to see your upright." Bunny chuckled. "Your wood and ivory. Something less than a Steinway."

"Uh, so, I guess it's your turn to do the honors this time around, huh, Bunny?"

"Guess so, Modecai. Since you're keeping count, man, not I."

Bunny inserted the key in the lock and pushed the door open.

"Home sweet home!" Bunny yelled, stepping into the apartment with his suitcase and horn case. "Said it when we got back from Paris, off our trip, and I'm gonna say it again, Modecai: home sweet home, man!"

"Oh, you're just a homebody at heart, huh, Bunny?"

Bunny creased his stingy-brimmed hat with his fingertips and then twirled his gold-plated pocket watch's chain like it had an appointment with time.

Modecai walked over to the piano. He wanted to say he was back, but he knew the piano knew that. But he did want to tell the piano something, but maybe the piano knew that too, what the three-day trip to Way City was about, why he and Bunny had gone back to Way City—what'd happened to Delores, why they were back.

Bunny was going through the mail.

"Mine, mine, mine, yours, Modecai."

Both knew who the envelope was from. A new month was approaching; the monthly envelope had arrived on time. It was always on time; never was it not.

Modecai's chest heaved up and then down. Bunny couldn't help but notice this ritual, this response whenever Modecai held the envelope his mother sent him.

"Ha, Modecai, look, man."

Bunny was swinging his gold-plated pocket watch around the world again.

"Bunny, not even once did you do that down in Way City."

"Hell no, Modecai. Them cats down there're too lame. Ain't never seen gold shine like mine, man!"

Modecai put the envelope on top the piano, not opening it since, apparently, he knew what it was.

Bunny looked at him seriously. "Know you itching to play something. Ain't nobody stopping you."

Modecai sat down at the piano. He heard the metal snaps on Bunny's horn case click open.

"You lead, Bunny. And I'll follow."

"Yeah, okay, Modecai."

They began playing something lean and angular. Something leaning toward the blues, melancholy, out of the way—practically deathly in sound, almost like a morning lament played in the late evening, the close of the day.

Modecai tried not to cry, but his fingers on the piano keys wouldn't let him do anything but. And Bunny, the way he was playing his horn, he, in his own way, loved Delores too.

"Man," Bunny said, snapping out his trance, "let me make some phone calls, Modecai. Around town. Harlem, man."

Slowly Modecai's fingers withdrew from the piano keys.

"Uh … uh, yes, Bunny."

"Gotta get in touch with the guys. Line up some gigs. Hell, step out of Harlem for a few days and cats around here begin to forget where to send your mail off to."

"Bunny …"

"Hell, Modecai, fame is fleeting. Very …"

Then Bunny went back to swinging his pocket watch around the world for a third time.

"Course, nobody's gonna ever forget who Modecai Jefferson and Bunny Greensleeves are, Modecai. We some bad Harlem jazz hep cats, ain't we!"

Bunny bounced over to the phone.

Modecai went back over and picked up his suitcase off the floor. He carried it into the bedroom. He'd call Corrine as soon as Bunny finished transacting band business over the phone. He'd call Corrine then, but now, he felt he could punch the wall's face in. He felt as lustfully violent as Bunny. The piano playing helped but not much. His system was still tight, piled high in anger. He didn't know how to get rid of it, spill it out his gut; but maybe he didn't want to, Modecai thought.

Modecai put the suitcase up on his bed. He unbelted the straps. Bunny played notes on his instrument he'd never heard played before. No, not ever. Notes as delicate as a teacup. Bunny knew sorrow. He'd lost someone dear to him. Delores wasn't dead, only Johnnyboy Daniels, but when the spirit dies—

"I wanted to pray with Delores. Who knows what good it would've done her. But it's all she has left."

Modecai's fists pummeled the top of the suitcase repeatedly.

"I wanted to do more. Damn, man, I wanted to do more for Delores!"

Modecai just stood there empty, as if his body had been hollowed out, his organs itching to die.

It felt good being back in Harlem, but not in this way. Bunny was happy to leave Way City, but not Modecai. He'd found something precious there, and it was still there. When the law enforcement people moved her to Foster City Prison, he would have wanted to follow her there too, not leave her side.

But now this was his hell, the mean face of it.

"Modecai, we're booked from now until the end of mankind!"

Modecai was lying on his bed.

"G-good, Bunny, good."

"Tired, huh?"

"Kind of."

"Man, shit, it ain't been easy on you. I know that shit, man."

"Did I tell you, Bunny, how much that jailhouse stank in the back?"

"Joe's gonna call the guys. If there's any problems with them cats, he'll get back to me on it, as usual."

"Good, good, Bunny."

Bunny leaned his back up against the door frame and fingered his trumpet.

"We got a two-week gig at Pearlie's joint. Then a week at Mister Ed's. And two at the Paradise Club—and they're just for starters. Start tomorrow night at Peaches. Ain't soon enough for me. Call Decca Records tomorrow. Them Ruby Record cats ain't got the only record label in town. To bankroll us. Can't kill a jungle lion with a peashooter, Modecai—gotta shoot the cat with an elephant gun, if you wanna lay him out, kill the cat cold."

Bunny didn't expect Modecai to laugh; he knew the kind of mood he was in, where he was—back in Way City with Delores. But even with this melancholy, this deep wound in Modecai, Bunny had to know something that he knew was affecting Modecai over a long haul of time—something he had been putting off and off, but not anymore.

Bunny walked into the front room and took the envelope off the piano. He looked at it. Maybe he was being selfish, uncaring about this, he thought. But he had to know. This feeling had permeated him, been troubling him and lingering in him for too long. Maybe it would be like kicking a man twice while he was down, he wasn't sure. Kicking the cat farther into the gutter; but maybe, just maybe it would help. Maybe Modecai finally had to square things with himself, needed a quick shot, dose of reality—see the truth for what it was and not be an ostrich whose head was stuck in the sand.

Bunny looked at the envelope again and put down his trumpet and walked back into Modecai's bedroom.

For now, Modecai didn't want Bunny back in the bedroom. For now, Modecai wanted to be alone, to think alone; he'd made this bed of his, and now it was time for him to lie in it.

Oh it was a cliché what he'd just thought, so literal. But he didn't give a damn. He wanted to wallow in misery, his own sorrow. It's one time he wished Bunny wasn't in the apartment with him. He wished Bunny had vanished, him, everything.

But Modecai heard Bunny as he approached his room.

"Modecai, you left your envelope on the upright, man."

Bunny extended his arm to Modecai.

"I-I know, Bunny."

Modecai made no effort to take the envelope out Bunny's hand, so Bunny, he dropped it down on Modecai's chest. It didn't bother Modecai in the least, Bunny's bad behavior.

"It's from your mother."

"I know that!"

"She sends it off to you monthly."

"I know that."

Modecai was getting rankled and Bunny knew it.

"Ain't gonna open the envelope, Modecai?"

"I know what's in it, like you said: it's my monthly money from my mother."

"Modecai …"

"W-what now, Bunny!" Modecai said, rolling over on his right side, as far away from Bunny as possible.

"Y-your mother … she's dead, is-isn't she? Is … ain't, isn't she, man?" Bunny asked the question as softly as he'd played his horn in the front room for Delores—as delicate as a teacup.

Modecai rolled back to Bunny, and there was no more acrimony in him. "Yes, Bunny, my mother's dead."

And right then and there, there seemed to be a load lifted off Modecai's shoulders and out his heart.

"How'd you know, Bunny?"

"You don't write her. Never. Not once. Gotta write her." Pause. "You don't call her. Pick up the phone to call her. Gotta call her." Pause. "Talk about her only when the envelope comes every month. When the money gets to you, you talk about her. Know you love her more than that, Modecai. Got to, man."

Bunny sat down in a chair off to the right of Modecai and leaned forward in the chair for he could hear Modecai's words.

"It's how I kept my mother alive all these years, pretending she sent my monthly money to me, her son." Pause. "She would have, you know. If Momma were alive.

"Momma died a year after Poppa," Modecai said, shutting his eyes. "Do you believe in someone dying from a broken heart, Bunny? My momma did. Charles and I had left home. Momma was alone. She knew she was going to die, so she got in touch with Mr. Webster Bannister, a real estate lawyer, and asked him to rent out our property for the family when she died.

"My mother, she was smart, a shrewd businesswoman."

Bunny smiled.

"When I was contacted and got back to the farm, Momma was dead. Charles, Charles … no one knew where Charles went off to—he'd disappeared. To this day I don't know where my brother is. If he's dead or alive. The money, I get monthly from Mr. Bannister. Faithfully, without fail."

Modecai looked over to his left and picked up the envelope. He looked at the return address on it.

"I asked Mr. Bannister if he would have the envelope's return address inscribed with my mother's name and family's address."

Modecai put the envelope down on the bed.

"This is Charles's money too. I have Mr. Bannister set aside what's equal to mine for Charles." Silence.

"I'm glad you know. That it's over—the pretense and all."

"Don't think of it like that, Modecai."

"Why try to pretend now, Bunny—because it's what I was doing all along."

"Yeah, but it was between you and your mother, man. Shit, ain't nothing as precious or real as that. Something between you and your mother. One who brought you into this world."

Bunny stood.

"Gonna take a catnap, in the mood, man. Think I'll stay in tonight. Do some writing." Bunny had reached the doorway. "By the way, phone's free. Ain't calling another soul tonight. Not even one in a gorilla suit. Yeah, Mr. Graham Bell is off limits to me. Ain't talking into another phone 'til next month."

"Tomorrow then?" Modecai teased.

"Yeah, that way off."

Modecai felt much, much more comfortable. He knew what Bunny was getting at: he owed Corrine a phone call. He looked at his watch; she was probably home by now, painting—the consummate artist. Why did he say it that cynically! he thought.

Modecai leaned over and put the envelope down on the chair Bunny had just sat on. Bunny was smart, so perceptive; nobody could get anything past him. But he wasn't trying, not with his mother. He'd been doing this for so many years it just felt natural to him. He was glad Bunny had found out. Happy as hell.

It was as though he had to find some way to keep his mother alive. It was just in his personality to do that, to deny reality when it was at its bleakest, at its lowest end of the scale; and now, he had to wonder, would he do that with Delores too? Pretend? Pretend she was in another time, in another place.

"I'm like Momma in so many ways. I hold onto my pain. I don't know how to let go of it!"

Modecai was frightened by what he'd just said. His mother died from her pain, from her heartbreak.

"I suffer with pain too. It killed Momma." Modecai looked down at his hands, his skin, and began imagining what it might look like if it were in the state of dying.

Delores, he would suffer with Delores's incarceration for the rest of his life. His body wouldn't be able to reject his pain. It would wiggle through him and make little noise. Burrow in him and bury itself there. Wake him at night when he least expected, at the oddest, most unattractive time. There was no pretense in loving someone too much. There was only honor, and sometimes torture—but never pretense. That, Modecai thought, was too damned smooth and painless and forgettable.

* * *

The smoke's shadow clung against the wall. It was, after all, a fair representation of how smoke actually drifts and exits a cigarette at a slow burn.

Modecai looked away.

"I disappointed you tonight, didn't I, Corrine?"

Corrine's light skin had red in it, like the tip of the Lucky Strike she was smoking. "Modecai, I just want to enjoy my cigarette," Corrine said, puffing on her cigarette. "It's all I want, really wish to do right now, is enjoy my cigarette."

"I'm disappointed in myself."

Corrine's head turned sharply to Modecai. "Self-pity, Modecai? Are, you're going to sit up here in this bed and wallow in self-pity?" Corrine asked.

Modecai brought his legs up under the sheets and blankets. He held onto them. It's when he rocked himself.

"I know what you're going through, Modecai." Corrine's voice was less harsh.

"Do you? Really?"

Corrine's cigarette dangled from her bottom lip. Then she took it out and put it on the side of the ashtray.

"Delores is in jail because of me."

"It has to cut deeply, that I know," Corrine said. "You have to feel her pain."

"Every night. Every day it's the same."

"Our relationship was growing. Sex between us was becoming so much better, Modecai."

Modecai stopped rocking himself.

"But tonight … sex between us didn't work, Corrine."

Corrine took a puff off the Lucky Strike and then extinguished it.

"When will this damned nightmare end?"

Corrine slipped out of bed.

"You know what, I think I'd better go," Modecai said. He got out on his side of the bed.

"Y-you don't have to, Modecai." Corrine said, turning back to Modecai.

"N-no, I-I think I'd better."

Modecai's clothes were on a chair; he began hustling them on.

"I want to apologize, b-but I did want to be with you tonight. I honestly thought things would work out better than this. What they have."

"Do you think you'll ever forget her?"

"I don't know," Modecai said, gripping his hands like they'd been plagued by crippling pain. "I know nothing about this thing that's consuming me. That I'm fighting."

"No, you wouldn't."

"May I call you later? On the phone?" he asked from the door.

"Uh … yes, of course. I don't see why not."

Corrine walked over to Modecai and kissed his cheek. For an instant, he held her slender body to him.

"Good night."

* * *

Modecai was in Harlem's cold. Would he ever get used to this kind of cold? He thought. He had his hat on and his overcoat (every button on it was buttoned), and the coat's flaps stood straight up as tall as rabbit ears.

Modecai laughed; he wished there was a tin can in the street he could kick. But he realized it was going to take much more than that to shake him out his funk. This was the fourth night since Way City he'd been in this kind of deep, dark mood. He and Corrine finally got together. He'd been postponing it, but tonight he invited her to Pearlie's and one thing led to another, and before he knew it, he was making love to her but failed: he couldn't get an erection. No matter how hard he'd tried—and Lord knows did he ever try—he couldn't get an erection.

Modecai's body continued to fight the wind like it knew it was going to win in the end.

It was a shock to him and then it wasn't—he was forcing things. He was trying to end something that had just begun. He was trying too hard, thinking too hard. Everything was Delores. Seeing her the way he did in Way City, in that jailhouse, with the smells and those kind of nigger haters. This would be her life: putrid smells and putrid people. All of it rotten. This is what Delores would wake up to each morning and go to bed with each night. This would be her life for thirty years. No wonder he was buried inside himself. No wonder he felt like he was a prisoner—looking ahead to a stretch of thirty years to life in his life.

Modecai had reached home. (It was debatable who'd won: the Harlem wind or Modecai.)

"You're always my solace, my comfort, aren't you?" Modecai said, sitting down at the upright piano. "You're always here for me. Unconditionally," Modecai laughed. "Like a mother. A mother's love."

Modecai didn't care how corny it sounded, because it was the right thing to say. His piano was like that, a mother's love.

"You let me express myself in the simplest of ways, don't you? Y-you let me uncomplicate things, my mind, make them clearer for me. I don't want to forget Delores, but in some way I have to. Momma died of a broken heart. It scares … still scares the hell out of me."

Modecai paused.

"Maybe when Delores and I write. Daddy was dead. He couldn't write Momma. Daddy was never going to come back to Momma. Delores and I will write. Will correspond." And then Modecai's eyes focused in on his piano.

"And then there's you, isn't there? I'll always have you. You'll always be here for me, won't you?"

Chapter 20

Bunny clapped his hands like an alarm had just sounded in the apartment.

"Modecai, I've decided, man: we're gonna have to get ourselves an agent! Tired of busting my hump every day!"

It was Sunday; they'd just finished eating breakfast.

"Ain't gonna be able to sleep at night though—them agents steal you blind, man!"

"I've heard all the agent stories too, Bunny. All I ever want to hear."

"And every single one of them is true," Bunny said disgustedly, pushing his plate away from him. "On the square. Ain't a lie in the batch." Pause.

"Gotta keep one eye on them and one eye on your mattress. Them agent cats got the bread spent before it's even baked good in the oven."

Bunny sat back down.

"So when do you think you'll start looking, Bunny?"

"Soon, Modecai. Got some feelers out now. Gotta be a white cat, though. Hell, colored cats know the same cats I know. Ain't gonna be a dog chasing his tail, man. Running around in circles. Besides, used to the white man stealing from me," Bunny said with a mean glint in his eyes. "Make me hate his white ass more!"

Bunny jumped back on his feet.

"And the only way we're gonna get downtown to Broadway, Modecai, is to dig down in them rich, fat white cats' pockets, man. Gotta get them to ante up the bread. One white cat knows how to talk to another white cat when it comes to money. Moola. Ain't gonna listen to no colored cat when it comes down to that kind of money, dough, Modecai, loot—kind we're looking for.

"If the show closes, don't want to think a colored man brought them down. Ain't their style. No colored cat's gonna do that to them, only their own. Bring them down."

Modecai got up from the kitchen table.

"It's never going to change, is it, Bunny?"

"Uh-uh. Not in this lifetime or the next, or the next. Like our music, Modecai: ain't nobody's gonna play it like us *but* us. Was born playing it. When you're used to something, grow up with it that way, hell, Modecai, I gotta say more?"

"No, you—"

"Modecai, haircut time," Bunny said, his hand brushing through his wavy brown hair. "Think I'll go down to the shop and let Little Phil snip and clip while I watch them fine ladies of the church pass by. Ain't nothing like church in Harlem on a Sunday morning. Hats, furs, and religion, man—in that order."

Bunny went and got his topcoat. Bunny was about to put it on, when Modecai took it out his hands.

"Here …"

And Bunny slipped one arm in one sleeve, and the other arm in the other.

"Thanks, Modecai."

Modecai's hand brushed the back of Bunny's coat.

Bunny stretched his brown leather gloves over the top of his hands.

"Mustn't keep them church ladies waiting." Bunny winked. "The Lord won't let me."

"The … n-no, you mustn't do that, Bunny."

Bunny saw this hollow look in Modecai's eyes. Lately, it would come and go.

Bunny knew why it was there.

"Just keep thinking of Broadway, Modecai. One day …"—Bunny spread his short arms out a mile wide—"one day them billboards gonna read …"

"Modecai Jefferson and—"

Bunny's elbow bumped Modecai. "Now don't start no shit, Modecai, not on Sunday morning!" Bunny brought his short arms down.

"It's gonna be great, man, soon as we get us a white agent to handle our business and them white backers with the cabbage—we're gonna be the baddest jazz cats on Broadway. Gonna have a long running show, hit," Bunny said, opening the apartment door. "Five, ten years running …

"Oh, hi, Earlene."

"Oh, hi, Bunny."

"Just wait and see, Modecai. Just you wait and see, man!"

Bunny was down the flight of stairs and, by now, out of sight.

Modecai was standing in his door frame and Earlene hers.

"Hi, Modecai."

"Hi, Earlene."

"I'm between heads."

"Oh. Where's Big Booty?"

"Down at Little Phil's."

"Oh …" Modecai grinned. "He'll probably bump into Bunny then."

"Wonder who'll win that collision," Earlene joked.

Modecai began drifting down the hall; he was in the mood for conversation.

"How's it going, Modecai?"

"Oh … fine, I guess."

"I mean between you and Corrine, honey. If … if I ain't overstepping my neighborly boundaries or nothing like that."

Modecai thrust his hands down in his pockets.

"I mean I did introduce you two," Earlene said maternalistically.

"Why you did, didn't you, Earlene?" Modecai answered pleasantly.

"So if there's something wrong in Paradise—"

"You'd want, be the first to want to know."

"Uh-uh, it ain't that, Modecai. It's—I-I really love you two."

"Well, speaking for me, and I'm sure Corrine, too, we really, really love you too, Earlene."

"I don't bring you up with Corrine in conversation when she comes for her hair—but I know something's wrong between you two. That something ain't right right now, Modecai."

"It's something all lovers go through, I guess, Earlene."

"Tell me about it, Modecai. Tell me about it, honey!" Earlene said, slapping her hefty leg hard with her hand. "Have had my share of romances, Modecai. Ups and downs in the romance department. Don't let this hair business fool you—Earlene's been busy as a beaver, baby! I ain't tangled up in colored women's hair all day long like I make it seem. Uh-uh."

"I know you have, Earlene."

"Love me some colored men, Modecai. Ain't about to tell you different. Love me some colored men!"

Then Earlene glanced down the hall and then back at Modecai.

"What's Bunny up to now?"

"Bunny, Earlene, oh, Bunny? Broadway, Earlene. Broadway. Bunny and I, we're working on the billing, that's all."

"Heck, get off it, Modecai: you know good and well who's gonna get top billing."

"Bunny!" both said then laughed in unison.

"One day you're going to make it to Broadway, Modecai. If Bunny says so, you will."

"We're going to give you front-row tickets on opening night, Earlene. How's that? Uh, you and your date, that is."

Earlene smiled.

"Ain't I gonna have somebody wash, set, and conk my hair on opening night, Modecai—besides me. Ain't I though!"

"You bet, Earlene!"

Modecai was making his way back up the hall.

"And things, honey … they're gonna work out between you and Corrine, fine, just fine, Modecai. Turn around. Give it time. Been in that slump before. You two just hit a snag, like you said, like everybody does—that's all, honey."

Modecai was back in the room, feeling trapped, knowing the mail wasn't delivered on Sunday. Benny, two days ago, over the phone, told him to have patience. He said he'd driven to Foster City Prison to see Delores. Benny told him Delores was doing okay, that she was adjusting to prison life.

"But how can, what's the address I can write to her, Benny, for Foster City Prison?"

"Not now, Modecai. Delores said she don't want to hear from you for now." "Why, Benny?"

"She's gonna write you, Modecai. Delores said she wants to do the first writing."

He couldn't recall what he said to Benny, but he was upset; his insides were all messed up. All he wanted to do was write Delores, it was all. He … but then he thought about it. It was he who wanted to give Delores strength, solace, provide her with some kind of spiritual strength. But then he realized that maybe it was Delores who was trying to find her own strength, who could best understand what was happening to her, explain it in better words than him.

It was Delores who was looking at thirty years in front of her, who had to make the days blend so they could become seamless, touch her tomorrows. It was Delores who had to find a balance, make do. It was Delores who couldn't count the hours, the minutes, the days, who had to lose track of them, discard them as if they didn't exist and then regain them as if each day counted, were golden—the end just down the road, around the corner.

It was Delores who had to do this. It was Delores who had to do this. Not him.

Not him.

Modecai was looking out the window, looking down on Harlem streets on a Sunday afternoon. The mail wasn't delivered on Sunday (not even up in Harlem, Modecai laughed). But tomorrow, or by the end of the week, he hoped he'd hear from Delores. He wanted to hear from her. He was eager to know how she was doing, and he wanted to write back to her bad, real bad, as bad as before.

* * *

Weeks later.

"Modecai!"

Modecai'd just stepped out the bathroom. Bunny had just burst into the apartment. "Let's dance, man! Rumba, fox-trot, cha-cha, don't matter!"

There was a towel wrapped tightly to Modecai's waist.

"Bunny …," Modecai said effeminately, "but I'm not dressed, darling!"

Bunny slapped Modecai's hand away. "Probably can't dance no way. At least I ain't seen you after all this time. Months. Probably got no rhythm. Probably Lindy Hop like a chicken."

Modecai laughed too.

Bunny was swinging his timepiece in front of him a mile a minute.

"Man, I never should've bought you that watch. It's proven to be the death of me. My downfall!" Pause. "Well … are you going to tell me or not!"

"Done it, man!"

"What, get—find an agent, Bunny? Booking agent?"

"No, uh, ain't found that white cat yet, but …"

Bunny's eyes teased. "But …"

Modecai's hands pleaded with Bunny for more.

"But found a white cat who just might produce a show for us, a Broadway show if the cat likes what he sees, hears."

"Wow … I, uh, I mean to say you … you did, Bunny? You did!"

Bunny's chest puffed out.

"How, how, Bunny?"

"Never mind the details, Modecai. I'm working in the margins, man. You know I know people who know people who … Hell, never mind the damned details, man." It's when Bunny's eyes became dreamy.

"Just think, Modecai, we're gonna be on the gravy train soon. Riding it. In the sauce. Like … hell, I told you, Modecai, this cat's gonna skip right over Fifth Avenue on that monopoly board and land on Park Avenue."

"Yes, only Park Avenue for you, Bunny."

"Hell, Modecai," Bunny said, winking at Modecai, "don't worry. I'll rent you out a room. And it ain't gonna be the servant's quarters—I ain't that cold!"

"When, Bunny!"

"When do we meet with this cat? In two days."

"Two days!"

"Hell, what you want, Modecai? Time to collect gold dust in your pockets. Two days!"

"No, no, not that, but …"

"We've got to get our tunes together. Presentable. Be like a, one of them, uh, Uh …"

"A résumé, Bunny."

"Yeah, that's the word I was after. Gotta have everything in tip-top order. Gotta hit the cat like a Jersey Joe Walcott jab!"

"Bunny, I—"

"You ain't dreaming, Modecai. We ain't dreaming. No, no, man. Promised you Broadway. And now I'm delivering on my promise—today."

Bunny scooted into the front room.

Modecai scooted into the bedroom and began dressing.

Modecai was halfway dressed, when he paused and the thrill of a Broadway producer, this person Bunny had found like a needle in a haystack, eased from out him. *Delores, will I get a letter from Delores today?* She still hadn't written him. Benny hadn't called him. There was no one to update him, bring him up to speed on things.

"Should I wait?" Modecai asked blankly. "I must respect Delores's feelings."

But every day he looked for that one letter from Delores. He didn't even know what her handwriting on paper looked like. But he wanted to know—God did he.

And when he got Delores's letter and he wrote back, he would have this good news to tell her about him and Bunny being Broadway bound.

Modecai buttoned his shirt.

"But maybe I-I won't tell her—I don't know. Delores is in prison. She's in prison."

No! Modecai protested vehemently. *No, I won't let Delores dampen my spirits. No! No! I'm not going to let her stand over me like a ghost.*

And then Modecai calmed down. *Delores isn't trying to dampen my spirits. Delores wouldn't do that. She'd lift my spirits. It's just my feelings; they're ambiguous, jumbled, all over the damned place.*

He had to get back in the room with Bunny. Listen to his sparks fly. See them.

Hear them. Let them light his eyes. Listen to more dreams and more possibilities. Listen to how to paint tomorrows with a beautiful brushstroke. Hear how special they are, how they make things grow wild and unexpected.

"Good, Modecai," Bunny said, sitting over a stack of sheet music. "Pulling out some of my best tunes out the stack, man. Best you get busy on yours too."

"S-some of your catchy ones?"

"Yeah, them showgirl numbers. Leggy dame numbers."

Modecai walked over to his stack of music sitting on the floor and pulled up a chair.

Bunny looked at him. Modecai's face was contorted.

"Don't know which sweetheart to choose, huh, Modecai? Pick out the rose garden?"

"How'd you guess, Bunny."

"Modecai, ain't easy leaving one in the stack, when you love all them cats equal. Meant so much to you at the time you wrote them. First laid down them tracks."

"Blood, sweat, and tears, Bunny," Modecai laughed.

"Joy too. Can't leave that shit out in the cold. Making love to a woman. Sweet love, Modecai. Picked out four so far," Bunny said, eyeing just that one stack of music—there were more.

"How many do you think we should carry with us?"

"Oh, hell, no more than say ten. Yeah, ten should do us just fine."

"Does this guy, uh, producer person, uh, does he know how to read music, Bunny? D-do you know?"

Bunny looked at Modecai like he had sixteen eyes. "How the hell am I to know that, any of that? This cat's got the bread, moola, the green stuff, the enchiladas, the—"

"I get the picture, Bunny. Bunny, believe me, man, I do get the picture."

"You're nervous, Modecai."

"It was a dumb question."

"Because you're nervous. Nervous as hell—who wouldn't be? But who the hell cares if the cat can read music or reads the *Amsterdam News* in his drawers at breakfast over coffee for that matter, as long as the cat's got the bread. The green cabbage, man!"

"You know, Bunny, I-I promised Earlene front-row seats on, for opening night."

"Damn, Modecai—no, I didn't!"

"W-what did I do wrong?"

"That means we gotta do the same for Big Booty too then, that's what!"

Modecai hadn't thought of Big Booty and Broadway.

"Damn, man! Four seats. That means four damned seats, Modecai!"

"How do you figure that, B-Bunny?"

Bunny bounced.

"How … you want to know how, Modecai? Two front-row seats for Earlene's big booty and two for Big Booty's. That's how. Just hope their big butts don't bust them four front-row seats on opening night on Broadway, man!"

Nope, Modecai hadn't thought about that at all, but Bunny had (even though Modecai hadn't told Bunny about Earlene's date yet, uh, making it, actually, five front-row seats overall, Modecai thought—not unless, uh, he had a big booty too!).

Chapter 21

Two days later.

There was another stupendous surprise in the Bunny Greensleeves, Modecai Jefferson household that Modecai didn't know about, for Bunny had (seconds earlier) cornered Modecai against the front room's wall like he was being mugged in Central Park by a crazed, furry-tailed squirrel. Trembling, perspiration was popping off Modecai's forehead. Modecai could taste his breath. Bunny had told him to shut his "pretty brown moons," then dashed out the room.

Now what was Bunny up to? What bunny was he going to pull out his hat this time? Bunny, who was up-tempo twenty-four hours a day, up-speed, on a fast track, only knew one speed. Who couldn't brake the A train, the express train, unless it might run off the track, or jackknife? That Bunny, Modecai thought. That hep jazz cat.

"Man, you look like something a cat'd find at the Salvation Army and reject. Wouldn't pack in his suitcase. Damn, man!" Bunny said now back in the room.

"Well, whatever you're doing, I hope you hurry up," Modecai said, tough-guyish.

Bunny cleared his throat as if there were an orchestra rumbling five minutes before curtain time.

"Modecai, on behalf of the Bunny Greensleeves's Big Bopper's Band and me, I'd like to present you with … *this*!"

And from behind Bunny's back came a briefcase, but not just any briefcase but a snakeskin briefcase.

Modecai was at a complete loss for words.

"One for you," Bunny said, "and one for me!" He pulled another snakeskin briefcase from behind his back. "We're going downtown today, Modecai. Ain't about to carry our tunes in a cloth sack, Jack!"

"Uh, Bunny, our briefcases aren't exact—"

"Never mind," Bunny said, handing Modecai his new briefcase. "Everything's first-class, Modecai. No second-class mail today, man. We're traveling first-class all the way!"

Modecai was staring, not looking at his new briefcase. His fingers felt it, how rich and fine its grain was.

"Man, Bunny. Man."

"And don't say they set me back some change," Bunny said, eyeing his.

"'Cause I already got me a nervous stomach with an ache in it. Banging it like a drum, man."

"No, I wasn't going to say that."

Modecai couldn't take his eyes off his brand-new handcrafted briefcase—not quite yet. Already, he was busy transferring his sheet music from his leather briefcase to his snakeskin one.

"Them tunes even sound better already, Modecai, don't they? Now?"

"Yeah, Bunny, yeah …," Modecai said like a Harlem nocturne.

Bunny and Modecai's downtown business engagement with this producer person was for one o'clock; it was twelve twenty. Bunny ducked into Modecai's room.

"Right on schedule," Bunny said, looking at his pocket watch. "Not a minute more or a minute less, man."

They walked into the living room to obtain the one last thing that would complete the ensemble.

Modecai picked up his snakeskin briefcase with his tunes in it, and then Bunny went and did the same.

"Feel like rich chocolate, don't it, Modecai? Like the mayor of New York City's tipping his walking hat at us. And his walking cane's tapping, making beautiful music.

"Ready, Modecai?"

"Been, Bunny."

"Then let's set sail to Wonderland and meet up with Alice and them seven dwarfs."

"Uh … Bunny," Modecai giggled, "I think that was Snow White and the Seven Dwarfs you're referring to. If I'm not mixing up my fairy tales."

Cavalierly, Bunny brushed aside Modecai's insistence on historical correctness.

Bunny bounced down the building's steps with Modecai following closely behind him.

They'd gotten a joyful send-off from Earlene, who wished them good luck and said "Broadway" about a hundred times.

"It's like I smell daffodils in the air, Modecai. In winter."

"Bunny, uh, uh, let's not get carried away today. H-how about it?"

"Hell, easy for you to say. You ain't meeting the mayor today, I am."

"We are going to the same place today, aren't we?"

"Don't know, Modecai, might decide to dump your black ass in the Harlem River! And drown you! Don't know yet …"

When they got to the street corner, Bunny stopped, but Modecai kept plowing ahead.

"Hey, uh, Bunny, aren't we—"

"We ain't taking no subway downtown today, Modecai. Alice don't ride by train. Chick and them seven dwarfs only ride downtown by taxicab. How the fairy tale goes."

Then Bunny placed his two fingers to his mouth and pressed his lips.

Tweet!

And a yellow taxicab suddenly appeared as if Bunny and Modecai were somewhere inside a fairy tale.

"SEE!"

"Bunny, how—"

"Hell, Modecai, don't ask me how," Bunny replied, just as amazed. "Just get in the damned cab, man, and fast, before the cat starts the meter. It runs hot!"

"So where to, pal?"

"Fifty-First and Tenth, and step on it!" Bunny chortled. "Push the pedal!"

Modecai and Bunny slapped hands, giving some skin, gleefully.

* * *

The taxi was moving at a good clip but stopping at red lights along the way, of course.

Modecai was as relaxed as anyone could be who was about to meet a potential Broadway producer.

"Are we almost there, Bunny?"

Bunny acknowledged Modecai's edginess.

"Don't worry, Modecai, you know I'm gonna do all the talking, man. Anyway. All you gotta do is sit in the corner like a mummy. Think you can do that?"

"Bunny, I-I have to say something, something to the man. While I'm there."

"Yeah, 'hello' and 'good-bye' in that order. All the other stuff in between, leave to me."

"You said Fifty-First and Tenth, right, pal?"

"Yeah. It's what I said."

"'Cause we're here with bells on."

"Hell, man, I knew that!"

Bunny reached back for his wallet. "How much we owe you?"

Bunny pulled out a ten spot.

"Hell, man, know it ain't more than five bucks. Keep the change!"

"T-thanks, pal. Thanks!"

The taxicab driver got out the taxi and opened the passenger door for Modecai and Bunny.

Modecai thanked him, but Bunny looked at him as if he could have done more.

Modecai and Bunny were on the corner of Fifty-First and Tenth.

"Is this it, Bunny?"

"No, Modecai, where we want, it's up the street. Farther up."

Modecai wondered why Bunny didn't let the driver drop them off in front of the building they were going to but soon realized why when he and Bunny began walking up the street that retained no deep, dark secrets, no mysteries laid open for interpretation.

The warehouses lined along Tenth Avenue sat dirty in the daylight—looked old and scruffy. The cold day making them as friendly to look at as a landlord nailing an eviction notice to a front door at midnight. Immediately Modecai felt his expensive handcrafted briefcase was out of place, shrinking in his hand like some sick trick a joker in a deck of cards would cook up in his darkest, most perverted dreams.

But the taxicab driver had to know how ruined looking, decayed this section of Fifty-First and Broadway was—he knew this street. But Bunny still walked on it with his head held high in the air, still out to slay the proverbial dragon, to lay the golden egg—still smelling the daffodils. Modecai kept stepping with him, stepping with him, stepping with him.

Bunny stopped and pointed. "This is the place, Modecai. This is where all our dreams are gonna come true, man. The dream factory. Ain't it sweet!"

If Modecai ever felt at odds with Bunny, for Modecai, it was now. If ever he felt Bunny was sprinkling gold dust when it should be table salt, it was now. If ever he wanted to quit this silly, preposterous adventure, for Modecai, it was now. Modecai's stomach felt queasy.

They stood outside the heavy wooden, windowless door. Bunny pushed the rusted button at the side of the door.

"Who is it?"

"Bunny Greensleeves and Modecai Jefferson."

Buzz.

Bunny pushed open the door and he and Modecai entered this thing that looked like a warehouse that should've been condemned by the city, or closed, but someone, instead, tried converting it into an office building (cash under the table, a sweetheart of a deal—bribe).

Right away Modecai felt his shoes getting dusty and his nose practically plug up.

And within seconds, two big guys with two big heads (one apiece) and shoulders to match opened the two doors that had to be opened in order to really get around, seemingly, decently in this place with the dusty floors, dim lights, and air twisting like a pretzel in a person's breath.

Bunny winked at Modecai and then cupped Modecai's ear with his hand. "Service, man!"

They went through a series of juts and turns (they'd stayed on one level of the many-leveled building) until these two bigheaded cats turned and looked at Modecai and Bunny like they hadn't eaten since Christ's Last Supper.

"The boss is in there!" the one said, saying it like he had snake food trapped inside his esophagus. The other bigheaded person slid back the heavy wooden door.

And the office, in this dusty pit bowl, was as clean as a pocketful of snowflakes. And the cat Modecai and Bunny were there to meet, this Broadway producer, kingmaker, who sat behind his tall desk and looked about as small as a mouse begging for a chunk of cheese, grinned at them like he'd just swallowed a big, fat alley cat out his cereal bowl for breakfast.

He was clean. He was in stripes (his suit, that is). And when he swung his chair off to the side, Modecai saw his pointy brown-and-white shoes (wing tips), which he quickly sensed could pop open a dream or deflate one—or anything else that might get in their way.

His voice was petite like a little princess; his hair, black and shiny. "Sit, gentlemen, sit." Pause.

"Thanks for coming down this afternoon. Hell, see you was on time too!" he said in his chirpy voice, looking up at his two employees who loomed over Modecai and Bunny like a dark night wearing brass knuckles.

"Can't strike up the band, not till the bandleader appears, Mr. Byerman!"

So that's his name, Modecai thought. It's funny he'd never asked Bunny this potential producer's name.

"Bunny, right?"

"Right, Bunny. Bunny Greensleeves."

"And you can drop the formality, Bunny, hell, and just call me Stuckey."

Bunny smiled like a bird of paradise in his yellow canary suit. "Yeah … yeah, Stucky."

Stuckey Byerman looked down at his pointy brown-and-white leather patent wing tips. He could stick someone with those shoes and they'd go *pop*!

Stuckey Byerman reached for a finely wrapped cigar from the opened burgundy cigar box. He snapped his short fingers, which elicited both employees to light the cigar on command when the cigar reached his pursed lips. Byerman puffed on his cigar until smoke puffed out his mouth like a smokestack. The room got full of dark smoke like a black cloud had rolled in from Kansas.

"Smell like hell, taste like heaven, "Byerman said, flicking an ash into the spit-clean ashtray.

"Them Cubans grow the best tobacco leaves there is." Byerman's eyes took in his Havana cigar in his hand admiringly. "There ain't no comparisons to be made." Then he pointed downward in what seemed to be a well-practiced routine. "Thumbs down!"

Then Byerman's eyes wandered over to Modecai. "You the silent one, I see. See them two beef-a-ronies?" Byerman said, casting his eyes on them. "One's silent as a fish, and the other one yaks as much as that duck uh … uh that Disney duck … uh … uh Daffy Duck, when there ain't nobody around. Can't shut the guy's freaking trap."

Neither one of Byerman's employees batted an eyelash, threw off a clue, so Modecai didn't know which was supposed to be like him and which one like Bunny.

"Guess you gotta keep balance in the relationship, huh, to keep the cylinders clicking?"

"Hell, don't worry, Stuckey, Modecai can talk for himself when the cat has to," Bunny said, glancing over at Modecai. "Modecai Jefferson ain't no shrinking violet."

"Me, I ain't got no partners." Stuckey Byerman took a healthy puff from his Cigar; he ran his hand over his slick hair. "Ain't gotta answer to nobody but me. Like it much better that way. That way you get to play the game by your own rules, not yours and somebody else's. Get my drift?"

A new, fresh smoke ring eased its way into the air.

"Hell, but you boys ain't come all the way down here to listen to Stuckey Byerman yap about his philosophy about things that ain't got nothing to do with why you come all the way down here from Harlem by subway to—"

"Wasn't subway but taxi, Stuckey—to set the record straight."

"Oh, pardon me, shit—by taxi, fancy-smancy taxi then, Bunny—to discuss business with me."

Bunny lifted his snakeskin briefcase off the floor and put it on the tip of his knee. Modecai's briefcase remained on the floor.

"We's here to discuss music, strictly music—Broadway. You gentlemen is jazz musicians, cats who put music in our ears."

"Yeah, cats who put music in your ears," Bunny said, "and your feet too!"

"Oh, pardon me, shit, Bunny—in our feet too. Gotta have dame numbers in a musical show. Them Cotton Club dames got some, *some* damned pair of stems!"

Bunny giggled. "Prettiest legs in the world, man. Them can-can chicks' legs in Paris, can't match them Harlem chicks' legs, right, Modecai?"

"Uh, right, right, Bunny."

"'Cause we've been there, to Paris. On the continent. Me and Modecai. Me—"

"So what you boys got? What you bring me in them, uh, them fancy-smancy snakeskin briefcases of yours? That must've set you boys back a penny. A pretty penny. Boys carried downtown here from Harlem."

"Brought you some of our show tunes, man."

"By the way, Bunny, you boys got a name for your Broadway show, huh?"

"No."

"Gotta theme? A storyline? A plot?"

Bunny said no to all three of Byerman's questions, and then he looked at Modecai again.

"See what I told you, Bunny, about partnerships."

"Hey, man," Bunny bristled, "you ain't gotta worry about Modecai and me. We on the same vibe. We're square to the peg, man!"

"Of … of course, Bunny. Of … of course, I ain't implying no different. You got all the angles figured. Covered. Ain't no clapping penguins. Square, yeah, square to the peg. Uh, on the same vibe."

"Yeah, man," Bunny said under tighter control. "Me and Modecai dance the Monkey. It don't dance us."

"Ha. I-I like that, like that there. Ha. D-dance the monkey, it … it don't dance you. Ha. I like that, Bunny. Like it a lot," Byerman continued laughing. And when he stopped laughing and his grin stayed wide and open, broad, Modecai could see the crooked teeth in Byerman's mouth.

"Yeah, Bunny, it's gonna be a great show, man. Great! One of a kind. Like I hear you play your trumpet: one of a kind. The greatest trumpet player on Earth. The greatest trumpeter in the world. World's greatest trumpeter. Broadway, Broadway won't know what the hell hit it!"

Bunny reached down inside his briefcase.

"This is what I brought you to listen to, man."

Again Bunny looked over at Modecai, overtly urging him to do the same as him.

Modecai was reluctant to, but when he did, whereas Bunny'd pulled out all of his tunes in the briefcase (ten), Modecai only pulled out three of the ten he had in his; and of the three tunes, Modecai knew exactly which three they were.

Bunny looked around the room for a piano.

"What you looking for, Bunny?"

"A piano. Ain't you got a piano, man? Something me and Modecai can play on. Bang our tunes out on. For you can hear … hear them?"

The tunes were on Byerman's desk, the ten of Bunny's and the three of Modecai's. Byerman was thumbing through them.

"These here songs are gonna be great. See you and Modecai's signatures on them, Bunny. Down on … uh, fat, big-as-a-swoll thumb, so I know they ain't second-rate. There's some gentleman I hire who'll play them through for me. Ain't short on thumbs!"

"Hey, man, the cat can't play them like us: they're our tunes!"

Byerman stood. "Calm down, Bunny. Calm down. It's how show business is …

Broadway and all that jazz," Byerman said like he was about to break out in a slow dance and shuffle down Broadway. Then his hand slid over for the Havana cigar in the ashtray.

"Now either you're in this with me, for this, or you ain't. Either you trust me on this here or you don't. I run a legit business," he said, puffing on his cigar. "I ain't got to cut nobody's throat, steal rings off a corpse." Byerman looked back down at his pointy shoes.

"You came to me, remember? Don't forget. It's my money you wanna use for me to stake on this here future enterprise, operation of yours with." Pause. "Then if so, you got to do business my way. My accountant pays the checks, Bunny. Attaches alla them pretty fat zeroes to the end of them fat checks."

Bunny's bounce reappeared.

"Hell, man, I just want me and Modecai to get to Broadway. The Great White Way, man."

Bunny looked down at Byerman. This was one cat Bunny was taller than and whose physique, in street clothes, looked five times more powerful than.

"Me and Modecai ain't looking for no handouts. Bargains out the bin. If you and them other backers put up the bread, stake it, you got a right to call the shots." Pause. "But don't fuck with us, man, or any of our tunes. 'Cause me and Modecai gonna play the game square, square as we can." Bunny took a look at his and Modecai's tunes lying out on top Byerman's desk.

"We gonna play the game the way you cats want us to, Stuckey, not unless you cats change the tune, mid tempo. Not unless it turns sour on us. Then, man, there's gonna be all kinds of hell to pay. Then it ain't gonna be Bunny Greensleeves, the world's greatest trumpet player but one angry black-ass motherfucker who's gonna cut your little white ass right the fuck into tomorrow morning!"

"Hey, Bunny, hey," Byerman said, looking at his two employees with the big heads and big shoulders and then taking a few steps over to Bunny and patting him on the back.

"Ain't nothing going down the pike, turnpike, like that there. Ain't no consideration. I respect the hell outta what you got laying there on my desk. I respect the hard work you and Modecai, here, your partner, done with your music," Byerman said, his eyes snaking over to Modecai. "Ha. You boys ain't come all the way down here from Harlem by taxi, like you said before, for you to kiss nobody's ass. I know that there. And your reputation preceded you, Bunny: you ain't no motherfucking low-ass ass kisser. I know that, Bunny."

"Yeah," Bunny interjected, "you can take that bread and bake it in the bank!"

"I know your reputation."

"Mine and Modecai's."

"Yeah, yours and Modecai's. Told that Big Hat Morrison motherfucker to take a fucking dip in the pool, didn't you? To take a fucking flying leap!"

Modecai wanted out of this place. He wanted out of this warehouse with dusty floors in it except for this room, this back section of the building as clean as white wax.

"Yeah, you're my kind of hep cat, Bunny," Byerman said, returning to his cigar and puffing it. "I-I ain't gonna fuck with a cat like you. A-a bad black cat like you," he said, again looking over at his employees.

"So I got your number and you got mine, right?"

"Right." Pause. "No need for you calling me before breakfast though," Byerman said, breaking the silence, "'cause I'll call you."

Stuckey Byerman blew some big, fat, black smoke rings in the air.

"We're gonna work good together, you and me, Bunny," Byerman said, sticking his hand out to Bunny. "Real good together."

Bunny shook Byerman's hand enthusiastically.

"Them dames—chocolate, brown babes on Broadway. Ha …"

"Prettiest damned legs in the world, man. Fuck them Radio City Rockettes' legs, Stuckey! Fuck them!"

"Yeah, fuck them Radio City Rockettes' legs, Bunny. Fuck them!"

Byerman stuck out his hand to Modecai. Modecai shook it.

"Thanks for coming down, boys."

"So when we gonna, me and Modecai, gonna hear from you, Stuckey? By phone?"

"Uh … oh … give me uh … give me no more than two weeks on this here, Bunny. Music, here. And lining up backers for this here Broadway show of ours.

"Uh, any more than two weeks, and it's a crime, gotta be a crime, Bunny," Byerman said, looking back down at his pointy shoes. "An absolute crime."

"Ready, Modecai?"

"Uh, you can see these two gentlemen here out."

"Yes, boss," came the response from who was probably the talkative one of these two moveable bookends.

"Thanks again for coming all the way down from Harlem, boys."

To Modecai, Stuckey Byerman's voice sounded like the rest of him was waving to him and Bunny, but he wasn't going to turn back around to find out. He and Bunny just held onto their expensive, new handcrafted snakeskin briefcases with his partially full but Bunny's empty.

"And don't forget to tip the cabbie on your way up to Harlem, Bunny—ain't a bad idea. Fucking two-bit scumbags!"

* * *

Tweet!

The taxi stopped at the corner of Fifty-First and Tenth. Modecai and Bunny hopped into the taxi.

"Where to, pal?"

"Harlem, my good man."

Then Bunny went to say just where in Harlem.

Bunny put his briefcase by his side on the backseat.

"Ha."

"W-what, Bunny?"

"Man, I can see Broadway in my horoscope, Modecai. Like a gypsy looking into her crystal ball. Crystal clear. Sign hanging from a star."

"You know, Bunny …"

"Lookit, I know what you're gonna say, Modecai, before you say it. Lookit, met worse cats than that cat back there in that warehouse setup before. But if the cat got the bread, then, shit, I'll be the motherfucker's goddamned boy for now."

Pause.

"Ha . . ." Bunny laughed again. "That was like some fucking gangster flick, wasn't it, Modecai?"

"Y-yes, it was."

"Goons."

"Goons?"

"Yeah, Modecai, they call them bigheaded freaks, cats Byerman got, pays at the end of the day, out his stash, goons. Do all his damned dirty work. Just like in them gangster movies we watch."

"Yes, I know," Modecai said anxiously. "Yes, I, why, yes—I-I forgot, I don't know how I suddenly—"

"That little pipsqueak ain't gonna do none of the shit himself. Blow on that little motherfucker, and he'll quiver like a feather, man. Only thing that cat could whip is a half-gallon of whipped cream in a bowl." Pause.

"Well"—Bunny's look was serious—"I don't like this no more than you, Modecai. Want to puke up on Byerman too. Sitting behind his desk. But it's gotta be this way for now. I ain't missed nothing that happened back in Byerman's office. Not a thing."

"I know it does, Bunny."

"Hell, I ain't letting my guard down. Ain't a fool in Paradise—ain't nobody's errand boy."

"But this is reality, isn't it, Bunny?"

"Yeah, Modecai."

"This is how deals are cut and made." Pause. "Yeah. I was the agent we ain't got yet in there. Cutting a deal. Negotiating for us. Business first. I mean I let Stuckey Byerman know where I was at, not even think about fucking with our tunes. Gonna be hell to pay.

"But then, Modecai, after that, man, I gotta follow the rules—"

"Like everybody else does, would, Bunny."

"Like all the cats do, yeah, Modecai."

Modecai was working his way out of his worry, his personal hang-ups.

"Well, you did great, Bunny. Just great, let me tell you, back there!"

"Yeah, man, I know how to talk to them Broadway producers. In their language. Know their lingo from *a* to *q*, Modecai."

"Like, like a King Oliver solo," Modecai laughed.

"Same damned way, man. Outdress them cats too."

* * *

Bunny was taking the flight of stairs two steps at a time. Modecai was taking his usual one.

"Hurry up, man! It'll be midnight soon!"

"Coming, Bunny. You know I'm not in the kind of shape you are."

"Piano players. Still glad you ain't a trombone player."

Modecai was still trying to figure that one out but, as always, couldn't.

And so the Bunny strut was on exhibit big-time. Bunny started down the hallway like he'd laid a golden egg.

"Oh no you don't, Bunny Greensleeves. Not by my door, you don't!"

"Don't you have a head in the chair to conk, attend to, Earlene?"

"Bunny ..."

Earlene came charging out her apartment with her hot comb in her hand full steam.

Modecai had gotten on the fourth floor's landing and was in the hallway and began cracking up.

"The Lord's gonna strike you dead, Bunny Greensleeves. I swear. If you pass by my apartment door without telling me the good news!"

"See," Bunny said, turning back to Earlene, "you already know the good news, Earlene!"

Earlene turned to Modecai sweetly.

Modecai winked and flashed two fingers as a victory sign.

"Two front-row seats on opening night, Earlene."

Earlene swooned, she and her pretty dimples. "Seriously, seriously, Modecai?"

"Seriously, Earlene."

Earlene was melting as fast as hot butter on steak.

"But just you, Earlene. Nobody else," Bunny shouted down the hall. "Not for that big butt brother of yours, Big Booty. Not for that big-booty cat, man!"

Earlene shook her fist at Bunny like she was going to knock him into next year. "I'll settle that score with you later, Bunny, Bunny

Greensleeves. You know you gotta pass by my door on your way out your apartment!"

"Not unless I jump out the window first!"

Modecai laughed during these verbal gymnastics between Bunny and Earlene all the way up the hallway.

When he got inside the apartment, he put his overcoat where Bunny'd put his, on the couch. Downstairs, Bunny'd taken the mail out the mailbox. He was going through it, as usual—the regular routine.

"Mine, mine, mine …"—and then Bunny paused for a long time—"yours," Bunny said quietly. "Y-yours, Modecai."

Instinctively, Modecai was sensitive to the shift in Bunny's voice.

Bunny handed Modecai the envelope. Modecai's heart began beating faster and faster.

Bunny looked at the back of Modecai, for he knew where he was going, to his bedroom for privacy.

Modecai wouldn't turn on the room's ceiling light, use the light switch.

Modecai was going to read Delores's letter under the night table's lamp. Modecai was floating as if on a cloud or on a stream. He sat down on his bed, switched on the table lamp, and lifted his leg off the floor, bending it ever so comfortably on the bed. Modecai was ready to do this. He'd waited so long, so patiently.

> Dear Modecai Im not going to start this letter off like Im on vacation because Im not. Im in prison. And Im not going to apalogize to you for not writing sooner simply because this is the earliess I could write you. This is hard. You know this is hard. Hard for you hard for me. Prison life is hard Modecai. Im not going to dress it up. I want to be honest. Like Ive always been about everything else. If I can put sumthing nice in this letter I will. But whatever I say I need to. And I want to say these things to you honey. To you and only you because you know what Ive been thru more then anyone else does. Its my mother thu Modecai. Shes the one I have not told whats hapened to me. That Im in Foster

City Prison. Ive been sent off to prison for murdering a man. Shes a Christian. But yes of course you know the details. I told you. I told you about my mother. How my mother raised me. I dont know what to tell her Modecai. How to tell momma Im in prison. That I killed a man. Really my lover in cold blood. How would you tell your mother. The days in prison are bleek. Its hard getting along with anyone so I keep mossly to myself. Thinking about the passed is good and then sumetimes not. Its bad. It can turn on you as well as help you. Sumtimes that happens. I cry a lot. Cry when I leass espect it at times. I don't want anybody to see me cry because Im supose to be tough. Its how I want them to think of me. The gards and the immates. Its how I protet myself. The immates know Im in here for murder. Killed a man in cold blood. In order to protet myself I have to pretend to be this tough black bitch all the time. I think Im going to write momma soon. Maybe tonight. Who knows. Im getting stronger. Stronger and stronger. You are the firss person Ive writen. Im going to write Benny hes been the bess freind anyone could have. I love you Modecai. I love you. I guess thats what keeps me going in here. At leass I like to think it is. I know Im fooling myself. People around here the ones who have been here a long time say you have to have sumthing on the outside to hold onto to keep you going on the inside. Guess well honey I have you. I guess Ill always have you. I don't know if itll make this prison any easser but then not much I dont think can do that. Modecai its time to say goodby. The letter Im going to end now. And when you write me back try not to feel sorry for me. This letter is depresing for you I know but dont let yours be to me. You are living life up north in Harlem. You and Bunny are chasing after things. Really going after things. Let me know all about it. Everything weve done and sacraficed together has been worth it. Its what

> I can hold onto. Its whats mine and yours inside here Modecai. Ill write to let you know about momma in the ness letter. Momma will write back I know she will. Love honey Delores

Delores's letter was sticking to Modecai's hand and shaking like fly paper.

"What do you want from me! What the hell do you want from me, Delores? I'm only human!"

This musician thing, always this musician thing. This thing that rises above everything else, above life's transactions, defines life better than life. *No*, Modecai thought, *I still have to live. There's still blood running through my veins. I'm still human. I make the kind of music I make because I feel everything, Delores. How can you deny me that? Expect so damned much from me!*

You're in prison. You're behind prison bars. I went to see a hood today who was posing as a Broadway producer. I gave him a little of my music, Delores. Bunny gave him a lot. He's a crook, Delores. An out-and-out crook. Bunny knows he's a crook but we're hoping, Delores, hoping for the best.

It's how free we are, Delores. Bunny and me. We make deals with crooks. We give them respectability because they have money, so they can call the shots any way they want. So they can operate, steer the dream, make it turn left or right—if they want. Make it work or not work.
"Damn, Delores. Damn. It-it's what I'm supposed to write about … about crooks, gangsters, g-goons? It's what you want to know about in the letter!"

From the desk, Modecai tossed the letter off to the side of the bed.

"I'm no better off than you. But I'll hide it. I'll disguise it l-like I did from Bunny and Earlene in the letter. I'll put a good face on it, Delores. I'll pretty it up for you. Dress it up in high heels and platinum blond wigs for you.

"Is it that you want? It's what the hell you want!"

Modecai fell onto the bed and rolled on top it and then stopped. He was flat on his back and remembering what he felt was a horrible day. A day filled with terror.

He didn't like Stuckey Byerman. He wished he'd never met him. He wished he and Bunny hadn't gone into that awful warehouse today. He wished it was an agent, anyone but him and Bunny to do it for them. He wished. He wished …

Modecai looked down at his still-dusty shoe tops.

* * *

Bunny was in the living room. What did Bunny expect? Why, to see Modecai soon, very soon—that's what.

He had to laugh about Stuckey Byerman today: the cat played the game to the hilt, to the nines, he thought. Told him he knew about Big Hat Morrison and that Fifty-Second Street shit. Today, he and Modecai were only one block away, south of Fifty-Second Street.

"Yeah, I could go after Big Hat Morrison, but it'd be just another nigger for them census cats to count. One more nigger left dead on a Harlem street."

Bunny went into his back pocket and felt what was back there—mean and steady and nasty and patient. "Kill me a colored man, sure. If I have to. Kill me a black cat. Ain't no sweat off me, my brow, man. Shit. B-but I've been looking at them white cats all my life killing off what's mine. What belongs to me. I-I …"

And then Bunny could see his knife slitting open a man's throat. And the man didn't have to have a face, just the color white. It's all. Blood was oozing out the cat, red as a red carpet covering a living room floor wall to wall. Red as swine's blood. Red as a sunset.

Bunny's hand let go of the knife handle. He could still feel its pulse and his own blood curdle. He could feel it like when he hit the high notes on the horn and what seemed the whole world applauded, fully understanding what he'd done like he'd made some pact with the devil.

Bunny turned his eyes into the kitchen, and what he saw, who he saw, was expected. The letter had come, hadn't it? Bunny thought. Modecai would write Delores as Delores had written him. Modecai had bought new stationery paper a few weeks back. He'd kept it out, wrapped it in plastic. It was visible; he'd seen it. Modecai still had the other stationery, the one he used for Way City. But now everything was different. Now everything was new and different for Modecai: Delores was in prison.

Modecai sat down. He looked up at the ceiling light. How do I begin this letter? was the question Modecai asked himself. He stretched his arms the length of the table, and then his hands gripped each side of the table. His body was tense as he began a review of the day in his mind a second time. Bunny, Earlene, Stuckey Byerman, goons—Broadway. And then Modecai thought of Delores and how ironic it was that it was prison that gave Delores the freedom to write him a letter, her first letter to him. Foster City Prison, but not before in Way City, Alabama, when Johnnyboy Daniels was alive.

Chapter 22

Two weeks later.

The bedroom lights flashed on.

"Two weeks on the calendar is up, Modecai!"

"Bunny …," Modecai said, rolling over to his right side of the bed, "have you gone crazy!"

"Two weeks, Modecai. That cat's had our music for two weeks!"

Then both of Modecai's eyes popped open. "It's … it's two weeks already?"

"On the nose," Bunny replied, touching his. "Right on the snoz, button, man!"

Modecai began to unwind and then propped himself up on the back of the wall like a rolled-up carpet.

Bunny was snazzily dressed. He flashed a piece of paper and recited the numbers by heart, like he was blindfolded. "Two, five, one, eight, six, two, four."

Modecai struggled to see the time on the clock. "Bunny, it might not be the wisest thing for you to call him, uh, Byerman at this hour, hour of the morning, man."

"Hell, Byerman should be up." Bunny frisked his fingers. "Counting his loot. His fucking scratch like a cat!"

"Only thing you're going to get at six twenty-two in the morning is—"

"Is a dead phone on the other end, huh, Modecai?"

"Right, Bunny."

Bunny's bounce slowed.

"It doesn't feel like two weeks."

"But it is, could count it backwards in my sleep."

"He did say he'd call. S-Stuckey Byerman, that is."

"Yeah."

"Well ..."

"I ain't sitting around for the cat to call me, Modecai, 'cause I'm gonna call the cat myself this morning."

"Not now though, Bunny."

"Uh-uh, not now. But when the clock strikes ten, Modecai, the white motherfucker's gonna be hearing from Bunny Greensleeves!"

* * *

It was a few minutes before ten o'clock. Bunny was pacing the floor in front of the black telephone in the front room.

Modecai was dressed. He was sitting at the piano composing, lost in thought and circumstance and, what seemed, time. He was hearing stuff, things he'd never heard before. Harmonics he'd never heard before. They were sliding through him and guiding him. They were perfectly packaged and pitched and arranged. And all he had to do was listen to them, this music of whispering angels and faint sighs and lovely—

"Time's up, Byerman! Yeah, motherfucker!"

Modecai turned, was shaken out his trance.

"Bunny, it-it's time already?"

"Yeah, Modecai. Byerman's time's up," Bunny said, grabbing the phone. "Time to hear how his ... his little puppet-sounding voice sounds like again. Ain't heard it in two weeks. Cat's voice better sound sweet as sugar and brown as maple syrup."

Bunny's eyes focused in on the numbers on the paper he was holding, and he repeated them aloud one by one.

"Two, five, one, eight, six, two, four ..."

Modecai watched Bunny's handsome face, the light skin and the curly brown hair atop his finely shaped head. And even while rattling in anger, Modecai thought, there was still this stunning *something* always in Bunny's face.

"Bunny, Bunny ..."

The phone had dropped out his hand. "T-that, that ...," Bunny stammered, his head seeming to be reeling, "that motherfucker. That little, little white-ass motherfucker!"

"Bunny, what, what—"

"White-ass motherfucker! White-ass motherfucker! White-ass motherfucker!"

Bunny looked at the phone; it was dangling. He looked confused, bewildered, infuriated, disbelieving. "It's disconnected, man. The phone's disconnected. The motherfucking phone's disconnected!"

Modecai's heart sank—the worst had happened. The one thing he'd feared.

Bunny was only temporarily distracted, disoriented, sidetracked—for he charged to the closet and grabbed his coat and hat.

Modecai leaped to his feet.

"The motherfucker's mine, Modecai! That little motherfucker!"

"No, Bunny, *no*!" Modecai said, flinging himself in front of Bunny. And even though Modecai wasn't near as physically strong as Bunny, he offered Bunny resistance. "You can't go down there!"

"Can't go, then try stopping—get out the way, Modecai. Get out the fucking way before I lay you out. The hell out, man!"

Modecai saw that look in Bunny's eyes, the way they'd look.

Modecai stepped aside.

Bunny ran to the door.

"It's my dream too, Bunny."

Bunny stopped in his tracks. "What you say? What'd you j-just say, Modecai?"

Modecai's back was to Bunny, so Bunny couldn't see his face.

"I said it's my dream too."

"Yeah, yeah, I know that, Modecai," Bunny said, releasing the doorknob.

"It was shady, Bunny. From the start. All of this. T-the building. The warehouse—I mean. The location. The dust on the floors. The …"

"Yeah, it's what you wanted to say in the taxi, wasn't it, Modecai? But I stopped you. Put my twist on it."

"Like I said, Bunny, it's my dream too."

"Yeah … all my razzle dazzle, man. All my strutting and … and peacocking, showboating, man."

"Bunny, don't do that. You're Bunny Greensleeves. It-it's who you are."

Bunny looked down at his shoe tops. "Yeah, yeah, I guess so."

"It felt like a setup, Bunny. I-I know I don't know anything, much about these things, but if anything ever felt like a setup, that did."

"Yeah, the little pea-ass motherfucker!"

Modecai chuckled.

"More reason to—"

"To what! What, Bunny? What? Because I know what you're going to do. I know what's in your back pocket."

"To—"

"Wind up like Delores! Is that it! Do a thirty-to-life stretch in prison!"

"I ain't Delores. Don't think that shit. Prison don't scare me!"

"Right, right, b-but who's going to play Bunny Greensleeves's horn? Who's going to do that!"

It's when Bunny looked over at his horn case and froze. He straight out froze. Modecai looked at it too. It was there on top the piano, the trumpet in its case—for now, unengaged.

Bunny felt the urge to go to it, so he did. His eyes brushed over it for a few seconds, and then he opened the case. *How many times have I done this?* he thought. But now nothing could be compared to it, this feeling he had. Bunny fingered the valves.

"Me and you, man. Me and you," Bunny said to the gold trumpet. "Come a long way together."

"He's not worth it, Bunny. Stuckey Byerman."

"Damn!" Bunny's anger had rebounded. "I had mean intentions, man. Nasty, real nasty intentions."

Bunny put the horn back in the case.

"B-but the cat's still got our tunes, Modecai."

"I know he does. But what can he do with them, when he can't even light his own stinky, smelly cigars!"

"Modecai, I don't know about you these days!"

Modecai slipped his hands down inside his front pockets.

"Let's just chalk it up to experience, what do you say, Bunny? As young as we are, huh?"

"Still like to …"

"Can't get to Broadway without you."

And even though Modecai had said it insouciantly, his heart meant every word.

"Ain't nothing gonna stop us, Modecai." Bunny paused. "That cat thought he was slick. White-ass monkey! But he ain't gonna be the monkey to stop this show. Uh-uh, not us."

Bunny walked over to a stack of music, which was building up off the floor (looked like an untamed jungle).

Modecai walked over to the stack of music which was building up off the floor (looked like an untamed jungle).

"Getting there, ain't we, Modecai?"

"Sure are, Bunny."

"Ha, down that road." Pause. "Do need us a name, though. The cat was correct on that score. Rang the bell."

"Right, Bunny, a name," Modecai said, scratching his head.

"Can't get a Broadway show on the boards without a name. Something catchy, jazzy, snazzy—make your heart pump oil!"

"Right. Right, Bunny!"

"And a story line, Modecai. A script, man. You're good with words. Shit, you're damned good with them. You can write out a script. Something pretty with a lot of pretty words in it. Cool. Pretty. Hep. Sublime."

"Right, right, Bunny."

"Broadway, man! Broadway. Close your eyes, 'cause here we come, ready or not, man. Here comes Bunny Odecai Greensleeves and Modecai Ulysses Jefferson—ready or not!"

"Right, right, Bunny!"

"Except, next time, I'm gonna find me the right cat. The right white boy t-to come up with the dough. The bananas. Write the checks. Ain't walking into no more warehouses, another one, with dusty floors—shit make me sneeze … Ahhh … Ahhh … *choo*! Dust up my shoe tops, Modecai. Cost too much for me to get Big Booty to shine them, plus the cat laying his big-ass mitts out for a damned tip? Cat's outrageous with his big-booty self, man. *Outrageous*!"

Modecai laughed and a kind of nonchalance swept over him. A kind of laid-back, satisfied look sat on his face.

But Bunny was looking at him. Bunny had Modecai in his crosshairs. "Hey, what you doing, man!"

"Uh … me, uh—who me?"

"Yeah, you!" Bunny said, thumping Modecai's chest. "Get busy. Back to what you were doing. Back to Broadway business. I shouldn't have to tell you that shit. We ain't getting to Broadway with you standing there like a lamppost. You got work to do. A whole lot of work. The music, the script …"

And so Bunny began rattling off things at first with his fingertips as digits to count on, and then his toes. Modecai was going to be one busy jazz cat according to Bunny's take on things. One busy jazz cat in Harlem!

* * *

Why was Modecai running so fast on 116th Street? A song, what else. A song had come into his head and heart, as usual. Something he had to get back to the apartment to put down on paper or possibly lose it. He couldn't take the chance, not with the melody rushing at him like a big, fabulous tidal wave. Not on your life!

He'd just had his first date since the "incident" with Corrine. They went to an art museum. They hit it off like ham and eggs. They were trying to lift off the ground again. It's like they had hit this bump in the road; it had stalled them, but today, it felt to him like they were back trying to recover what they had had—see just what lay ahead for them.

In fact, they'd had sex at Corrine's place. Modecai had no problem with an erection or with enjoying sex with her—none whatsoever. So he was more than upbeat about that.

And as for Delores, three weeks ago he did hear from her. She said she was adjusting to prison life, that things in Foster Prison had improved for her. And she'd written her mother and said the good thing, what really lifted her spirits was her mother had written her right back. Her mother said she understood what'd happened to her in Way City with Johnnyboy Daniels. Her letter said God would forgive her. She said her faith would carry her through. She said she would visit Delores in Foster City Prison in what was this month of March.

"Hey, Modecai," Little Phil said, running out the barbershop with scissor and comb, "tell Bunny, would you, he's on for two o'clock tomorrow afternoon, okay? I squeezed the cat in!"

"Okay, Little Phil," Modecai said, hustling across the street, dodging oncoming traffic. "Will do!"

"Cat's got me cutting his hair by appointment only now," Little Phil mumbled. "Bunny. That damned cat …"

Modecai heard the mumbles with his perfect pitch intact and was howling unreservedly.

Modecai zigged his way here and zagged his way there. If you were in a overhead blimp looking down onto the streets, you'd swear Modecai Ulysses Jefferson was like a balloon losing air, steam, and then going absolutely crazy by sheer will and design.

Chapter 23

Two months later.

This was rare, Bunny and Modecai walking together on Harlem Streets on a Saturday afternoon at twelve fifteen. Of course they walked the streets of Harlem to and from local jazz gigs, but not this. Even they found it strange, taking note of it.

"Stravinsky—gonna get some of that Stravinsky cat's music, Modecai. Love that long-haired Russian cat!"

It was mid-March. The March wind was blowing down buildings and kicking out teeth as bad as a pack mule after lunch.

"Can't get enough of him, huh, Bunny?"

"Cat's bad, Modecai. Got a ear. A pair of mitts. Think the cat's got an antenna hooked up to the moon. If anybody gets up to the moon, Modecai, it's what them cats'll be playing: some of that sweet Igor Stravinsky's long-haired shit."

"But who can think about the moon, when we've got this … this Harlem wind to contend with today, Bunny."

"Yeah, making noise. A lot, man. Keeps your teeth chattering in tune, don't it, Modecai? Like Hamp playing his xylophone. Uh, said it correct, didn't I?"

"Sure did, Bunny," Modecai said, his teeth chattering in tune. "It's spelled just like you pronounced it: x-y-l-o-p-h-o-n-e," Modecai laughed.

Modecai and Bunny were heading over to Mr. Silverman's record shop, Silverman's Records, at 126th and 6th. They were off to buy some old and new, some tried and true. Mr. Silverman's record store had quite a wide variety of records in its record bins for any record lover to pick from.

Marty's, a few stores down from Silverman Records, played its jukebox extremely loud all day through a speaker system. Folk on 126th Street liked it like that. The jukebox was playing loud now. The sound waves knifed right through the March wind, whipped right into the heart of it.

Suddenly Bunny stopped on a dime. He stopped as if he were shot by a gun.

And Modecai stopped on a dime too, like he too had been shot.

Bunny's body trembled. His hands covered his ears as if he were trying to ward off the sounds coming out Marty's speaker system. He kept doing this as if he were fighting beasts and demons out on 126th Street.

"My ears, Modecai! My fucking ears!"

"Bunny, it's your—"

"My tune, Modecai! My tune! FUCKING TUNE!"

How could Modecai calm him when he was hearing the same thing blasting out Marty's, knifing through the March wind like it was cutting into its heart.

"I'll kill him. KILL HIM!"

And out on 126th Street, Bunny yanked it out his back pocket, and it stood in the March wind shiny, bloodless, Bunny clenching it seemingly in a state of complete magnificence, extreme ecstasy.

"Bunny, Bunny, put it away!"

"The motherfucker stole it, Modecai. He's dead, Modecai. Stuckey Byerman's dead. He's a dead white man!"

"Now, now, put the knife away now!"

"Gonna find him, Modecai. Find the cat. His white ass. Gonna cut him, man. Slit open the motherfucker's throat. I'll find him. Byerman. He ain't long for living. Ain't, Modecai, ain't …"

* * *

Modecai and Bunny were back in the apartment. Modecai had gotten Bunny to bed.

"Corrine, yes, I'm glad I-I caught you."

"What's wrong, Modecai? What's happened!"

"Bunny, he's out of control. But who could blame him? Who … a record, Corrine. Bunny and I heard a record today. Some guy was singing. I—we, I don't know his name. But it was Bunny's … Bunny's tune, Corrine. They stole it …"

"Stole it!"

"Stole it. What would I do? Byerman, Stuckey Byerman—he's the one, he's—"

"I remember the name. The Broadway producer. The—"

"I didn't leave my, what were my best tunes with him. B-but Bunny did, Corrine. Bunny did."

Pause.

"And he's going to kill him. Bunny's going to kill Stuckey Byerman. Find him and kill him.

"What would I do if someone stole my tune? What would you do if someone stole your painting or, or forged it? W-what would anyone do? And Bunny vows he'll kill him. Slit his throat!"

"Where's Bunny now, Modecai!"

"Byerman has goons, C-Corrine. Tough guys to protect him. Paid killers. Stuckey Byerman has goons, paid—"

"Modecai, Modecai, where's Bunny now?"

"Paid—"

"Modecai, listen to me, honey! Where's Bunny now!"

"In the bedroom. I got him, got him in bed. I—"

"Oh …," Corrine sighed.

"But what the hell does it mean?"

"In the past you've told me of Bunny's violent side."

"I have." Pause. "It's in him like his music."

"Maybe Bunny will—"

"Get over it? No, he won't. Music's saved him up to now. Being what he is, who … a, the greatest trumpet player anyone's ever heard has saved him." Modecai looked over at Bunny's horn case.

"His horn. But now none of it matters. I saw it in his eyes: Bunny's willing to give it all up, t-to forsake it, all of it if he has to."

"How could someone like Bunny, I mean as …"

"Street smart? S-streetwise?"

"Be duped. Make himself so vulnerable. Fall for—"

"Easy, Corrine. Bunny wants to live on Park Avenue."

Pause.

"Corrine, I'm going back into Bunny's bedroom to check on him. I'm just thankful I had you to talk to."

"Maybe … Dammit, Modecai, I hope everything works out. That Bunny comes to his senses. Killing scum like Byerman isn't worth it."

Modecai was off the phone. Had he given Bunny enough time to cool off? he asked himself. He needs a cooling-off period. Maybe, like Corrine said, he'll come to his senses. Maybe he'll put his music, which has always been first, above his violence.

"I don't know how to handle this, but I must. I'm his only hope. He'll destroy himself if I don't help him. If I don't come up with the right words, the … the right things to say."

This was pressure. This was life at its worst. Modecai turned toward the kitchen. Bunny's room was just beyond the kitchen.

Modecai stood on shaky legs. He just didn't want his voice to be the same as his legs. Would Bunny be asleep or awake? Would he still be in a deep panic? How should he walk? How much noise should his body make, actually make?

He was in the kitchen and then out again. Modecai didn't understand how to carry his weight, this slender body of his—how to control it, how to make it work for him. Bunny, he'd been dealt the dirtiest of blows: Stuckey Byerman had beat the hell out of him.

"Modecai … Modecai … is, is that you?" His voice was pale, enervated.

"Yes, Bunny."

Modecai could see Bunny's outline in the bed. Bunny's body looked like a small bundle of laundry. It's what came to Modecai's mind—it was immediate, spontaneous.

"Thought … thought so …"

Modecai wasn't going to switch the room's light on.

"Ain't … ain't making the gig tonight, Modecai. P-Pearlie's. A-ain't playing tonight. My horn tonight."

"Not tonight, Bunny. No, not tonight."

"Got all this shit in me, Modecai. Bad shit in me." He shivered. "Feel like an addict, Modecai. Like one of them dopeheads … fiends you see out in the streets. In Harlem streets. One of them cats. Arm's full of dope. Except, but it's violence f-for—in me, Modecai. Got violence in me, Modecai. I'm doped up with violence."

Modecai's head dropped.

"Stole f-from me. H-he stole my music, my music …"

Modecai could feel Bunny's eyes, how they were bleeding, and saw his hands reaching up to them. Modecai moved over to Bunny's bureau, pulled the top drawer out, and then walked over to Bunny's bed.

"Thanks. Thanks, Modecai," Bunny said, taking the handkerchief out Modecai's hand.

"I called Corrine, Bunny. I had to talk to someone. So I called her."

"S-she understands, Modecai? Corrine understands? If one of her paintings …"

"Yes, we—it was brought up. Corrine and I got around to that."

"I ain't running from nothing." Bunny's voice hardened. "I ain't hiding from nothing, Modecai."

"No, I know you're not, Bunny."

"This ain't me." Bunny's natural voice was returning. "I don't do this kind of shit, man. Lie in a dark room like I'm hiding, man. A-afraid of what's outside the door. This ain't me, Modecai. I don't do this, this, man …"

"I know, Bunny. You did it for me. Me, Bunny," Modecai said, his voice panicky.

"For you and us, Modecai. For you and us and the band and, and the future."

"Yes, yes, Bunny, all those things. All those things."

Bunny grabbed Modecai's arm. "You're trying to save me, Modecai. You're trying to save me, man. I know you are!"

"I have to, Bunny. I have to try."

"But it … it almost feels like dying though, Modecai. Feel myself dying."

What am I doing to Bunny? What am I accomplishing? He is this person, this—

And suddenly Bunny rolled out the bed and onto his feet. "I'm playing tonight, Modecai. I'm fucking playing tonight!"

Fear shot back into Modecai.

"You—"

"I'm playing my horn tonight. Pearlie's. At fucking Pearlie's. Playing it as loud as I can. Sweet as I ever played it. Make my ears ring, Modecai. Make my ears ring, man!"

Bunny folded the handkerchief in a neat tent fold.

"Wear this shit in my suit jacket tonight. Gonna look sharp as a tack, Jack. Gonna blow down a fucking mountain, Modecai. Set the world on fire. Make my ass wiggle, man!"

Then Bunny walked up to Modecai and held his shoulders.

"Ain't nobody gonna steal my tunes again. This is the last time I'm gonna let you talk me out of killing a cat, Modecai. The last fucking time."

* * *

A few more weeks passed, and with their passing, newer revelations had developed.

First, Bunny's tune had shot, in record time, to the top of the Billboard chart (Billboard was the record industry's meticulous ranking system for record sales). Bunny's tune had become the number one best-selling record in the country. Therefore, after three weeks of the record maintaining its top perch on the Billboard chart, the same young hotshot singer released a new record and instantaneously, the record zoomed to the number five spot on the chart. Most industry insiders had now predicted it was just a matter of time before his new record would be sitting pretty atop Billboard's chart. Most industry people agreed—how lucky could one guy get.

Only, no one knew the tune (not the lyrics) was written by Bunny Odecai Greensleeves. No one knew that but Modecai, Bunny, Corrine, Stuckey Byerman, and the songwriters who penned their names to Bunny's tunes and had gotten credit.

Second, everyone was cleaning up. Everyone was making money hand over fist, as fast as a mint machine. Everyone was slaying the golden goose—everyone, that is, but Bunny, the songwriter.

When Bunny became aware of all of this, he'd said, "I'm gonna get my bread. What's mine. Gonna get what Stuckey Byerman, what the white motherfucker took. What that white motherfucker owes me, Modecai."

And all Modecai could do was shake his head, knowing that everything was just a matter of time … was a ticking time bomb, for Bunny had said it so coolly, restrained, so ice-cold, at the time.

* * *

Bunny had just come out Mr. Silverman's shop. He was carrying records in both hands. Not one was his, the ones the hot singer had recorded—he'd heard those records on the Harlem jukeboxes enough to know they were still selling like hotcakes. Bunny was alone. Over the past few days he was finding being alone more and more suited to his liking. It wasn't that he was melancholy but that he was bitter. Stuckey Byerman had shitted on him. Plain and simple, shitted on him. It's how his mind would remind him, rewind that scenario over and over like a broken record.

But all of that would end. When? Bunny didn't know—but it'd be soon. How did Bunny know this, because he'd put the word out three days ago on Harlem streets, through the grapevine, that he wanted to meet with Byerman. That he wanted to sit down to talk to him.

Bunny chuckled, oh, yeah, Byerman, that motherfucker, knows by now. It's been spooned to his ears. He's a gangster, a hoodlum, all right. A kingpin. He'd set the cat up: gangsters, kingpins want to see their victims squirm, to sweat it out. Byerman was no different.

Yeah, he'd put the word out on the streets, saying he wanted to sit down to talk with the cat. Stuckey Byerman would want the meeting, the confab as badly as him, Bunny had figured. For he could see the sucker he'd set up again. The sucker who bought all of this, his line—the goods.

He'd remembered Byerman's pointy shoes even though pointy shoes were in fashion, in style (wing tips)—everyone was wearing them, but Stuckey Byerman would wear them even if they went back to square-toed shoes, for Stucky Byerman wanted to stick people with his. The cat wasn't through.

Bunny scooted into a malt shop. The jukebox was playing the number five Billboard record in the country, which would soon zoom to the number one record in the country according to record industry experts. Bunny picked up the pay phone and dropped a nickel in its slot.

"Yeah, Bunny. Got any word yet, Stew? The fish take the bait yet, man? Yeah. Yeah. Be at the apartment? Call on the hall phone, man. Number I gave you." Bunny looked at his gold-plated pocket watch. "'Bout an hour—what? Two? Okay, Stew. Okay, can wait. Waited this fucking long, man."

Bunny hung up the phone. Then *his* tune played through his ears.

"Yeah, you owe me, Byerman. Owe my black Mississippi-ass big-time, man."

Modecai heard the front door open and close, and man, was he ever relieved. Whenever Bunny went anywhere without him now, he was a total wreck. And when he came back, it was like God handing him back something beautiful.

Modecai scurried out the bedroom. But then he didn't let his anxiety show; he mustn't let it show, not to Bunny. Modecai relaxed.

"Hey, Bunny."

"Hey, Modecai."

"What records did you buy at Mr. Silverman's?" Modecai asked while looking at the record albums Bunny was carrying.

"You know I got that Stravinsky cat, Modecai."

"Yes, I know that for a fact, Bunny."

"Mr. Silverman turned me onto a French cat, uh … uh …" Bunny was looking at the album jacket. "Rav—"

"Ravel. Yes, I've heard of him. He's quite an orchestrator."

"Yeah, Mr. Silverman spoke of those same fine qualities."

"Wonder how we missed him when we were over in France, Bunny?"

"Wonder, Modecai. Maybe I can learn something from the old French cat, man."

Bunny now looked at Modecai. "See you all dressed. You and Corrine again? Stepping? Walking the boulevard?"

Modecai nodded.

"In a groove, huh, Modecai? Playing in the key of C, I see. Swing-swinging …"

"No sharps and no flats, Bunny—as you always say. No sharps and no flats."

"For now, Modecai. But watch out for that drumroll, man. Drummer's always got something, a trick hiding behind his back while keeping time. While banging them skins, you don't always know about."

Modecai looked at Bunny. Was he being deceived? Duped? he thought. Was Bunny as happy, as lighthearted as he seemed?

Bunny came over and hugged him, what seemed just for the heck of it. But then Bunny said, "Modecai, I ain't gonna be your best man—so scratch it off your calendar now, right now. Ain't standing in front of an altar, under no circumstances."

"How about a trumpet solo then, Bunny?"

"Hell, Modecai, God ain't heard me play my trumpet in church, just in clubs. Might just knock the Big Cat out the sky!"

Modecai laughed more.

"Rehearsal's at six o'clock, but you know that, don't you?" Bunny asked, winking out one eye.

"Yes, I do, Bunny. I know that, man."

Bunny pulled out his pocket watch. "Ain't gonna have to clock your Hamlet, North Carolina, ass, am I? Put you on the clock?"

It was a Saturday. Corrine and Modecai were going to take in a movie.

"Modecai …"

"Yes, Bunny?"

"Have—you and Corrine have a good time, man. Do it up right."

Modecai thought Bunny was going to say more. The expression in his eyes suggested as much.

"Thanks, Bunny. We're going to take in a movie this afternoon."

Bunny had his trumpet in his hands, his fingers loosening the three valves.

"What, what are you going to do, Bunny? Do while I'm out?"

"Who me? Guess I'll go and put that long-haired Stravinsky cat on the phonograph and then Ravel. And then some James P. Johnson, man. Feel in the mood for some of that cat's music striding through Harlem on a cool Saturday night."

"Yes, James P. Johnson does, Bunny."

Modecai was at the apartment door. He took this look at Bunny, and both he and Bunny felt it, whatever "it" was, simultaneously.

"Go … Modecai. Go. Don't worry about me. Corrine's waiting, man. Probably already got her movie stub in her hand, man."

And it's when Bunny said something Modecai thought was quite profound, quite significant.

"I'm a man, Modecai. Always been a man." Bunny used his hands to demonstrate this. "From since I was small, always felt like a man. Like I had to take care of business. Take care of myself. My responsibilities. Had a momma and daddy, got them—but felt I had myself first, man.

"Modecai, I've never felt different about it since the first day I was born. Never."

Modecai studied the sharp, crisp crease in Bunny's light green slacks—the quintessential Bunny Greensleeves, Modecai thought.

"See you, Modecai."

"O-okay, Bunny."

"Have you a good time at the cinema. You and Corrine."

"Real French, Bunny. Cinema."

"Yeah, real French, man."

Modecai opened the apartment door.

"Love you, Modecai …"

Only, by then, Modecai had already hustled down the hall and exchanged pleasantries with Earlene who had a head, as usual, in the chair.

Modecai was walking fast like he was trying his best to keep abreast of his own footsteps. Like he was pushing, merging twelve twenty-two Saturday afternoon into six o'clock Saturday evening. As if he were back on his way to the apartment, back home from his date with Corrine, back with Bunny and Bunny Greensleeves's Big Band Boppers. Modecai didn't want Bunny out of his sight, but neither he nor Bunny could live that way: the constant watchdog, keeping Bunny under constant surveillance, ever distrustful of Bunny's every move. It, this was no way for either of them to live.

Bunny wanted a piece of Stuckey Byerman—it was Modecai's fear. Bunny wanted to kill Stuckey Byerman. He wanted to slash his throat; it was his only wish, his only desire.

Was Bunny giving him false hope? The note he'd played on the trumpet was the sweetest note he'd heard Bunny play. It rang in his ears; all his heart and soul was in it. Today Bunny had Stravinsky, Ravel, the records he bought from Mr. Silverman's record shop. Bunny was going to play them. He was trying to learn more about orchestration, just as he was. And then Bunny said he'd listen to James P. Johnson. They both loved James P. Johnson striding through Harlem. And the band, it rehearsed at six o'clock.

Bunny seemed happy. He seemed secure. Modecai wanted to feel Bunny was safe. Modecai wanted to feel secure in the knowledge of knowing that much about today, what it offered. If he and Bunny were just buying days, it didn't matter. It was each day that mattered. Each day gave them another day. It added up to another day. It's how Corrine saw it—this way also.

* * *

"Bunny, man, it's for you. By now, thought everyone in Harlem knew you and Modecai got you a phone in your apartment. But guess not," Mr. Clarence said resignedly.

Bunny was at the phone.

"Yeah, Stew. Yeah. Okay. Okay. Yeah, yeah, I got the info, man," Bunny said, his voice dissolving into the phone.

"Hell, Stew, you do good work, man. Damned good work. Thanks. Thanks."

Satisfied, Bunny hung up the phone and proceeded down the hallway.

Bunny bounced.

"Broadway, Bunny? That, that wasn't Broadway calling, was it!"

"Yeah, Broadway, Earlene! Big as a lollipop, Earlene. Red as a flame. Grand as a string of Grandma's pearls. Yeah, was Broadway, Broadway calling, all right!"

"Bunny, Bunny, I can't believe it! Broadway, Broadway! D-does Modecai know, honey!"

“No, Earlene. Gonna surprise him, the cat. So … uh listen, listen, don’t say nothing to him before I do, okay? Keep the info under your hat, uh, okay, Earlene?”

“Uh, you mean under my wig, don’t you, Bunny?” Earlene laughed.

“Your wig, yeah, under the red wig you sporting you today.”

“You know I won’t say nothing to Modecai. Not a peep. Y-you don’t have to worry about me,” Earlene said earnestly, her skin practically turning a deep purple. “My mouth’s sealed as tight as, as … uh, as tight as Grant’s Tomb, Bunny!”

Bunny laughed.

“Two tickets, Bunny? Right, honey?”

“Two tickets it is, Earlene.”

“Two front-row tickets on opening night, Bunny!”

Earlene clapped her hands and joy leaped across her pretty black face.

Bunny was back inside the apartment. He ran into his bedroom, opened the closet door, and pulled out his white suit as if he were heading off to a king’s coronation.

“Gotta look sharp, man. Gotta look pretty. Pretty as ten white doves flying in a formation.”

Bunny began shedding his clothes, and when through, he had the white suit and shoes on and looked as pretty as ten white doves flying in formation.

“Hell, man, just another day on Wall Street. Just another motherfucking day down on Wall Street!”

Bunny pressed both hands down on the white suit’s lapels. He didn’t want to ruin it for Earlene, not Earlene. Bunny and Modecai hadn’t told her about the Stuckey Byerman fiasco. They didn’t want to take the anticipation, the hope and joy out of her. Modecai told Corrine, but he and Modecai knew Corrine could be trusted not to tell Earlene: Corrine was as solid as gold. Bunny looked down at his white vest: should he leave the top button buttoned or not?

“Man … decisions …” He laughed.

Bunny left the top button unbuttoned. Then out the closet came his white overcoat and hat. Bunny put both on with extra care.

“Hell, think it was Sunday, man. But Saturday’ll fucking do!”

Now it was time to traverse the hall, pass by Earlene, and she would understand why he was decked in white, looked as pure as snow.

Bunny walked into the front room and picked up the snakeskin briefcase. But as soon as he did, he stole his eyes away from everything else in the room but his horn. And Bunny was transported into a flight of thought and fantasy and meaning, of this and that and everything else in his life.

"I love you more than any woman," Bunny said, opening the horn case. "But I ain't never loved a woman. You never let me. Gave me a chance to. You know that, don't you? Shit … shit …"

Bunny looked at Modecai's piano.

"Me and Modecai went down to Way City for you? Man, a jazz cat's ax, man, is all that life gives the cat. To live or die for."

He put his trumpet back in his case.

"Come into this world, though, to do what I gotta do. Ain't always a wish but a promise."

Even if he could play a final note out the trumpet right now, Bunny felt too sad to play it.

Bunny snapped the horn case's metal clamps shut.

"Earlene, I'm going out to slay the dragon!" Bunny said, standing outside apartment 4B.

"Oh, Bunny, you're—"

"I know, Earlene. I know. You ain't gotta tell me: look as pretty as the Hope Diamond!"

"Prettier, Bunny! Much prettier!"

Earlene was between customers, even if remnants of burnt hair were in the air.

"Uh … Earlene …"

"Yes, honey?"

"If Joe and the band show, and me and Modecai ain't here, let them in the apartment, okay? You still got Big Booty's key, right?"

"Yes."

"And another thing, uh, if you would, uh, Earlene, don't say nothing to them cats either about Broadway, okay? The Broadway show. Still keep it—"

"Under my wig!"

"Right, Earlene. Under your wig."

"Oh, uh, of course not, Bunny. I won't. Modecai should know before anybody else. Ain't gonna say a word, honey. Not a peep like I said."

"Right. Good girl. Thanks."

"Bunny …"

Bunny pressed his fingers onto the tip of his hat.

"Two front-row tickets? One f-for me and my date. R-right, Bunny?" Earlene asked, reconfirming what'd been already agreed on only minutes ago.

"Yeah."

"Bunny … you do look pretty."

Earlene was the only person who could make Bunny blush—and it's what he was doing. So he walked up to Earlene and kissed her on her broad, beaming cheek, causing Earlene to turn cherry-red too.

"Broadway, Bunny!"

"Yeah, Broadway, Earlene!"

* * *

Bunny was out the apartment building on 116th Street. He looked both ways from the front stoop. He spotted a taxi.

Tweet!

The taxi skidded in the street, in front of Bunny, like it'd hit a patch of ice.

Quickly, Bunny was in the taxi's backseat. Bunny was more than set, ready for his trip downtown into Manhattan.

The taxi was there. The time was right.

Bunny was in the taxi's backseat salivating and then leaned forward to pay the cabbie the fare.

Bunny stepped out the taxi.

"Yeah, I'm here, Byerman. Motherfucker!"

The sucker fell for it hook, line, and sinker, Bunny thought. There's a sucker born in the universe every second as P. T. Barnum announced. Bunny had to laugh as he gazed at the building: wasn't this what he'd expected? Didn't he know it would be classy? Didn't he know the building's characteristic, its single most distinctive trademark would be class? In no way was Bunny disappointed.

Bunny was in the building's extravagant lobby but could not be admitted beyond that particular point unless he saw the young man at the round marble installation in the middle of the lobby, the sign so instructed.

"Good afternoon, sir."

"Good afternoon."

"How may I help you?"

"My name's Bunny Greensleeves. Got an appointment with Stuckey Byerman for two."

"It's one fifty-nine, sir—I'll ring Mr. Byerman." Pause.

"He's expecting you, sir. But said wait in the lobby, he'll be right out."

"Thanks."

Bunny knew what that meant, "he'd be right out." Bunny knew who to expect to escort him to Byerman.

It was no more than twenty, twenty-five seconds later. And Bunny's two bigheaded escorts had arrived. First he wondered what Byerman fed them and then wondered if he should kiss them or throw roses at their feet.

The talkative one (Bunny still assumed) said, "Follow me."

But Bunny was sure the cat meant he should follow the two of them.

There were no stairs to climb, no elevator to take. Apparently, Bunny Byerman's office was on the first floor. But they were walking down a couple of long corridors. Bunny was squeezed in the middle of these two bigheaded goons. He was almost tempted to hold onto their arms and swing from them like they were thick tree branches, but then his frolicsome mood shifted fast, real fast, when Bunny remembered why he was there in that building—what shit Byerman had done to him.

The elegant wooden doors opened. This part of the big building seemed far from everything, as if what went on back there was in secret, covert. And then the wooden door opened out to a new door. And then Bunny was walking on a plush red carpet and the little cat with the black, slick, shiny hair behind the big desk wheeled around like a carnival's pinwheel.

"Bunny, Bunny. So nice to see you, Bunny!"

Bunny looked around, his escorts settled in around him.

"Yeah, Stuckey, nice digs you got you, man."

"The best, Bunny. Only the best."

The desk was new. The cigar box on top the desk was new. It was just the cigars, Bunny wondered—he didn't know if Byerman had changed brands (not that Bunny knew that much about cigars).

Bunny's question was answered in the short term though, when Stuckey Byerman snapped his fingers after he'd lifted one of the cigars out the velvet-covered cigar box. The nontalkative goon lit the match to light the cigar.

"Havana, Bunny. Gotta be a jewel of a place, man," Byerman said, blowing out his first fat ring of smoke. Byerman watched it climb to the tall ceiling and then pancake out. "Jewel of a place."

And then Byerman looked at Bunny's snakeskin briefcase.

"What you bring me, Bunny? What? New music to play for our Broadway show? Them Broadway babes? What you got for me in that snakeskin briefcase of yours?"

Bunny took it upon himself to sit in one of the chairs, the one to the left of the desk. One of the goons shifted with him. Bunny removed his white hat and put it atop the briefcase.

Byerman took another big puff on his Havana cigar. "Thought you knew, Bunny, I'm in the record business now. Playing platters."

The chairs were new too, Bunny noted.

"Gave up that Broadway crap. Not enough fucking money in it, man!"

Yeah, Bunny thought, he expected all of this. He was going to let Byerman have his fun. This was how he saw the big picture in his dreams unfold. It was all being played out according to what he'd imagined, in that world of dreams too.

"Got me a pad on Park Avenue, Bunny."

And it was like a blade stabbing Bunny's gut. How did Byerman know about that dream? Or was it coincidence, mere coincidence? Was it? WAS IT?

"Got off Fifth Avenue. Lowlife on Fifth Avenue, Bunny. Scum. Plain fucking scum. Takes money to live on Park Avenue. Moola. Dough. What you jazz cats call it? Bread, man?" Byerman said.

"Life's sweet, ain't it, Bunny? Just gotta know how to shuffle the deck right. Open the right doors. Make the right deals."

Bunny crossed his leg.

"By the way, Bunny, you look real pretty in white. Real, real pretty in a white man's white suit."

Byerman coughed.

"Now what the hell are you down here for, Greensleeves! What fucking business do you got with me that I know of? Is on my fucking calendar!"

"You owe me money, Stuckey. Bread. A little table salt."

"And listen, quit with the Stuckey crap, Greensleeves, and address me proper. Call me by my proper name from now on: Mr. Byerman, man. Mr. Byerman, to fucking you."

"Stuckey."

"Oh … so, so … you're gonna be one of those kind of niggers, are you?"

"You owe me big-time, Byerman. Big-time, man!"

"Hell, Bunny, you're back on Fifty-Second Street, ain't you? What else you want? I let you come back on my street, didn't I? Moved over from Fifty-First just for you, Bunny. Ain't that enough? Good enough for you?"Pause.

"The hell with Big Hat Morrison. The hell with that nigger. Harlem nigger. Nigger scum. Scumbag. Plate of scum. He don't run the show down here—I do. Stuckey Byerman! I ain't gonna let him ban Bunny Greensleeves and Modecai Jefferson from playing on Fifty-Second Street no more, man!"

"I want my bread, Byerman, all of it. Every last cent. Down to the last crumb off the fucking table."

"What, for you can throw it away on them nigger girls, broads, Bunny? Crap? Them white-skinned Cotton Club chorus girls, dames with them long, shapely legs, Bunny?"

"You owe me, motherfucker!"

Byerman's fist smashed the desk. "Owe you? A monkeyshine nigger like you, dressed in a white man's suit!"

Bunny was about to jump out of his chair, onto his feet but, instead, felt the oppressive nature of the two bigheaded freaks standing over Byerman as if he were a stolen treasure.

"Don't fucking make me laugh, Greensleeves. Don't make me fucking howl!" Byerman dashed out his Havana cigar in the ashtray.

He snapped his fingers.

"This is how I live, Greensleeves … This is how Stuckey Byerman fucking lives …"

A new cigar was lit.

"Twenty-four hours a day. Every day of the fucking week."

"You owe me, white motherfucker!"

"Listen, man," Byerman screamed, rising to his feet, "it is what you niggers in Harlem say, 'man,' isn't it? A-ain't it? You brought your fucking music to me. You was looking to me and some other assholes to jerk around. Use our money on a nigger show, some black-faced crap. P-piece of nigger shit. Well, no dice, no fucking deal, Greensleeves. I'm no sucker, Greensleeves. I wasn't born yesterday in a fucking circus trunk. I ain't no candy apple in a barrel. You left it, I took it, I used it—it's how we do business down here!"

There was a big bay window directly behind Byerman, about two feet away.

"Just like you're doing now, Greensleeves. Dumb nigger. Bringing your music to me. When are you gonna learn, man? When are you niggers up in Harlem ever gonna learn nothing!"

It's when the bigheaded freak with the big neck, who'd moved from Byerman and to the right of Bunny, snatched the briefcase off Bunny's lap.

"Yeah, open it. Open that shit up and see what the nigger brung us! Open it!

Open it, I said!"

"Nothing, Byerman! Nothing! Fucking nothing!"

"You fucking—"

"Nigger!"

"N-nigger!"

"You got a stack of air, man, you white motherfucker! Nothing but air, Byerman! Nothing but fucking air, a stack full of air, motherfucker!"

"Is this your fucking revenge, Bunny?" Byerman asked, putting out his cigar slowly. "A fucking briefcase? Empty fucking briefcase? Is, is this it?"

Pause.

"Music. You put your whole life in it, don't you, Bunny?" Byerman leaned back in the chair. "Uncle was a musician, ever tell you that, Bunny? My father's brother. A violinist. Uncle Bernie, Bernard Leonard Byerman—ever heard of him? Wanted to play at Carnegie Hall one day. Was a tailor by trade. Worked Manhattan, the lower East Side. Poor sap. Goddamned sap. Practice. Practice. Practiced at night. All fucking night. Yeah, my uncle Bernie was a sap, all right. Thought the world was gonna make him a world-famous violinist—when all he was, was a fucking tailor, a fucking piece of crap. Shit. He—"

"Your uncle Bernie didn't know how to steal," Bunny said. "How to take what another man owns. Works for, man."

"Uncle Bernie was a tailor, a fucking violin player—what you expect? I'm a crook. I'm a fucking hood who—"

"Who lives on Park Avenue and works on Fifty-Second Street."

"Yeah, and makes no fucking bones about it. Aches about it. Who's got fucking credentials to prove it."

"Who steals, man!"

"T-that hotshot kid, he sings your fucking songs good, don't he, Bunny?

Beautiful. Just beautiful. Discovered the kid myself. Cut him a deal he couldn't refuse. The kid leaped at it."

"Like me, huh, Stuckey?"

Bunny's eyes gleamed. His throat was tight. His heart was beating a thousand heartbeats per second. This was different than playing a high note on his horn; this was more thrilling for him than anything he'd known before. It was more beautiful inside him than music—this extreme, freeing, multinoted violence that was cresting in him.

"Yeah, Bunny. Except I paid the kid peanuts. Candy wrappers. Yeah, I know, but he … more than what I paid you. Wasn't no free ride. Paid, ha, paid him for singing both your fucking songs, Greensleeves. Put me on Park Avenue!"

Bunny shot to his feet.

"Sit that nigger down! Sit that fucking nigger down!"

One of Byerman's goons clamped his hand to Bunny's shoulder, trying to strong-arm him, but Bunny's powerful hand slapped it away.

"Get the little monkey! Get him!"

Bunny bounced away from the bigheaded freak. His hand slid down into his back pocket, and like a flash it was out in the open, the ruby-handled knife.

"He's got a knife. A fucking shank! Get it! Get it!"

One of the bigheaded freaks grabbed Bunny's arm, but again, Bunny was far too powerful for him, and when his hand grabbed the desk, holding onto it for leverage, Bunny brought the blade of the knife down and ran it straight through the heart of his hand.

It's when the other freak ran at Bunny at full force. But Bunny saw him and took the knife's blade out the other freak's hand, wheeled, and aimed it at his heart and ran it straight through the heart of his heart.

He died instantly.

Bunny smiled.

The freak on the floor was writhing and screaming in pain.

Byerman's body had frozen. Byerman couldn't move. It seemed a wonder if his ears even heard the bigheaded freak's wild shrieks from the floor.

The blade's knife had new blood dripping from it.

"Now it's your turn, Byerman. It's your fucking turn, motherfucker!"

Byerman couldn't move, defend himself. But suddenly his hand went into his desk drawer and he pulled out a gun.

Only, Bunny let him; he encouraged Stuckey Byerman in getting but so far with it.

"Uh-uh, Byerman," Bunny said, slapping the gun out Byerman's hand and off to the floor. "Uh-uh, no cat dies that easy!"

"Y-you can have the money, Bunny! Y-you can have it—all, all of it, Bunny. All of it, f-fucking it!" Byerman said, pushing himself, his back up against the edge of the big bay window.

"I don't want it, man. Don't want it now. I-I said you can play on Fifth … Fifty-Second Street," Byerman stuttered. "Y-you and, and Jefferson. You and Modecai Jefferson."

"Don't want it now, man, me or Modecai."

Byerman was out his chair, on his knees.

"Please … take the money, Bunny. Take the fucking money. Take it. All, all of it. I don't want to live on Park Avenue!"

"Me neither, man. Once did. But don't anymore. Scum … lowlife record producers live on Park Avenue." Pause.

"Get up, Stuckey …"

"Bunny, y-you, y-you …"

"Ain't gonna hurt you. Not a hair on top your head, man. Uh-uh, not a strand."

Stuckey Byerman trembled. And soon Byerman was on his feet. And suddenly Bunny was wiping him off carefully, purposefully.

"T-thanks, Bunny. F-fucking t-thanks." Byerman was trembling.

"And I-I ain't gonna say nothing about this here little caper, skirmish to no one, n-nobody, Bunny. Nothing. S-squeal nothing t-to nobody. Nothing's gonna come of this here. This here little incident, Bunny. From my lips. Nothing. Nothing. To no coppers, authorities, police. No fucking coppers or, or nothing. I'll clean it up myself, Bunny. The whole fucking thing. Never, it never happened as, as far as I'm concerned, Bunny, fucking concerned, between you, you and me. Don't worry about fucking nothing, Bunny. Nothing. This here is between you, fucking you and—"

And then Bunny grabbed Byerman by his suit's lapels, jerking him off the floor, lifting him straight above his head, and pivoted; and Bunny hurled Stuckey Byerman through the plate glass window head first.

The glass smashed, shattered, and there Byerman lay in the junky alleyway, butchered, his face torn by glass. But Stucky Byerman was still breathing, still alive.

And now Bunny hurdled himself through the gaping, smashed-out window and out into the back alley, landing catlike onto the balls of his feet.

Byerman was crawling on his hands and knees, trying to get away, to escape Bunny, as he saw Bunny pressing toward him, pursuing him, his feet cracking through glass blanketing the concrete floor.

"Don't worry, Byerman, ain't gonna be long …," Bunny said, his knife still leaking blood over his white suit. "For you to live. Ain't gonna be long for you, man. Gonna end your misery. Gonna make the world fucking safe again!"

And Bunny grabbed Byerman by the foot, pulling him back to him.

"Please, please, Bunny! PLEASE, DON'T, DON'T, BUNNY!"

Bunny had Byerman by the leg, dragging him closer and closer to him.

"My knife can, it can taste you, Stuckey. My knife can taste your white fucking flesh … skin, man."

And then Bunny's arm caught Stuckey by the neck. Bunny's arm was wrapped solidly around Stuckey's neck.

The bloodied blade was pressed against Byerman's slender throat.

"Modecai … Modecai …"

And Bunny heard Stuckey Byerman breathe in what he knew would be his last breath of air on Earth out his lungs.

And Bunny heard heaven in his heart.

"This is for you too, Modecai. Y-you too!"

Bang!

The bullet blew a hole in the back of Bunny's head.

The bigheaded freak stood in front of the smashed-out window with Stuckey Byerman's revolver in his good hand and blood rushing out his bad one.

Stuckey Byerman looked up at the bigheaded freak in the broken-out window and smiled behind his bloodied face.

Bunny was dead.

* * *

"Bunny's late, Modecai!" Joe Crawford said.

It was six ten.

"Finally caught the cat by the tail. Bunny always riding us about being late for rehearsal. Always dangling that doggone gold pocket watch at us, but it looks like the cat finally fell into his own can of Beeswax."

"Or … he was messing with one of them young chippies—and she didn't know when to quit. Come up for air. Got him in her squeeze box, and she ain't letting go," Specs Sherman said, sitting behind his drum kit. "Like a bee catching a honey bear with honey."

The Bunny Greensleeves's Big Bopper Band was in stitches.

Modecai stood at the window. He was looking east and west on 116th Street for Bunny.

"Give him a-another ten minutes. There's got to be a reason why he, B-Bunny's late."

Modecai could picture Bunny stepping out a taxi, anything that would get him back to the apartment as fast as he could for rehearsal.

"Bunny's never late."

Modecai kept looking out the window, down onto 116th Street.

"Ten minutes is up, Modecai."

"Yes, yes, I know, Joe," Modecai said nervously, disappointed, glancing at his watch. "Okay, this is new music," Modecai began explaining to the band. "It's Bunny's. He wants us to play it at Pearlie's tonight."

Each band member, when receiving the music, kind of let their eyes riff on it.

"Dog-doggoneit, Modecai—this is some great stuff!"

Modecai was sitting on his piano stool, adjusting it, looking at Bunny's music too.

"Yes, I know, Joe," Modecai replied.

* * *

The band rehearsal was over. The band was packing its instruments away. Joe was kind of lingering behind everyone else. Modecai pulled him over.

"Joe," Modecai said, taking Joe Crawford into his confidence, "would you do me a favor? Would you take the music to the club tonight?"

"Sure. W-what, any-anything wrong?"

"N-no. There, uh, it's all there," Modecai said, handing the music to Joe. "Plus encores."

"Right, Modecai."

"See you tonight."

"Oh—yeah … yeah, Modecai. Yeah. You and Bunny"

Joe was the last band member to leave the apartment. The gig at Pearlie's was at ten. Modecai stepped back over to the window. It was seven thirty-five.

"Where is he? Where the hell is Bunny!"

Knock.

"Come in."

"Bunny's not home yet, Modecai?"

"No, uh, Earlene."

"Oh, thought I might've missed him come in."

"Uh-uh. No, you didn't."

"Oh … I guess he's …"

And then Earlene remembered she wasn't to tell Modecai what was the good news, that it was to be a surprise. That it was to come from Bunny and only Bunny.

"He … he's out catting around."

"S-suppose so, Earlene."

But Modecai knew he was faking it, that Bunny never let anything get between him and rehearsal and a gig, not even a long-legged, stacked dame.

"Bunny'll be storming down the hall, through the door any minute now, Modecai. You just wait and see," Earlene said reassuringly. "Gonna be swinging that chain of his. Watch, uh, I bet you!" Earlene said while all her thoughts contained Broadway and her two front-row tickets for opening night.

"It's all right to leave the door open, Earlene," Modecai said, seeing Earlene was leaving.

"Okay, honey."

Modecai was alone again.

"Where the hell are you, Bunny? Your briefcase is missing and your white suit and hat and topcoat. Y-you were, were supposed to be listening to records, records. It's what you said when I left the apartment!"

Modecai felt like going to bed. It's why he gave the music to Joe Crawford.

He felt like sleeping. He didn't feel like going off to Pearlie's. Something was wrong, radically wrong.

Bunny would be here, he thought. He'd never miss a gig. He wanted to play. Every night Bunny wanted to play the music, be the star, wow the audience, hear the one thing in the world that made sense to him.

Modecai stood and then sat right back down.

What if Bunny was with Stuckey Byerman? What if he found him, Stuckey Byerman!

Modecai looked over at Bunny's horn case.

"Oh no. Oh no. Oh … oh …"

Rap. Rap.

"Modecai, you got a call in the hall. Swore everybody and his brother in Harlem got you and Bunny's phone number by now. Second call to come in through the hall phone today. First one was for Bunny. Come in for—"

Modecai ran to the door. He opened it, but Mr. Clarence was gone. The phone was off the hook.

Second call! Mr. Clarence said it was the second call that's come in through the hall phone today. Who made the first call? Who!

Byerman. Bunny. Byerman. Bunny. Stucky Byerman.

"Yes, yes. T-this is—"

"Jefferson!"

"Yes, Jefferson. M-Modecai—"

"Looking for somebody, Jefferson!"

"Yes … I'm, who's—"

"Your pal!"

"Bunny, Bunny—"

"Greensleeves!"

Silence.

"C-can you tell me where he is? Where Bunny is!"

"Yeah." Pause. "Greensleeves needs a fucking friend, Jefferson!"

* * *

This was lower Manhattan on a Saturday night down at the piers, peopleless, as dark as a stretch of black 2:00 a.m. snow.

"You sure we're in the right place, buddy? Awfully dark back there. Desolate too."

"Wait for me, okay?" Modecai said.

"You want me to wait for you? Got rats down here behind them warehouses. Warehouse rats big as cats. Here's a flashlight, buddy. Can navigate better back there. Carry one in the glove compartment in case of road emergencies."

Modecai wasn't scared. He wasn't afraid of anything. Rats? Rats as big as cats? He'd twist their heads off their necks like chicken.

But he was scared, wasn't he? Byerman. Bunny. Byerman. Stuckey Byerman.

Bunny had gotten a call on the hall phone today. He took his snakeskin briefcase. He wore all white. His trumpet and case were left on top the piano.

The flashlight shone down on the pavement.

A rat, big as a cat, leaped from out of nowhere.

Modecai didn't flinch.

The air, Modecai didn't want to breathe much of it into his lungs. Fish. The air had a strong fish smell.

Modecai looked back over his shoulder; the cab was still there, the only light other than the flashlight on the docks.

Modecai's foot speed quickened. It was almost as if he were running—it's what it felt like.

Hoodlums. Gangsters. Mobsters. Ku Klux Klan. White mobs. Crackers.

Southern lynchings.

Bunny was hurt. He needed his help. He needs a "friend's" help.

Another rat, big as a cat. The air, like fish, was in it—fish air.

He could hear Bunny's trumpet, his horn, his music playing in Pearlie's. Yeah, in Pearlie's, man. Joe Crawford and Bunny Greensleeves's Big Bopper Band were playing like crazy at Pearlie's.

But now he must find Bunny. Bunny was in his white hat, suit, topcoat.

Modecai stopped walking; he could smell it as clearly as fish air.

He turned the flashlight to his left, and there Bunny lay.

"Bunny …"

The flashlight shone down on Bunny's face. The rats ran off.

"Bunny."

Modecai wanted Bunny off the cold ground and in his arms. He bent down for Bunny and lifted him. Modecai 's nose smelled Bunny's dried-out blood.

"The band's at Pearlie's, Bunny. P-playing at Pearlie's. They have the charts, Bunny. The new tunes. I gave them to Joe before Joe left the apartment."

Modecai turned. He began walking toward the taxicab parked at the end of the pier with the flashlight pointed to the ground.

"We rehearsed the tunes today. At the apartment, of course. You were late. First time, Bunny. First time. Everything, we figured you had to be doing something. Something to be late."

Modecai kept walking, carrying Bunny in his arms and hearing the music the band was playing in Pearlie's.

"They blew a hole in your head. D-didn't t-they, Bunny? S-Stuckey Byerman's goons?"

Modecai kept walking until he reached the black-and-white taxicab, opened its passenger side door, and got in.

"You can take me and my friend Bunny—take us home. Back to 116th Street in Harlem."

The taxicab driver started the taxicab. He looked back over his shoulder and into the dark cabin at Modecai and Bunny in the backseat.

"Your friend ain't dead, is, is he?"

* * *

All of Harlem was at his feet, bowing, paying homage to its king. All of Harlem was shocked by the news, shocked by the murder of Bunny Greensleeves. Harlem had yet to recover from the news but knew enough about Bunny Greensleeves to know how he would have wanted to be remembered after his death.

It was four days after his murder.

Modecai had made all the funeral arrangements.

Modecai wanted the funeral to be as big in scale as Bunny's life.

Chapter 24

The black hearse had ridden along Broadway, along Park Avenue where the rich lived.

There wasn't a motorcade, only a lone black hearse, specifically, with only Modecai and the driver in it. Then the hearse was driven back to Parnell Brothers Funeral Home in Harlem to join the other cars and then lead them in a motorcade through Harlem streets.

A huge contingent of cars were parked in front of the church premises and beyond. The casket was open. Modecai was to be the last person to leave it. It was the back of Bunny's head that had been affected. It was the back of Bunny's head Modecai knew no one would see.

Modecai looked down at Bunny's dark sunglasses reflecting light from the church sanctuary's overhead lights. He'd had the mortician dress Bunny in all white. A white suit, a white hat tailored for his head. And Bunny, his gold-plated watch, was in the vest pocket, exposed. Modecai had found it among Bunny's belongings—as if Bunny knew not to wear it to Stuckey Byerman's office, as if the visit presaged certain danger for him.

And now Modecai's fingers touched Bunny's gold trumpet. Bunny's hands held it. The trumpet lay across Bunny's stomach and chest. The bell of the horn pointed diagonally up to Bunny's left shoulder, where Modecai's fingers were.

Then Modecai looked down into the casket, down at the gold-plated pocket watch that looked up at him, reflecting him. Joy swept over Modecai not unlike when he heard a Bunny Greensleeve's solo soar skyward; above all else in the world. Modecai turned and walked back to the front-row pew where Corrine, followed by Earlene, Big Booty, and Sticks Cooper, sat to the right of him.

"Are you all right, Modecai?" Corrine asked.

"Yes, Corrine."

Earlene's head turned to her left, and she looked at Modecai with concern too.

The Bunny Greensleeves's Big Bopper Band played Bunny's music.

Jazz musicians were in attendance. Luminaries. The greatest jazz musicians in the world. It was a roll call for all the greats of jazz.

The service had concluded. Six pallbearers (band members) carried Bunny's casket on top their shoulders. Harry "Sweets" Edison led the procession out the church, playing his trumpet a capella. Modecai, Corrine, Earlene, Big Booty, Sticks, and the mob of mourners followed Modecai up the church aisle.

Modecai kept his head down until he reached the church's vestibule. But then something bizarre happened that was not only weird to Modecai but for the other jazz musicians who knew the Modecai Jefferson and Bunny Greensleeves story.

This was like some confrontation brewing, singularly, powerfully, now resurrecting itself from the recent past, only, Modecai understood it must not in any way detract from Bunny's funeral, this collective celebration of Bunny's life.

"Modecai, man, you can come back downtown. The ban's off, man. Lifted. Been … I put on—it wasn't, never was about you no ways, Modecai. Fifty-Second Street—the ban was never about you, just Bunny," Big Hat Morrison said.

"No, not without Bunny. Bunny, man."

Modecai's hand touched the back of Bunny's casket as the procession continued down the church's gray stone steps.

* * *

Bunny's body was to be shipped to Philadelphia, Mississippi, for burial tomorrow, to be received by the Greensleeves family.

It was later in the day.

Modecai's body was stretched out on the living room couch. His eyes were shut. Corrine was with him. She was holding his hand. Her head was on Modecai's chest, but she'd raise her head to look at him.

"Don't you want to go to bed?" Corrine had asked Modecai the same question earlier.

"I-I will, Corrine." And he'd said the same thing.

Modecai's eyes opened—they were bloodshot.

"I'll undress you."

"No. I'm not a baby. I can still un—I'll get up onto my feet, okay."

Corrine got off the couch.

"And then … I can't, Corrine! I can't!"

Modecai could only move his torso; below the waist he felt paralyzed.

Corrine ran out the apartment.

"Modecai …"

Modecai saw Earlene and Big Booty.

"Big Booty will help you," Corrine said.

"Don't you worry none," Big Booty said. "I'll take care of you, Modecai."

Modecai was in bed. Corrine had undressed him.

"Do you think, can I fix something for you, honey?"

Corrine was at the edge of the bed.

"We buried him, didn't we, Corrine? Bunny? Didn't we today?" Modecai's head was flat to the pillow.

"Yes, Modecai."

"It was a beautiful service, wasn't it? The band played beautifully, d-didn't it?"

"Yes," Corrine said, fighting back her emotions.

"Bunny would've been proud of the guys."

Silence.

"Sweets Edison, Bunny always loved Sweets Edison's sound. He played beautifully too, didn't he?"

"Yes."

Silence.

"Clifford Brown died too young, too, like Bunny. Both trumpet players, Corrine." Pause. "Do you know of any painters w-who died young, too young like them—they did, Corrine?"

Corrine bit her bottom lip and then shook her head.

Modecai broke down. Corrine held him.

"He … I bought him a new white suit and hat. I-I bought Bunny a … a …"

Corrine rocked Modecai back and forth.

"All of Harlem came out. Everyone, everyone in Harlem who is someone knew Bunny. Bunny was the mayor of Harlem, Corrine."

Corrine pressed her head to Modecai's.

"I don't hate white men, the white race," Modecai said in between tears. "I-I don't hate p-people … Just Stuckey Byerman."

The story came back to Modecai. People who knew people told Modecai what had happened four days ago on Fifty-Second Street. How it all went down.

"At least Bunny killed one of them, Corrine. Killed one of those bastards. He would have killed Byerman too if only …"

"If he'd only killed the other bastard!"

"Yes. Bunny would've killed the three of them. Byerman would be dead. Bunny would have killed him!"

Modecai hadn't told Earlene the story. He'd found out from Earlene what Bunny had left her with, the illusion, the impression of things to come, of Broadway and her two front-row seats on opening night for her and her gentlemen friend. No, Modecai had decided not to kill this illusion of hers, to burst the bubble Bunny had so carefully crafted.

Corrine now was rocking Modecai.

"And Big Hat—"

"Yes, Big Hat, Corrine."

"He—"

"But he's not the culprit here, Corrine."

"But he tried to kill Bunny's—"

"Spirit?"

"Yes, Modecai. He did …"

"Try, but no one could kill Bunny's spirit. It made him stronger. Things like that always made Bunny stronger, not weaker. Like he needed people in the world like Big Hat Morrison, Morrison."

Modecai sank his head back into the pillow.

"It was Stuckey Byerman who killed him. Don't ever forget that, Corrine, who killed Bunny. Stuckey Byerman who had Bunny dumped down on the pier, behind a warehouse—with rats."

"I don't know that world."

"But it's all around us, Corrine. Bunny saw it. Bunny knew it, about it. Even if we, you and I didn't. Bunny was prepared for it."

"But it killed him, Modecai."

Modecai shut his eyes. "It didn't matter. All that mattered was that Bunny never let himself pretend it wasn't there. Not for a day of his life, Corrine."

* * *

Corrine had wanted to stay the night with Modecai, but Modecai said she didn't have to. He wanted to think; nothing was more sacred to him now than his own private thoughts, solitude, almost trying to find peace through suffering.

The bedroom lights were on. Modecai was sleeping with them on. He hadn't moved out his bed, not even to the bathroom—not that he had to use it, because if he did, he felt he had enough physical strength to get there and back. But what do you do when you lose a friend? What do you do when you lose someone you love? What do you do when you lose someone like Bunny Greensleeves?

Modecai trained his eyes on his long, sinewy fingers. He hadn't touched the piano since last Saturday, since after rehearsal with the band the day Bunny was killed. It was like it was Way City all over again, as if it was that time of his life again—where he and his piano were separated by events beyond his control, time-warping them again.

When would he be able to play his piano again? When would music come springing back to life inside him?

"Yeah, I knew it was one of Stuckey Byerman's men I was talking to over the phone. But I was pretending, trying to fool myself, trick my—"

When would he be able sit down and block life out his head, look away from things he'd never allowed his life to. *It was always the difference between us, wasn't it, Bunny?* Even though Bunny dreamed, even though he fancied things, even though his head was stuck as far in the clouds as his, Bunny wasn't afraid of failing—not like him.

Modecai heard the apartment door open, and before he knew it—

"Hello, Modecai."

"Hi, Earlene."

Modecai struggled to straighten himself.

"I'm going to cook for you, Modecai. I'm gonna fix something for you to eat, honey."

"Don't, Earlene, I'm—"

"Modecai, honey, I'm gonna cook for you. You gotta eat something. Put something in your stomach."

"Earlene …"

Modecai pointed to his closet.

"You don't have to get up. Can serve you your meal in the bed. Right where you are. Ain't a bother. None at all, Modecai."

Modecai kept pointing his finger.

"My robe, Earlene. Would you hand me my robe, please." Pause. "Thanks, Earlene."

"Modecai, I'm gonna be in the kitchen cooking if you should need me."

Earlene hadn't been in the kitchen long. She was trying to settle in, fry pork chops and do the other things, but was finding it difficult. She heard Modecai when he entered the kitchen.

"It wasn't the suit … the white suit …" Earlene's bottom lip quivered. "Bunny wore last Saturday. He looked so pretty in. Bunny wasn't buried in that suit, was he, Modecai?"

Earlene was breaking down. Modecai went to her and held her.

"No, Earlene. It wasn't the white suit Bunny wore last Saturday."

"He was so happy, Modecai," Earlene said, her eyes tearful. "All the time."

Modecai held her. Modecai felt it was his turn to rescue someone.

"I loved that man. Loved him," Earlene said, wiping her eyes with the back of her hand. "So very much."

"He loved you too, Earlene."

"M-me and my big butt, you mean, Modecai," Earlene said, pulling away from Modecai.

"Here, Earlene." Modecai had a handkerchief for her.

"Let me finish cooking for you, Modecai. The cooking … I-I ain't getting too much done at this rate."

Modecai sat at the kitchen table. Earlene was really good to him, he thought.

Damned good to him.

Now Earlene had left the apartment. Modecai was back in bed, under the covers. The pork chop and the gravy odors remained in the apartment.

"Bunny's funeral was today, wasn't it? It's been a long day, Bunny. It's been such a long day for us. You were king today. You wrote your name across the Harlem sky."

Struggling to get out of bed, Modecai still had his robe on.

"D-Delores has to know," Modecai said, his footing not sure, almost stumbling across the floor as if drunk. "She must know."

Then Modecai turned back and went into the nightstand's drawer. "I must write her t-to let her know."

Modecai had the pen and paper and was heading for the kitchen table. The kitchen light was on.

Modecai sat down in the chair.

"I must spare her nothing."

And then Modecai's hand moved feverishly as if he were writing music.

"Nothing, do you hear me?"

* * *

The establishment Over Easy was cozy and modest in scale. It was a nice, quiet place on Lenox Avenue in Harlem to spend time after a hard day's work.

Corrine sipped coffee from the cup and then took a puff on her Lucky Strike. Her hand glided across the top of Modecai's.

"Were you able to write music today, Modecai?"

"Yes."

"Much?"

"Some."

"Y-you worked at the piano?"

"Yes, mostly."

"H-how did it feel, darling?"

"All … all right."

Corrine drew back in her chair and took another puff on her cigarette.

This was the third time they'd dated like this, Corrine and Modecai, since Bunny's death, and each time it'd been this way: Modecai practically nonresponsive, practically monosyllabic, always totally depressed.

"Are we ever going to be able to talk about it, Modecai?" Corrine asked, her eyes gazing as hard as diamonds into Modecai's.

"What? Talk about what!"

"You've already cried, I saw you, Modecai—I was with you. The one who held you, honey." Corrine took her time. "But when are you, we—when are you going to be able to talk to me about it?"

Modecai shrugged his shoulders.

"You're living there, Modecai. In the apartment. M-maybe—please don't be angry with me, but maybe you should move, honey—out the apartment."

"No!"

Modecai's eyes boiled.

"You won't stop torturing yourself, will you? You don't want to find peace."

"I wrote a letter. I wrote Delores. I discussed it with Delores!"

"Delores! Delores! Y-you wrote, you mean you discussed it with Delores!

What, you—"

"My feelings, Corrine, my feelings. That's what!"

"Damn, you, Modecai, damn you!"

Corrine jammed the cigarette down into the ashtray and then hopped up to her feet.

Modecai grabbed her arm. "Sit down!"

"I won't!"

"And stop making a scene!"

Corrine broke Modecai's grip. She ran over to Over Easy's coatrack, grabbing her coat, rushing out the door.

Modecai jumped up. He rushed money out his pocket to pay the bill, ran over to the coatrack, grabbed his coat and hat, and then ran out into the street in pursuit of Corrine.

She was running up Lenox Avenue.

"Corrine, Corrine! Wait! Wait!"

"For what! Tell me!"

"Please, please!"

Modecai, when he finally caught up with her, grabbed her by the arm again. He was rough with her.

"That's the second time you've done that," Corrine said, glaring at Modecai.

"That's not like you!"

"No … no … it … it isn't …" Modecai let go of her.

Corrine kept walking up Lenox Avenue.

He kept walking. And then Modecai stopped.

"I'm sorry. I'm so sorry, Corrine."

Corrine hadn't stopped walking.

"I-I feel as though, as though the whole world's caving in on me. The whole damned world, Corrine."

Corrine hadn't turned to look back at Modecai; she was still walking quickly up Lenox Avenue, putting herself farther and farther away from Modecai.

* * *

Modecai was a half block from home. He'd finally gotten a letter from Delores. She'd apologized for the delay, for she said there was a mix-up with the mail in Foster City Prison, that she'd been lucky to receive it, but then apologized for using the word "lucky."

After rushing through her apologies, it was when she expressed the pain Bunny's death had brought to her. She said she was deeply saddened by his death and, that night, cried a lot. But then her letter went on to say she knew how Bunny felt about being cheated out of something. It's how she felt before she shot Johnnyboy Daniels, as if he'd cheated her out of a life.

Delores's letter went on, and she likened herself to Bunny without his obvious predilection for violence but with his determination to right things. It'd put her in Foster City Prison, she said, and Bunny in a grave.

Modecai was on the apartment building's fourth floor.

"Modecai, here, honey," Earlene said, handing Modecai a sealed envelope. "It's from Corrine. Earlier, she was by."

Earlene watched Modecai walk up the hallway with Corrine's letter. *What now?* Earlene thought to herself. *What now, Modecai? Honey?*

Modecai unlocked apartment 4D's door. He hadn't spoken to Corrine since the Sunday afternoon at Over Easy, when he grabbed Corrine's arm, got physical with her. Time had traveled. Now this.

Modecai wasn't going to torment himself. He wasn't going to be his own worst enemy. Modecai opened the envelope.

> Dearest Modecai,
>
> In two days I'm leaving for Paris. It's spring! I'll be in Paris in the springtime. When the flowers grow. It wasn't supposed to be this spring, this early, I know, but it's turned out that way anyway. A painter belongs in Paris. Her heart, I guess.
>
> Please forgive me for saying good-bye this way, but it's because I don't think I am capable of doing it any other way. I hope we can remain lifelong friends. I hope we can correspond with each other as soon as I get settled there. (At least I'll write you.) I don't know how long I'll be there or how long my funds will hold out or how my life will play itself out in Paris: job, career, et cetera.
>
> It seems I can't help you with Bunny's death or make you forget Delores.
>
> I love you, Modecai. That much I know. I unmistakably love you. I guess I always will.
>
> Your friend forever,
> Corrine

Modecai refolded the letter and stuck it back inside the envelope. Modecai half laughed and half cried. The letter didn't surprise him, not one bit. It was either going to be a letter (as it was), a phone call, or a one-on-one talk; but either way he was going to lose Corrine. He knew this the other week (however many days ago it was), that it would be over between them. He loved Corrine, but it was still Delores. He exposed that to Corrine the other week. His most profound feelings he exposed to Delores, after all. Corrine took a backseat. She was no fool. He'd all but declared his greater love for Delores.

Corrine was smart enough in this affair of the hearts, to hold onto her dignity, Modecai thought, before she let him destroy it. She was smart enough to take hold of her life, regain control, take charge of it again and not wait for him to decide about them or whatever vague notion, amorphous thing it was he was now doing to their relationship. Yes, she loved him but was unwilling to put up with his mental malaise, the vicissitudes in his life, sacrifice her sanity, her life for what, by all overt signs from him, was no future with him.

Indeed his life felt as if the whole damned world were caving in on him.

"Modecai … are you all right?" Earlene had stepped into the apartment.

"She's gone, Earlene. I mean, Corrine's leaving for Paris in two days."

"Paris, Paris, France, t-to stay, Modecai?"

"Yes, possibly," Modecai said, hiding the envelope, putting it behind his back. "If things go as she'd like them to go. Work their way out for her over in Paris."

"It's been Corrine's dream, hasn't it, honey? Like it was for Bun— oh … oh … sorry, Modecai, I …"

"You weren't about to say anything wrong, Earlene. To apologize about."

But Earlene stood at the door suddenly looking skittish.

"I wish her luck, Earlene."

"Me too, Modecai. God's speed."

"Uh—yes, God … God's speed." Pause. "You know when Bunny and I went to Paris—"

"It was cold, Modecai," Earlene laughed.

"Brrrr … f-freezing!"

"Like a Harlem winter, Modecai?"

"At times, Earlene, it seemed colder, even colder than that, a Harlem winter."

"It was your first one, wasn't it, honey?"

"Yep, Earlene. Uh, my first Harlem winter all right," Modecai said proudly. "My first one," he repeated fondly. And then he said in a cheery voice, "But there're going to be plenty more to come. A lot more Harlem winters for me!"

"Uh … uh, Modecai, I better get back to my head before the girl lays me out!"

"Uh, okay, Earlene. Don't want you out of a job."

"Heaven forbid!" Earlene kept laughing. "Earlene Bailey without a beautician's job!"

The apartment door closed. Modecai rose. He looked at the envelope. He pressed it to his hand, put it up to his nose, and smelled it like it was bathed in perfume.

"Paris …," Modecai sighed.

Then Modecai walked off to the upright piano.

"In the springtime."

Chapter 25

Four months later.

"Modecai, maybe if I dididlaleeda on that A—extend it some ..."

"Uh, Lee, let me see," Modecai said, marking the sheet music with his pencil and then his teeth gripping it again. "Mmmm ... let's try it that way," Modecai mumbled. "Uh, yes, give it a try." Pause.

"Great!" Modecai exulted after the flashy flourishes executed by Lee Bates's horn. "It works great there. Great suggestion, Lee."

"Just call me the 'idea man,' Modecai—who couldn't write a song that'd fit the tip of a pencil!" Lee Bates chuckled.

"Full of suggestions though!" Specs Sherman shouted from behind the drum kit. "Full of them, like a crackerjack box, huh, Modecai?"

The band was all there, filling out the apartment.

"Hey, Specs, they just come to me from out of space."

"Like little green men, huh, Lee? I get you."

Band rehearsal had concluded. It'd been a sensational rehearsal, Modecai thought. Just sensational. The band was really, really cooking. It was even better than what it'd been before Bunny's death.

Modecai grabbed the pencil, and black love notes began dashing through his head and down onto the sheet music like it was running a sixty-yard wind sprint. Modecai's brain was exhilarated, light as a feather, high as a kite, dizzy as a weathervane in a one-hundred-mile-an-hour hurricane. He felt like dancing on Harlem rooftops, laughing at a Harlem moon, packing his suitcases and taking a trip from Earth to Mars no matter how despairingly scientists of the day spoke of how cold it must be, alien to the human species, earthlings.

He could write into the sunset, into the dawn, into summers and winters and springs. He could write until all eternity ended and blessed itself and began again.

And whenever he heard Bunny's golden trumpet play majestically in his ears at the upright piano while composing music (like now), the sound of Bunny's trumpet was astonishingly fresh, had soared to new heights that only he could hear, knowing Bunny was only responding to what he heard him doing, that there'd been a connection between heaven and earth, and that music never really ends at one point and begins at another, at least not black love notes or a true friendship that endures and lasts the distance.

Epilogue

The jazz cat was jamming away on his instrument. He was cut in a cool funk groove.

The dusk was settling, slipping down; it was in a comfort zone.

The heads in the crowd bobbed and dipped as if tethered to one body. The music seemingly warming over their skulls like a low-sitting sun on this muggy, sticky August evening in Harlem.

The park's loudspeakers carried the music from off the bandstand to the crowd, most of whom were standing on their feet looking up at it. If you whispered something tenderly into your lover's ear, it'd sound like a crackling rim shot laid down by a drummer's drumsticks in breaking the mood.

His dark sunglasses hid his eyes, and he was in a cool cap that could be worn in both summer and spring. Modecai stood far back in the crowd as erect as new oak (at least a fifty-year-old one). He was digging Art Blakey and the Jazz Messengers up at Grant's Tomb along with everyone else. He was digging the cat on piano and, particularly, the young cat who they'd said was this Wynton Marsalis cat on trumpet—who was laying everybody out, down for the count.

The group had been playing for about forty-five minutes or more. Modecai had heard some old and new tunes. And out of nowhere the band played one of Bunny's tunes, and then one of his. The crowd liked them—it really did. And so it made Modecai's heart beat extra fast.

Modecai would have to get to walking soon, get in step. He would have to get back home soon. There was something he had to get back home for, something, it seemed, he'd been waiting for forever.

The Jazz Messengers kept playing even as Modecai tipped his cool, tan cap to them with a gentle regard and great appreciation.

“Ex-excuse me,” Modecai said, breaking the spellbinding silence.

“Sure, mister. Step light now, to the tasty tune.”

Modecai moved off to the curb. He turned back around to listen to one of Art Blakey’s driving drum solos kick up the August air.

“Bohena still plays great drums,” Modecai said. “Rhythm’s as steady as a banker’s clock. Him and Max Roach.”

Modecai was going to walk home since he had time. On a night like tonight it would be great to sleep on a beach, in the sand, and here he was walking on the streets of Harlem, Modecai thought. Of course Modecai didn’t know what a beach breeze felt like, just Harlem’s sweetly manufactured air.

“Wouldn’t have it any other way. Uh-uh. No other way at all.”

(Will my underarm deodorant hold out? Of course it will. Without a doubt!)

Modecai walked down the street’s short incline and looked up at the overhead train rails. Even though it was a subway station overhead, it made Modecai think of a bus station, of the Greyhound bus, as a train rumbled loudly above him.

Young jazz cats were still flocking to New York City, not necessarily Harlem but New York City. They were cats still rumbling loudly into Harlem with their axes. Probably more of them were coming in by plane and train than bus (whichever ticket their parents opted to buy). But Modecai was more than sure some still rode the bus in, arrived by Greyhound at the Port Authority Bus Terminal, were keeping the tradition alive.

No Bunny Greensleeves yet, but you couldn’t hold the Greyhound Bus Company liable for that—hold its feet to the fire.

Modecai felt refreshed. These days, cats were playing jazz music in the parks. Hey, a jazz cat plays music wherever a jazz cat can get a gig, Modecai laughed to himself.

Harlem jukeboxes … that was a thing of the past. Black queens and kings still walked the streets of Harlem, but things in Harlem, in general, had changed. Black folk dressed differently, looked different, acted differently in this age and time and space.

Modecai drew in his breath, and his emotions too, and kept a stiff upper lip—for he and his size fourteen and a half shoes had passed the

Apollo Theatre. His band, the last one Modecai led as bandleader, had played its final gig there some two years ago at the Apollo Theatre (a Harlem landmark).

He'd stopped performing. He'd retired from playing in public. Retiring from public performance only upset him for one night, that special one on the Apollo stage. Playing for Modecai was always a means to an end: he just wanted to hear the immediacy of his music being played (like Haydn). Writing, composing, it's what held the upper hand; what regrets could he possibly have?

Jukeboxes. Harlem's jukeboxes. Modecai laughed. Regrets? He laughed again. Corrine, yes, Corrine would now and again pop back up in his mind. He hadn't corresponded with Corrine in over twenty years. Turning back the clock, Paris turned out to be to Corrine's liking, Modecai thought. She married a black man in France. An expatriate like her. An intellect. She'd become a successful painter.

Five years back, Modecai'd read where Corrine Calloway Barnwell had moved stateside, back to the United States, was living in the Washington DC area, teaching art at a university. Corrine and her husband were still married and with children.

Modecai looked at his watch; things clocked out fine, perfectly. When he got back home he would be able to sit down and catch his breath.

Modecai was home. He stood on the apartment building's brick stoop and tipped his hat off to Harlem, this time his best friend, her ladyship, for getting him home safely.

Modecai walked up the three flights of stairs until he got to the fourth flight. He didn't look for Earlene anymore (something which always broke his heart): Earlene was gone; she'd moved out of Harlem, apartment 4B, thirteen years ago. Earlene found herself a man (Vernell B. Battles, a fellow Chattanoogan), married him, and moved back down to Chattanooga, Tennessee, and opened a beauty salon simply called Hair Stylings by Madam Earlene, a salon Earlene was successfully running up to this day.

As for Big Booty, he lived in the apartment alone until his death. Big Booty died of diabetes less than three years ago. His body was shipped back to Chattanooga, Tennessee, for burial in the Bailey plot down there.

Modecai opened his apartment door, 4D. He turned on the light. All day he'd been in a pensive mood. Art Blakey didn't bring it on but helped, moving in and out of old tunes like he did. It was like he was moving in and out of the old and new today, into shadows and light then out again, time being shifted forward then back, forward then back, like a metronome keeping life's steady, unimpeded beat.

How does one sum up a jazz man's life? Modecai thought. By his music? By the sum and total of his music?

Stacks of sheet music rose high off the floor. Modecai looked over at his upright piano; he started leafing through the bundles of sheet music.

Not all his music could fit in the apartment anymore, so he rented out space in a Secaucus, New Jersey, warehouse. By now Modecai had written enough charts for ten Broadway shows.

Modecai walked over to the opened window to get a breeze, only there was little breeze to look for or anticipate this evening.

"But not without Bunny. Uh-uh. There'll be no Broadway shows without Bunny."

It was last year when Modecai drew up a will stating the authorization for his show tunes to be published after his death and not before, not under any circumstance.

Modecai turned and removed his cool cap, laying it on top the piano. His dark sunglasses stayed wrapped to his face. He looked back at the window.

"Man, am I full of reminisces today," Modecai said wistfully. "Must be getting old and musty. Must account for how I feel today."

Then Modecai tested his legs' elasticity by doing a repetition of deep knee bends at a slow cadence. "Yep, old and moldy."

Modecai looked back down onto the 116th Street, and darn't if he didn't expect to see a few bubbly, young eyeballs with golden halos encircling them, looking right back up at him with awe and wonder. The apartment was a jazz landmark. It'd become a jazz shrine. People from around the world, far and wide, but especially young jazz musicians, came to visit and see just where the great Bunny Greensleeves had once lived in Harlem—one of Harlem's many legends, heroes. They came to pay homage to Bunny, to their king, no matter how short he lived or how young he died: he was a big part of Harlem's grand-scale history.

Modecai wouldn't move out of apartment 4D for all the world, even if the owner dynamited it, he'd say. And at times the building's tenants thought he was kidding, and other times thought him even more serious than how he'd said it.

Now he sat down on the couch and waited. Modecai was waiting for what was to happen next in his life. He took another glance at his watch: it should happen soon, very soon, he thought.

"Funny"—the idea blindsided him—"I still haven't written a song for Miss Tallulah Brown in Way City, Alabama, after all these years. But what jazz musician in his right mind would write a song for a landlord who threw him out of his apartment for making noise? Certainly not me, to be the first!"

If Modecai were to be honest, his eviction from Miss Brown's apartment in Way City, Alabama, still stung him. It still left a bad taste in his mouth. He could joke about what happened in Way City, Alabama, but forget? No, that was just too hard for him to do even now after so many years had passed in perfectly clocked stages. Time that marches forward, and memories roll back.

Modecai shut his eyes and wouldn't open them again until the phone rang.

His blood was running hot, and it had nothing to do with his walk from Grant's Tomb or the deep knee bends since it all had to do with life, his life, yes, the shadows and light—the stepping in and out of them, making a life in general, but living a jazz musician's life in particular. Turning himself over to the will of something else, stronger, smarter, mightier, which still ran its course as if it would not stop until he died; and that would be the reward, that the gem set in the crown, for him, at least, that he was never a burden to it, that he was responsible to it, that he—

Ring.

Modecai leaped off the couch, in no way anticipating his rash reaction, for he was supposed to be calm and cool, rational, but, instead, was badly shaking.

"Oh … man …"

And what he couldn't believe before Modecai was believing now with all his heart.

Ring.

Modecai stood there and hoped his voice wouldn't tremble, cause an earthquake within the room when he spoke into the phone.

"Hel-hello … Hello …"

"Modecai, is that you … honey?"

It'd been thirty years that Delores had served her jail time in Foster City Prison for murdering Johnnyboy Daniels in Way City, Alabama. Tomorrow, at ten o'clock sharp, Delores was to be released from Foster City Prison, and Modecai was to fly down to Foster City to be with her.

"Yes, it's me, baby … Modecai, Delores."